The Stars In The Sidewalk
My Demons Don't Die Easy

A Novel
Craig Matthews

 Craig Matthews Media

The Stars in the Sidewalk

Copyright © 2021 Craig Matthews Media

Scriptures taken from the Holy Bible, New International Version®, NIV®. Copyright © 1973, 1978, 1984, 2011 by Biblica, Inc.TM Used by permission of Zondervan. All rights reserved worldwide. www.zondervan.com The "NIV" and "New International Version" are trademarks registered in the United States Patent and Trademark Office by Biblica, Inc.™

Permissions for quotations or use may be sent to:
Craig Matthews Media
P.O. Box 611235
Port Huron, Michigan 48061-1235

Visit www.CraigMatthewsMedia.com for news and information on this and other exciting titles.

What people are saying about The Stars in the Sidewalk:

"LOVED IT!! I couldn't put it down. The Stars in the Sidewalk is a very somber and intriguing story of one man's trials in life. The story is engaging, thrilling, and at parts heartbreaking, but this adds to the experience of the read... I would recommend this book to family and friends alike." Jill H. Boca Raton, Florida.

*

"The Stars in the Sidewalk is a story that will pull you in and keep you guessing. Craig's characters draw us to them, as we watch the underlying work of God in their lives. This book is one you won't soon forget!" Lori P. Plano, Texas.

*

Another fine job by local author Craig Matthews! Once I got started, I couldn't put it down. By the time I reached page 15, the characters— many of whom felt strangely familiar— were alive and the story threads had me hooked. Scooter's journey wasn't easy. His challenges were more than most of us will ever know. It is a story of faith and redemption. A story that will both warm the heart and make you do some serious thinking. Definitely worth reading and I'm glad I read it. btw - read this one from the beginning and don't skip forward. Let the author guide the story. Dean S. Berkley, Michigan.

*

"An intriguing thriller where demons, evil, and revenge surround the broken characters; but threads of hope and restoration keep emerging. I was mesmerized by the character development and enjoyed it immensely!" Mary S. Richardson, Texas.

*

"No matter how far we have come and how much we have accomplished— we are still plagued by unresolved "demons." Failures, hurts, and regrets, continue to raise their ugly heads! The Stars in the Sidewalk challenges us with hope in resolution." Bob T. Davison, Michigan.

6

"WARNING: Make sure you have time to read this unique novel before opening it. From the opening bell in chapter 1, "Bloody Stars" to the final bell of "Star Shine" your mind will be wrapped and twisted around the depths of one individual, tormented by caring in his jagged world.

Technically, I noticed amazing consistency and depth of character in every action and word uttered, while emotionally capturing that depth in so few words.

You'll explore brutally honest stories in an interwoven tapestry of personalities, strengths, and weaknesses from the concrete world through the spiritual world of souls on their own nebulously guided journeys.

You'll recognize personally familiar virtues and vices as the author artfully and delicately lifts the veil of pretense over raw reality. Your tears cannot be jerked when they so willingly flow.

I feel honored and improved having enjoyed this classic in the making. Wayne F. Petitto Scriptwriter, Spartanburg, South Carolina.

*

"You have an enemy. He wants to destroy you and all that you hold dear. If you are at a place where you are ready to honestly face your own demons then I recommend Stars in the Sidewalk to anyone regardless of religion or faith. In this novel Craig Matthews takes you on a journey encouraging an introspective look at your own demons, and leading you to engage with God at a deeper level. Nothing and no one is beyond His reach." Tracy J. Lapeer, Michigan.

*

This is not the book you are expecting. It's not a pretty fairy tale or fantasy about stars in the sidewalk – it's a gut punching, throat grabbing thriller.

An early question, "Can someone be broken beyond fixing", grabs the reader and encourages him to think about the magnitude of the question. Is it possible, is it even feasible that someone who has hurt people, harmed others, escaped from reality by any means possible – can be fixed? Can you be fixed – can I be fixed. Wait, you may say – "I'm not broken - I'm doing pretty well, all things considered." Are you? When you look at your truth – are you?

This is not a moralizing or preachy novel; it is a heart written story of someone who wants to survive – and to survive with integrity and honor. His journey takes him into the darkness where he must look at what he hopes for. In spite of his very real humanity, he has hopes. Can he learn how to achieve these hopes in a world which seems intent on destroying good. Is it possible to learn how to heal from the inside out?

Craig Matthews has written a modern parable which will resonate with any of us who want to find the answers to our brokenness. We learn we cannot fix ourselves in isolation – we learn to find those people who will walk with us through the darkness and guide us as we find our light and our answers. This is more than a story of adventure and intrigue, although those qualities make this a compelling read. This is a story that grabs the reader and asks the pertinent question – is change possible? Is it possible for you? Read and discover more about you in this story of a broken man.

Perhaps you will learn that you are a mess – and that is not the end of your story. You – we all – are a mess; and we're loved by the One who always reaches out to us.

Pamela Quay, Detroit, Michigan. Author of the upcoming dystopian thriller *"Escaping to the Trees"*

*

8

Many Thanks

Writing a novel rarely happens in isolation, (well the writing part of it, for me, actually does happen in complete isolation) but what I mean is there are a bevy of people behind the scenes in the makings of any good book. This work is no exception to that rule.

There have been so many people involved at various stages of this project and I am forever in their debt:
Bota your friendship and editing work have been life giving, both to me and this story.
Mark your work on the cover and art design in the middle of your crazy, busy world, humbles me.
Lori Price you are THE Grammar Fanatic, going way above and beyond the call of duty.
All of my Beta readers taking on the job of helping a brother out, is so inspirational.
Most of all, my wife Connie, who has endured too many hours of a closed office door and then me prattling on about scene ideas, characters, while enduring my reading of the manuscript and stressing her out with a thriller.

Thank-you is hardly enough to all of you. Thank-you for bringing this story to life and to light. My prayer is for this work of fiction is that it would somehow begin to help wash away lifelong darkness in peoples lives with waves of renewing light of hope and inspiration. I believe genuine life is found at the intersection of our messy lives and God's redeeming grace.

This book is a work of fiction. Although I hope you wonder if I was writing about you, I can assure you all the characters and situations are imaginary. Any resemblance to anyone living is an unintended coincidence.

The Stars in the Sidewalk

10

Dedication

This book has been written with two groups of people in mind. First and foremost, those who are struggling through life. Carrying around the weight of shame and suffering is tiresome. When it feels like the entire world is aligned against you, freedom seems like a distant candle flicker. Don't give up! Reach for help.

Secondly, the group of humble, servant leaders that reach out to the hurting one Monday evenings. They invest countless hours in the shadows, praying, reading, and preparing for the opportunities to bring freedom, hope, and healing to the broken. They have inspired me while they reflect the relentless love of God.
It is a honor to serve with them.

The Stars In The Sidewalk
My Demons Don't Die Easy

A Novel
Craig Matthews

Chapter One
* Bloody Stars *

A bell on the door rang above his head and caught him off guard, its high-pitched jingle brought childhood memories flooding back. The recollection was from a store called Jason's. It was a small-town convenience shop located on the main road through the village and its bell chimed every time the door was opened. That sound conjured up a mysterious old woman from the darkness of the back room to investigate the signal. The check-out lane was located at the rear of the long narrow building, with its low, white counter acting as the only barrier between the worker and the rest of the world.

"Can I help you find something?" was the worn-out phrase from her tired voice. She had no intention of ever coming out from her fortress to help a couple of scrawny kids. He recalled a time when his buddy Jet was with him, and they were after several candy bars, but only had money for one. Regret flooded over the incident, as he remembered all of the theft his group of friends had committed in that store. As he walked toward the counter to pay for one treat, he intentionally blocked the old woman's view, and Jet filled his pockets with chocolate bars.

The building in the memory shook violently, shifting and narrowing, stretching out in front of him, pulled like warm taffy. Hundreds of exaggerated pairs of living, blinking, eyes appeared high on the walls, protruding from the block. The twisted and familiar scene glared at him with a sardonic smile, acknowledging this remembrance of failure. The eyes of shame locked onto his mental movement toward those past sins, surging with an electric intensity to remind him of their power and the strength of their grip.

"Why? Why would you put the check-out counter in the back of the store?" he asked the memory with a shudder, trying to shake free from the pain again, while the hair on the back of his neck stood up. The sudden need to escape exploded inside his chest.

"Sir, can I help you?" Asked a different, real woman, interrupting his panic and snapping off the vision. She was seated behind a sliding glass window wearing a look of uncertainty, waiting for an answer to her question. Her mouth continued its smile but her eyes gave away her annoyance at the intruder.

"Oh, sorry. The bell . . . It reminded me of something . . . I think I should go." The residue of the vision pushed at his feet to flee.
"Are you here to talk to someone?" She interrupted his escape plan.

"I . . . I'm here to see Angie," he said.
"Do you have an appointment with Miss Barnes?" she asked.
"Yes."
"For what time?"
"Sorry. Five o'clock."
"You must be Mr. Lawrence," she stated.
"Yes ma'am."
"I see you haven't been here in a-while."
"Right, a long while."
"Is all your information still the same, Mr. Lawrence?" she asked, while looking over the top of her reading glasses— the kind with the beaded chain hanging like a Christmas garland around her neck.
"Yes, I believe so."
"Well, I need to be certain, so I'll print out what I have, give you a clipboard, and you can have a seat to double-check what we have on file."
"Sure," he said and nodded uncomfortably.

Within a minute, she handed him a brown clipboard with two sheets of paper and a pen affixed beneath a chrome-spring contraption which looked somewhat like a mouse trap, but large enough for a human hand.

He wrestled to release the pen from the death grip of the clip while he sat down. The pen came free and the metal bar snapped hard against the paper. The noise caused a woman in the small waiting area to glance over at the familiar scene and offer a conciliatory smile.

Returning the smile, he placed his attention on the sheet and made a couple of corrections with the red ink. Retracing his steps to the sliding window, he replaced the clipboard without attempting to reattach the pen into the vise.
"*Gina,*" according to the name tag, was talking on the phone and mouthed a "thank you," while holding the receiver with her head

scrunched to her right, pinching the phone between her cheek and shoulder to free up her hands for note-taking on her meticulous desk.

Turning on his heels, he sought out the safety of the brown-cushioned seat. *"They've redone the waiting room,"* he thought to himself. The paneling had been removed and replaced with drywall painted an off-white hue. The dusty, wooden mini blinds were gone from the two windows, and several paintings adorned other walls. A couple of antique lamps on square end tables had several magazines fanned out on top of them, like napkins on a sports bar. The table next to his chair had a few, but most were for women and a new "Holiday Makeover" was of no particular interest.

"How long has it been since I've talked to Angie?" he asked himself.
"It has to be four years," the answer came whispering through.
"Mr. Lawrence, Miss Barnes will see you now," Gina said.
"Thank you," he said. He stood and crossed the room like a man who wanted out of an uncomfortable situation. He grabbed at the door expecting it to open, but it was held tight in a wooden death grip, so he released it and something in the wall buzzed. He reached out and pulled just as the buzzing stopped but the door didn't move.

"You have to pull with the buzz, Mr. Lawrence." Gina leaned out from behind the opaque glass.
Now, with a red face, he managed to pull during the vibration, and the door swung wide with little effort.
On the other side, Gina smiled just a bit to herself at his embarrassment.
"Sorry," was all he wanted to say, but didn't.
"Last door on the right," she called to his backside as he pressed forward.

"The hallway hasn't changed," he thought, which was the exact moment he noticed his work boots. They were leaving a trail of dried mud pebbles with each step he took down the narrow hallway. Fear gripped him as he looked back over the mess he had made, stuck halfway between the entry door and his destination.
"Now what?"
He bent down to pick up the larger pieces close to his feet, but there were so many. And every time he moved more black bits fell on the glossy white tile. He used his hat as a bucket, then decided to remove

16

his boots, but forgot about his sweaty socks in the process. As he
stepped out of his work boots the moisture from his now-exposed socks
left wet imprints on the floor.

"Crap!" he said, louder than what he intended.
Trying to navigate through his mess, the dampness from his socks
muddied the dirt from his boots.
"I gotta get out of here," he said, letting embarrassment take over. The
need to flee pressured his legs to turn.

"Mr. Lawrence!" came the familiar voice from behind him.
He spun with his boots and bent hat in his hands. With a bright red face,
he saw Angie standing in her doorway.
"I made a mess," he said.
"That's okay. Come on in here, I'll get that cleaned up— don't you
worry about it," she said with a full, genuine smile and a wave of the
hand. "It is so good to see you again."
He took a few steps forward, drawn by her presence.
"Don't worry about the mess. We want you here, dirty boots and all!"
"I feel so stupid."
"It's fine." She meant the mess, not the reaction.
"I was running late from work and I forgot about the boots," he said
while standing in the hallway.
"My socks are sweaty, too."
"Of course. You were working!"
"Yes, I was," he said.
"Come on in I'm not afraid of dirt. By the looks of it, you must still be
working construction."
"Yes, ma'am," he said.

Walking in through the door, the situation became familiar, and he felt
more at home.
"So do you have a big job that you're working on?" Angie asked while
closing the door behind them.
"Yes, we're working on a pool deck."
"Like a wooden deck?"
"No, a concrete patio around an in-ground pool."
"Wow, sounds like quite a project!" She noticed he was keeping his
blonde hair longer now. "Just set the boots down anywhere," she said,
pushing past him to her chair.

Her scent was fresh and pleasant on his dirt-encrusted nostrils.
"Sorry," he said, while sitting in the thick-cushioned seat. The wide
comfortable chair sat next to the wooden office door and invited his
tired body in. He noticed the carpet looked brand new while setting his
boots and dirt-filled hat down with a cringe.
"Don't worry for one second about the carpet," she said.
"I forgot how perceptive she is," he thought.

*

The sun was up over the Sacramento Mountains when the bell rang for
recess. Boys and girls charged out of the white, brick building onto the
dusty playground. Four students had been given a sacred soccer ball to
carry. Every grade was assigned one new ball for the entire year, which
they had to guard like a precious jewel. Different students were tasked
with carrying the orange cones that were used for goal markers at the
ends of the dirt fields. Since the second through fifth grades all had the
same recess time, there were four simultaneous games.

The process for choosing sides was efficient and ruthless. The rules
were handed down from the staff in an effort to eliminate arguing.
When a student was picked they had five seconds to make a selection
for the opposing team. If they failed to choose, the opposing team
selected someone for their own side. In this process the weaker players
were assigned to the opposition, so the one picking could take the
stronger players for their team. The first person was selected by the
teacher before recess and served as the team captain for the entire day.
This position was rotated among the whole class throughout the school
year, so everyone had to assume the role several times each year. The
soccer game was the highlight of the day for many students. It was
played religiously and, with almost three hundred days of sun a year in
Alamogordo, New Mexico, the games were never canceled.

Bobby was small for his age and not the most popular kid at
Oppenheimer Elementary. He also hated playing soccer, preferring
baseball to the European sport. His dad had played baseball as a kid
growing up, and Bobby hung onto that shred of information as sacred.
He dreaded the days he had to carry the ball and be the captain. Most of
the other kids groaned when he got the call. It wasn't that Bobby lacked
athletic skill for his size— he was just a few sizes too small for his age,

even though his mom had held him back in kindergarten to give him a chance at *"catching up,"* as she liked to describe it.

On this particular day the teams were selected, then the teaching assistant with the dreaded assignment of "official" for the game, blew the whistle and turned to talk with another aide. Within the first few minutes an injury was guaranteed. A kick in the shin, glass in the leg or a hundred other varieties of sport-induced terror. All wounds were inflicted by willing classmates trying to prove their moxie in the beloved sport, which would win them bragging rights for the day.

During the first injury time-out, the teacher's aide was tending to players while the game continued because each team was down a player. Slamming shins without guards could be painful— two boys were trying to walk off their dead legs.

It was at this point that the most popular soccer super-star broke in on the goal— the goal Bobby was defending. With all of the confidence of Pelé, he sprinted in and let fly a hard shot. Somehow Bobby got a hand on the attempt at the last second. The ball ricocheted off of Bobby's outstretched fingers and flew over the eight-foot-high fence, to the amazement of everyone on the field.

The student making the shot needed to save face and challenged Bobby, throwing him to the ground. He was the most popular kid in the second grade, so no one came to the defense of under-sized Bobby. Punches were thrown and the goalie was knocked out of the game with the beating. Laying fetal in the dirt, not one student would tell the assistant teacher what had taken place for fear of retribution by the soccer stud.

At the end of the school day beneath a cloudless robin's-egg blue sky, Bobby— sporting his black eye and ripped shirt— met his sister in front of the school to board the bus. The buses were late, like always, because the yellow units transported both the high school and the middle school passengers first, before making their way around to Oppenheimer.

"What happened to you?" Bee demanded, both hands were on her hips.
"Nothing."
"Really, Bobby?"

"I fell down playing soccer," Bobby said.
"A fat lip and a torn shirt doesn't happen when you fall down."
"Let it go, Bee!"
"No way."

Bobby knew she would never let it go. She didn't have a "quit" switch in her body.
"Was it the Gonzales kid again?"
"Let it go, Bee! I don't need your help," he said.
"You can't let them treat you like this, Bobby."
"You will only make things worse for me."
"Bull crap!" she said as she pushed through the swelling crowd of kids, looking for the culprit.

Bee knew where the soccer stud lived because his older brother shared her fifth-grade class. She walked over to the students waiting for the northwest bus.
"Hey!" she said.
"What do you want, pretty girl?" said the second grader, displaying his bravado in front of his group of friends and older brother.
"What did I tell you about picking on my brother?"
"Your brother is a punk, because of him, our soccer ball is stuck in the drainage ditch."

Bee walked up to the boy. She was more than a head taller, and pushed her finger deep into the middle of his blue "Chivas" T-shirt.
"Hey!" he said. His reaction was the invitation for his older brother to step in.
"Bee, back off."
"Armando, you had better tell your brother that I will beat the crap out of him in front of all of these girls if he doesn't lay off Bobby!"
"I don't think you're going to do that, Bee." Armando stepped in close.
"I'll do it right after I knock you on your butt." Bee glared.
Armando made the first mistake of the day. He pushed Bee and she stumbled from the unexpected contact. Oppenheimer School has a distinct, no contact rule on the school grounds.

Dropping her backpack, without regard for its contents or the rules, Bee walked up to the boy who was four inches taller and kneed him in the groin. With a sudden gasp he fell to the ground. The younger brother charged at Bee for dishonoring his family. He was met with a prompt punch to the face. His nose crunched and bled upon impact. Large droplets of crimson blood splashed on the bright white concrete. The bloody Gonzales soccer stud crumpled to the ground, screaming in pain, pawing at his blood. The children surrounding the fight winced in unison at the sight.

Bee moved in towering over him. She bent down, grabbed the whimpering student by a handful of black hair, yanking upward with just enough force to grab his attention.
"You had better leave Bobby alone, do you understand?"
He nodded in compliance. Turning to Armando, she grabbed his reddened face by cheeks and whispered, "Don't make me hurt you, Armando. Tell your brother to leave Bobby alone, you got it?"
"Puta!"
"Call me what you want. I'm not the one on the ground grabbing at himself."
Bee turned and snatched up her backpack, walking past her horrified, but adoring, brother.
"Let's go, Bobby."
The crowd of students parted and let the pair pass.
Bee put her arm around her sibling and with her mouth close to his ear whispered, "You and me against the world." Bee waited for the customary response.
"You and me, Bobby."
"Together," he said and bumped fists with a guarded smile.

*

As Angie sat down in her cozy chair, Scooter's mind went on a journey back to a familiar place. It was her other office across the hall. He was thinking about the first time he had met her, some fifteen years ago. In front of her again, he couldn't identify one thing different about his counselor.
"You haven't changed a bit," he said.
She took the compliment and didn't respond except with a slight upturn in her smile.
"How are you doing?" she asked.
"Um, okay," he replied, not remembering in the moment he had made the appointment the previous week.

"So, what brings you in today?"

"*Straight shooter*," was his first memory impulse.

"Gina said you sounded a bit unnerved when you called in," she said.

"Yeah. I was."

"What had triggered you?" Angie had her notepad and pen at the ready to jot down some thoughts. Her long black hair ended with curls on her shoulders.

"Well, it was a rough day. But it didn't start out that way."

"Why don't you start at the beginning and walk me through it," she said.

"We started a new job. It's an older home on the north side of town. We got there with all of the equipment to tear out their patio. We've done work in other homes in the neighborhood so I was somewhat familiar with the best place to park my rig. I'm driving the dump truck now, so hauling equipment to the job site is part of my job," he said to update her on his progress and promotion.

Angie nodded and her eyes narrowed as she listened.

"The tool truck, pickup, and I got to the street. I was the last in the line of vehicles and trying to spy out the best place to unload the Kubota from my trailer."

"The Kubota was the machine you're hauling, I assume?"

"Yes. It's our small loader. We use it to get in tight places."

"Okay." She nodded.

"Mack pulled up and stopped in front of the house."

"Your boss?"

"Yes, you have a good memory."

"And?" She made a notation.

"So, Mack sets his brakes, just past the driveway and Layne swung the pickup with the air compressor into the driveway. There were some overgrown bushes along the side of the drive where I couldn't see the actual concrete, only the approach and sidewalk. I was glancing back in the mirror to make sure my trailer was close to the curb and so I didn't block the neighbors driveway. As I looked forward a kid on an orange bike darted out from the driveway across the street, right in front of me. I thought I drilled him."

"Oh my!" Angie said and sat forward in her green chair.

22

"The only thing I could do was slam on my brakes," he said while his right hand experienced a slight tremor, which he tried to hide. "I didn't even have time to blow my horn," he said.
"Did you hit the child?"
"I heard a thud. He went flying off his bike onto the pavement and started screaming like I'd ripped his arm off."
"Was he injured?"
"I got out of the truck and went to him. There was some initial movement as I approached. He had blood all over his face and neck. I thought he was dying."
"Oh, no!"
"Then the idiot stood up and said, 'Gotcha!' He hopped on his bike and took off, leaving an empty ketchup packet on the ground."
"So you didn't hit him?"
"I don't know how I missed, but I think I did. It looked like my hood swallowed him whole. The sight of the ketchup blood. . ." he trailed off.
"I'm sorry."
"It was just a dumb prank by a stupid kid," he said.
"That was a crazy way to start your week," she said.
"It got much worse," he said, looking at the floor. He returned to clenching his jaw.
"Okay, what happened next?" Angie asked.

"I wanted to scream at the kid for being so thoughtless. It turns out he lives next to the house that we're working at. Mack thought I had run him over, said he saw the whole thing in his mirror. He came charging out of the truck with a red face and loaded for bear," he said.
"He started his daily yelling session at me out in the street. Telling me to slow down and watch what I was doing. Ranting and raving, which is par for the course. Scooter this and Scooter that."
"How did that make you feel?"

"Well, never good, but I'm used to it and usually I let it run off my back. But with what had just happened I yelled back at him and threw my hat. I don't really remember what I said. My face was red and my heart was pumping. I had to turn away from him and walk back to the trailer. I started taking the chains off the machine so I wouldn't do something stupid or say something I would regret. I was so mad I could see stars."
"What do you mean?"

"I was so angry. I was seeing white flashes," he said as his face flushed from the memory. "Like my blood pressure had gotten too high or something," he said, looking at her with his steel-blue eyes.

"Wow. Okay. Did you pass out or lose your vision?"

"No."

"I hope you see that you've made progress," she said and scribbled more.

"How so?"

"You didn't throw a fit or a fist, when in the past that may have been the way you would have dealt with the situation."

"I need the job. I can't be ringing up the boss, even though there are plenty of days I would like to," he said.

He took notice of the small coffee table between them. It looked familiar but he couldn't place it at first. Then it struck him like a bolt of lighting— it was just like the one from his grandmother's living room. The stark memory ushered in a buried fear.

"So, they call you Scooter now?" she asked with a slight smile.

"Yeah," he said, trying to ignore the memory the table whispered to him. "It's the guys on the crew. When I have to leave in the truck to go get something or haul broken concrete away, they say I am 'scooting' out again. Like I am getting out of work by doing my job."

"Are you okay with the label?"

"Yeah, they don't mean anything by it. I guess I would be worried if I didn't get a nick name," he admitted.

"I like it. So, Scooter—" She smiled at him now. "May I call you that?"

"Sure, Doc."

"What happened after the screaming episode in the street?"

"While I was working on getting the machine off the trailer, the whole thing just kept running through my head. I wasn't seeing stars anymore, but I was determined I was going to find the kid or say something to his parents, if I got the chance."

Angie nodded, while her pen danced.

"I mean, I could have killed him." He was intense in the memory, leaning toward her.

"I get it. You were shocked. You thought you'd hurt a child," Angie said.

"Plus, I was concerned backing the machine off of the trailer. My head was on a swivel, kind of paranoid, looking out for everything," he continued.

"I bet you were! What happened next?" Angie asked.

"I remember driving the loader up the driveway and seeing the other guys scurrying around trying to get ready to begin cutting concrete with the big saw. The saw looks like a white box with two handles. It has a spinning, screaming blade of death on the front when it's all assembled."

"It sounds frightening."

"It's loud— it can kill you— and it cuts through concrete like butter," he said.

"Yikes. Okay. Got it— danger." Her eyes widened while she held her hands out in front of her.

"So, we got started pulling out their patio. We have a saw running along with the jackhammer busting up some of the concrete close to the house. We had to get all of it out so they can dig the hole in the ground to put the pool in.

"That has to be loud."

"It is. The entire first day the family stood at the window watching us work. The homeowner and his wife, along with a younger boy. The couple is in their sixties, so I assume it was their grandson or something."

"Is the watching unusual?"

"No, not at all. Happens all of the time. It is not everyday people have work done on your home. When it comes to getting a new in-ground pool, it usually happens once in your lifetime," he said.

Angie nodded.

"It was another hot day," he said

"We've had quite a few of those this year," she responded.

"But we got lucky this summer because we had just finished up a large project up on the lake. That job was a custom patio with walls, multi-level sitting areas, and a seven-foot-wide walkway all the way down to the beach."

"Wow, fancy!" Angie took notice of his dark tan and calloused hands.

"The place spoiled us. Cool breezes, dry sandy work area and pretty scenery."

What Scooter didn't admit to was that most of the best scenery was in motion. Countless photos were clicked when Mack wasn't watching. Boats, clear-blue water, and bikinis were the main distractions of the day. Those beach projects made getting up and going to work a little easier.

Scooter went silent— thinking about the aspects of the job, rather than talking to Angie about it. He remembered the guys getting busted snapping photos and they certainly didn't want the rage of Mack to come down on them for screwing around when they were supposed to be working. Several times the boss lost his cool on that patio. Mack tried so hard not to get upset, but it came so natural for him. Layne got barked at a few times for gawking and Scooter for frequenting his lunch box. Scooter smiled at the memory.

"Hey, where did you go?"
"Sorry, I was thinking about the beach job," he said, embarrassed.
Angie waited.
"And I was thinking about the guys on the crew."

"Continue with the story about the kid on the bike. You were on the machine?"
"Right. Um, I remember Mack barked to fire up the compressor. He wanted me to use the jack hammer and get the broken piece busted up and put in the dump truck, while he made a couple of relief cuts by the corner of the house."

"So, I was pounding away at the concrete with the heavy hammer and I caught another glimpse of the orange-bike kid in the yard to the south. He was sitting on the back steps of a dilapidated house watching us work. Judging by the looks of him, he was ten or twelve years old, but his young face contradicted his appearance. He had a cocky demeanor. With long hair and a stocky build, he carried himself with an attitude that was much older."

"Like he was the tough kid in the neighborhood?"

"I thought he was the jerk in the neighborhood, if I'm being honest."
"Please. Honesty is the only way it works in here," Angie said.
"He was the type who thinks they've been born to keep the rest of the world in line, especially those younger and weaker."
"Which triggered you?"
"The scene was familiar to me. The kid just smiled. Not a real smile, but the kind that says, '*I burned you and you can't do anything about it,*' which ticked me off all the more."

Explaining all of this to Angie came easy for Scooter now. Several years in the office across the hall had helped him get a better grip on his life.

"So, you think the kid on the bike is a bully? What does it have to do with you?"
"He's a bully all right. I can see right through him."
"What does it have to do with you?" Angie insisted.
"Nothing!" he snipped back. "It has to do with Ronnie!" His hand tremor returned.
"Okay." She paused trying to remember. "Tell me about that."

"After we ripped out the concrete, we went back a couple of days later to start working on the patio. Pour some steps, get the drains set— those kinds of things," he explained.
"Is the pool is in at this point?" she asked.
"Yes, it's a tub pool. They set those in with a crane. It's one piece."
"You're the pool guys, too?"
"No, that's another crew— we only deal with the concrete part of the process."
"Oh," she said, looking confused.
"The pool company subcontracted with my boss to do the concrete work."
"Got it!" she said with a toothy smile.
"When we started working again, the kid started hanging around."
"The neighbor kid, the one on the bike?" she asked.
"No, the kid from inside the house."
"Oh, the grandson?"
"Yeah, except he isn't a grandchild. He's a foster kid."
"Okay," she said. "How do you feel about that?"
"It's screwed up."

"What is— the household?"

"No, they seem like nice people. They were putting in the pool for their own grandchildren and this kid got thrown back into the overwhelmed foster care system. The couples' daughter is a caseworker and mentioned Ronnie was getting returned for the third time in a year, so they stepped up to help," he said.

"That's amazing!"

"They've had other foster kids through the years but had stepped back during retirement. They told me they felt compelled to help Ronnie."

"What is the screwed-up part, Scooter?" Angie asked, knowing the session time was running short.

"Ronnie was a six-year-old kid who'd been forced through the system because his mom was an addict and couldn't get her life together. Dad is gone."

"Okay." She was not seeing the correlation to his anger with his situation.

"Which is bad enough, but not what the real problem is," Scooter said.

"So what is the real problem?"

"I got close to this kid over the next few days. Joking around and teaching him a little about construction, swinging a hammer, using a tape measure, things like that."

"So you felt a connection with him?" Angie asked.

"Yeah, I did. Even shared a few snacks from my lunch. Got him a little hammer off of the truck to let him help us pound stakes."

"Pound steaks?" Angie contorted her face with confusion.

"Stakes are the steel pins we use to hold forms in place," he said. Angie nodded.

"When we were working, he was having fun, maybe the time of his life. Dell had said as much."

"Dell is the homeowner?"

"Yes."

"He said the only thing Ronnie wanted to talk about when we left for the day was how he was going to grow up and be a concrete worker."

"How adorable!"

"I thought so, too." Scooter paused as the story caught in his throat.

"So, we showed up in the morning— this must be the third or fourth day on the job— and Ronnie was nowhere to be found. The house was shut up tight. That was a bummer. We thought they had stuff to do— no big deal."

"We unloaded the truck, carrying the tools to the back yard like every other day and came around the corner. . ."

Scooter choked on the words. "There was blood splattered everywhere."

"What?" Angie said.

"Yeah. Blood all over the sand. On our forms. On the coping around the pool."

Angie shifted in her seat at the image Scooter painted.

"It looked like someone had taken a savage beating."

"Oh my," she said.

"I immediately thought the kid on the bike had something to do with it, and felt sick."

More notes were written on the yellow pad.

"A few hours later, the homeowners came driving into the garage that sat back by the pool."

"I thought you took the concrete out?" Angie asked.

"We took the old concrete patio out, but left the drive way in. The garage sat thirty feet back from the house," he said.

"Gotcha."

"Exiting the car, Dell and Sharron had strained faces, pale even. Ronnie got out with a bandage wrapped around his head."

"Oh no," she said.

"He was bruised all over his face and arms. His lip was blown up twice the size, his nose was bandaged over and one eye was covered."

"You've got to be kidding?"

"I asked Dell what had happened. He told me the neighbor boy was playing with Ronnie after we'd left for the day. Someone starting throwing sand, then Darrell began wailing on Ronnie with both fists like he was possessed or something."

"Who is Darrell?"

"The kid on the bike!"

"Oh! Okay. Now I get it," Angie said.

"I was so pissed off— I wanted to knock some sense into the kid myself," he said.

"Your intuition was right about him being a bully. How is Ronnie doing?"

Scooter thought for a moment.

"The kid is resilient, but when I bent down to look into his swollen face, he jumped in my arms and started crying," he said. "For a split second I didn't know how to react, but I held him tight and let him cry on my shoulder. The rest of the guys didn't know what to do. I just rubbed the kid's quivering back. Sharron was crying with both of her hands over her mouth."

"How did you feel in that moment, Scooter?" Angie asked.

"Like I never wanted to put him down. I turned away so the guys couldn't see me tearing up."

"You were afraid of what they thought?"

"They're construction workers, Angie. They don't have a handle on their emotions. They wouldn't understand, plus they'd never let it go."

"I get it."

"As I was holding Ronnie, he whispered in my ear, 'They look like stars,' while he was pointing down to the forms."

"'What does, buddy?' I asked him and he just pointed. It took me a minute to figure out what he was talking about. But it was the blood splatters on the wood. His blood splatters." Scooters eyes dropped a couple of unexpected fat tears onto his shirt.

"Which upset you?"

"Yes, they looked like bloody stars. It just took me right back to all of my issues," he said.

"So how do you think Ronnie is doing?"

He thought about the question.

"I think he's a strong kid."

"Is he? Or maybe he's hiding from his pain?"

"Maybe."

Angie remained silent.

"I'm sure you're right," Scooter said.

"Sound familiar, Scooter?" she asked.

"I want to kill that kid, Angie."

"Why?"

"To protect Ronnie," he said.

"Do you see yourself in him?"

"Yes." Scooter's hand shook with the thought.

✽

Chapter Two
* Magic Stars *

"The big truck sure is loud!" shouted Ronnie from the porch.
"You bet it is," Scooter said, walking past the bruised boy. Ronnie was wearing his superhero pj's.
"Why aren't you sleeping?" Scooter pointed the question at Dell and Sharron, who looked exhausted, rather than at the enthusiastic child.
"'Cause you guys are making the concrete today!" Ronnie answered anyway.
"Been up since five," yawned Dell from his over-sized porch chair.
"Ouch!" Scooter kept on walking back to the truck to grab some more tools.

The crew had met the mixer at the jobsite to begin the first day of pouring. The concrete truck showed up half an hour early, but the men were not ready when the truck arrived. So, the scramble-fest began in earnest. Tools had to be unloaded, bulkheads had to be set, rubber expansion joint cut.

Mack was stationed high up on the truck putting the powdered color into the drum. He was rinsing down a bit of mess from opening the palpable bags of fine black dust, all the while watching everyone out of the corner of his eye to ensure they would be ready to go. Every time the concrete showed up, Mack's blood pressure increased by twenty points. His cheeks turned a deep purple. The coloring of his face was the signal for shouting to commence. It continued throughout the morning's pour.

"Fire it up!" Mack barked to the driver.
The motor revved. The red and white drum on the truck began its ten-minute spin, mixing color into the concoction of stone, sand, water, and cement, while guys dashed to and fro.

"Come on, guys, let's get the lead out!" Mack was shouting, descending the narrow ladder by the cab of the mixer.
"There he goes again," Layne said to Bull.
"What?"
"He gets nervous every time we pour."

"Like we've never done it before?" Bull responded while wrestling a rubber boot that was one size too small.

"He's gonna blow an artery," Layne said from up inside the tool truck.

"And I know, your phone don't dial 911 for that," Scooter interjected.

"Da. . . rn right, Scooter!" Layne checked his language for the kid's sake.

"Can't get your fat feet in your boot there, chubby?" Scooter quipped, watching Bull struggle.

"No, but I know where I can stick it," Bull said.

"Just take your socks off and grease up those cankles," Layne suggested, implying Bull's ankles were so big they were just extensions of his calf muscle. No longer ankles— they were now cankles. It had been a running joke for the entire season.

"Shut up, Lamer," Bull shot back from his place on the rear bumper of the tool truck. He was huffing and puffing while pushing his foot through the concrete-encased boot.

"Maybe washing your rubbers, every once in a while, would help there, Bully— Bully Boy," Scooter said with a condescending English accent.

Bull was a strong oaf of a man, the kind every concrete crew loved to have. Picking up weighty things was all a part of a day's work in the trade and the big guy could pick up heavy things with the best of them. Bull wasn't the guy to figure out grades, drains, or the amount of concrete needed for the job. He was there to transport things— to the truck, from the truck, into the loader bucket. It was like God made him for lifting, shoveling, and washing tools. Simple physical work. Bull work.

"Hey! Somebody fire up that loader," Mack thundered.

"Yeah, yeah," Layne said, going after the machine that had been resting all night in the backyard.

Ronnie was standing at the railing jumping up and down with anticipation for the next part of the project to begin. Layne gave the kid a high five on the way by.

*

Ding, Ding. The cursed pneumatic bell was summoning again.

James had zero motivation to be at work on this cloudless Saturday. He had spent the night before partying too much to be awake, let alone to be waiting on customers at the station. He lifted himself up off of the chair and made his way up front when the bell rang again.

"UGH, what do you want?" He yelled in the back room, before going through the door to the front reception area.

He was angry that he had to open on another Saturday for his stupid boss.

Not one, but two boats had drifted into the dock at his station at the mouth of the river.

"How can I help you?" he asked as he exited, trying to be polite.

"Need some fuel, buddy."

"No kidding?" he said, removing the hose from the pump and reading the guy's mind.

The spotless-white cabin cruiser was shimmering in the early morning sun. The stained teak and shining chrome highlights glistened from a recent waxing. The reflections off of the Black River were splashing beams of light all over his face, as ripples from converging wakes danced from shore to shore. Boating season was in full bloom and James was going to be stuck servicing rich people all day long with an incredible hangover.

James loved working on the water through the summer and he hated working on the water throughout the summer. Today, it felt like the hate was going to win— again.

"Hey, is that premium?" asked his plump customer.

"Sure is," he managed to say back, knowing it was not premium fuel he was dispensing into the guys seventy-five-gallon tank.

"Are you sure? The pump says that it is regular," he stated.

"Listen, I've been working here a long time and I know which pump is the premium. The label never got changed. This is the good stuff," he said firmly.

"Okay," said the unconvinced man.

James wished he had remembered to grab a few sugar packets off the coffee stand in the back to give this customer an extra special gift in his tank. He smirked at the thought.

"Screw this guy," he said to himself.

The fuel tank access on the craft named *Emma Mae* was on the port side, back near the stern. Hungover, James stayed on the dock to service it, wishing for a speedy end to his day.

The second boat was just tying off in front of the white classic being fueled. The long hull of the speed boat was canary-yellow and had eight chrome exhaust pipes reaching for the sky. The name *Yellow Submarine* was plastered down its side in bold black letters. It was loud and brash — everything James hated.

Two young guys jumped out on the dock to tie off and James assumed that they were rich kids. When he got a closer look, one of them was a spoiled beach brat. The other was Ron, a kid he knew from his high school days.

"Ron, is that you?" James asked, squinting against the sunshine.

"Hey, Moby, what's going on?"

"Just livin' the dream. Working another gorgeous day, making a ton of money for my boss— when I should be on the beach," he said.

"Yeah, that sucks. This job looks good on you Moby."

"I've lost a few pounds since high school," Moby said.

"I don't miss those days," Ron admitted.

"Me neither. Where did you get the boat?"

"Are you kidding? It's not mine."

"The *Yellow Submarine* belongs to my dad," said the tall skinny guy with a visor. "Can you fill it up?"

"Yep," he said. "*Arrogant turd*," is what he thought.

"Where did he get the awesome name?" James asked sarcastically.

"He loves the Beatles and owns a company that does underground work, so, since it's yellow. . ." he trailed off.

"How cool," James deadpanned.

"When do you get released from boat jail?" Ron asked with a smirk.

"At four," James said.

"We're going to a big party up by Lakeport. If you want to come hang out, we could catch up on life after high school," Ron said.

"Gonna be lots of chicks," the skinny guy with no name said, grinning with a goofy plastic smile.

James loathed the pinhead already.

"Hey, my pump clicked off a few minutes ago. Can you stop talking with your friends and do your job?" The rotund impatient guy chirped with a reddened face, as he climbed back aboard his expensive craft.

"Yeah, one second. I love my job," James said sarcastically and lumbered back to the waiting boat.
Lifting the nozzle out of the tank, he quickly depressed the lever again so gasoline splashed on the shiny exterior of the *Emma Mae*, running down its hull and leaking off into the water, sending a rainbow-colored slick across the surface.
"That will teach you," he said to himself and smirked while replacing the cap. He wiped the cap clean with the red rag from his back pocket for show.
"Using a card today?" he asked the arrogant hulk on the other side of the craft.
"Yes, Master-card," he replied as he handed it over.
"Be right back with your receipt."

James knew what he was going to do to this oaf. He slid the card through the reader, punching in the $430.00 charge. While it was processing, he grabbed a blank receipt and gently rubbed a pencil over the paper that he held on top of the embossed numbers of the credit card. James flipped it over and copied the rest of the info. He slid the new graphite copy under the old metal register and walked outside whistling a new tune.

"Have a nice day," he said to the impatient idiot who then stepped over to fire up his motor.
"Another rich guy in a panic to relax. Good thing credit card numbers are worth money these days," he thought, as he tossed the line to the guy's crabby wife and smiled his secret "gotcha" smile.

"That guy is a real jerk," Ron said to James, as he made his way back over to the Submarine.
"I deal with idiots like him all day long," he said. "How did you get hooked up with this guy?" James was pointing with his eyes down the dock.
"Oh, Phil?"
"Yeah, good old Phil."
"He's a neighbor to my aunt and uncle who live up on the lake," Ron said. "He offered a ride in the boat-- said we'd definitely get some girls to ride along."
"That's a true statement. Is he going to that party?" James asked.
"Yeah," Ron said.

"Well, maybe I'll meet up with you guys."

"Cool. Do you know about the hidden beach north of Jeddo Road?"

"The one in the ancient cemetery?"

"That would be the place!"

"Should be a good time," James said.

"Yeah, it should."

James already had in mind what was going to happen at the party, but his idea was different than Ron's definition of a good time.

＊

"Come on, guys, you gotta get that pulled down!" Mack shouted from his seat on the Kabota. He was busy stuffing his face again with a peanut butter sandwich, while barking random commands between bites.

"A little water would be nice, Mack. This stuff is stiff as—," a winded Layne shot back. He managed to self-edit due to the young audience, just as Bull tripped on the wire mesh again.

"Whoa, Mr. Bull almost fell down!" Ronnie said to Dell just inside the sliding glass door. They were locked into the concrete crew's every move.

"Mr. Bull, are you okay?" Layne quipped in a feigned kids voice. Everyone laughed.

"I hate wire," red-faced Bull said.

Layne and Scooter were pulling the concrete down with a ten-foot screed, while Bull tried to keep up with the rake. They were pouring a section of the pool deck between the pool and the sun room on the rear of the home. It was farthest away from the driveway so it needed to be poured first.

"You gonna need more mud?" Mack asked, striking up an after-snack cigarette. The boss was not only overweight, but he smoked like a chimney. He began coughing after asking the question.

"Those things are gonna kill you, Mack!" Bull said, to deflect attention off of himself.

"Shut up, Bull, and rake faster!" Mack shot back.

"Looks like we're good here. Are you gonna add some water for the end?" Scooter said as he removed his sweaty hat and wiped his forehead with the sleeve of his T-shirt.

"You guys are pansies," Mack said, as he backed up the loader.

"Says the guy sitting on the machine with the big butt," Layne shot back.
"Dell, what does that mean?" Ronnie asked.
"It's a joke, Ronnie," Dell said.
"Mack, even the kid don't get your jokes," Layne smiled.
"You're lucky he's standing right there."

The morning progressed. The guys managed to finish getting the two sections put down as the sun came over the trees. Bull was busy rinsing off tools in the bucket of the loader, using the hose from the concrete truck. Mack was in the cab of the tool truck talking on his phone. Layne and Scooter were using hand floats to smooth out the concrete and edgers to push the aggregate down next to the form.

Ronnie and Dell had moved outside for a closer look at what the concrete guys were up to.
Ronnie had a million questions bouncing around in his bruised and bandaged head.
"Scooter, why are you doing that?" he asked.
"This helps close up the surface, so the concrete sets up. Do you want to try?"
"Are you sure?" Dell asked.
"He can't hurt anything at this point," Scooter said. "Come here."
"Okay."
"This is called a hand float. You don't have to push down on it, just let it glide across the surface— like this."
Scooter demonstrated for the enthusiastic boy who was hunched down, resting his hands on his knees.
"Now you try it." Scooter offered it to the lad.
"Always tryin' to get out of work, huh, Scoot?" Layne said.
"Says the pot."
Layne smiled as Scooter had used one of his favorite saying against him.
"Let it stay flat. You're just trying to fill in any dips and holes from the bull float guy," Scooter said.
"I heard that!" Layne said.
"Good bull float guys don't leave gorges along the form," Scooter explained, digging at his coworker.
"Good thing I'm a good bull float guy, Ronnie," Layne said.

"I don't know bout that Mr. Layne!" Ronnie said, and everyone laughed.

"You're a good judge of character, young man!" Scooter said to Layne's huff.

"So, when are you going to put the small stones in?" Dell asked. "Do you seed them on the top?"

"They're already in."

"Oh?" Dell looked confused.

"This mix uses pea stone as the aggregate instead of limestone," he said.

"I don't get it," Ronnie said.

"Well, to make concrete strong, rocks are used in the mixture, along with cement, sand and water. The rocks in this concrete are very small. Do you see them?" he asked.

"Yes, there must be a bazillion of them in there!"

"I think there are a bazillion and two-hundred-fifty," said Layne from across the pool.

"No way, Layne!" Ronnie said with a six-year-old sass.

"So, if the rocks give it strength, is this type of concrete weaker?" Dell asked.

"We add more cement to make up the difference. So, instead of six-hundred pounds of cement per yard, we order seven hundred pounds of cement in each yard."

"What is cement?" Ronnie asked, continuing to push the mag around the top of the mixture.

"Well, cement is baked limestone powder and it's one of the ingredients in concrete. It reacts with the other ingredients and together they become solid over time," Scooter said.

Ronnie was thinking.

"All right, buddy. I have to get working so we don't lose this slab."

*

There was no official bus stop at Trinity Hospital, yet the dusty, yellow bus— number 322— made its daily stop just inside the parking lot to let the final two riders off.

"Thanks, Patty!" Bee smiled and gave the woman driver a high five, before descending the three steps to the hot asphalt. Bobby gave the high five without looking up at his mother's best friend.

"Hey! What happened to your face, Bobby Miller?"

"Nothing, Miss Patty."

"It don't look like nothing to me." She was glaring the way any concerned mother would look at their eight-year-old son who was obviously lying to their face.

"Bullying is not acceptable," she said, with her hand on his shoulder.

"Bee took care of it."

"Okay, Bobby, but you can stand up for yourself."

"What about Pastor Jerry?"

"What about him?"

"At church last week he was talking about turning the other cheek when someone slaps you."

"That is important. But Jesus never said we couldn't defend ourselves from a bully, young man."

He was confused by the apparent contradiction.

"That verse talks about if people are mistreating you because you believe in Jesus, then you endure it, knowing God will protect you."

"He wasn't telling us not to fight?" His forehead scrunched with the idea.

"We try to do everything we can to avoid fighting, but sometimes there is a good reason to stand up."

"When?"

"When people are taking advantage of others, especially the weak."

"So, what Bee did was a good thing?"

"I'm not sure what she did, but standing up for those who can't defend themselves is brave."

"Oh." Bobby was thinking.

"I know you can stand up for yourself, Bobby. You have a kind heart which is a good thing. Don't ever lose that part of you."

"Okay."

"There are those times you'll have to turn into a ferocious warrior to defend the weak."

Bobby considered what she was saying.

"Do you understand?"

"I think I do," he said, looking at his smiling sister standing at the door of the bus.

"Be brave, kiddo." Patty pulled the boy into a hug.

"I'll try, Miss Patty."

As the pair walked toward the hospital, Patty smiled and left.

"You and me," Bee said.

"Together," Bobby replied and they touched knuckles.

As the doors to Trinity Hospital's special oncology building opened magically in front of the pair, a whoosh of cool conditioned air struck their sweaty faces. Turning the corner, they headed for the stairway, preferring it to the elevator. Three floors up they raced, giggling at their exaggerated echos in the concrete stairwell. They gathered themselves before they opened the door to the "serious" floor. Their mother had scolded them several times for their lack of empathy and they did not want to have that extended discussion again.

"Hey, guys," said Old Man Willie, from behind the check-in desk. "Hey, Willie," the pair replied in unison with smiles. They never repeated the "Old Man" part of his name out loud while he was within earshot. Mom had said it was a respect thing.

Willie was helping a woman with some paperwork, so Bobby and Bee tiptoed their way to the vending machines on the far side of the waiting area. Mom had given them each their daily dollar to spend any way they wanted. They deposited their backpacks at their usual table and proceeded to negotiate with each other. Two dollars brought many more choices within reach, but they would have to share whatever they chose. Back and forth, each sibling gave the reasons for their selection. Most days they could decide on what to buy for their after-school snack, but there were a few days they couldn't come to a consensus and each bought what they could for a buck.

Settling in after a snack of corn chips and a Coke, their mother required them to work on homework or to be reading something worthwhile. Their table was the farthest away from the television, which was showing a daily doctor's talk show. The large windows next to the table opened to the far western horizon. Nestled up in the eastern hills, the third-floor oncology waiting room of Trinity Hospital held a commanding view of the area. The crisp north-south streets, many named for states, were perpendicularly cut by numerical roads which began counting from the city center some twenty-five blocks south.

The shimmering white gypsum of White Sands National Park stood out like a beacon and naturally drew the eye from their vantage point. The

Park attracted many visitors to the area throughout the year, but the average temperature of a balmy seventy degrees kept them around.

Dotted in rows to the north were several pistachio farms, each with their own roadside stand selling their nuts to visitors traveling along US 54.

Far to the southwest, the White Sands Missile Range Testing area would occasionally send streaking missiles off into the distance. Old Man Willie seemed to know when the facility was going to be launching, so he would alert everyone over the waiting area intercom to be watching the western sky.

Mom was an oncology nurse who arranged her schedule to be five eight hour days, unlike the usual rotation of four twelve hour shifts on, then four off. That schedule constantly moved the nurses' weekends and was impossible for single mothers to adapt their home lives around. A couple of nurses were in the same situation and had pressed the administration for the consideration.

Two hours a day during the school year, Bee and Bobby occupied the same table in the waiting area, with the ever-present Old Man Willie standing guard.

*

By nine o'clock, the hidden Lake Huron beach was filled with teenagers from all over the area. A radio was rocking out some tunes from the tailgate of a pickup truck. There was a large fire surrounded by bikini-clad girls and teenage boys. The mood was festive as the end of summer was drawing close. Half of the kids were celebrating heading off to college in a couple of days.

The lake was calm and twelve boats were anchored close to the shore, lined up in two rows. The older relics were closest to the beach. The expensive crafts had a row all to themselves, farther out in the lake. The crescent moon hung low over the eastern sky as people danced, played with a glow Frisbee, and hung out by the fire.

The famous red cups were held by all or were in close proximity. The keg sat in a kiddie pool filled with ice in the back of a silver pickup truck. Six teens were splashing around in the lake, as a lone couple walked into the woods, holding hands and carrying a blanket.

This was the scene that James cruised into with his pickup truck's exhaust thumping. He was trying to be as discreet as he could, idling into place in front of the silver beer truck.
As his vehicle went silent a teenager dressed in a black hoodie strolled to the passenger window.
"Dude, you're parked right on a headstone. You may want to move," he said through glassy eyes.
"Naw, the dead guys don't care," James said, and got out of his ride.
"Isn't it like desecration or something?"
"I don't care, man. You seen Ron around?" James asked.
"I don't know who that is," he slurred.
"Good talk." James said and walked away. He spotted the free beer pool, taking advantage of the opportunity to fill a red cup with the frothy beverage.
"Hey, Moby! You made it," Ron said. His expression gave away the fact he had been drinking for hours.
"Looks like you've been here all day, champ."
"No. The real party started at six. That's when the beer showed up," Ron said, downing the rest of his cup and swaying over to the keg.
"Everyone seems really young," James said, looking around.

Three driftwood logs were arranged around the fire, with ten people sitting on them. One guy was strumming a guitar, with four girls gathered around him fawning. Other couples were lying in the sand on the far side of the fire, swapping spit. It looked to James like they were attempting to eat each other's faces off. He winced, knowing he was in his mid-twenties hanging around high school kids for fun.
"I may as well make the best of it," he said to himself, knocking back the cup.
"Ron, where is old Phil?"
"I think he took some girl out to show her his boat," Ron said.
"You mean Daddy's boat?"
"Yeah. Come on over and I'll introduce you to a few people."
"A few high school chicks?"
"No, these girls have graduated. They're heading off to college next week."
"Oh, well, by all means, lead the way. They're eighteen?" James asked.

42

"Yeah," Ron said.

Walking over to the end of one of the driftwood logs, Ron introduced
James to Colleen.
"What happened to your friend?" Ron asked the girl.
"She went for the boat tour with Phil," she said, using quote fingers.
"Oh, right!"
"This is my friend— Moby."
"Moby?"

Ron clearly had too much to drink so James sat down close to Colleen.
"Hey, beautiful," he said with all of the charm he could muster, lying
through his teeth. Colleen wasn't even beautiful in her own eyes and not
that many found her attractive. Exactly the kind of girl James was
looking for at this party. Insecure, drunk, and homely was James's
dating trifecta.

"I'm James. Drunk Ron tells me that you're headed off to college?"
James asked, acting very interested.
"I thought you were Moby?" Colleen said.
"Not tonight."
"Yes! I'm heading out of this crappy town. Going to—"
James cut her off.
"Don't tell me! I have this gift and you'll be amazed," he said with a
broad "game show" smile which revealed a chipped front tooth.
Colleen took the bait.
"Let me guess, you're going to—"
"Wait! We should make this a bet or something," she said, feeling the
effects of the alcohol.
"Okay, what should we bet? This is an impressive gift I have," he said.
"Loser has to swim past the boats and go under-water."
"Great!" James said. Ron was lost in a fog and sitting on the ground in
front of the log.
"You're going to— wait! Let's make it a two-part bet," James offered.
"What do you have in mind?" Colleen asked.
"A swim for the loser of the first bet on the college that you're going to
attend. And a second bet for what you're going to be studying."
"What is the second bet?"
"Um, a walk through the cemetery at midnight!" James said.

"Deal!"
They shook on it, which was exaggerated for effect.
"For major bragging rights and the loser has to swim— my first answer is, Wayne State."
"Final answer?" Colleen asked.
"I was going to say Michigan State, but no, my final answer is Wayne."
"Aha! Wrong-o. You gotta go swim! Should of went with MSU. Woot! Woot! Woot!"
"Well, that's disappointing," he lied.
"Are we going to have the second bet now, or after you get wet?" she laughed.
"Let's have it now and up the stakes!"
"Ooh, a gambler!"
"Slam a beer and a walk in the scary cemetery!"
"Deal!" she said.
"You're going to be a special education teacher!"
"WHAAAT? How did you know that?"
"I told you I have a gift."
"Apparently your gift only works half of the time, Mr. Swimmer!"
"Yeah, yeah, yeah. When I get back, you're going to get an overflowing cup of beer, missy!"
"Bring it on, Mr. Swimmer."

James pulled his T-shirt over his head, dropped it in her lap, and then kicked his sandals at her feet. He was already in swim trunks so he ran the thirty feet to the water and kept on chugging through the shallows. James finished off the payment with a shallow dive in the cool, flat lake. Colleen watched and hooted from the log while he disappeared in the night between two anchored boats. James was searching for the *Submarine.*

In the pocket of his swim trunks, he had placed what he needed for this part of the celebration. A few long strokes later he came up behind the *Yellow Submarine.* James was silent as his head broke the surface of the water, listening for any sounds coming from inside the boat. There was some soft music playing and he lifted himself up far enough to see into the craft. The cabin door was closed.
"Perfect," he thought.

44

Reaching in his pocket James pulled out the wrench he had brought for this job. He had been planning this surprise all morning. Pulling in a quick breath he dove down behind the boat and felt for the transom plug. Placing the wrench James spun the plug free. He grabbed the brass plug, stuffed it in his pocket and swam away from the anchored craft. The *Submarine* was bubbling furiously into the night, taking on water. James had helped himself to the half-inch wrench at work, which he dropped to the bottom of the lake on his way back to the beach.

"My debt is paid," he announced to Colleen with his arms spread wide, bowing to drip water on her feet and legs.
"Wow, you took a long swim! Is that why they call you Moby?"
"It felt really good. It was my first bath in a month," he said, ignoring her question.
"Gross!"
James grabbed his T-shirt and touched her bare leg in the process. He glanced around at the activity. Seeing no one was watching, he pitched the brass transom plug as far as he could throw it. He used his T-shirt to dry himself off in an overt display of his ripped body.
"Colleen-the-college-girl has to pay up her debt now!"
"I'm ready, big boy!" she smiled.

James made sure he filled up her red cup as full as he could make it, pulling off the foam head. He also slipped in a tiny red pill from the zipper bag in his pocket, knowing it would put Colleen over the edge. He figured fifteen minutes after she slammed this beer, he could take her out into the cemetery and collect the second thing he showed up to this lame party for. He stepped over drunk Ron on the return trip to his perfect target girl.

*

"What are you spraying?"
"It's called surface retarder," Layne said.
"What does it do?" Dell asked.
"It stinks!" Ronnie said.
"You're right, young man."
"It smells like rotten eggs," Ronnie said.
"Indeed it does," Layne said.
"Your sniffer still works, kiddo," Scooter said and smiled.

"Yeah, at least Darrell didn't break that," Dell said.
"What happened to the kid?" Scooter was asking Dell so Ronnie, who was standing by Layne, wouldn't hear.
"Nothing. He's only ten and said someone else started it," pointing his eyes to Ronnie.
"Even if he did, that wasn't justified," Scooter said, looking to the boy.
"Exactly what I thought," Dell said.
"Where are the kids parents?"
"Different guy every month— the mom has some real issues," Dell said.

They both shook their heads in disbelief.
"Now a young kid has to pay for that, insane."
"We're having a fence put in just as soon as you guys are done," Dell said.
"Don't blame you," Scooter said.
Scooter moved to Layne and pointed to a spot he had missed with the spray.
"So what does the stinky yellow stuff do?" Ronnie asked Scooter.
"Well, it slows down the top of the concrete from getting hard but lets the rest rock up."
"Why do you need that?"
"Because Mr. Dell here is having custom concrete put in. It's called exposed aggregate."
"Supposed egg-gr-get?"
"Close enough, kiddo. In a little while we're going to wash it off and you'll get to see some serious magic happen," Scooter said.
"Cool!"
"And tonight you'll see even more cool tricks!" Scooter said.
"Tonight? Awesome!" Ronnie beamed.

*

"Moby, what the hell did you do?"
"What are you doing here, Ron?"
"I know you screwed with the *Yellow Submarine* last night at the party."
"What are you talking about?"
"Phil's boat is sitting on the bottom of Lake Huron, in ten feet of water!"

46

"No way! Kind of appropriate, though, since it's called the *Yellow Submarine*."
"I'm serious, dude! His dad wants to kill you, man," Ron said.
"I don't know what you're talking about," James said.
"B S. Why would you do something like that?"
James refused to respond.

"And what happened to Colleen?"
"What do you mean?"
"She was there with me then you walk in and charm the pants off of her."
"What? She was nice and all, but way too ugly for my taste."
"That's not what Maggie told me this morning. She said that you and a very drunk Colleen went for a walk in the darkness."
"Who is Maggie?"
"Colleen's friend that was on the sinking boat with Phil."
"Never met her," James said, finishing up with a customer.

"She said you two went for a walk and had sex in the cemetery, then you called her fat and ugly. She was so drunk; she just sat there while you walked off with her clothes."
"What?"
"Who does that, man?" Ron was getting loud.
"Not me," James said.
"Moby, you've always been a mean son of a gun. I thought that maybe eight years out of high school you would have changed."
"You're not my judge, Ron."
"If Phil's dad gets his way with the cops, they'll be hauling you in front of a judge in downtown Port Huron soon enough."
"What are you talking about?"
"The cops are investigating the sinking and a possible sexual assault!"
"They won't find me connected with any of that," James said.
"You took a nice girl—, who I liked— out into the darkness and took advantage of her."
"No, I didn't!" James glared.
"Did you drug her?"
"The sex was totally consensual— we were both drunk!"
"I ain't buyin' it, man! You screwed with her head just enough to get in her pants."
"Bull crap."

"I know you, Moby. I know that you did it. You are a sick freak! You hunt for victims, man. You always have."
"What goes through that twisted head of yours?"

Ron's fists balled up. He considered taking his growing anger out on James, right there on the public dock in front of God and the dozen people watching the shouting match.
James stuck his finger right in the middle of Ron's chest, just above his solar plexus with enough force to grab the man's attention.
"On the day you think you're big enough, I'll meet you any time, any place, and we can settle this thing that's been brewing between us, once and for all," James said.
"I'll be back to take you up on the offer, Moby Dick."
"Looking forward to it, Ron."

*

"So, what happened after confronting him on the dock?" Angie asked the skinny, younger Ronny Lawrence sitting in her first office.
"I was so mad at Moby. I didn't know what to do, so I went home thinking the cops would sort it out. I tried to call Colleen several times, without an answer. I was worried about her, hoping there was some way I could make what happened to her better— like I could fix it."
"Can you fix what happened or her?"
"I don't know about fixing anyone or anything."
"Can I tell you a story? It's short."
"Sure," Ronny said.

"A counselor friend of mine used to speak at conferences around the state. He liked to tell a story a guy told to him. He said this man had done some time in county jail for a long sentence. When he was inside, he had to participate in classes for anger management. While in a small group of eight guys, they were talking about what we're sharing here today. An inmate in his late fifties spoke up after one of the young men said he was just trying to 'change' his girlfriend. *If she would just change, then everything could go back to normal.'*

So, the Black fella couldn't take it anymore, stood up looked right at the guy, and said,

'You're going outside of your AOC! You've got to learn to stay inside your AOC, man!'
The guy asked him what he was talking about.
'Your AOC is the three feet that surrounds you and it's called your area of control or AOC. The only place in the entire universe you have any control of is that three foot circle you occupy. You can't change your girlfriend, man— you can only change you, cause you're the only one in your AOC!'"
"My AOC, huh?"
"Exactly," Angie said.
"I like it," Ronny said.
"So, where was Moby in relationship to your AOC after the party?"
"Inside."
"What?"
"Definitely inside."
"How do you figure?" Angie asked.
"I wanted to get so close to the mean, son of a whore, so I could strangle the life out of him with my bare hands. I wanted him inside my AOC, Angie. That, I can control!"

*

"Fire it up, Layne!"
Layne gave the ancient power washer a couple of strong tugs and she popped to life, spitting and sputtering for a few seconds, then "Old Red" was off to the races, shaking itself down into the soft sand just outside the form. Scooter pulled the trigger on the wand as the water spit out hard for a brief second, then coughed a couple of times before it started coming out at a steady pace.

"What are you guys doin' now?" Ronnie wanted to know, from inside the screen door far away from the loud and shaking power washer which was down at the other end of the pool.
"Makin' some magic happen, sonny!" Scooter said with a smile.

With that, Scooter began washing the concrete. As he did, the bright-yellow spray which had dried in the afternoon sun was pushed off in front of the strong spray. Scooter was making sure he held the tip of the wand at least a foot above the surface of the newly poured slab. Back and forth he worked the piles of yellow muck and gray sand. Layne joined him on the concrete. Using a broom, he pushed the sloppy mess off the edge, away from the pool. He was careful not to push down too hard.

"Look, Dell! Scooter and Mr. Layne are washing the stinky stuff right off!"
Dell smiled.
"LOOK!" he shouted. "There has to be a gazillion little rocks!"
"Well, would you look at that? Pretty cool, huh, kiddo?"
"Yeah! They told me this was 'supposin' the egg-ree-get.'"
"Making magic," Dell said, smiling behind the bruised boy, with his hands resting on Ronnie's shoulders.
"Yeah, makin' the magic happen!"

The six-year-old was mesmerized by the washing ballet.
"Mr. Layne is funny!" Ronnie was pointing at the concrete guy dancing with his broom.
Dell smiled.

Layne was the unofficial comic of the team— every quality crew had one accomplished, funny man. Most of the time Layne worked along just fine, yet he was always angling for the humorous— like when Bull was trying to finish some concrete and his pants were riding low around his hips, exposing what is known in the trade as a plumber's crack. Layne made his way over and sprinkled a handful of hot sand down his back side, sending laughter all around. Everyone except Bull, that is.

While funny, Layne was a strange cat. In his late forties, he still acted like he was twentysomething. He had tattoos all over his arms and legs, and the cream of the crop— was the skull in the middle of his back which announced to the world "Death is Forever!"

He was a guy most would think had a mean disposition, based on his appearance, but in truth he was a pushover. He was forever seeking ways out of work, trying to convince other, not-so-intelligent members of the crew to do his tasks, or taking on the hardest aspects of the job. Layne would be the guy to put a smudge of grease on the steering wheel or under a door handle. It would get worse when he would find your gloves and insert various objects in the fingers for kicks.

Bull had chased him around the jobsite after figuring out Layne had tied a toilet paper string on his belt. He couldn't figure out why the neighborhood kids were laughing and pointing at him throughout the day until he saw the shadow and heard the laughter. A classic Layne move.

*

Next door, inside the broken-down garage behind the house, young Darrell was peering from the back of a stack of old boxes. From the shadows, he was keeping a close eye on the exuberant kid with the bandages.
"I'm gonna beat the smile off of your dumb face, Ronnie." While he watched, a new mantra over-took his thoughts. The chant became more powerful as he repeated it. He began stabbing an old stuffed animal with a rusty steak knife as he spoke out his poem of death.
"Two in the chest, one in the head."
"Two in the chest, one in the head."
"Two in the chest, one in the head."
"Then you will fall and there lay dead."

*

Chapter Three
* Stars in the Sidewalk *

"Mr. Dell?" Ronnie was near the top of the stairs looking down at his elderly foster parents. They were both passed out in their recliners, leaving the television talking into the night.

"Mr. Dell?" He called one more time, not wanting to wake them— only making certain they were sleeping sound. If they stirred, he planned to ask for a drink of water. Neither moved a muscle.

Ronnie was on a mission to see the magic Scooter had told him about earlier in the day. He didn't want Mr. Dell or Miss Sharron to tell him how long he could be out in the middle of his highly anticipated dream. Moving back to his room, Ronnie threw the blanket over the pillow to make it look like he was in the bed. Grabbing his comfort blanket from the floor, he carried his shoes and closed the bedroom door.

He knew that in order to get past the sleeping fosters he would have to be quiet as a mouse. Earlier in the day, he had walked around the house to find the creaks in the floors and on the stairs. Now, Ronnie needed to remember where to place each and every step, all the way down to the landing, through the long hallway, and back to the dining room. The sliding glass door was quiet enough, but he was concerned about how heavy it was going to be.

Each step Ronnie took was a personal challenge to him. He had tried this maneuver many times in his other foster homes, but every other escape attempt had been thwarted by a suspicious and overbearing despot.

Today, he had been able to soften his fosters up by overplaying his pain and garnering their sympathy. He still hurt from the beating Darrell had given him— but he liked the attention he had received.

"Foster kids call it survival," he repeated to himself, descending the fourteen steps.

The head bandage covered his swollen left eye and impeded his progress in the darkened house. Step by careful step, he tiptoed down the hall with a cautious smile spreading across his face as he neared the dining room. He paused because the lights had been left blazing in the room. Sharron had left a partially finished puzzle— a picture of a field of intense-yellow sunflowers— splayed out over the monstrous dinner table. Ronnie made his way to the sliding glass door, which had been left ajar so the cool August evening could refresh the home.

Ronnie slid his skinny frame through the doorway, while gently rolling the screen aside.
"Success!" He smiled at his accomplishment and bent his ear back to the screen as he closed it. The fosters were still snoring away. He had escaped.

"What does magic look like?" he thought, and turned his attention to discovering what the concrete guys were talking about. Glancing around the back yard work site, he pulled his little blanket around his shoulders. The light from the dining room was flooding out on the new steps he was standing on. They felt warm to him for some reason he didn't understand. Pulling his shoes on without tying the laces, Ronnie stepped into no-man's-land and felt the wire mesh compress beneath the soles of his feet. Walking intentionally toward the pool, he was convinced the real magic had to be out on the new stuff the guys had poured today.

The sound the wire mesh made from each step reminded him of the cheap mattress springs on the bunks in the Children's Home. The memory flash made little Ronnie shudder while creeping into the darkness. The water was stirring in the pool next to him. The pool pump was singing its quiet song next to the garage. Ronnie stepped over the piles of muck. Scooter told them to avoid tracking the wash onto the slab because it would stick to the new concrete and leave ugly footprints.

Looking around, Ronnie was expecting something to turn on or jump up.
"Where is the magic?" he wondered aloud. As Ronnie's eyes adjusted to the darkness he could see stars up in the clear sky. Crickets were chirping in the grass behind the house while mosquitoes buzzed their malicious intent around his face. Then, Ronnie noticed the new concrete

beneath him. It was glowing with hundreds of blue stones shining up past his feet!

"There are stars in the sidewalk! There are stars in the sidewalk!" he said. He had to cover his own mouth to keep from yelling into the night.

Ronnie's sudden proclamation was heard from inside the garage next door by Darrell-the-vicious, his sardonic smile glowing in the darkness.

*

"No work today?" Angie asked Scooter, noticing his clean tennis shoes.

"Nope, today was a rain day for us," Scooter said.

"Are rain days welcomed or frustrating for you?"

"Sometimes they're frustrating because of the money, but we've been going hard for the entire summer, so getting an extra day off in the middle of the week is a good thing today. Until next Friday's paycheck, that is."

"Right." Angie said.

"And I may have to work Saturday for straight time," he said.

"So, we were talking about your work frustrations and things that had triggered some emotions last time," Angie started.

"Yes."

"You mentioned near the close of the session you thought about hurting the bike kid."

"Darrell, the sadistic neighbor kid."

"Right— Darrell." She made a note.

"It felt like what happened to Ronnie flipped a switch inside of me. It was replaying scenes from my childhood."

"Okay."

"What was the word you used when I put thoughts and feelings from my experiences onto another person or into their life?"

"Transference."

"That's it! I've been trying to remember the word all week," Scooter said.

"In what ways did you engage in transference last week?" Angie asked.

"Well, Darrell beating up Ronnie made me feel just like I have many times when I was young," he said.

"What emotion surfaced with the memory?"

Scooter thought for a moment.

54

"Out of control. I felt out of control." He tugged at the legs of his pants. "Control of what?"

"I guess it goes a long way back. I was about ten, at the orphanage— I mean the home for kids without parents," correcting himself.

"I remember touching on the subject," Angie replied.

"Well, part of what I never told you was I met this other kid there. I can still see him walking into the cafeteria for the first time. He had a small head with a pointy face. Everyone called him "The Rat" as soon as he showed up."

"Not flattering at all," Angie said.

"You're right, but the scrawny dude liked it. He wanted everyone to call him Rat. He wore it like a badge of honor."

"Okay."

"Well, Rat and I were bunkmates for a year. We got to know each other's stories, all of the good and ugly stuff. The thing about Rat-man was he had such a filthy mouth. Every thing was 'F this' and 'F that.' It wore on me so much that I started avoiding him."

Angie nodded.

"He would get busted for talking like a truck driver all of the time," Scooter said. "Then our room was getting into trouble and having extra chores, because this guy couldn't shut his trap for five minutes."

"How does this equate with what happened to Ronnie?" Angie asked.

"That part doesn't, but you needed to know the history in order to understand what happened next."

"Oh, okay."

"So, one night after we had cleaned the toilets for the fourth night in a row because of Rat, me and the two other guys in the room decided we were gonna teach him a lesson."

Scooter wasn't sure that he wanted to continue and paused.

"Go on," Angie said.

"We took full-size bars of soap and slipped them into socks. Then we beat the living crap out of him."

"You took part in that?" Angie's eyes narrowed.

"Kinda."

"There really isn't any middle ground here, Scooter. Either you did, or you didn't," Angie insisted.

"I hit him a few times, but I couldn't get past the sound the bars were making on his ribs and head."

"Wasn't he screaming or calling for help?"

"He was knocked out cold with the first hit. Jimmy beat the snot out of Rat. He was enraged, landing blow after blow after blow. We had to knock him down to get him to stop. He would have killed him."

"Why did you stop hitting him?"

"The kid was a pain in the neck, but he didn't deserve to die," Scooter was tearing up with the convicting memory.

"So, what is the connection to Ronnie?"

"It was like Darrell was an enraged Jimmy and The Rat was Ronnie. I felt like I needed to protect the kid or he would have died. Like I needed to knock Darrell off Ronnie the way I had tackled Jimmy."

"You felt so powerfully about that issue, you decided to come in to see me again?"

"I think so. I've been asking myself that question since it happened."

"What happened to the kid?"

"Which one?"

"The Rat, as you called him," Angie cringed.

"He was still my roommate. I told the truth and they let me stay. Jimmy and the other kid got moved to another room."

Scooter paused, holding back his emotions. "The poor guy was so beat up, but he thanked me for saving him," Scooter admitted.

"How do you feel about that now?" Angie asked.

"I have regret, but not for what you think."

*

From the shadows Darrell watched Ronnie dance and flop around like he was a character in a kids fantasy movie. Young Mr. Bruise was beside himself with joy, overflowing with happiness. Then Darrell recognized what Ronnie was dancing on. The new concrete had shiny-blue lights glowing all over it. The scene appeared to Darrell like Ronnie was lost somewhere in the vast universe, able to walk among stars and dance with the galaxies. Darrell felt a stream of burning jealousy burst through the night and grab hold of his aching, empty heart. He was witnessing a beaten, broken down kid experience unadulterated joy and wondered how it was possible. How could such a loser be so happy? The question lingered only for a moment. Because Ronnie was alone, Darrell crept closer.

The light in the dining room went cold and Dell could be seen shutting the door, flipping the lock and pulling the blinds. Ronnie had stopped in his tracks for the moment of commotion, then was back into his far-away galaxy, dancing, and spinning to a silent rapturous tune encased in his heart.

Darrell was trying to plan what to do next. Glancing around the yard, he noticed it was a huge mess in the middle of the large project. There were plenty of dangerous objects lingering for Ronnie to get hurt on. All of the steel stakes holding up the forms were pointing blunt ends up into the night sky. The wire on the ground inside of the forms could stab into feet or hands. The pool itself was a threat for a young boy to drown in. Darrell thought about charging over and finishing what he had begun, but there was an orange construction fence up around the whole area, separating him from the ball of twirling bandages.

Then, fate twisted its ugly head. In an instant, Ronnie stepped off of the concrete, tripped on the wire, and fell face down, landing with a thud. Darrell almost laughed out loud and would have if he hadn't covered his own mouth. He was watching Ronnie from the dark corner of the garage next to the humming pool pump.

"What the—?" Darrell strained through the night, trying to see the brat on the ground. Ronnie wasn't moving.

"I bet he knocked himself out with all of his stupid dancing," Darrell whispered. "I need to finish this."

*

"How do you know what I think?" Angie asked.

"I guess I don't."

"You guess?"

"I don't know, Angie."

"So why do you have regret?"

"I regret saving Rat," Scooter said.

"From the beating?"

"No, later throughout my early years. I let him stay in my life, and looking back, I should have walked away much sooner."

"What do you mean?" Angie asked.

"He was a drain on everything," Scooter said.

"How so?"

"All the talking, cussing, and swearing. Like he was constantly vying for my attention. It sucked the life out of me."

"What did you do?"

Scooter wasn't sure if he could trust Angie with that information yet.
"Let's just say that he's dead to me now."
"Really?"
"The Rat is dead. End of story."

*

"James, you're only ten years old. Do what your father says," she said.
"Mom, I don't want to pick up the trash around the yard," the boy
replied.
"This is not about what you want, young man. This is about you
learning to obey your parents!"
"He's NOT my father!"
"He works hard and gives us everything we need," she insisted.
"He's a drunk and a loser!"
"You had better watch your mouth!"
"I don't."
She cut him off. "Enough!"
"But—"
"Not another word! Or you'll be picking up every piece of trash around
the entire block and I will walk with you making certain you do it!"
"That's not fair!"
"And you'll wear a dunce cap the entire time you're outside!"
"I am sick of this. It's not my trash laying around the yard," James said.
"It doesn't matter! This isn't about who owns the trash— this is
punishment for the hateful way your treat your brother, the kids at
school, and us!"
"I don't care. I hate you all!"
"You will do as you are told, James! This has to end."
"I will run away!"
"Not before the trash! I told you to get me a beer out of the fridge, then
get the garbage picked up!"
"This sucks."
"Right now! Or do I have to get out Grandfather's belt?"

James sulked off to the kitchen to fetch his scrawny, alcoholic mother
another beer. He was thinking if he got her enough wobble pops maybe

she would forget about the punishment. Then another idea hit him in the face. Before he stepped into the kitchen he bolted into the bathroom and rummaged in the medicine cabinet.

"There it is," he said, grabbing the small brown bottle. It was only half full of the blue-green capsules. He took two, replaced the lid, and exited.

"How many are left?" Mom shouted over the T. V. She was talking about the beer.

"Five," he said pulling the door of the grimy fridge open, not caring to count.

"Bring me two!"

He grabbed hold of two cold brown bottles and set them on the counter. Opening one, he emptied both capsules into the bottle and smiled. "That should take care of the trash," he said.

Half an hour later, James put one unopened beer back into the fridge so it would cool before "the guy" got home from work. Mom was passed out on the couch while he hatched another plan, which required a plastic trash bag.

Down the hall, his brother was napping.

"Hey! Get up now!" James's stern words shook the boy from his slumber.

"What do you want?" yawned the boy.

"Mom is on the rampage again and said if we didn't get the trash picked up in the yard she was getting the belt out for Dad, and giving him permission to give us a beating."

"Why? What did I do?"

"I'm not sure, but we have got to get going right now!"

"I don't want to!"

"Do you want to feel the belt snap across your backside again?"

"No! I'm going to ask her."

"You go ahead. Wake her up and she'll box your ears again."

"She's sleeping? I thought that she was yelling?"

"She was screaming for you and has been drinking a lot. You know how mean she gets when she has had too many, right?"

"I don't want to pick up the trash!"

James slapped the boy hard across the face.

"Don't speak to me that way!" James screamed.

The crying could be heard throughout the house, but it didn't matter to James anymore.

"I'll beat you stupid if you don't get up right now and pick up the trash." James towered over the boy who was three years younger. He was bent on getting the yard cleaned up and would do whatever it took to impose his will over the crying brat. He slid the black trash bag over his brother's head and twisted.

"You had better do what I tell you," he whispered to the side of the squirming bag. A surge of adrenaline pushed through his head, confirming the vow he had made to himself. *"People are a means to an end, a product to be consumed."* The die was cast in young James.

*

Just as Darrell was about to move from the shadows to get a better view of Ronnie, a light clicked on upstairs.

Dell and Sharron had finally made it off of the recliners and up the steps to their room. Sharron paused to look in on Ronnie from the hallway. She smiled, convinced he was sleeping in the midst of the pile of blankets and went to get ready for bed.

"Did I tell you about Darrell?" Dell asked Sharron, who was in the adjacent master bathroom.

"Tell me what about him?" she asked, pausing to hear.

"I caught the little deviant talking to Ronnie."

"When?"

"It was after dinner when Ronnie went outside on the front porch."

"I thought he was coloring at the table?" Sharron asked.

"He was."

"What happened?"

"Darrell must have thought Ronnie was alone. I was sitting on the couch reading and I heard someone whispering."

"Whispering?"

"It was hard to hear, so I got up and crept over to listen without being seen."

"And what did you hear, Dell?" Sharron asked, looking at him now, with her hand on her hip.

"Darrell was telling Ronnie he was sorry for beating him up. Something like, 'I don't know what comes over me sometimes.'"
"Really? Did you believe him?"
"Not for a second. Then he said they should play together again."
"How did Ronnie respond?"
"He just said, maybe," Dell said.
"I'm not going to let that psychopath anywhere near Ronnie again!" Sharron said.
"I agree," Dell said with his hands held out, with a "don't kill the messenger" attitude. "He asked him if he wanted to come play in his fort."
"Fort?"
"Supposedly it's in his garage," Dell said.
"There is no fort in that garage! I bet he just wants to get him alone again."
"I'm not sure, Shar."
"How did Ronnie respond?" she asked.
"'I don't know,' is all he said."
"What did you do?"
"I moved over to the front door, walked outside, and asked Ronnie what he was up to. Never heard anymore from Darrell. I didn't even see the kid," Dell said.
"He was probably hiding in the bushes. That kid scares me, Dell. He has a real problem."
"He was never like this before. Something has set him off, or he's been really good at hiding his rotten side for a long time."
"Do you remember how long they've lived here?"
"It's only been a year and a half, but he's never done anything like this before."
"That you know of," she said.
"Fair enough. We have to keep our eye on him."
"And Ronnie," she said.
"I'm going to have a talk with Darrell's mother tomorrow."
"That is a good idea. We can't have our foster kid living in fear. I'll never let him around our grandkids."

*

"Come here, boy!"
"Yes, sir," James said.

"Who do you think you are?"
James didn't reply with words, only defiant eyes. His stepdad recognized the simmering insubordination in the urchin. Lurching for the boy's neck, he pulled him over to the basement stairwell and, like an armful of dirty laundry, threw him down the flight. James instinctively reached out for the handrail, but failed to catch it in time. He bounced on the third and seventh steps, fracturing his left arm and chipping a tooth on the damp concrete floor. His stepdad followed down after him, pulled him to his feet, and beat him unconscious with several blows to the head and a few more to the ribs.

Dear old dad was certain James would never put a plastic bag over his son's head again. He deposited the limp body into the dank pantry beneath the stairs and forced the swollen door shut. Retreating to the main floor, he calmly closed the solid basement portal and clicked the lock in the clasp.

"Did you teach that no good kid of mine a proper lesson for what he did to me?"
"Message received," he said with a noxious smile.
"How long will you give him in lockup?"
"This one is going to cost him three weeks."
"Seems about right," she said.
"Beer?"
"Thought you'd never ask."

*

"Hey, Mom, can you help me?"
"What do you need, Bobby?"
"I have an assignment for history class."
"What is it?"
"Mr. Blaine wants us to do a family tree."
"Oh," she paused. "And what do you want to know?" Kim asked.
"I'd like to know more about my dad."
"What do you need to know?"
"Mom, I know losing him was hard and, if you don't feel like talking about this I can tell my teacher what I know about your side of the family."
"That side is a dead end."

"What are you guys talking about?" Bee joined from the couch.
"Our family tree."
"For school? Isn't it a fifth-grade thing?" Bee remembered.
"Yes, and our family tree looks like a telephone pole on paper," Bobby said.
Laughter from Bee, not Mom.

"I figured this day would come." She paused from cutting the tomato for the dinner salad.
"I've been wondering for a long time," Bobby said.
"You have?"
"Of course."
"Why haven't you asked me?"
"I think I asked about five years ago, but you got real quiet and sad. I decided I didn't want you to feel bad, so I just learned to live with the idea of not knowing much."
"You have a kind heart, Bobby," Kim said and reached for his face.
"Do you remember anything, Bee?"
"Not much. I have this flash memory of being held by a man who I think was Dad. More like a dream, really. He was swinging me around in circles and singing. Then he blew into my neck and I laughed, the bill of his baseball hat hit my cheek— that's it," Bee said.
"What did the place you were swinging around in look like?" Kim asked.
"There was wood all over the walls and crazy yellow carpet."
"That was the house we lived in when we first got married. He was so proud he was able to get enough cash together to buy the place."
"Really?"
"How old were you?" Bee asked.
"We were both twenty-three. We were so in love it hurt." A smile washed over Kim with the thought. "After dating for only five months we decided not to wait any longer. We knew we were meant for each other. So, we rushed off to Mackinac Island and got married."
"You got married on an island?"
"Yes, a romantic island in Lake Huron. No cars are allowed, so horse and buggy or bicycles are the only way to get around. We managed to spend our honeymoon night at the Grand Hotel." The memory brought another smile.
"The famous one with the huge porch?" Bee asked.
"One and the same."

"So, do you have questions?" Kim asked Bobby.

"What about my dad's parents?"

"He grew up in an orphanage near Detroit. I don't know anything about his biological parents. He had a foster mom who adopted him when he was a teenager."

"Is she still alive?"

"I don't know. When we left after your dad's. . . demise, I think I heard she may have passed away a few years later."

"So you don't know much about him?"

"No, I know everything about him, just not much about his family."

"Did he have any siblings?"

"No," Kim said. She didn't enjoy lying to her kids.

*

The sand still felt warm beneath him. Ronnie knew he had taken a fall. He could remember the rush of the ground. His arms were wrapped in his favorite blanket as he had stepped off of the concrete. He had forgotten about the wire mesh that tripped him up.

"I should have stayed on the magic sidewalk," he thought to himself.

Looking down, he saw his limp body. He knew he had two holes in his chest and one in his head. A large pool of his dark-red blood soaked the ground. Ronnie was confused by the scene. His body was motionless, yet he was standing over himself.

"*What was this feeling*?" he asked no one in particular. Then it dawned on him.

"*I feel like I'm still dancing in those stars, but better. Or maybe, more!*" A great peace washed over the six-year-old soul, unlike anything he had ever experienced.

"Hey kid." The voice came from behind him.

Ronnie wasn't startled or afraid of the deep-baritone voice filling his new reality.

"Hey, mister. Where am I?" Ronnie asked.

"What do you mean? You're right here."

"But where is here? Because it isn't there," he said pointing at his lifeless body.

"Well, we're here and not there at the same time."

"Huh?"

64

"The body you've taken leave of, remains there, but you— you're here."
"Where is here, then?"
"Here is a place between there and home."
"And what are you doing in this halfway space?"
"I've come to bring you home."
"What if I want to stay here?" asked Ronnie to the tall man sitting on the back steps.
"We can stay for a minute, Ronnie, but then we have to be on our way."

Ronnie considered the idea.
"I know I want to go home, but I feel weird about leaving here."
"Both are true."
"They are," Ronnie agreed.
"Exchanging the familiar for the obscure feels difficult."
"Dell and Sharron are good people," Ronnie said looking up at the house.
"Indeed."
"This is going to hurt them."
"There will be purpose in the pain, Ronnie— as with all pain."
Ronnie thought about the statement.

"Do you know why this happened?" the deep voice asked from behind him.
"Yes. It was my time," Ronnie said.
"You have faith, kid."
"I asked Jesus to help me and He has," Ronnie said.
"It's not so easy for most people, Ronnie."
"I wonder why?"
"The word 'childlike' comes to mind," he smiled.
"I guess."
"Many things get in the way of seeing," the voice said.
Ronnie turned to face the mysterious character.
"My eye was swollen shut and Jesus let me see," Ronnie said.
"How long have you been able to see?"
"When Darrell was beating me with his fists, I thought I was going to die."
"You have a great faith."
"I don't know 'bout that," Ronnie said.
"Trust me, you do."

"What's your name?"
"People call me Bob."
"Hmm. I thought it would be different."
"Really?"
"Like Gabriel or something from the Bible."
"I hear that a lot," Bob said.
"I bet."
"Say good-bye. We have to go."
"Okay."

Putting the old world behind him, Ronnie took Bob's hand and they left for home.

*

Chapter Four
* Death Star *

"Mom wake up!"

"What's wrong, Darrell?"

"I just got a call from Pete."

"Pete?"

"You know, we lived at his house for a while? He had the huge black dog. Down in South Park."

"Pete Vargas?"

"Yeah, Pete!"

"What does he want?"

"He said he was at the Griz having a few with some friends."

"That's nice, honey."

Darrell shook her. "Mom, Donny is out!"

"What?"

"Donny is out! Pete was having a few beers with some of his work buddies and Donny came into the bar."

She sat straight up, propelled by fear, and trying to comprehend.

"Donny got out of prison and Pete said he was looking for you. Looking for us."

"Crap. You're not kidding?"

"We've got to get out of here right now. Pete was calling from the toilet stall inside of the Grizzly bar. We have about ten minutes."

"Only grab what you need." She threw the sheet off and pulled on her pants. Smacking herself on the face, Tina tried to focus.

Darrell ran out of her room to his. The mattress held his small duffel bag which was already bulging with everything he cared about. Five minutes later, the two of them pulled the squeaky doors open on the worn-out, blue Ford Focus. She slammed her door without regard for noise— fear had overtaken the booze— while Darrell gently closed his side.

"Come on, Mom, let's get out of here!" He played the fear card perfectly.

"Blueberry" fired up on the second try. Tina wished the piece of crap had a better muffler as they backed out of the driveway. She slammed into the neighbor's mailbox across the street and snapped the pole clean off.

"MOM! You ran over the mailbox!"

"Shut up, Darrell! I'm doing the best I can. You . . . you remember Donny is a homicidal maniac, right?"

"Yeah."

"Shut up, and let me drive," Tina screeched.

"Maybe you shouldn't have drank so much," Darrell pushed back.

"Stop it!"

"Where are we gonna to go?"

"I don't know." She was trying to think with a woozy head.

"What about Canada?" Darrell asked.

Tina considered the idea. "Okay— good idea. . . As a felon, he won't be able to cross the border!"

"You smell like booze, Mom. They won't let you in, either," Darrell said.

"I don't have my ID!" she said.

"I grabbed your ID. We can stop to get a coffee and gum, then drive down to Marine City and cross over on the ferry."

"Nah, nah, they shut that ferry down. I guess her neighbor got transferred out of there up to the Soo."

"Huh?"

"Sault Ste Marie. In the Upper Peninsula!"

"Crap," he said and panic jumped right in. Darrell knew he needed to get out of the country. His shoes still had some of the ooze washed off from the concrete by the pool at Ronnie's.

"There's another one in Algonac— we can cross there and go to a friend's house in Wallaceburg."

"Don't stop in town. There's the twenty-four-hour gas station south of St. Clair."

"Good idea, kiddo," Tina smiled at her fast-thinking son.

"How did your bike get in the car?"

"I put it in before we left—" Darrell didn't say how long before.

*

"Morning, sweetie," Dell said.

"Morning."

"Let me get your coffee." He stood up from the table, leaving his morning devotional.

"Where's Ronnie?"

"Still snoozin' under the blankets."

"Kind of warm for that?"

"I know. You want the French Vanilla creamer?"

"Just a splash. I figured the boy would be up bouncing off the walls with the guys coming back."

"So did I," Dell said. "Wanna sit on the porch?"

"Sure, that's why I got all dressed up."

"You got dressed for the neighbors." He smiled at his own wit.

She plucked his cheek with a kiss, and they went outside through the front door. The sky was crystal clear while the breeze was tender warm. Song birds greeted them from the ancient maple tree on the front lawn as a golden finch jumped out of the holly bush off to their right. Cicadas were buzzing out their primal songs, announcing the coming heat.

"This is my favorite time of year," Sharron said, pausing and breathing in deep through her nose.

"We should run Ronnie over to the beach later. It's going to be a warm one. The hot bugs are out," Dell said, taking his place in his Adirondack chair.

"Good idea."

"We would have to go to Lakeside. I think Lighthouse would be too strong for him."

"The current is really strong with the water being so high."

"The beaches sure have been taking a beating these last couple of years."

"But the water sure is pretty."

"And the boaters love it."

"You miss the boat," she said and sipped, looking his way with a shift of her eyes.

"On days like today I do," he said with a melancholy smile.

"I do, too."

"Look, here come the troops," he said.

"Only two trucks today?"

"Their loader is already here."

"Oh yeah, I forgot about that. How much longer do you think it will take them?"

"Mack was saying it would be another week before they were out of here."

The air brakes on the International set with a sudden whoosh, as the tool truck parked in front of the home. The pickup pulled in front of the large panel truck. There were two guys in each vehicle. Scooter and Bull in the pickup, Layne and Mack in the truck that looked like a big billboard, complete with a picture of a thin smiling Mack plastered all over the side. The bright red lettering declaring *"Mack's Concrete"* could be seen from a block away. Ten descriptive pictures decorated the sides of the rig. Individual squares identified the type of work they specialized in, complete with action photos of the smiling crew. Dell had taken the tour through the images just the day before.

"Morning!" said a waving Bull.
"Morning, guys!" Sharron said.
"Ready for the heat?" Dell asked. "Gonna be almost ninety today."
"I may accidentally fall into the pool," Layne quipped.
"Whatever you need to do!" Dell said.
"Scooter, go get the loader fired up, so we can take the tools back in the bucket," Mack said and stretched.
"Right, boss."
"The key is in the ashtray."

Scooter grabbed the key and headed to the back yard. He was thinking about Darrell, wondering if the kid was going to jump out at him from the row of green hedges which followed the drive back. Scooter pictured him covered in ketchup and yelling, *"Gotcha!"*
"Dang kid," he thought as he rounded the corner into the back.

At first, the scene didn't compute for Scooter. *"Why was Ronnie lying on the ground?"*
"Why was there dried blood?"
"HEY!"
"SH— Oh my God!"
"HELP!"
"What happened, little buddy?" Scooter raced over, smashing through the temporary orange fence, to the boy who was still wrapped up by a blanket around his shoulders. The skin on the side of his face was a horrid shade of gray. Ronnie was lying face-down with his forehead resting unnaturally on a form. His head was stuck on a stake.

Scooter didn't know what to do. His mind was racing, so he reached in to feel for a pulse on his neck.

"Oh no!" Scooter recoiled from the feel of the cold flesh.

"Oh my God! Oh my God!" He turned his head and threw up his morning coffee into the pool, losing his grungy baseball cap in the process.

Layne entered the gory scene and ran into an invisible wall with the ungodly sight. The shock stopped him in his tracks. Bull was right behind, followed by a huffing, red-faced Mack. Scooter was on his knees next to the lifeless boy with one hand on the blood-stained sand and the other on the little guy's back, weeping without regard.

"What the hell?" Layne said, shaking his head, fighting an instant swell of rage.

"Oh no!" were the only words Bull could manage.

Mack did an about face, hoping to run interference for the foster parents. As he reached the corner to look down the driveway, he ran into Dell with Sharron a few steps behind.

"Wait, guys! Please— please wait," Mack pleaded.

"What is it?"

"It's horrible and you won't want to see it."

Dell rushed past his outstretched arm and rounded the corner. He had already witnessed plenty of horrible in his life. Vietnam made sure of it.

"Sharron, please!"

"What is it, Mack?"

"The little bo. . ." Before he could finish the word, an ungodly shriek came from Dell in the back yard.

"Dell!" Sharron pushed her way past Mack, forcing herself onto the scene.

Mack grabbed for his phone and dialed 911.

The screaming from Sharron commenced as a female voice came to life in Mack's ear.

"911. What's your emergency?"

A neighbor raced past Mack as he tried to talk.

"What's your emergency?"

"A little boy—"

"Sir?"

"There has been an accident," he managed. "I... I think he's dead."

Mack hung up his phone, slid down the wall of the house, and put his face into his hands.

"Wait!" Scooter shouted at Dell just as he was bending to grab the boy's body.
"His head is stuck. . ."

Sirens were racing in close within a minute.
Two police cars slid to a stop in the street next to the drive. Before they had crossed the sidewalk in a full-out sprint, an EMS truck stopped at the end of the driveway.

Dell and Sharron were reaching for the boy, as the first officer came around the corner.
"Wait!" the cop shouted. "Is there a pulse?"
"No, he's gone. By the looks of it, for quite some time." Layne said, bending over with both his hands on his knees.
"I need you to back up! I'm sorry, but we have to do this."
"Everyone, back up— now!" The second, shorter cop said with a calm authority.
"We need you to get back in case there's any evidence to collect. You three move over against the house," he instructed Scooter, Layne, and Bull.
"I need to know who you are and your relation to the boy."
"I'm Sharron. This is. . . this is my husband, Dell," she said wiping at tears.
"Who is the boy?"
"He's our foster child," Dell said, as tears rained down his face.
"Who are these other guys?"
"Those guys are working on the pool, and he's the neighbor," Dell said unable to control his emotions.
"I thought you said he was sleeping, Dell?" Sharron was frantic.
"I looked in on him just twenty minutes ago," he said.
"A detective is on the way folks. We're going to need statements from everyone," the tall cop said.

*

"Hi, folks, my name is Donna McBride. I'm a detective with the Port Huron Police Department. I am very sorry for your loss. I need to interview everyone. I'm not accusing anyone of anything. I want to understand— better said, I need to understand— what has led to Ronnie's death. The interviews will be ongoing until we get to the bottom of what happened. I want to honor this boy's life by getting to the truth of how this all took place. Thank you in advance for your cooperation."

The crew leaning against the rear of the house was in shock as the detective made her announcement. A blanket had been placed over the body near the pool as a shroud of disbelief descended on the scene like a pall over a casket. Dell and Sharron were sitting on the new steps, retreating into their own worlds of fear and regret.

"Detective!" Scooter spoke up, breaking the eerie silence.
"Yes?"
"I think there's something you should know."
"You are?"
"Scooter. Part of the crew working here."
"Scooter?"
"Yes, ma'am."
"I'm not old enough to be called a ma'am yet," she smiled, attempting to bring some levity while noticing his red eyes.
"Okay, sorry."
"Call me Donna." She offered her hand.
"Donna, it is."
"I wanted to tell you, this young boy was having a problem with the neighbor kid next door."
"What do you mean?"
"The neighbor's name is Darrell. He's about ten or eleven, twice the size of Ronnie and had literally beaten the snot out of him just a couple of days ago."
"Okay." She was taking notes.
"Darrell has been hanging around whenever we're here," he said.
"Hanging around where?"
"He's been watching us like a hawk. All day long we notice him looking over at what's going on. He keeps to his own yard, but he's always interested. Today, his house appears abandoned."
"Do you know his full name?"
"No idea."

"Okay, I'll have an officer look into this right away. Thank you, Scooter. I need to talk to the parents first, then I'll get back to you guys."

"Okay," Scooter said and turned to leave.

"Did you see the beating?" The detective asked before he took a second step.

"No, I only saw the results of it, but I think Dell did."

"Dell?"

"The foster dad. The homeowner— sitting over on the steps," Scooter lifted his chin in Dell's direction.

"Right. Stay put and we'll talk in a bit." Donna managed an obligatory partial smile.

*

"Thanks, Patty, for taking the kids camping."

"It was a blast! Have you ever been up to Ruidoso?" Patty asked.

"Not formally. I think I drove through coming over from Portales."

"If you came across 70, you went right through it. How long did you live in Portales?" Patty asked.

"I finished up my degree at Eastern New Mexico."

"Go Hounds! My brother-in-law went there," Patty said.

"Oh. I lived there for three years. After college I had a job in a clinic in town."

"Yeah, I knew about the clinic job," Patty said. "More wine?"

"Yes!"

"Bobby told me he had to do a family tree, but said it looked like a telephone pole."

"Ha ha, yes, it kinda does. He was asking me questions about his dad for the project."

"Oh yeah?" Patty said.

"I haven't ever told them the real story. I always dance around it." The wine had loosened her lips.

"Well, you've never told anyone that I know of."

"I know, I'm sorry."

"Hey, I don't ever want to pry into your business," Patty said.

"No, I'm just so ashamed," she said.

"Why?"

"Well, Patty, I left the love of my life because he was a drunk and had no motivation to change."

74

"I'm so sorry. Out here in the wild west it happens all of the time."
"Yeah, working at the hospital, I see it too."

The wine warmed. "If the truth be told, I've never stopped loving him."
"Do you miss him?" Patty asked.
"Not too much any more. When I start to feel lonely, I only have to remember the drunken crap and I snap right out of it in a hurry."
Both ladies laughed.
"So, the kids— they believe he is dead?" Patty whispered.
"Yes. It was the convenient lie after Bobby came along."
"So. . . is Bobby?"
"His kid?"
"Yeah? Or did you have a fling in the hustling metropolis of Portales?" Patty said and laughed.
"You've seen the town, right?"
"Yes, I have— that's why it's funny," Patty said.
"No, I left Michigan when I found out I was pregnant. There was no way he was going to ruin another child."
"That's a hard life, girl," Patty said.
"It's why I had to take three years to finish one year of college."
"Right."

*

"I am so sorry for your loss. I'm Detective Donna McBride and I need to ask you some questions to understand what took place here."

"I'm Sharron, and this is my husband Dell." Both were visibly distraught.
"You're the home owners?"
"Yes."
"This is your full-time residence?"
"Yes."
"How long have you lived here?"
"Twenty-three years."
"What's the boy's name?
"Ronnie," Dell said, handing the officer Ronnie's small case file he had retrieved from the downstairs file cabinet, while Sharron shook with grief.

"You're his foster parents?" Donna looked into the envelope, pulling up a couple of documents to examine.

"Yes."

"How long has he been under your care?" she was asking while searching through the file.

The question stung the foster parents like a punch in the gut. "Just a couple of weeks. I have the exact date written on the calendar inside," Sharron managed.

"I'm sure it's in the folder," Dell said.

"How would you describe Ronnie's behavior over the last couple of weeks?"

"He's been well-behaved," she said.

"And you, sir?"

"He's— was— a good kid. He was confused about many things. He needed some stability in his life and I think he found it here."

"What do you think he was confused about?"

"He had no cohesion, no order— it was like he was craving it."

Donna took more notes. "Is he your first foster child?"

"No, we've had many over the years," he said.

A uniformed officer brought them tissues, and the pair nodded in appreciation.

"We haven't fostered in the last fifteen years or so," Sharron said. "Our daughter is a case-worker and asked us to come out of retirement for this little boy."

"Who is your case-worker? I know it can't be your daughter."

"Kenisha Wexler. I have her card inside."

"I'll need her number." Donna studied the couple.

Sharron nodded.

"When did you last see the boy alive?" She wanted to see their reactions to the question.

"Last evening. We tucked him in around nine." Sharron lost control. "I checked on him around eleven thirty."

"What do you mean?" Donna wasn't taking notes on the paper now, just in her mind.

"I opened his door and looked in."

"What did you see?

"I saw a pile of blankets that looked like he was asleep in bed." Sharron looked right at the detective.

"Did you see him?"

"Pardon me?"

"I need to know if you actually saw Ronnie sleeping or just a pile of blankets?"

"Only blankets." Sharron briefly covered her face in shame. "With his injuries and not sleeping much the night before, I didn't want to disturb his rest."

"That's what I saw when I looked in on him this morning," Dell said, as tears cascaded down his face.

"I need to have a look in his room."

They made their way up to the bed room.

Enveloped in a state of shock, Dell and Sharron still took notice of two inquisitive cops inside their house.

The veteran detective scanned the bedroom and held up her hand for the couple to stop.

"As you can see, the blankets were arranged by someone to make it appear that Ronnie was asleep in his bed."

"I do."

"So do I," Dell agreed.

"Do you know who would do this?" Donna asked.

"No."

"No. It was dark in here. Ronnie refused to have a nightlight."

"I need photos of everything in here," Donna said to a cop behind the couple.

"Don't touch anything! People, this is an active crime scene— do not touch anything!" Donna yelled from the top of the stairs. "Let them know outside."

"Roger that," a cop said.

"Dell, how was your relationship with Ronnie?"

"It was great. We had a lot of fun. We were planning to go to the beach today," he said, dabbing at his snot.

"What about the fight with the neighbor boy?"

"That kid is troubled." Dell glared.

"Where does he live?"

"Next door, but the place looks empty today."

"What is the boy's name?"

"Darrell— not sure of his last name," he said.

"It's Patrick," Sharron spoke up from her tissue. "Darrell Patrick."

"Tell me about the alleged altercation between Darrell and Ronnie. When did this occur?"

"Two days ago. Darrell came over to play with Ronnie, which they had done a few times. They started playing with some trucks in the pile of sand behind the pool. We were inside making dinner when I heard Ronnie screaming."

"I ran out and found Darrell sitting on top of Ronnie, punching him in the face. It was vicious."

"What did you do?"

"I shouted and pulled him off."

"Ronnie was trying to protect his head. His lip was split and his eye was puffing up."

"When you pulled him off, what was Darrell's reaction?"

"He had a smirk at first, but then quickly blamed Ronnie for starting the fight, claiming he threw sand in his face. But I didn't see any sand on Darrell."

"How did Ronnie react?" Donna asked, jotting down another thought.

"He just held on to me. I asked him later what had happened and he said they were both throwing the sand."

"What did you do next?"

"I told Darrell to go home and tell his mother what happened. And said I would be over to talk to her as well."

Donna scribbled.

"Then I took Ronnie inside and cleaned his wounds."

"Did you take him to a doctor?"

"We were going to, but he pleaded not to go. He was terrified of doctors and wanted us to fix him up." Sharron said, as guilt tore through her heart. "We told him we would try, but if it was too bad, or if he had a headache, then we were going to take him in to see the doctor."

"We ended up taking him early the next morning because he wasn't sleeping well and said he felt like he had to vomit," Dell said.

"What did the doctor say?"

"Mostly just bruises, a fat lip, and swollen eye. They wanted to see him in a couple of days. We have the report."

"I need to see the report. Anything else I should know?"

Dell and Sharron looked at each other.

"Not that I know of."

"No."

"I know this is hard. I appreciate you talking with me. I have to go out and check the scene. I need you two to go out on the front porch while I gather information."
"Okay."

Donna came out to the backyard through the dining room's sliding glass door. She took some mental pictures of the area from that perspective. "Hey, go ask whoever was first on the scene to come back here," she asked a uniform, then moved over to the victim.

"Scooter, we meet again."
"Yes, … Donna. Detective. . . Donna," he was stumbling and grabbing at his damp hat.
"So, what did you see when you first came back here, Scooter?"
"I was coming back to get the loader so we could load the tools."
"Tools for what?"
"We were going to pour more concrete around the pool today."
"You guys are the concrete crew?"
"Yes."
"When you got back here, was this construction fence up or down?"
"It was up."
"Are you sure?"
"Yes. I knocked it down running to Ronnie."
"Walk me through how it all happened."

Scooter gave her a step-by-step replay of the all details he could remember.

"Okay, thanks, that helps," Donna said.
"Do you know who owns these footprints in the bloody sand area?"
"No."
"They're too small for your feet."
"It appears so."
"Did anyone younger come back here?"
"Not that I'm aware of."
"Interesting. . . Do you see the bottom of Ronnie's shoes?"
"Yes."
"Do you have any idea what the black and gray substance is?"
"I know exactly what it is. It's the cement and retardant we washed off the surface yesterday."

"The concrete looks unique," she said.
"It's called exposed aggregate," he said, then explained the process.

"So, it looks like Ronnie, or someone with the same shoe size, was all over the concrete with this wash-off cream on his feet?"
"Someone was walking on the concrete with dirty shoes."
Donna noticed a different print as well.

"I think I may have said some things that led to this."
"What do you mean?" Donna asked.
"I was telling Ronnie we were making magic on this concrete yesterday," Scooter said.
"Magic?"
"Yes, we worked glow stones into the top of the concrete. They appear white during the day, but at night they glow blue. They look like stars."
"And?"
"I think he may have come out here to find the magic I was talking about."
"Okay." She scribbled a note in her book. "Thanks for being honest."
"It would kill me to think this happened because of what I said," Scooter said.

"I need you to answer a few more things and, unfortunately, they're going to be difficult to look at."
"Okay. I already puked out breakfast into the pool."
"I wondered about those floating chunks," she said.
"Sorry."
"Not a problem."
"It appears the young man was impaled through his eye socket. Could you tell me if he is on one of the metal things?" She said pointing to another stake.
"The stake?"
"Sure."
"They hold up the two-by-four form to grade."
"How are they attached to the form?"
"They're screwed in."
"Are you sure?"
"Yes. I installed them."
"We're going to need to get the screw out."
Scooter nodded his head.

"How long are the stakes?"

"Two feet."

"How hard do these stakes pull out of the ground?"

"In the sand, by the pool, they come out easily."

"I need you to look and tell me your opinion." She double-checked his reaction to her question.

Scooter nodded, then looked at Ronnie as Donna lifted up the blanket. "Do you see what I'm saying?"

"Yes, it looks like the stake has punctured his eye socket," he said gagging and jerking away. Scooter exhaled loud and long to compose himself. He bent to retrieve his hat which had escaped his head with the sudden move.

"Can you tell me how high the stake is above the form?"

"About six inches."

"Thank you. I know it isn't easy to look at."

"You're welcome."

"One more thing. Could we get the proper tool to get the screw out?"

"Sure."

"Thank-you. You can wait with the others. I'm certain I'll have more questions."

"Okay." Scooter glanced one last time at his lifeless buddy before he left.

*

The single-wide trailer sat bathed in thick darkness beneath the branches of oak and ash which blocked out the crescent moon. Scooter was alone, absorbed in the blackness. He poured another glass of cheap whiskey. The day's events were on rerun and refused to pause, pushing against his sanity. He had stopped at the party store, instead of reaching out to his sponsor. The pain was overwhelming, and his current plan had a single objective— becoming numb— sobriety be damned.

"Ronnie was a sweet kid," he mumbled and touched his face. "A sweet kid. Why did I tell him about the magic?"

A door slammed outside. The sound was so close it was hard to discern distance because the walls in his ancient trailer were paper-thin. Noise, cold, and heat, easily penetrated the aluminum shell. Nothing was private or sacred in this trailer park. All the "Lovely Acres" mobile home park consisted of was a dead-end street and twenty-two small trailers.

Located behind a popular shopping center, people constantly walked through the park, searching for a better way in or out of the mall. Strangers knocked on his door several times a week looking for one thing or another, many of them drunk.

Right now, Scooter wasn't moving a muscle for anyone. His tiny couch was littered with the mail from his box he hadn't bothered to check in over a week. Most of the contents were junk mail and held no interest for a single guy, except the pizza coupon.

One real letter was from the friend of the court reminding him of his payment for child support. While current, he still had a thousand dollar loan from his sister for last winter to pay back. The notice caused him to take another long pull on the gut-burning concoction, draining the glass. "That poor child didn't deserve this!" he announced to the darkness. Pairs of scowling eyes appeared, popping through the paneled walls, watching the man sink again.

"I wonder where the devil kid ran off too?"
Scooter was convinced Darrell killed Ronnie and cycled through the facts— no one was home, the house looked abandoned and even more dilapidated than usual, the neighbor's mailbox was snapped off and in-line with their driveway, the blue car was gone, and the bike was missing. He had recently beat the crap out of Ronnie, was a known bully, according to the cops had multiple Child Protective Services cases through the years, and mom was an unfit alcoholic who had lost custody of him when he was a baby. In Scooter's mind, everything pointed to this kid— everything.
"Where are you, Devil Boy?" Scooter shouted toward his ceiling.

"Your Honor, the evidence in this case is overwhelming!" He was playing out the court scene in his altered mind.
"I will prove beyond any reasonable doubt this loser bike-kid, also known as 'Darrell the Vicious,' is guilty of premeditated murder and should be hung from the gallows," as cheers of adoration from the packed courtroom went up. *"Here, here! Bravo!"*

The bottle was half gone before he had bothered to open his hamburger. The fries he ate right away, because who likes cold french fries? He slid off the couch and sat on the floor in front of his makeshift coffee table, laid his head on the cool wood and started gnawing on the salty, grease-soaked burger, while his face became numb. His trusty hat fell to the floor, but he didn't notice.

After the burger was gone, a thundering truck rolled into the park and went silent. It was close. Scooter thought they had parked on his lawn and wanted to look out of the front window over the kitchen sink. The room was spinning a bit as he used the table to boost himself upward, wiping the remaining burger grease from his cheek.
"Less booze," he said.
As he made his way past the tiny kitchen table and to the sink, a loud rapid pounding blasted the door he had just passed. Under normal circumstances it would have startled him, but his reactions were running at about twenty percent capacity.
"Lawrence!" said the muffled whisper on the other side of the door. "Lawrence!"
"Shut up man. You're going to get me in trouble," Scooter yelled at the backside of the closed door.
"Open up!"
"Who is it?"
"It's Jimmy!"
"No, you stay outside." Scooter was pointing at the back of the door.
"Come on— open the door. I won't get you in any trouble."
"You shouldn't be here, Jet. Jimmy the Jet!"
"Come on. We don't have to go anywhere or do anything. I just want to catch up with my old Denton buddy."

Deep down inside, Scooter knew he would regret letting him in, but the booze made him click the lock and nudge the door open for his former friend. All of the eyes on the walls disappeared.
"Lawrence! Man, it's good to see you!"
"How did you find me?"
"I saw you walking down Griswold a few hours ago, brown bag in tow."
"Really?" Scooter was wobbly.

"Sure did. I had to go take care of a few things before I could get back and catch up! Man, give me a hug!" Jimmy grabbed the man and lifted him off the dingy-yellow carpet in a bear hug.

"They don't call me Lawrence anymore," drunk Scooter said.

"Why not?"

"It's not who I am. Like we call you Jet, not Jimmy."

"What do they call you, then?"

"Scooter."

"What? And you like it?"

"Yeah, it's okay. Better than the old me."

"Whatever you want. Looks like the old you is here right now."

"What have you been up to?" wobbly Scooter asked.

"Tryin' to stay out of trouble."

"How's that working out?"

"What are you celebrating with the really cheap booze?" he asked, ignoring the question.

"Nothin'."

"Wait, you aren't celebrating anything, are you? You're down in the dumps. What's got you?"

"You know me so well." The statement came with a raise of his eyebrows and his glass.

"What happened?" Jimmy the Jet asked.

After a long pause. "It's, a kid. . ." The piercing eyes returned, glowing with intensity.

Scooter told Jimmy the story from start to finish, including all of the gory details. As he recounted, a seething anger welled up inside of him. An anger he hadn't experience in many years slammed into his willing heart. Scooter launched the whiskey bottle at the glaring eyes, smashing it against the wall, sending a shower of shards and brown booze all over the living room wall and entry door.

"Dude!" Jet said, ducking.

"Sorry man. I'm just so pissed off right now. This world sucks!"

"You're right. You want to go take out some frustrations on someone?"

"Who?"

"We could go to the Griz," Jet said.

"No, I really don't need anymore booze." Scooter rubbed his head, wondering where his hat had gone.

"We could go over to Ted's and get some coffee."

"For what?"

"Just to get some coneys and coffee. Sober you up."

"I said I wasn't going anywhere with you, Jet, and I meant it."

"Okay. Fine." Jimmy held up his hands in front of him. "I'm glad you opened the door. I've missed hanging out with you."

"Don't make me regret it, Jet."

"I won't. I'll let you sleep this off," he said, picking up Scooter's hat off the floor and dropping it on the coffee table.

"Thanks."

*

"Scooter!" Angie pounded on the white trailer door.

"Come on Scooter. We need to talk!"

Inside the tin house, the body splayed out on the disheveled bed, stirred at the recognition of the distinct sound the hollow door made when beat against.

"What do you want?" he said into his bare mattress. Scooter pushed himself up from the heap and began the march to the door, wearing only his black boxer briefs and a headache.

Boom, boom, boom — came the call again.

"Scooter, wake up!"

He didn't recognize the muffled voice through his closed door but he did hear his name.

"What do you want?" he said forcefully as he yanked the door open. Angie was startled by the swiftness of the movement.

"Good morning," she said, clearing her throat at the sight of the man standing before her.

"Angie? What are you doing here?"

"I was on my way to work and I heard the news, so I wanted to check in on you."

"You did?"

"Yes. I'm concerned for you."

"You're aware how early it is?"

"I am very aware it's morning." She maintained direct eye contact.

He didn't have a clue. "So you're making house calls now?"

"I've always made house calls."

"Well, I'm okay," he lied.

"No, you are not," she said.

"Why would you say that?"

"I can smell the booze, Scooter, and you gave that stuff up years ago."
"I know," he said, rubbing his throbbing head.
"When we're under stressful situations it is likely we'll feel tempted to go back to old ways of coping."
"I got past the temptation part very easily," Scooter said.
"I figured."
"Now what?" Scooter asked.
"I have time today. We can sit down and talk through this."
"Why would you do this for me, Angie?"
"I care for you. I really do and I want what's best for you."
"Well thanks. It's a rare commodity these days."
"I don't think it's rare. I think people are so distracted, so they fail to recognize it."
"Could be."
"Remember the last time we stopped talking?"
"Yes."
"And we still haven't talked that issue out."
"I'm aware." He grabbed at his pounding temples.
"I want you to hear me on this, Scooter."
"Okay." He was hanging onto the side of the door with one hand.
"If I were the perfect, mind-reading thief who was determined to ruin your life, this is the place I would plan to sabotage you. This is the time I would attack you and destroy you."
Scooter didn't respond.

"I'll make time in my schedule for you," she said.
"I appreciate it."
"Call me after work," Angie smiled.
"Mack gave us the day off, otherwise I would be up already." He smiled.
"How thoughtful."
"He's paying us, too."
"Even better," she said. "One thing. . ."
"What's that?" he asked.
"Pants are required in the office." She smiled again.
"Gotcha."
"Call me." Angie turned and left.
Scooter smiled, closed the door, turned to walk away, and buried a shard of whiskey bottle into the bottom of his foot. "Crap! What the hell?"

*

Chapter Five
❋ Dark Stars ❋

"Can I get you a coffee, Scooter?" Gina asked from her rolling desk chair.

"Thanks but I'm not really a coffee guy."

"Well how about some cocoa?"

"Sure, that would be nice, Gina," he nodded.

"Whipped cream and cinnamon?"

"Wow, fancy. Yes, a little bit of each, please," he said.

Gina returned with an over-sized, bright-blue mug with the bold *Blue Water Clinic* freighter logo.

"Thank-you," Scooter said.

"We gave up on the throw-away cups and switched to mugs. It saves so much trash," she felt the need to explain. "I think everything tastes better when you drink from a real mug."

"It does, but I bet it makes for lots of dishes." Scooter sipped through the pile of cream dusted in the aromatic brown spice.

"I have plenty of time to do them during the day, so it's no trouble at all." She waved him off, smiled and returned to her fortress.

"Hey, you wore pants!" Angie said with her genuine greeting. She was dressed in a conservative dark blue skirt and white buttoned-up top, looking rather business-like standing behind her desk.

"I've got to tell you, I'm so pleased we are meeting today." She came around to her chair and sat. "And I want to let you know I have an open hour after this. So, if we need to keep on going, or we run late, we're able to do that."

"Thanks, Angie," Scooter's face flushed because he felt awkward. He knew his screwed up life would require additional work from her. "I still can't believe you came to my place and woke me up," he deflected from the shame.

"You are important to me and I wanted to make sure you understood."

"I hear you loud and clear." Scooter nodded his head in appreciation.

"The last time we stopped talking with each other, I tried to reach you, but kept striking out."

"It was my fault. I got the notes. I even heard you stop by. I just wasn't having any of it."

"Why do you think that was true?" she asked.

"I was hiding."

"From whom?"

"You, obviously. God. Anyone who wanted to get close to me," Scooter said.

"Anyone else?" she asked. It was a sincere question.

Scooter thought for a moment. "I think I was hiding from myself, as well."

"Why?"

"Um, because I felt unworthy of friendship. Any friendship."

"How did it work for you?"

"Pretty well. No one came around after a while." His sarcastic smile shone over his mug.

Angie laughed. "That's not what I meant."

"I know."

"You were building walls," she said.

"Yes. I guess I was."

"Why do you think people build them?"

He thought briefly. "To protect ourselves. To hide. To keep people away."

"All good answers and true as well." She smiled at his insight.

"Yeah, I didn't want anyone close enough to see how broken I was."

"Makes sense," Angie said.

"I read it in the stuff you gave me," he said. "Not sure if I do now, either."

"I understand, but you showed up."

"I do want to get better. To be better," he admitted.

"Then you may have to trust me, Scooter."

Long pause, then another sip at the sweetness in the mug.

"Okay."

"What is at the root of this brokenness, Scooter?"

"I don't ... know," he stammered to think.

"Something caused you to feel broken?"

"Probably has something to do with how much of a disappointment I was, I guess." He shrugged.

"To whom?"

"Everyone."

"Be more specific, please."
"My parents for starters. They were good people and I felt like a big screw-up who couldn't get his life together." Scooter hung his hat on his knee.
"Your feelings of brokenness are because you're a screw-up in your eyes?"
"And their eyes, I would say."
Angie looked up from her note taking.
"How do you know this, Scooter?"
"Well, I could see the disappointment when they look at me."
"Oh. Have they ever said they were disappointed in you?"
"Not in those words."
"Have you asked them about it?"
"No."
"Why not?"
"Well, my mom's husband passed a few years ago."
"You weren't close?" Angie said.
"How did you know?"
"You just referred to him as your mom's husband, not step father."
"Yeah, I've never liked him much."
"Did you ask your mom how she felt, then?"
"No."
"Why?"
"I didn't want to face it, I guess." He was using the mug as a shield, holding it up in front of his chin.
"Do you think you owe it to her to find out what she truly thinks, rather than jumping to conclusions based on a look or a feeling?"

He stared at her for a second, lowering the mug.
"That's one of the reasons I like you Angie. You don't pull your punches. It's also one of the reasons I don't like you."
She laughed at his honest assessment. "Thank you, I think—." She tilted her head when she answered. "What about the question?" she asked.
"Yes, I suppose I owe it to her, to actually find out what she's thinking," he said.
"Then we can work through any issues that conversation may bring to the surface after you talk to her."
"Right."

Angie engaged in a brief period of silence for effect.
"So when are you going to ask those questions?"
"Soon."
"Really?"
"Yeah."
"When?"
Scooter felt trapped.
"This weekend."
"I'll ask you next week," she said, and made a note.
"I know, believe me, I know. Are you sure you don't want to make a house call, to make sure?"
"Touche. So, have you been a disappointment to anyone else?"
"I'm certain I have been," Scooter said.
"Who?"
"I don't know."
"Yourself?" she pushed.
"Yes. Only everyday I'm alive."
"That's brutally honest."
"Just the way you like it dished up, Doc," he smiled.
"In what specific ways have you disappointed yourself, Scooter?"

That knife cut deep. A pair of eyes appeared on the wall behind Angie's head. He sipped at his mug again, trying to find some wiggle room and not looking at the shame-filled eyes. She continued her unrelenting gaze. It felt like she could see into his heart. Scooter decided to crack open the door. He took a deep breath and tested the water with one, apprehensive toe.

"I feel like a loser for being over forty and living alone in a crappy trailer for most of the year."
Scooter went past the toe and stepped in with both feet. "I feel like a loser because I wanted to drink again. I need to own a car and I don't. I feel broken because the only woman I ever loved, I chased away. So far away, in fact, she's hiding somewhere in Texas. My daughter is gone. I'm disgusted at myself for being so weak I continue to cope with life the way I did when I was a teen—" gravity pulled his tears from their bonds and his chin toward the floor.
"We have a break through!" She handed him the box of tissues. "Thank you, for trusting me." Angie said with her head forward.
"You kinda forced me, Angie."

"Fair enough."

She needed to push a little more and straightened up in her seat. "Do you expect talking through these emotions will help you learn to deal with them when they arise, or is the better strategy hiding, like you've been doing for forty-some years— like you said?"
"I guess I have to decide if I want to be stuck in the same hole all my life or do I bust a move?"
"Good assessment."
Silence.

"Do you want to?"
"I don't know if I can do it," Scooter admitted.
"Well YOU can't, alone. But WE can," Angie smiled with the emphasis. It did feel good to Scooter to get some of his stuff off his chest, but he was still a guarded skeptic. The eyes on the wall appeared to freeze with fear, then they faded away.

*

"Sir, are you the owner of this house?" Donna asked the gentleman with the slicked-back black hair.
"Yes."
"Here's the warrant. We need to look around inside."
"Okay. I have the master key."
"Well that's better than having to bash the door in," Donna said with a smile.
"But not nearly as fun," a nearby officer quipped.
Donna rolled her eyes at the three uniformed cops behind her.
"There you are," the undernourished homeowner said.
He reminded her of Squiggy— or was it Lenny— from the old *Laverne and Shirley* show.

"Can I get a look-see, too?" he asked.
"Maybe, as soon as we're done, I'll try to get you inside. We may have to red tag the home, depending on what we find."
"How long is that gonna take?"
"Not sure. This is a murder case, so we want to spend the time and get it right the first time."
"So I can't clean the joint out today?"

"No. Not for a while. Check the warrant. It explains some things more clearly, or visit the website."
"The longer it sits, the more money I lose."
"I understand and am sorry about that, but we didn't ask for this case either."
"I know."
"Thanks for understanding, sir."
"Sure thing."
"Before you go, I need to get your phone number."
"Right."
"In case we have to come back."

The house was well-worn and needed updating throughout. This house stood out like a sore thumb on the long block of proud mid-century homes. Taking notice of the yard and exterior, Donna was certain the neighbors wanted the place condemned— it looked bad. Inside, she was mildly surprised by how orderly it was.
"Outdated in its decor, but not too disgusting," she thought walking through the front doorway.
"Looks like they left in a hurry," observed one cop.
"Sure does," she said. "They left a lot of belongings behind."

Inside the team gathered evidence over the next several hours. They took hundreds of pictures and two DNA samples from hair found in the bathroom sink. They bagged several pieces of suspicious clothing. What set them off the most were a couple of foot prints on the old rug at the back door of the house. Small prints from a kid. They scraped away some of the dry material off of the fibers and into a sample bag.

"I need to see if that matches the surface material the guys washed off of the concrete next door," Donna said to the officer who was on his hands and knees taking the sample.
"Right, boss."
"Don't you cuss at me!" she replied, smiling.
"This place is a mess, eh?" another officer said.
"Not as bad as most of them."
"Remember the one over on John L?"
"That place was rancid!"
They all laughed and groaned from experience. All except one.

"There had to have been thirty pairs of women's underwear thrown in the corner of the bedroom."

"What?" said the new guy collecting the rug evidence.

"At least thirty."

"That's disgusting. Why?"

"The woman of the house didn't wash her underwear," Donna said.

"Like it was against her religion or something," quipped another.

"They were all filthy, as if she wore them for a few days and kicked them up off into the corner."

"Gross."

"The smell was gross."

"There had to have been a few months' worth, all steaming in the pile," he exaggerated.

"Poor George, he was gagging while bagging all those up." Donna laughed.

"Yeah this is heaven compared to that place," replied George the gagger.

"Why were you there?"

"Drug bust."

"Go figure."

"Get this— during the day the lady worked as a professional at a hospital," one said.

"No way."

"How do you go that long without bathing?"

"And not have your coworkers squirting you off?"

Laughter helped them cope with the difficult cases. Not one of them wanted to remember Ronnie's dead body or what they had to do to get him off of the metal stake, especially since the screw stripped out. Yet, at the same time, remembering what was done to the boy motivated them to figure it all out. This case had become personal.

*

At the end of the first hour, Scooter needed to pee and excused himself. "Too much liquid."

He returned a few minutes later with a couple of bottles of cold water, courtesy of the ever-vigilant Gina.

"Thank you," Angie said, smiling at the gesture.

"It was Gina."
"Can we talk about the boy?" Angie wasted no time, as Scooter's butt hadn't finished sinking into his seat.
"I guess so."
"Tell me about your relationship. Did you know him before the job?"
"No, I met Ronnie the day we started."
"Okay. Tell me about your connection with him." Angie was twisting her pen, waiting.
"We got along great. He made me laugh with his never-ending questions and antics."
"What do you mean?"
Scooter cracked the seal on his water bottle. "It started out about building things— concrete, forming, shoveling, wheel barrels. You name it, he wanted to know the names of all of the tools and what they did."
"Cute."
"That's what we all thought at first, but this kid was serious. It was like he was studying for is contractors test or something."
"Interesting. How did you feel about his curiosity?"
"I though it was great. Not too many kids want to learn about our job."
"Why is that?"
"Because it's hard."
"Like today, for you, here?"
"A different kind of hard. It's a difficult trade to be in. Most of the guys working on crews have had made some awful decisions in their lives and as a result go to jail or prison. When they get released they figure out pretty quick there are very few places that will hire someone with a record. That's the main reason the trade is littered with drug addicts and drunks who bounce from crew to crew."
"I didn't recognize that pattern before," she said.
"Those guys are just trying to survive and most can't break away from the addictions, let alone the shame."
"Is that why you struggle?"
"Not really. I like my job. It's hard on my body, but my stuff began long before the concrete came along."

"When did your difficulties begin, Scooter?" Angie opened her water.
"Well, I know this is going to sound sacrilegious or something."
"Go on,"
"My troubles started the day I was baptized."

"Really? Tell me about that." Angie set her water down and made a note.
"It's not like I didn't have any problems before that day."
"Help me out. How long ago was this?"
"About fifteen years ago," he said.

"I was baptized in the lake, right out in front of God and everybody. It was by this old fellow from the north end of town. He was a friend of the family and a pastor at a church. My wife had left me a few months before I was succeeding in becoming a big-time drunk. Everyday, I was asking my boss for a few bucks so I could stop on the way home and get a forty or two."
"Forty?"
"Forty-ounce beers. So I could get buzzed up and not have to think about what I had done."
"How often were you drinking?"
"Four to six nights a week," he said. "Maybe seven."
"Okay, so everyday."
"I haven't felt like that until Ronnie's passing and one other time."
"What does 'that' feel like?" She used finger quotes.
"Like everything is beyond repair. Broken past fixing."
"I like the phrase— broken past fixing." She wrote it down. "So how did you meet the pastor?"

He chuckled. "One Sunday, I went to church because my sisters kid was singing in the worship service for the first time. They asked me to go, so I went. Man, did I stink of the beer that morning. I had deteriorated to a point where I didn't care about anything— other than the beer, that is. My wife and daughter were gone, and I didn't know any better way to deal with the emptiness I was feeling."
"What happened?"
"I was in church hung over. Stinking like alcohol, so bad it was coming out of my pores. I was sweating because I thought I was going to get kicked out— or worse, get my sister's family kicked out, whatever they call it."
"Excommunicated."
"Excommunicated." He didn't like the word.
"Did it happen?"
"No, the opposite, in fact. I was sitting, listening to some preacher talk."

“It wasn’t the older guy?”
“No, he rarely preaches, but takes care of reaching out to people that visit and the sick. Things like that.”
“Okay.”
“So, this preacher gets going and all of a sudden I think he’s talking directly to me. Like I’m the only soul in the place. I was actually worried my sister had told him my story. I start sweating even more. I wanted to leave, but I was sitting in the middle of the row. I was stuck.

Then the shame I was feeling for all of my stuff was lifted off of me when I heard about Jesus dying for my sins. I had heard it before from my grandparents back in the early days. But this preacher was talking to me like we’re talking here. Almost every objection I brought up in my mind he was answering within a few minutes. I couldn’t get over it. I knew it was the answer I needed in my life.”

A long pause filled the room.
“Yeah. All of a sudden, my life made sense like it never had before.”
“What do you mean?” Angie asked.
“I knew in that moment, I needed Jesus. If I was going to survive, I really needed Jesus to rescue me from my broken life.”
“What did you do?”
“I didn’t know what to do, so I stood up. Even before the guy was done talking. I told him I needed to have the Jesus he was talking about— if he would have a drunk like me.”
“That was bold.”
“Desperate, is what I call it.”
“All of it sounds good, Scooter, but how was your baptism in the lake the day all your troubles began?”
“Well, like I said, it really wasn’t the day my troubles began. It turns out, I was way worse than I had ever had imagined. I had so many things to overcome in my life and before that day, I was unaware of what they were. It seems like, from that day forward, I just keep on stumbling over things I need to change. I’m constantly tripping over my weakness and sin.”
“It’s true for every human ever conceived, Scooter. Except Jesus, that is.”
“You think so?”
“Absolutely convinced.”
“Then why do I never make any progress?” he asked.

"I think you are making progress. I don't think you can see it."

"You don't know one tenth of my issues," he said.

"I'm certain you think that's true. Yet, I know you are human and people are filled with sin and insecurities. The sin has to do with the fallen nature and the insecurity has to do with how much importance is placed on what other people think."

"Especially people in the church," he said.

"True."

Scooter poured some water into his mouth.

"So, what are some of your tripping points, Scooter?"

"Drinking for one. I get a handle on it for a good long time, but it's hovering in the back of my mind."

"God hasn't removed the temptation from you?

"No. Most of the time I'm good. No desire to be drunk. I can even have a beer with dinner."

"Okay."

"For years I didn't use the sauce to cope."

"Good news, right?" Angie asked.

"Yes. But there have been a few events which pushed me, to the point where I was trying to escape."

"So, what's the real issue then?"

"What do you mean?" He shifted in his chair.

"Is the issue drinking or something makes you believe drinking is your answer?"

"I wouldn't say answer. Just medicine, I guess, like a muscle relaxer."

"So you just figured it out."

"Huh?"

"Alcohol is not the sickness. It's merely a way to cope from what is really digging at your heart."

"Hmm." He was deep in thought as he swallowed more cold liquid.

"How do I do that, Angie? I mean, how do I get down to what is really going on? I'm sick of the merry-go-round," he said with a shrug and his palms opening upward.

"I think I would like to point out to you first, what you've been doing has brought you to today. It hasn't been a waste. Maybe God needed to demonstrate to you the futility of your thinking? You've engaged in broken coping methods for so many years perhaps He needed to

98

demonstrate that in a dramatic way, so He can change you from the inside out— which is the only way real change happens.”
“What?”
“Maybe you needed to come to the end of yourself, Scooter.”
“Hmm.”
“To see your way doesn’t work.”

He had no idea how to respond.
“Maybe it would be helpful to consider the way you’ve chosen to cope has been the means by which you’re going to see your greater need for Jesus. Instead of a merry-go-round, like you describe, it has been a trail up the side of a mountain. The path has a ton of switchbacks, which make it seem like you’re going in circles, but, in reality, you are making progress toward rounding the bend of change. To the place where God will say it’s time to move on from this unbelief into faith. And He will equip you to live in a different way.”
“It is a lot to swallow right now, Doc.” He swallowed more water.
“I know. Sometimes we like to be stuck, Scooter. It’s a familiar pain, in a familiar place. Being stuck can be our broken attempt to control the uncontrollable.”
“I don’t know how much I can trust her,” he thought.
She saw his eyes glaze from over-stimulation. “I know this has been a double whammy today, but don’t you quit on me, Scooter!”

*

“Who is the hottie and where’s your hat?” Layne asked.
“She’s a friend of mine and my hat is gross,” Scooter said.
“You have friends?” Bull poked.
They were all watching the woman with the extraordinary figure walk away from them, toward the parking lot.
“Who knew?” Mack said admiring the view.
“I’d like to run into her coming out of my funeral,” Bull tried humor, but wasn’t very good at it.
“You’d be dead, you idiot!” Layne quipped.
“Not with her in my life.” Bull tried to redeem the joke, but it was too late.
“Your ugly self is dreaming to think you could ever get someone like that,” Layne said.
Bull huffed.

"So, are you two a thing?" Layne asked Scooter.

"She is a really good friend."

"Rea. . . lly?" Layne said. "Can she be my really good friend, too?"

"Sure. Why not? It would be good for you, Layne."

"You know it would!" Layne gyrated and laughed.

"Stop acting like concrete workers and let's pay our respects," Mack barked in discreet tones.

They all walked into the rear entrance of Frederick's funeral home and were greeted by an elderly gentleman asking them which family they wished to visit. The question didn't make sense to Scooter since there was only one viewing going on that evening.

"Ronnie."

"Yes, all the way down the hall on the right." The man pointed the way, fulfilling his duty.

"Thanks," Mack said, and pressed past the greeter.

In the viewing room, Dell and Sharron were off to the left, away from the small casket.

Layne pointed out that Ronnie's "custom bury box" was surrounded by flowers and vases.

None of the guys knew what to do next.

Mack whispered to Scooter, "Sorry, man, this must be hard for you, considerin'." It was meant to comfort, but it wrecked him on the inside.

"Thanks, Mack," he managed. Scooter went to find the bathroom. The other guys went to wait in the line to console Dell and Sharron.

Within minutes,Scooter joined the quiet trio as they stepped up to talk to their grieving customers.

"I'm so sorry for your loss," Mack said. He hugged Dell, but was shaken up.

Bull was uncomfortable with the whole ordeal and would not have showed up if Mack hadn't insisted they go together. "I'm sorry," was all that he could say to Sharron, which was enough.

Layne said the same things plus he hugged both of the mourners.

Scooter came close to Dell but lost control of his emotions— he cried out loud. Sharron comforted him by wrapping her arms around him. Dell put his arms around their convulsing shoulders and they all had a long cry together. Without words being exchanged, they still spoke volumes. The three other men who made up Mack's Concrete gazed at the carpet, pushed out of their comfort zone.

Bull walked to a side table and grabbed a box of tissues, ready to offer to the hugging mass as soon as they disengaged.

"I'm so sorry. I really liked that kid."

"We know you did, Scooter," Sharron said.

"Thank you for caring for him. You could have pushed him away," Dell said.

"He had so many questions," Scooter laughed.

"Yes, he did."

"Thank you for being patient," Sharron said.

"All of you guys," Dell said.

"Yes, you've all been wonderful. And you work so hard."

"My gosh! The job you do!" Dell said.

"You're so good at what you do, on top of it," Sharron said. "Seems like you guys get along really well."

"We do," Mack admitted.

"It shows. People like having crews that get along working on their homes," Sharron said.

"Life is too short to be grumpy all of the time, right, Mack?" Layne joked to break the tension.

"Right." Mack managed a smile through his thick mustache.

Bull offered the tissues and the three criers thanked him.

"So have you heard anything from the police?" Mack asked.

"They came to Darrell's house and went through the place with a fine tooth comb."

"They were there all day," Sharron said.

"What about Ronnie's family?"

"We haven't heard one word from anyone."

"Of course, CPS has been over several times," Dell admitted.

"CPS?" Bull whispered to Layne.

"Child Protective Services," Layne replied.

"The case is still open, so they can't tell us anything," Dell said.

"Are they gonna do something to you guys?" Layne asked.

"We don't know." Sharron began to cry again.

"I would testify for you in a minute," Layne said. "I watch people with kids, and you guys were great to that boy— and I would tell anyone who wants to know."

"Me, too," Bull said.

"We may need you guys to do that," Dell said.

"Let us know where to say it and we all will," Mack said. The guys agreed.

"Ronnie told me you were nice people," Scooter said.

The line was building behind them so the men were preparing to move away.

"We'll finish the project, guys. We just don't know when that will be," Dell said.

"Don't worry about it. You take your time and we'll be ready when you are," Mack said.

"Thank you," they both said.

"We're going to get out of your hair."

"Thanks, you guys, for coming out. It was very kind."

"You're welcome."

The four construction men walked up to the front to where the closed casket was positioned. The polished maroon metal gleamed in the bright lights. Ronnie's picture was up on a stand in front of the pall. The group paused for a few seconds, then left in silence.

*

"Did you get it?"

"Yes. The picture from the parking lot in Algonac clearly shows the blue Ford entering the ferry at 7:42 a.m."

"Perfect. So, what do we have?" Donna asked.

"We have the victim being in a known altercation with the suspect, with the suspect causing physical harm to the victim."

"Which points to motive," Donna said.

"We have footprints on the new concrete which show a shoe size consistent with the suspect."

"We have evidence showing the same muck from the pool on the rug of the suspects house," Donna said.

"Now, we have confirmed traces of blood on the rug as well."

"I think we can present a solid case to the prosecutor— that young Darrell is responsible for Ronnie's death," Donna said.

"I agree."

"We need to find the kid. I've got to get a hold of someone with the RCMP."
"To see if they have video of the suspects coming off the ferry?"
"And to check if they have any known whereabouts for our young suspect and his mother."
"I would think she's going to be charged as an accessory to murder."
"We shall see," Donna said, lifting her perfectly sculptured eyebrows.

*

"Thanks, guys. I'll put an extra hour on your check."
"Don't worry about it, Mack."
"See you guys tomorrow," Mack said. "Scooter, you sure you don't want a ride home?"
"No. I want to walk and think for a while."
"It's like three miles home."
"No, only two."
"I guess you gotta get a job that makes you more tired," Layne said, as they got into Mack's truck and drove off.
Scooter forced a smile and waved.

He wanted some time alone to think about everything that had happened, plus all of the stuff he had been talking to Angie about. The guys were right— she sure was beautiful. He hadn't really noticed before. Attractive sure, but tonight she was stunning.
"How is that going to play out?" he wondered.
He thought it was really nice she would stop to visit the family.
"I guess we live in a small town and she knows tons of people," he mused.

The sidewalks in this old part of town were new because of the sewer work that had been done last year. Walking was easy, not having to worry about tripping on every rotten flag.
"The new stuff looked good enough for a city sidewalk," he thought and was glad he didn't have to be on the crew.

The phrase Angie used in their last session came back to tap him on the shoulder. *"Sometimes we like to be stuck."*
"Do I like to be stuck?" Scooter thought about the statement over the course of the next few blocks, walking with his hands in his pockets.

"Do I like to be stuck?"
"Am I stuck?"
"Do I like it?"
"Do I like to be stuck?"
"Maybe you need to come to the end of yourself, Scooter," also ran
through his head.

He walked into the Wolverine, a small party store on his route some ten
minutes later. The workers knew him simply as Forty— the guy that
used to buy a lot of forties.
"Not tonight," he thought. *"I want a Vernors."* It was a sweet gingery
treat he had liked since childhood. For some reason it was a comfort to
drink it, reminding him of his grandmothers house, when he was just a
boy.

"This is it, Forty?"
"Yep, it's all I want," he said and paid the man.
Pulling the door open the bell rang and he glanced up at the old brass
signals as he left.
"Bells," he said under his breath.

Condensation gathered on the green and gold label. The bottle opened
with a short burst of pressurized carbon dioxide, forcing the familiar
smell of aged ginger to his nostrils. "I love Vernors," he said with a long
and loud burp.

A lifted black pickup slammed on its brakes in the middle of the two-
lane street right out in front of the party store. Oak Street was a one-
way road, so there was no danger of a head on crash, but horns rang out
at the selfish move by the driver. A one-finger salute was flashed by the
guy who had been cut off in the move. But the truck driver didn't notice
or care about any of it— he wanted one thing.
"Scooter!" The truck pulled into the party store parking lot and stopped
within inches of the startled pop drinker. The horn blasted Scooter and
both doors swung open.

"Jet? What the heck?"
"We saw you and wanted to stop."
"We?"
Out from behind the passenger door came a long-lost friend.

"Tums? Is that you?"

"What's up, Lawrence— with no hat?"

The two bros hugged, shaking each other's hand while patting on the back with the other.

"So what have you been doing?" Scooter asked.

"I'm back, brother!"

"Back to good old Po-Ho?"

"Yep."

"You've been gone a long time."

"You should know, you gave me my going-away party, like six years ago."

"Yeah, you are right. Almost forgot."

"Well I haven't. What's up with the new nickname— Scooter?"

"Yeah, came from the guys I'm working with."

"Sweet." The sarcasm dripped.

"So, where are you staying?" Scooter asked.

"With Jet."

"You two are back living together?" Scooter laughed and looked at both of them.

"Just for now, until I get a job and stuff."

"Like old times, Lawrence," Jet said.

"Lots of places are hiring right now, so you're in luck, Tums."

"Where you are working, Lawrence?" He wasn't comfortable saying his old friend's new name, even though he had gotten the rundown from Jimmy the Jet on the story.

"Mack's"

"The concrete guy?"

"Yeah. It's a good job. I mean, we work hard, but he pays every week and I get unemployment in the winter, if I am not plowing snow."

"So is he hiring?" Tums asked.

"Mack?"

"Yeah."

"Tums, you want to do concrete?" Scooter was skeptical.

"It would be a job."

"Naw, dude."

"What do you mean?"

"It would never work, us two working together. You'd hate it and I think we would end up killing each other."

"Really? I'm so surprised you would say that!" Tums' tongue was planted in his cheek.

"Serious."

"So, Lawrence, you want a ride? We could hang out."

"The three of us?"

"Yeah, like old Denton days, minus a few guys."

"No way."

"Why not?"

"Because I have to work tomorrow, and you jerks would keep me up all night."

"Come on."

"No way, can't do it."

"Maybe this weekend then?" Tums said.

"I don't know, guys," Scooter said. "I guess we'll just have to see how it goes. Later, Jet. Tums." Scooter lifted his chin in acknowledgment and walked away, leaving his two friends offended. The sky was shimmering with the end-of-the-day brilliance as Scooter pointed his feet toward home.

*

Chapter Six
✱ Star Of David ✱

"Thanks for staying late, Angie."

"This isn't late for me, Scooter. I often have clients later than this. People who have jobs need counseling during the evenings. This is normal."

"So you had clients up until now?"

"Not today. I went to dinner and came back so we could talk," she said. "I appreciate it."

"Looks like you cleaned up, shaved, and you have a respectable hat!" Angie said with a gleam in her eyes.

"I was pretty ripe after work but I hate shaving. This hat is the cleanest one I own."

"Well, thanks for the favor!" Angie was smiling wide.

"Sure."

"How have you been coping this past week?" she asked.

"Okay. I didn't drink at all."

"Progress. How have you been feeling?"

"Depressed, I think."

"Describe that for me." Angie raised her pen to the ready position.

"I've been focusing on the fact I told Ronnie to go look for the magic the night after we were done pouring the concrete."

"What was the magic you wanted him to see?"

"We put these stones that glow in the concrete. They're a cool feature that look like you're walking on stars."

"Oh, that does sounds like magic," Angie said.

"But by me telling him, he went out and got himself killed," Scooter said.

"Do you know that?"

"Not for certain."

"Then what do we do, Scooter?"

"Get all the information?"

"Yes." Angie nodded her head, making her curls bounce. "Why would you want to get all of the information?"

"So we can base our choices on fact rather than guesswork."

"Right."

"So, when you talked to your mom. . ." Angie broke off that question. "Scooter, do you call her Mom?"

"Yes, I do," he said. "She's the only mother I've known. Sure, she was my foster mother, but she adopted me in spite of all of my issues."
"When was that?"
"I was in Denton, the home for troubled kids."
"Or kids with challenging life issues." She redirected his thinking again.
"Right. I was twelve."
"Okay. How did speaking with your mom turn out?"
"It went really well. I asked her if she saw me as a failure or screw-up — I think is how I worded it."
"And?"
"She said she never has. In fact, she thought I was a tough kid for dealing with everything that was thrown at me and not falling apart."
"Really? You don't say?"
"I think it's what kept me from drinking this week."
"How so?"
"Just hearing my mom say that about me really helped me to see I'm stronger than I thought."
"So, all of these years thinking you were seen as a major disappointment?"
"Wasted time. Wasted life," Scooter admitted.
"What's the best news in that discovery?"
"Huh? I don't follow."
"You now recognize believing untrue things is a waste of your time and a waste of your life."
"True. I hope I can remember."
"You will."
"How do you know?" Scooter was skeptical.
"I'm going to remind you, Scooter," she said, smiling with her welcoming eyes.
"I still feel responsible for the kid," he said.
"I know you do."

Later, Angie closed her session with a prayer. She prayed Scooter would know how much he was loved, that he would fight the feeling of disappointment with the truth of faith, knowing he was a child of God, loved and redeemed.

*

"I saw you here the other day," he said to the woman's back.

"Yeah, what's it to ya?" She didn't feel like putting up with any crap. Tina was hungry, hung over, and needed to get a few things at the store. So, pumping gas was the first problem needing to be fixed, apparently the second was some jerk making rude comments behind her. Tina imagined another horny guy ogling at the backside of her low riding pajamas as the gasoline fumes touched her nose.

"You're from 'Pure Michigan,' I see."

"What's it to ya?" Tina said turning to face the jerk. Her "pervert" was a Royal Canadian Mounted Police officer.

"Knowing who is in our humble country is my business, missy. Now, I need to see your identification."

Tina knew she was blown and started thinking on her feet, like usual.

"Sorry. I had a rough morning. My ID is in my purse. Let me get it for you, Officer."

"Okay. Just keep your hands where I can see them."

"Yes, sir."

As Tina reached into the car, she gave a quick glance into the station to see if Darrell had caught a glimpse of was happening. She was still trying to protect him from Donny at all costs. Her gas pump snapped off as she hoped her plan would work.

"Here is my ID, sir. I really have to pee. Can I go inside and take care of it and my monthly issue, while you run this?" She was holding out her drivers license and a small white tube so he could see it.

"Um, sure." He was uncomfortable with her showing him such a personal item.

"Thanks. I'll be right back."

"Stay where I can see you. Here to the restrooms and no deviation from the path, understand?"

"Yes, sir. Thank you."

Darrell was walking toward the door when his mom came through them.

"They're running my information," she whispered.

"Okay."

"If anything comes up they're going to take me into custody. You need to leave. Go back to the house, and stay hidden. I don't want Donny finding you. I'll come back for you, Darrell, like I always do."

"Okay," he said. His mind was racing— he knew he would have to remain calm in order to get away from the cop. Darrell paid for his snacks and exited out the door with feigned confidence, right after his mom disappeared into the restroom.

The cop was seated in his car immediately behind the Blueberry, so Darrell walked across the front of the store and around the corner to be out of view of the man. He needed to cross the street in front of the station in order to get back to the house where they had been staying. In order to do that, he walked six blocks out of the way, then ran back to safety.

His bike was laying in the backyard which is how he figured he would make his escape. He grabbed a few items out of the house, mounted the bike, and left. He was going to head north to Sarnia, to try to get over the border into Port Huron. Darrell didn't know how any of this would work out, but he knew he needed to get back to the States to have any hope. He witnessed his mother getting cuffed, then put in the rear of the police cruiser. Darrell peddled for twenty miles down back roads and through farmers field's, trying to remember to keep the sun at his back as much as he could.

He passed many homes along the way— much of it looked like Michigan. He was making steady progress north until a pickup truck full of teens drove by at high speed, spinning their tires. They scared him off the road and into a ditch. Darrell flipped head over heels and the bike crashed hard into a concrete culvert, popping the tire. The front fork was bent, as was the rim. If he wanted to save the bike, he was going to have to drag it back home.

Darrell wasn't a kid that cried much. Countless number of stepfather-types had beat the desire out of him over the years. But sitting in a Canadian ditch with a broken bicycle, bruised shoulder, and arrested mother, fear finally caught him and he broke down, sobbing.

The line of trees hid him along one side with the tall grass on the other. He laid down and wept like he never had before. A few hours later, darkness crept over the area and Darrell made his way from his wreck. He held a small, cloth shopping bag in his hand with a few clothes and some snacks from the store. The disposable water bottle was empty, but he held onto it.

As Darrell walked, he kept to the shadows as much as possible, hiding when cars passed. When the moon was high in the sky a stench hit him in the face. It was from a farm that was lit up and bustling with activity, even at the late hour. A mile later, he crossed the entrance to Smith's Pig Farm as a semi-truck was entering the road into the facility.

Darrell hid in the darkness beneath some trees which lined the street. He watched for a while until he fell asleep, camouflaged with his back resting up against a small pine tree. Waking a few hours later, the moon was low on the western horizon and Darrell shivered from the cool night air.

The "farm" was a distribution hub where trucks were loaded with unhappy pigs and the rigs shipped out on the same road they came in on. Darrell remembered a boyfriend of his mom was a pig hauler. Transporting the animals across the border was his main job. His trailer was three levels high and always reeked from animal waste. Darrell's mom made fun of him when he wasn't around by calling him "Mr. Piggy." He wasn't a large man, just a smelly one, so the nickname stuck.
"Maybe this is Mr. Piggy's farm." Darrell thought.

Darrell knew he needed to get moving if he was to hitch a ride with an unsuspecting driver. Walking down the road, he found a spot where he was hidden so he could observe. Now he needed to wait until a driver left his truck to close the tailgate. He thought he would have enough time to run to the trailer and hide with the beasts on the top level. There had to be a hundred pigs per truck, all making the journey to becoming sausage and bacon. It was his way back.

"Bacon." He couldn't think about food because he was famished. Darrell knew if he got arrested they would feed him and the thought was tempting, but he knew he could not get caught. He would be blamed for the kid's death and be sent away for the rest of his life. His plan had to work. He was forced to concentrate and wait for the right truck at the right moment.

About forty-five minutes later, with the eastern sky becoming lighter, a truck driver got down out of his cab to make his way to the back of his rig. Darrell jumped from the bushes with his bag, and ran as fast as he could toward the front of the truck. Fifty yards never felt so far.

He heard the gate on the rear of the trailer squeaking and made a break for the space between the truck and trailer. The pigs were all riled up over being forced onto the transport, while the diesel engine rumbled through twin exhaust pipes.

Darrell grabbed for a handhold to boost himself up onto the catwalk between the tractor and the trailer. Hearing the gate bang behind him, Darrell knew he was running out of time. He lunged for the side of the trailer, hoping to catch his hands and feet into the slits that ran horizontal along the sides of the unit. When he hit the side with a thud, he didn't have enough strength to hold himself up. He slid down the trailer, landing on his back in the smelly mud. His clothes were covered in pig dung and the driver was closing the last gate. Soon, the driver would be walking up the passenger side of the rig to do a final safety check before hitting the road.

Darrell army-crawled through the muck beneath the trailer, scrambling and searching for a way to get out of his mess. The tire rack hung low on this model of pig hauler. Two spare tires were held in an enclosed area. The mud-caked boy crawled his way into the tight space, preparing for the ride back to Michigan.

An hour later, the driver, named David, according to his door, pulled his Star Truck Line rig into the USDA inspection station in Wadhams, Michigan. This was his required stop to have his pigs checked over. The government building docks were full of trucks, so David had to pull into the truck stop next door, backing into a spot along the last row. After the air brakes were set, Darrell, complete with his dry pig mud covering, slithered out from between the two tires. He made his way into the woods behind the busy truck center.

*

"Good night." Scooter waved to Angie as she got in her car. He had refused a ride, telling her he needed processing time, and that the walk home was helpful to him.

As soon as she pulled off, Jet raced in front of Scooter, blocking his way.
"Wut up, Scooter?"
"Hey, guys," he said, noticing four bodies in the truck.
"I'd offer you a ride, but you'd have to hang out in the bed with a bunch of scrap."
"I need the walking time."
"You've been doing a lot of walking lately," Tums said.
"Hey, Tums," Scooter acknowledged his old friend in the front passenger seat.
"Lawrence!" came from the back seat, behind Jimmy.
All four doors opened up as Jimmy the Jet cut the motor.
"Holy crap," Scooter said, as the four men piled out around him.
"Look, the old Denton gang!" Scooter said.
"Got us back together again!" Tums announced.
"Just missin' the Moby," Jet said.
"He's locked up," Tums said.

"I. . . I. . . I haven't seen you in a long time," Johnny said to Scooter.
"It's been a while, Johnny Dog." The two men looked at each other with uncertainty. They simply nodded their recognition.
"And J-Law, with the beard— I didn't even recognize you, dude," Scooter said.
"Yeah, just sick of shaving."
"For a really long time," Tums quipped.
"So, Scooter, who was the hottie?" Jet asked Dog's question.
"Wow, she is fine!" J-Law said in an over exaggerated manner.

Scooter was experiencing a familiar feeling of uneasiness wash over him as they talked in the circle. These were his people, 'the boys.' These men had been some of his closest friends. They had always been present since they were in Denton State Home together. Through high school, they were closer than brothers. The secrets they shared, along with the stupid things they had done together, could fill volumes of books. They all knew no one wanted to write down the colorful story of a bunch of degenerates.

Scooter felt the old familiarity flowing around the circle, but it was intertwined with a new reality these guys didn't share in. He had gained a new sense of self from a life apart from these guys and their steady influence. He had been trying to move on from his old life— move on from these old friends— for a long time. The pressure the Denton Boys brought upon him made him feel like he was less of a man. The feeling of being stuck clung on him like the stink of dead fish. No, he certainly didn't buy into the mantra of "*the good old days*" anymore.

"She's a good friend of mine," Scooter said.
"We saw you come out of the counseling center," Jet said.
"Is she your counselor or something?" J-Law laughed at the thought.
"Screw off," Scooter said.
"Oh! So sensitive! It must be true," Johnny said.
"He's been this way ever since he found Jesus, guys." Jet said.
"Yeah, I remember. Come on— leave the man alone." Tums said.
"Don't you want to hang out with us, Lawrence?"
"No. I've got to work in the morning, guys. You know it."
"So what?"
"We can catch up," another said.
"I've got to go, fellas."
"You've changed, Lawrence," said J-Law.
"You're weird now," Johnny said. Scooter ignored him.
"Hey, do you think your girl counselor would want to go out?" J-Law poked.
"You leave her alone, J-Law," Scooter said.
"Or what, Scooter— Lawrence?"
"Or you'll answer to me," Scooter said.
"Oh. Big man!"
"Don't push me on this one." Scooter was serious. J-law threw up his hands flashing a smile. "And don't you even think about her, Dog—."
Scooter called out the little man, pointing right at his face.
The teasing continued for a few minutes, then Scooter waved them off and walked away.

"Man, what has gotten into him?" Tums asked.
"He's too good for us now," Johnny said.
"I told you guys," J-Law said.
"What are we going to do about that?" Jet asked.
"He's always been one of us," Tums said.
"He's the one walking away," Jet sneered.
"His girl counselor is fine," Johnny Dog said.

114

“Yes, a true statement!”
“Probably shouldn’t mess with her Dog. He just might kill you,” Tums warned.
“Yeah, yeah. Nothing I haven’t heard before. He can’t get rid of me, and he knows it.”
“I think I’ll pay her a visit,” J-Law said.
“You need some counselin’ now, J-Law?” Tums laughed.
“Yes, I believe I have seen the light!” They laughed, while Jet sneered at Lawrence’s back, now a block away and out of earshot.
“He isn’t one of us anymore,” Jet seethed. “He walked away from the Denton Boys.”

*

“Mom! Mom! Mom!” The front screen door slammed. “I got it!” Bobby was holding up yellow papers as he walked into the house that smelled of fresh spaghetti sauce.
“Got what, Bobby?”
“I got on the Tigers!” Bobby’s nose lifted toward the enticing aroma.
“Is that the team you wanted?”
“Yes, it’s my favorite team. They have the best coach!”
“That’s great honey. When does practice start up?”
“In two days.” Bobby sat down at the round kitchen table, looking over the papers.
“I really need someone to be my athletic supporter this year, Mom.”
“Really?” She tried not to laugh at her son.
“Yes, so maybe if you can’t make it to the games, then Bee can?” He looked at his sister who was reading.
“Okay?”
“Good,” he said.
“Wait— do you know what an athletic supporter is?” Bee asked from the couch.
“I thought I did.” Now Bobby was uncertain.
“Honey, it’s something you wear, like underwear, that holds a protective cup in place to guard your man parts.”
Laughter commenced between the two girls at Bobby’s expense. He retreated to the refrigerator.

“I thought you were a Diablos fan?” Bee asked, chomping a crisp carrot.

"I still am, but they're in the minors."
"Well, I thought you liked the Texas Rangers," Mom said from the
stove.
"I did, but now I have a new favorite," Bobby said.
"The Detroit Tigers?"
"Yep."
"They were always my favorite baseball team."
"Really, Mom?
"Sure. I grew up in Michigan, so of course they were, silly."
"Did you ever go to a real game?"
"Yes, a few."
"That's awesome!"
"I have a picture somewhere of me sleeping at a game. It has the date
written on it."
"You fell asleep at a Tigers game? I could never do that!"
"I was tired and it was a 1-0 pitching duel."
"So, was it in the new park or the old?" Bobby asked.
"The old, but I've been to both."
"Which one did you like better?" he asked.
"I liked old Tiger Stadium better because you felt like you were so close
to the action, unless you were a bleacher creature in center field."
"Center field was 440 feet deep," Bobby said, repeating new knowledge
born from his baseball curiosity.
"And the flag pole was actually in the field." Mom wanted to show
Bobby she knew a thing or two.
"Cool!"
"The game I slept at was the last game of the '87 season against the
Blue Jays. The Tigers won the game and the American League East
Pennant."
"What? You fell asleep while they won the pennant?"
"I did. The teams were tied before the game. They were big rivals
during the '80s. But the game was boring, so I took a little nap. But at
the end, the stadium was filled with electricity. It was very exciting!"
"That's cool. I didn't know you liked baseball."
"I do, and your dad loved it, too."
"Really?"
"Sure did. Do you want to hear a funny story about your sister?"
"Of course, I do."
"Wait," Bee said getting up off of the couch to join in.

"Your dad played softball when we were first married. He had an equipment bag in our closet. One day in the winter your sister came out from searching around in our bedroom with a new toy."

"What was it?"

"She had your dad's cup over her face, like it was a mask."

The groans and squeals were heard by the neighbors as they all had quite the laugh.

"She thought she was Darth Vader!" Mom said, nearly crying from the joke.

"Darth Vader!" Bobby said pointing at Bee, laughing uncontrollably, with tears in his eyes. "Luuuke, I found your cup!" he said with his hands cupped over his mouth.

*

"I thought that was you," Donna said.

"Hey, Detective Donna," Scooter said taken aback by her beauty.

"Donna is fine, Scooter. How are you doing?"

"Okay."

"I see you guys are back to work." She nodded toward the truck.

"Yes, we are. We have a job up on Riverside Drive."

"Nice area."

"It is."

"Do you have a minute for a couple of questions?" Donna asked.

"Sure, this thing has a huge tank," he said, now pumping the gas.

"On Ronnie's case, did you notice there were two sets of footprints on the new concrete?"

"I thought it looked like one set was all over and another set walked across the slab once, close to the pool."

"Right, that's what we saw, too."

"Are you done with the crime scene now?"

"Why?" Donna asked.

"They're going to want to get their pool done at some point. We have to tear out the stuff we poured."

"The cool stuff with the glowing stones?"

"Yes."

"Why?"

"We can't get the footprints off it because it has been too long."

"Ohh." Donna scrunched her nose while clenching her teeth.

"Plus, I don't think they want that kind of concrete anymore. Bad memories and all."

"I understand," She paused. "I'm trying to tie up loose ends on the case," she said.

"Okay."

"Where were you that night?"

"The night Ronnie died?"

"Yes."

"I was home."

"Which place? I saw information that you own two places."

"Yes, there are two. The second home is in Smiths Creek. I inherited it from my grandmother. I was at the trailer in town, though."

"Okay." Donna wrote down a note in her book.

"I usually only stay in my grandmothers house during the winter. After the concrete season is over."

"Can anyone confirm you were home?"

"I don't know. My neighbors maybe. I live alone."

"Right."

"I went shopping at the mall behind the house earlier that evening."

"Do you have a receipt?"

"I should, at home."

"If you can find it, that would help."

"Sure. I'll look after work. Have you found the neighbor kid?" Scooter asked.

"Darrell?"

"Yes."

"I am not supposed to comment on an ongoing investigation."

"Yeah, but it looks like I'm part of it." Scooter was uneasy by Donna's avoidance.

"Not yet, but we have good leads," she conceded.

"Officer Donna McBride," Mack said, approaching the vehicle with two large white fountain drinks and a hearty smile.

"Hey, Mack," she said. "Just asking Scooter a couple of questions about the case. I need to ask you the same thing."

"Shoot," he said.

"Where were you the night Ronnie died?"

"I was home all night. The wife will confirm it."

"Okay. I have to make sure I cross all of my t's and dot all of the i's. For the report."

118

"Gotcha."
"You two take care." With that Donna turned toward her unmarked police car and left.

"Weird," Scooter said.
"You didn't like your visit from sexy Barbie cop?" Mack said, using the name the guys on the crew had given to Donna.
"She's something else," Scooter said with raised eyebrows.
"It was a little weird, though," Mack said. "Frozen coke?"
"Tanks, bawss," Scooter said in a cartoon-like voice.

*

Mack and Scooter were driving to pick up a mixer from a jobsite south of town. The stretch of road cut through farmer's fields and long sections bordered by thick woods. Gratiot Avenue was one of the original roads that pinwheeled out from Detroit, sixty miles southwest. Because Interstate 94 followed the same route, the road known by locals as "Old Gratiot," had very little traffic and almost no police presence.

Mack's antiquated truck was loud and unreliable. Its normal parking place was in the yard, waiting for someone to buy it to rid the company of the ongoing need for repairs. The *"Death Dodger,"* as it was known, had a knack for needing steering corrections while driving. The wheel felt so loose because the steering parts were worn out again. The truck was far too used for Mack to invest his time, so he had been attempting to sell it for the last couple of years. The yard location was on a lonely, secondary street out in the township that got little traffic, which meant the tired flat bed spent most of its days shared with fields of thistle and golden rod.

Today's trip was different. Mack thought he may have an interested buyer for the Dodger, so he wanted to put a few miles on it to make sure it ran. After a jump and some ether, the truck lumbered down the road like it always had. Mack's muscle memory returned as soon as he pulled out on the road, fighting the wandering beast after every bump.

About ten miles out of town, old Gratiot got rough. The guys were just chatting about life while sucking down their frozen drinks. A car pulled next to them, into the oncoming traffic lane, with the driver honking and waving for Mack to pull over. Mack slowed to a stop on the side of the road, and jumped out to chat with a pale, frantic woman.

"I thought you guys were going to blow up!"
"What? Why?"
"Your gas tank is dragging on the ground and sparks are shooting out from the steel!"
This was the same moment Scooter smelled strong gas fumes inside the cab.
"Scooter, GET OUT!" Mack yelled, red-faced and waving his arms.

The lady pulled away in a hurry, stopping a hundred feet down the road, as Scooter pushed his door open. Mack reached in to switch off the truck.
"Holy crap!" Scooter said, looking below the vehicle. He had to grab his hat and dance out of the way, as a wave of gasoline washed toward the ditch. Mack, glanced for traffic and got down on the ground to have a look for himself, from the driver's side. He was struck with fear.

The back side of the tank was dragging on the asphalt— both of the straps had broken free. The front of the tank was being held up by the gas lines to the engine. The entire corner of the tank had been ground off by the pavement. The guys hadn't heard the dragging steel because of the loud exhaust on the beast.

Mack's immediate concern— after not blowing up— was the huge fine for thirty gallons of gasoline washing into the ditch, so he jumped into action. He had replaced the metal gas line a few years prior and made a quick decision to cut the new rubber line as close to the tank as possible. Scooter pulled the reeking, empty tank free and threw it in the back on the bed with the junk and twisted forms.

Mack grabbed the full five-gallon gas can out of the toolbox next to the driver's door, setting it in the cab on the passenger floor. Then he pulled on the rubber fuel hose, which was being held in place by zip ties. Using his pocket knife to cut the plastic fasteners, Mack freed it from the underside of the truck. They fed the hose through the open window and stuck it down into the neck of the gas can.
"Scooter, try it," Mack barked.

The Dodger fired up on the third try and the two guys waved to the waiting woman.
She got out of the car and asked if everything was okay, clearly shaken from the incident.
"Yes. Thank you— you may have saved our lives."

It took another few minutes before reality sunk into the grateful guys who occupied the *Death Dodger*.
"Man, we could have died," Mack said, wiping the back of his hand across his sweaty forehead.
"Yeah, it was close," Scooter admitted.
"Did you look at these steel tank straps?" Scooter had brought them inside the truck.
Mack glanced over, then looked over the top of his reading glasses. "Somebody cut these."
"Recently." Scooter pointed to the clean slices in the metal— ninety percent through the strap, with no rust in the cut.

*

Chapter Seven
* Twinkling Star *

The distinct sound of film being pushed along by plastic gears, clacking through the machine, and over the powerful light, still excited Johnny. Those combinations of sounds transported the man back in time to his friend's basement, where he was first introduced to adult films. What he witnessed on the portable movie screen was burned into his soul. The expressions of ecstasy on the actors' faces as they engaged in different acts were etched on his psyche. Everyone appeared thrilled in the movie that now never ended. Johnny thought about what they were engaged in, convinced sex was the key to happiness. His unconscious conclusion was that acceptance and approval were found in sexual acts.

He was confident every other person would be just as excited about his discovery as he was. Sure, there had been the stash of magazines he found in various places. He had enjoyed looking at them and reading the stories of fantasy encounters. He would place himself inside of those stories, dreaming of all the willing women who would make him feel good about life and love. This became his religion. Now, films made the fantasy even more real, more believable than ever before, while his twelve-year-old brain began searching for ways to feed the growing need of self worship.

Johnny began collecting films from wherever he could find them. Dumpsters, garage sales, even stealing them from friends' parents. He searched anywhere and everywhere. He developed an eye for seeing the hidden, sexual secrets of the people around him. He hung around seedy stores hoping to pick up some fallen fruit from the tree of his new life. At home he hid his precious discoveries in the drop ceiling over his basement room, dragging them out to stimulate himself several times a day.

During the next couple of years, he accumulated hundreds of items—films, magazines, photo copied pages, stories, toys, and drawings. Every tool was meant to excite himself, and build his hidden life around what he worshiped. Soon his porn stash became legendary among his school mates. Students knew if they wanted smut, Johnny was the guy to go to. He was buying, selling, trading and stealing the stuff all of the time. It helped that his dad was nowhere to be found. Johnny pilfered all of the old man's magazines from his stockpile in the attic of the garage. His mother was so wrapped up her own boring and pathetic life — he considered her advice useless.

By high school, he was hosting porn parties on a regular basis. These gatherings often included drinking and drugs, frequently ending with awkward teenage orgies. He lived for those parties. Soon they were not enough to satisfy the growing monster with him. Only new and more tantalizing acts with various people seemed to get him back to feeling accepted and believing again.

Johnny's fantasy world came crashing down on a Saturday morning after one of his crazy parties in his basement. It turned out some of the girls he had engaged with the night before had been drugged and were not consensual partners. Johnny was discovered. His stash was confiscated. He was prosecuted as a minor and shunned by polite society. The label of "pervert" was hung around his neck. Even the Denton boys called him Horn Dog, or just Dog for short.

This humiliation should have ended his fantasy world, but it only served to fuel his need to get back to the place where he was being satisfied. *"It's just a natural thing."* He used the logic to convince himself over and over again. Those were his darkest years— the time when he experimented with all of the available depravities that never satiated. Young and old. Male and female. Inanimate and living. Everything was meant for his own pleasure. It was a rare moment for him to consider where this life was leading him. He slammed those doors shut a thousand times, as he turned to numb the wretched pain, instead of facing it. Potent dopamine flowed as he flicked on his favorite old film projector again and metaphorically bowed down in worship.

*

West of the Family Truck Stop and next to the USDA Import Inspection Center, Darrell managed to crawl five hundred yards through thick woods. Reeking of pig feces and mud, exhausted from his ordeal Darrell crashed while laying beneath a pine tree next to a small man-made lake. A deep pit was dug to mine the sand for the interstate with water filling the hole. Now, the deep-blue waters shimmered in the hot afternoon sun. On the far side of the lake, about a half a mile away, a solitary log home lay nestled by an old growth forest of oak, maple, and ash. A small dock with an upended rowboat rounded out the scene.

When Darrell woke three hours later, his thoughts sunk into a minefield of doubts and fears over his situation. The one thing he knew for certain was he needed to go swimming. He couldn't stand one more minute of the stench. Keeping everything on except his shoes, Darrell waded into the water to rinse away the stains and stink. The self-reliant kid removed his clothing one article at a time. He rubbed each filthy item vigorously between his submerged hands, hoping to dislodge all evidence of his trip. The mud looked like plumes of smoke being released into the crystal waters.

When Darrell had finished washing, he tossed each piece of clothing onto the grassy shore. The interstate traffic was whizzing past off to his left, but the vehicles were unseen, hidden behind trees. Scents of wild flowers and goldenrod mixed with the cattails that stood at the shoreline. Other than traffic noise, the serene scene calmed him. Birds chirped in the trees, toads croaked out their lonely sonnets, as iridescent purple dragonflies and black bumble bees heavily laden with pollen, buzzed past his head. Remaining low in the water, he scanned the entire shoreline for signs of life. Finding none, he looked back to the log home and studied it. After gazing for three long minutes, no one appeared to be home. Darrell slipped out of the water, refreshed and renewed. He moved to arrange his clothes on a bush in the sun as his clean skin glistened.

Darrell searched inside his dirty, green bag for something to eat. He found a smashed bag of chips and a granola bar he stole from the house in Canada. He knew his wallet carried two Canadian dollars. He needed a plan, but the only idea flowing into his mind was a growing hunger. So, he forced the chip dust into his mouth, hoping to stop his stomach's protest. The dry granola bar was next. He needed water in his empty bottle, so he decided to fill it with what the lake offered.
"You gotta think, Darrell."

*

Scooter had admired the picture on Angie's wall ever since he began counseling with her. The lighthouse worker was opening a door to check on a storm. The surrounding ocean was in a rage with waves crashing over the stone breakwater, threatening the lighthouse itself. But the artist depicted the keeper with a cup of coffee in his hand, like he was watching a show on television without a real care in the world. Scooter was growing in his belief that Angie's office was becoming the lighthouse for him. With all of the difficult and nasty things he talked to her about, she remained just like the keeper of the lighthouse— calm in the middle of the storm, trusting the rock on which she stood.

"Hey, where did you go?" Angie asked.
"I was thinking about your lighthouse picture." Scooter pointed with his chin.
"And?"
"I think you're the guy with the coffee cup in his hand. Calm in the middle of the raging storm."
"I try to be that guy," Angie said with a smirk and looked down to her notepad as a finger twirled in the ends of her hair.
"You are for me." He smiled.
Angie used the pause in the interaction to prepare her next question.

"So, it seems to me, you've wanted to tell me something for the last couple of sessions, but haven't been ready to talk about it."
"You're intuitive, Angie." Scooter wiped at the corners of his mouth.
"What's going on?"
"Um, drinking isn't the only thing I struggle with."
"You mean believing drinking will solve your problems, rather than mask them?"
"You're reading my mind," Scooter said.
"Good." Sitting with her legs crossed, she smiled and bounced her dangling foot a couple of times.
"I have a problem with women."
"What do you mean?"
"I know women aren't the problem— the way I look at them is," he said, with a growing embarrassment.
"Okay, what is problematic with the way you look at women?"
"When I was young, I began looking at pictures." Scooter stirred in his seat.
"You mean erotic pictures, Scooter?"

"Yes. Playboy and the like."

"What do you think the problem is?"

"Those magazines put women into a box I use to make myself feel better," Scooter said.

"When do you do this?"

"Usually when I'm feeling bad about myself."

"Bad?"

"Rejected, I guess. I use the mindset to escape from reality," Scooter said.

"What are you running from?"

"Huh?"

"You used the word, 'escape.'"

"Um, the emotions of feeling rejected, I guess."

"So, to overcome feelings of rejection, you turn to pornography to escape?" Angie said.

Angie paused to let her synopsis sink in. "Does it work?" she asked.

"For a minute," Scooter admitted.

"Are you saying the Band-Aid is a genuine solution?"

"No, that can't be right. But the intense feelings and the sexual drive I have need something."

"Freud believed our sexuality was the defining feature of our lives," Angie said.

"Do you?" Scooter asked.

"I think he's full of crap. Sexuality is a part of life. Some choose to elevate their sexual proclivities to a place of prominence, but I believe in so doing, you're allowing a piece of who we are, by design, to define the totality of your existence."

"Okay," Scooter said, looking up and pondered her statement.

"You have legitimate needs, Scooter." His face flushed, and she continued, uninhibited. "But choosing to meet those needs in illegitimate ways will never bring you peace."

"Hmm."

"The porn industry reduces a woman to an object. Objects are by nature things to be used. In this case, used for another person's pleasure."

"I understand. It describes Johnny Dog to a T."

"Do you think it is a healthy view of women?"

"No."

"Okay. Why?"

"Women are human beings— no one deserves to be treated like an object."

"Created in the image of God, and all," Angie said, adding to his thought.

"Yes."

"Having said that, Scooter, you are made in the image of God, too. Part of your manhood includes a sex drive. Denying those feelings is to deny part of who you are."

"So, I should get with women sexually when I have the need stirring?"

"Never. That is exactly the problem I described. I believe God made them male and female, for each other, within the bounds of marriage. That is the sexual expression God designed, Scooter."

"But it's not how the world operates, Angie."

"Is using porn to get off helping you become a better version of yourself?"

"No."

"Precisely. And it never can, because you would be asking a part of who you are to become the motive for the whole of you. Whenever you do that, you become addicted to the means to make it happen, to the exclusion of the rest of your life."

"You're talking about being out of balance again?"

"Indeed— and self-absorbed."

"So, you're not saying stop looking at porn, 'sick pervert?'" He used finger quotes.

"What am I saying?"

He considered the question for a moment.

"To look into the deeper issues that push me to believe objectifying women is the answer."

"Answer to what?" she asked.

"My loneliness?"

"What about your need for intimacy, Scooter?"

"I don't know! I just thought I had an issue with looking at porn a couple times a month."

"That's only a symptom, my friend." Angie was being intentional, wanting him to squirm.

"So how do you deal with it?" Scooter asked.

"With what?"

Scooter realized he opened his mouth before thinking.

"It's okay to say what you're thinking," Angie said.
"You're a beautiful woman, Angie. How do you deal with all the people objectifying you?"
"Thank-you for being honest. It's not easy sometimes, but it comes down to the fact I am not responsible for what others think."
"The old AOC lesson again?"
"Yes. And we can't control how people respond. I do have control over how I act towards others. If I walk around wearing suggestive clothing, then I'll get more people reacting purely out of sexual instinct. I had no choice over my genetics. The only choice is how we use what is given to us."
Scooter nodded in reply.
"Plus, beauty is certainly not only about attraction and outward appearance, but what we are like on the inside. The connection we have. The idea of intimacy is we get so close— into-me-I-see."
"Intimacy is something I haven't had in a very long time, Angie."

*

"I've always wanted to ask you something, Mom."
"Oh yeah?" Kim sat next to Bee and pulled her daughter's blanket over her legs.
"Yes," Bee said.
"You know you can ask me anything, honey."
"Why do you still wear your wedding ring?"

Kim thought for a few moments
"I think there are several reasons."
"Okay."
"First, it's a habit, and it makes me feel normal, I guess."
"Okay." Bee was taking mental notes.
"Another is it reminds me of what your dad and I had together," she said, looking at the ring.
"But doesn't that make you sad?"
"Sometimes I get sad over what I lost— sure."
"Must be hard."
"Sadness is part of our life on earth, honey." She caressed Bee's hair.
"I know."

"Another reason I still wear this ring is it helps keeps creeps away. For the most part." Kim smiled.

"You have creeps?"

"All women have to deal with creepy guys."

"Really?"

"Yes. There have been creepy people I didn't want anything to do with, and me flashing my ring lets them know I'm taken."

"And back off!" Bee said with a laugh.

"Right. Plus, I think marriage is a sacred thing. Death may separate you from your loved one, but the love I had in the beginning remains." Her heart was warmed by the connection with her daughter.

"Have you ever thought about dating?" Bee asked.

"A little."

"What has stopped you?"

"I think it would be too hard. Maybe after you guys are out of the house."

"Don't let me get in the way of your happiness," Bee quipped.

"Jesus is my happiness, and you only make it better, my beautiful girl!"

"What about him?" Bee pointed to Bobby and laughed out loud. He was laying on the floor in front of the television with his hand in the front of his pants.

"Bobby! Get your hand out of your pants. You have to eat with those!" The girls laughed. Bobby was embarrassed.

"Not so much right now," she said to her daughter with a smile. "Are you gonna share the popcorn, missy?"

"Sure, but not with him!"

*

Donna was headed out of the basement of the white six-story municipal building where the command center of her police unit was located. The massive St. Clair River pushed past the eastern side of the complex and was the place the six-year veteran went to think. The stainless-steel guardrail had served as her counselor for many cases over those years, especially when a clear head was required to see past the clouds of evidence to catch the bigger picture Donna often found the obvious answer was looking right at her. The river had a knack of hypnotizing her distractions away to reveal the truth.

"Detective!"

"Hey, Shirley." Donna watched her peace evaporate in a split second, with a single word.

"Sorry to interrupt your break."

"It's not a break— just trying to clear my head," she said, still looking out over the river toward Canada.

"I thought you needed to know Mrs. Patrick's deportation is happening within the hour."

"Good news! Homeland bringing her here?"

"They want a crack at her first."

"That's a load of crap! And they know it!" Donna turned to face Shirley.

"Fleeing across an international border gives the Feds jurisdiction, Donna."

"I know, I was just hoping. Did they say where they're taking her?"

"They're coming here," Shirley smiled.

"That is good news! Maybe they will let me in on the interview."

"If you flash them that pretty smile of yours, anything is possible," Shirley said.

"Whatever it takes. If God gave me this nice smile and fine physique, I intend to use it, Shirley."

"You go, girl," the fifty-year-old receptionist replied with a bright smile.

"Thanks for hunting me down." Donna turned back to the water.

"Wasn't much of a hunt. I can read your face when you need some fresh air."

"Then thank-you for looking out, Shirley."

"It's my pleasure, Donna."

*

The familiar bells chimed their goodnight to Scooter as he passed through the door of the counseling center. The sky was crimson as the sun was tucking behind the western horizon. The scattered clouds were aglow with red and violet hues. Stepping off the curb while looking up almost sent Scooter sprawling across the asphalt parking lot. When he regained composure, his cheeks flushed and he glanced to see if anyone had witnessed the clumsy move. Then he noticed the Honda in the corner of the lot. He knew who occupied the vehicle and anger surged inside of him. He took a direct line to the gray sedan.

The driver made him knock on the window before he would acknowledge his presence, feigning ignorance, as low rhythmic beats poured from the car, vibrating the trunk lid.

"Dog?"

"Hey, Lawrence."

"What are you doing?"

"Just listening to some music," he said, as his eyes darted.

"Right."

"What are you talking about?"

"You know exactly what I'm talking about. You're here to follow Angie."

"Get out of here," he replied.

"I saw it in your eyes the other night. The moment you saw her, your face lit up with the weird look you get whenever there's a pretty girl around."

"Screw off! You don't know me anymore."

"The heck I don't— that look of yours hasn't changed."

"What?"

"You want to follow her to see if you can find a way to talk to her and seduce her."

"I don't know what you're talking about!" Dog tried anger as camouflage.

"Bull crap, dude. You've been this way ever since I've known you," Scooter shot back.

"No way. I've changed." He was gripping at the steering wheel.

"No, you haven't. Change is hard but you aren't willing to put in the work, Dog. You have the same look in your eye now as you always have had whenever you're on the hunt."

"On the hunt? Okay, Scooter." He rolled his eyes and turned away.

"Listen, you'd better beat it, Dog. Leave her alone."

"You're crazy, man."

"No, I am perfectly sane, and you are still a pervert, dude."

"I'll tear you up, Lawrence."

"Get out of the car and we'll see about that," Scooter said without concern for his increasing volume.

"You're always giving me crap, Lawrence. Why do you think we haven't been hanging out?"

"We haven't been hanging out for years because you have a problem you refuse to take care of."

Scooter was allowing his anger to fester. "You're sick," Scooter said pointing.

"That's why I'm here. I was trying to work up the nerve to get an appointment with your doc so I can start working on things," Dog said, changing tactics.

"I don't believe you."

"Fine, I don't need your approval."

"Find a different counselor, Horn Dog." Scooter meant the disrespect.

"I want her help."

"I bet you do."

"Shut up."

"You're an idiot. You haven't changed one bit," Scooter said.

"You don't know me!"

"You need to get out of here before I drag you out of the car and beat the crap out of you, just like the last time."

"You got lucky last time."

"There was no luck, you short, little punk."

"You think she's gonna fall for you, Lawrence?"

"It's not like that Johnny. She's actually helping."

"You're weak. You've always been weak."

"You may be right, but I'm not too weak to kick the crap out of you."

"I ought to climb out of my car so we can finish this fight we have been dancing around for the last fifteen years."

"I think you should. Please do."

"You don't want to get rid of me. You need me." His eyes flared.

"No, I don't, and now you've pissed me off." Scooter went for the door handle but it was locked. His Napoleon-sized nemesis' car squealed away and left.

"You better go, Johnny Dog!" he yelled after the car.

Scooter glanced back to the counseling center's door where Angie was standing in the glass watching the ugly scene, just as he had feared.

"I wonder how long she was there?" he asked himself while walking back to explain.

Angie held the door open. "Are you okay?"

"Yeah. I know that guy. He's a real dirt bag and I think he is stalking you."

"Why?"

"Because he saw you the other night and commented on how hot you were."

"It doesn't mean he's stalking me," Angie said.

"I've known him for a long time. He's thinking he could woo you with his charm, and flattery."

"Woo me?"

"Into bed, Angie." Scooter was looking into her eyes. "Please lock the door at least. I can stay with you until you leave."

"Should I call the police?"

"It's up to you," he said. "I'm not leaving until I know you are okay."

"I'm not afraid, Scooter."

"Okay, Angie, but your fear has nothing to do with this."

Scooter watched her for a reaction. "I tell you what," he paused.

"What?" she said.

"Do you have any more clients to see?"

"No. You were the last."

"Then I need a ride home tonight, Angie. Can you do that for me?"

"I suppose I could."

"You offered the other night." He smiled.

"You're right. Let me gather my things."

*

"Hey, man, where you at?"

"Hangin' out at the Griz with Tums."

"Can I stop in?"

"Sure, Dog. What ever you need."

"Thanks, Jet."

"How long until you're here?"

"Five minutes."

"I'll get you a cold one."

"Okay, thanks."

Four minutes later the gray Honda sedan pulled into the *Grizzly Bar* that was just west of town. The hangout was a local favorite— a country music-loving, red-neck bar, with an imposing stuffed grizzly bear peering from over the top of the impressive line of booze.

"Busy— must be dollar beer night," Johnny said, looking for a parking spot.

A couple minutes later, Johnny let the first taste of the cold ale wet his dry mouth. Jimmy the Jet was hanging out with Tums.

"What up, Johnny Dog?" Tums had been drinking with intent.

"Ran into Lawrence tonight."

"Good old Scooter," Jet sneered dragging the name out.

"Whatever. The guy has turned into a real head case," Tums said.

"Where did you see him?"

"We just had a screaming match in the parking lot of his counselor friend," Johnny said while checking out a couple of women bent over at the pool table.

"The counselor girl is fine," Tums said.

"You said that!" Johnny said, continuing his observation of the women.

"So, what were you doing over there, Johnny Dog?" Jet asked.

"I don't know, just hanging out," Johnny's head spun back to Jet, knowing he was caught.

"Yeah, right."

"I was chillin'— just listening to some music," he said, with his palms opening to the ceiling.

"Yeah, okay," Tums said.

"What did Scooter say?" Jet asked.

"He thought I was there to chase after his counselor girl friend."

"Do you think she is his girlfriend?"

"I think he wants her as his lover," Dog said.

"Wouldn't that be against the law or something?" Tums asked.

"It would be an ethical violation for sure," Jet said.

"You should turn him into the cops." Tums laughed over his empty mug.

"He drives me nuts," Dog said.

"I hear you." Jet said.

"He's turned into a real tool."

"The counselor chick is smokin' hot, though."

"For certain."

"What was he saying to you?"

"He was screaming in my face, wanting to pull me out of the car to fight."

"Lawrence wanted to fight? He must have been really mad," Tums said.

Jimmy the Jet's face contorted. "He needs to be taught a lesson in respect— Denton style."

"Preach it!" Dog said, as he turned back to the two desirable objects shooting pool. He got out of his seat and walked over to the women, as his personal film projector clicked away in his mind.

*

Scooter's heart was still pounding from the confrontation as he stood next to Angie's car.
"Sorry, it's a bit of a mess. Let me throw those files in the back."
"Don't worry about it." He smiled, enjoying the view down her shirt for a brief moment.
"Clean cars have never been my strong suit," she said.
"It's not all that important, if you think about it."
"You're right, sir. Until this very moment," she smiled.

She slipped into the driver's seat. "Get in. Where are we going?"
"I think we should go to your house."
"Excuse me?"
"You should drive home. I'll make sure you get in, then I'll walk home from there."
"Oh."
"That sounded a bit forward, but I just want to make sure I've scared Johnny off."
"I will be fine."
"I know, but please let me do this. It will help me sleep better, knowing."
With a resigned sigh and a deep breath Angie said, "Only so you can sleep better, Scooter." She smiled and fired up the engine.
"I don't know too many women that drive manuals," he said, watching her thigh flex as she pushed in the clutch, noticing her skirt had slid up, revealing more of her long legs.
"You don't know many women, do you?"
"No, I guess not."
She smiled and pulled out onto the road, accelerating hard to make the light.
"Thanks for being a protector," Angie said, looking forward and shifting.
"You've done so much for me, Angie. It's the least that I can do."
"Chivalry is an uncommon trait these days, Scooter," she commented as she glanced at the stubble on his chin.

Scooter had no idea how to respond. Inside he was stirring, not feeling chivalrous at all. His attraction to his counselor was taking over his heart and his ability to think. *"What would I do if she invited me inside her house?"* He was hoping it would be true and glanced wantonly at her body again.

"How do you feel after the confrontation?" Angie asked, breaking his obvious stare.

"I don't know," he said.

"Eyes forward, take a couple of deep breaths, and relax," she said.

"Okay." He knew he would do anything for her. The pressing issue for him at the moment was the incredible urge he was having toward Angie. *"What would happen if I kissed her?"* He had crossed over into lusting now.

"What were we talking about tonight, Scooter?" She interrupted his hedonistic thinking.

"A bunch of things."

"Yes, but we focused on one particular thing," she pressed.

"My struggle with porn."

"Your struggle with what?"

"With the way I view women," he corrected himself.

"And what was the struggle, specifically?"

"That I see women, or my perceived image of women, as the answer to my loneliness."

"Okay. When do you think you are most likely to feel that way? You said it in the session."

"When feeling rejected."

"Do you like conflict?"

"No, I hate it."

"Right." She had known the answer before he said it.

"It's the last thing I want to do," Scooter said.

"Precisely."

"What does that mean?"

"Answer this, 'When I am forced into a conflict, I usually feel. . .'"

Angie took off hard from the light, pushing Scooter back into his seat which made him smile. *"She is perfect,"* he thought.

"When I am forced into a conflict, I usually feel," she repeated.

"When I am forced into a conflict, I usually feel angry, frustrated, and confused."

"Okay, does that make you want to run to, or run from, the person you were having a conflict with?"

"Run from."

"What?"

"I want to run from them. Avoid them," Scooter said.

"Do you feel like conflict causes you to to be attracted to the person or rejected by them?

"Rejected. Definitely rejected."

"You're feeling rejected right now?"

"I guess so," he said.

"When we go through stressful situations we will fall back into what I call our default settings, like a computer. Under stress we reset to our default settings."

"Okay."

"If I'm right, under stress you will most likely do what, Scooter?"

"Drink. Objectify women. Isolate."

"Precisely. Which of the three are you doing right now?"

"*She was reading my mind*," he panicked. "I don't know!"

"I do."

"Really?"

"Yes. It is our enemy's oldest play in his worn-out book," she said.

"What is?"

"Under stress we revert back to our old ways of coping."

"This is hard," Scooter admitted.

"Indeed. Our biggest mistake is thinking life is easy."

"So, me sitting here feeling attracted to you is all a play of Satan?" There it was.

"Not entirely. Your choices throughout your life have led you to think a certain way. To react a certain way to different stimuli. The enemy knows this, and is crafty enough to use it against you every time you let him get away with it."

"But these are powerful feelings." There was no going back now.

"I know they are, Scooter. But what you feel is not necessarily the truth of how life actually is. You are not your feelings. You have emotions and experience them in powerful ways and much of the time they are pointing to something that is going on inside of you."

"Every time I leave your office my brain is smoking," he said pressing his palm against his forehead.

"What do you mean?"

"You make me think more deeply than I ever have."
"That's a compliment. Thank you."
"I'm thankful for you and for the smoking brain thing," he said.
"Good."

He swallowed hard, considering if he was going to say everything he was feeling. "I am really attracted to you, Angie. I think about you all of the time. You're beautiful. You're smarter than anyone I have ever known. You make me laugh and cry, which has never happened before."
"Scooter, I'm your counselor. I'm humbled you think about me in those ways. I think right now, you have already said what you're experiencing."
"I did?"
"Yes. It is called intimacy. Remember "into-me-you-see?"
"Yes."
"Intimacy is a powerful reality. It shakes our soul to know someone cares for us. It changes things inside of us when we believe we are loved and lovable. Our world is twisted toward good when we are heard. That's what you're experiencing right now. It's new and it's powerful."
"It is."
"The challenge for you in this moment, is you're reacting with your base instincts to something entirely foreign."
"Huh?"
"You told me you haven't experienced intimacy in a long time."
"Yes."
"You're feeling sexual arousal because of the wiring of the human heart. God designed that level of physical intimacy for one relationship — your wife. Our enemy twists that into knots all of the time. A spiritual connection can be just as intimate, Scooter, without the sex."
"I can't see the distinction, Doc. Don't both the spiritual and the physical happen in sexual relationships?"
"Exactly. That's why sex is so powerful. In our world it has been turned against us by a crafty enemy. There is much more than a physical act happening during intercourse. It is a spiritual bond people share. The oneness. When the enemy convinces us to go outside of God's construct for sex, the beauty is lost in the drive and children of the King are left feeling broken, hollow, and cheap."
"That's a real buzzkill, Angie."

"The key to a good marriage is when both the physical and the spiritual connection are happening inside each partner, as they are seeking to live a life of love for God and humanity."
Scooter blew out air between his lips, making them flap.

"I feel your frustration. I also know the next thing you're going to experience is feelings of shame and rejection." She placed her hand on top of his. "I'm not rejecting you, Scooter. I want what is best for you. I'm glad to call you friend, and always will be."
"Okay," he said, but he didn't know what to believe as his heart sank into his stomach.

"You've been through so much stress, Scooter. There is every reason to expect a wide range of emotions. They aren't bad. You're not bad or deficient in anyway. You're a child of the King of Kings. Bought by blood of the Son of God. He has not rejected you, even though you have felt the things you have felt and done the things you have done. It is all covered under His blood, Scooter. The cross of Jesus redeems us and frees us. The problem is believing you really are, in fact, His. God loved you so much He came and died for you, and has promised that you belong to him. Nothing can separate you from His love. Walking in the truth, instead of the old lies— that whisper you will never measure up, you will never be accepted— is the greatest challenge of life on earth. You have been accepted. You have been redeemed. You are a child of God. Will you believe it? Will you believe it right now? Will you walk in truth, or remain in the old way of thinking?"

Scooter had not realized the two of them were sitting in a parking place at Angie's house.
"I feel like a child," he said.
"You are His kid, Scooter, and you can rest in that fact. Thank you for being brave and wanting to protect me."
"You're welcome," he said looking toward his feet.
"Will you do me one more favor?"
"Anything. You know I would do anything for you."
"Will you be brave and believe your genuine identity in Christ, instead of the lie that you are only your failings and sin?"
"I'll try."
"Try is good." Angie patted the top of his hand.

*

Scooter was five miles away from home, so he decided to ride the bus. He waited at the stop for almost half an hour when he abandoned the idea and left on foot. Mulling the conversation with Angie over and over, he walked on. The battle inside him was raging against the strong urges that were conjured up when thinking about her. His lustful glances had fed those urges and brought him to the place he was placing God-like expectations on their relationship. He was convinced Angie was the ideal woman. In his mind, she was perfect in every way. *"It may be true, but it doesn't mean she'll fix me. It cannot mean she's my answer, but I want her. I need to concentrate on what she said to me."* He was talking out loud to himself now, sounding crazy. *"I cannot remain the same. I am a child of God,"* he said. *"God help me with my crazy way of thinking — my selfish way of believing. I feel so broken, Father,"* he said as he looked up and noticed countless bright stars, twinkling away.

It was almost eleven o'clock when he made his way past the lit trailer park sign. He was exhausted from the long day, wanting nothing more than his bed and the solace it promised.

Checking his mailbox he found a few things inside and turned for home. He was the sixth trailer on the left, precisely in the middle of the row. Something didn't feel right. Scooter looked around the outside of the trailer, even walked back to his shed at the rear of his home. It was dark in the backyard, but everything looked normal to him. "Just tired," he said.

Up on his metal steps, he reached for the door handle and noticed it was loose, broken in fact. He reached his hand in to find the light switch and clicked both the outside and living room lights on at the same time. He gently pushed the door open with his left hand and grabbed for his pocket knife with his right, clicking the tool open and stepping inside.

Scooter's place was destroyed. Everything was overturned and tossed around. The entire house was the in the same condition. He wasn't sure if anything was missing but went for the electric water heater— not because he was concerned that his water was hot— but the hidden nook was where he kept his important things. Scooter had learned early on, when you live in a trailer park, the things you care about need to be locked up in a secure and isolated location. The piece of paneling in the corner of the back closet was still in place. The screws had not been removed, or if they had been, the bandits took the time to put them back in.

"I doubt it," he reasoned. Still, he went looking for the Phillips-head screwdriver. Five minutes later he found one in the kitchen, stuck in the wall right through the bill of his favorite, albeit filthy, hat.

"What the heck?"

Back in the bedroom he closed the blinds. *"At least they were still hanging on the window frame,"* he thought. Making short work of the three screws, Scooter found everything in place just the way he had left it. A deep breath calmed him. He needed to alert the park about the break-in. What he didn't know was if he was going to call the cops.

"Pete, you up?" Scooter knocked on the first trailer home across the street in the park.

"What's going on here?" the man asked, touching his Santa Claus beard. He opened his door only a crack, until he recognized Scooter.

"Sorry to bother you so late, Pete."

"Scooter, what's going on?"

"Someone broke into my place and threw everything around."

"Oh! Is anything missin'?"

"Can't tell yet. Mostly just tossed about, as far as I can see."

"We haven't had any of that crap lately, Scooter. I'm sorry to hear it."

"Thanks."

"You gonna call the cops?"

"Maybe in the morning. Right now, I'm too tired to deal with it all."

"They have a habit of not showing up for vandalism," Pete said, like he had real life experience with the matter.

"I know a detective," Scooter said.

"Then you may get lucky."

"Yeah, well luck didn't break into my place."

"True enough."

"Night, Pete."

"Sorry, Scooter. Let me know if you need somethin'."

"Thanks," he said and left.

The Stars in the Sidewalk

*

Chapter Eight
✳ Beautiful Star ✳

"I'm Scooter," he said holding out his hand.

"Matt. It's good to finally meet you, Scooter."

"He has a firm handshake," thought Scooter. Matt stood about two inches taller, fifty pounds heavier, and, Scooter guessed, five years his elder.

"You too, Matt."

"Pastor tells me you're a busy man," Matt said.

"Yes, the concrete season is in full swing. People are panicking now the kids are back in school. They want to get things finished up before winter."

"So you do concrete work? Who do you work for?"

"How many are in your party, gentlemen?" interrupted the high school-aged hostess.

"Just the two of us," Matt replied.

"Right this way, please."

"Can we get a booth over in the corner?" Matt asked.

"Sure, anywhere you'd like." She feigned a smile, but didn't make eye contact with either man.

"What are you having to drink?"

"Coffee, for me," Matt said.

"Water for me. Thanks." The hostess walked away.

"Not a coffee drinker?"

"No, not really. I work for Mack's Concrete," Scooter said, pointed to his grungy backup hat.

"He has a very good reputation, but your hat has seen its better days."

"Yes, he does, and I've been meaning to pick up a new hat." He smiled. "What do you do there?"

"It's a small company so I do a bit of everything, including driving the dump truck."

"Nice. Do you like it?"

"I do. We're a good team, which makes a big difference."

"What do you do in the winter?"

"We get laid off usually the second week of November, depending on the weather."

"Do you collect unemployment then?"

The hostess brought their drinks and silverware.

"Yes. And we plow snow."

"Do you like plowing?"

"Not really, but it gives me something to do. What about you, Matt?"

"Designer by trade. I work for a small company down in Chesterfield."

"What do you design?"

"Automotive connectors. The composite wingnuts and fasteners. Most of the stuff you don't see unless you're working on a car."

"Gotcha. I don't have a car right now to work on," he said it like he was confessing some grievous sin.

"They're a pain in the neck," Matt said and sipped at his steaming mug. "I've had plenty of them, but not right now."

"Makes it hard getting to work."

"Most of the time I ride a bike the three miles but a coworker has been picking me up this year. He only lives a few blocks away."

A waitress walked by carrying a serving tray. The aroma of bacon and eggs curled in her wake.

"Boss man lets me borrow a truck if I really need to, plus the bike keeps me in shape" Scooter said.

"Cool. Doesn't the job keep you in shape?"

"Yeah. It's a running joke. I don't work hard enough, so I ride the bike for exercise."

Matt laughed. "Does not having a car makes it hard to get to church?"

"Yes, especially up in Lakeport."

"Right. I don't recall seeing you there."

"I make most holidays. I tag along with my sister Jan and her family."

"Jan Clemons?"

"Yep."

"I know Jan and Bill very well."

"Good people," Scooter said.

"Do you guys know what you want for breakfast?" The quaint diner was filling up early on a Saturday morning.

"What's the 'Super Saturday Special' I saw on the sign?" asked Matt.

"Three eggs, potatoes, toast, ham, bacon, and sausage patty, for six bucks."

"Sounds great. Over medium with rye."

"I'll have the same."

"Thank you, guys. I'll bring more coffee."

"Thanks."

"What is this thing my sister thinks would be so great for me?" Scooter asked.
The sound of a glass shattering in the kitchen echoed behind them causing many to look and Matt to wince.
"We're trying to come along side the men in our church."
"Meaning?"
"We realized, as a culture, we are drifting further and further apart."
"True enough," Scooter said.
"To combat the isolation, we're trying to be intentional about getting to know the guys in our church and become known by them."
"Sounds simple enough."
"It is just that simple," Matt said, spreading his hands.
"You're not trying to sell me something or take me away on a creepy retreat to some remote island?"
"Nothing to sell here, although the remote island thing— maybe Fiji in February— sounds pretty good."
"Yes, Fiji would be good. Sign me up! So Matt, are you married?" Scooter drank some water for the first time.
"Yes. Twenty-three years. We have three kids. The oldest is going to SC4 here in town, and the other two are in high school." Matt's eyes lit up.
"High school!"
"Yeah, so I may need to vent a bit myself."
"Vent. I think you may need more than that."
"So true."
"Girls or boys?"
"Oldest is my son, the younger two are my girls," Matt said with pride.
There was no way Scooter was walking down that road yet. "Wow."
"So you're a single guy?"
"Yeah. My sister keeps bugging me about that."
"Any prospects?"
"Not really," Scooter said and thought of Angie.

The first meeting of the two men from different walks of life lasted a little over an hour. They agreed to meet every couple of weeks, then exchanged phone numbers for emergencies. Matt had one of the new fancy phones, while Scooter busted out his archaic flip phone. Matt didn't say a word but Scooter felt behind the times as they stood in the parking lot of the diner.

Before they parted, Matt asked Scooter to hang on while he dug a plastic bag out of his back seat and tossed him a new black hat.
"See if that fits," Matt said and smiled.
"Perfect," Scooter said. He had a real weakness for new baseball hats. The black cap was fitted to size and had the word *"Present"* embroidered in white across the front. The "P" and the "n" were in blue, so if only the white letters were read it said "reset."
"We had a few made up for a group of guys at church. We've been trying to learn to be more present in our lives. You know, not distracted. We discovered to live a present life we need a reset, something to remind us of our life in Christ."
"It's a nice hat, Matt. Thanks."
"My pleasure."

*

"Tina Patrick, I am Detective Donna McBride with the Port Huron Police Department."
"Okay."
"You're a hard woman to track down."
"Why?" Tina thought the detective looked like a runway model instead of a cop. Noticing her perfect figure and flawless makeup made her feel frumpy and ugly.
"I'm not sure. Why don't you tell me?"
"Not sure what you're getting at. I was spending some time at my friends house in Ontario. There's nothing illegal about that, is there?"
"Not necessarily," Donna said. "I received your friend's information from Homeland Security." She flicked through the file.
"Do you know why you're here today?" Donna asked.
"Not really." Tina thought the dank space smelled like a musty locker room.
"Have you been read your rights?"
"Yes."
"Do you want an attorney to be present?" Donna asked.
"Do I need one? I can't find out what you want with me."
"Do you remember Ronnie?"

Tina thought for a moment. "Ronnie? Dell and Sharron's foster kid?"

"Yes, that would be the one."

"Sure. Seemed like a nice kid. Kept to himself from what I noticed." She bit at her thumbnail.

"Do you know anything about the whereabouts of your son, Darrell?"

Tina Patrick put her head down on the cool metal table and began to sob.

"Tina?"

"I left him at the gas station," she whispered.

"Where?"

"In Wallaceburg."

"Why would you do that?" Donna wrote a note.

"To keep him safe," Tina was trying to compose herself.

"From what?"

"From the psychopath."

"Who is that?"

"Donny O'Flannery."

"Who is Donny O'Flannery?" Donna scribbled the name on the inside of the file folder and circled it.

"He's an old boyfriend who beat the shit out of me and my Darrell." She wiped at her face with her orange sleeve.

"Why him and why now?"

"Darrell woke me in the middle of the night screaming Donny got out of Jackson early. Donny was at a bar asking if anyone knew where I was. A friend called and warned us, so we took off to Canada where we knew he couldn't follow us."

"Why couldn't he follow you?"

"He's a felon, so he can't get across the border," Tina said and raised her head.

"Right. So, you're saying you left Darrell at a gas station to keep him away from this Donny O'Flannery character?"

"I told Darrell to go back to the place we were staying."

"When did you tell him?"

"I told the cop I had to pee, so I could warn Darrell off."

"So you lied?"

"I did have to pee, but yes, I lied to protect my son. I knew I would be sent back."

"So, you left Darrell in the care of your friends to protect him?" Donna clarified. "What did the RCMP say to you?"

"Say?"
"You crossed the border with your son— didn't they ask about him?"
"I lied to them," Tina locked eyes with the detective.
"And I'm supposed to believe you now?" The elegant detective's eyes flared more than she intended.

Tina didn't know how to answer.
"When was the last time you saw Ronnie?" Donna sat forward.
"The neighbor kid?"
"Yes— Ronnie. The only Ronnie I've been talking to you about."
"I don't— . . . the day before we left, I guess. I remember Darrell telling me about getting into a scrape with him. Why are you asking me about this kid?" Tina was rubbing her temples now.
"Because he's dead, Tina. We have reason to believe your son Darrell was involved in his death."
The information felt like a bomb going off in Tina's fragile head.

"That is ridiculous." She slammed her hands down on the table.
"We have solid evidence putting your son, Darrell Patrick, at the scene during the time of Ronnie's death. We have evidence Darrell had beaten the child mercilessly not forty eight hours before his death. We have evidence your child was stalking Ronnie all throughout the previous few days before his death. We have evidence of Ronnie's blood on your rug." Donna let that sink in, while the officers from Homeland Security watched from behind the mirrored glass.

"Tina, we have a solid case against Darrell. Where is he?"
"I don't know!" Tina felt like she was going to throw up.
"We need to find him!" McBride pushed.
"So do I!" Tina glared at the attractive, Black, officer.
"I need your cooperation, Tina. It's your only hope."
"What do you mean?"
"You're facing a long time in prison."
"What? Why?"
"Aiding and abetting a murder suspect across an international border. Fleeing and eluding. Interference in a capital crime investigation. Criminal neglect of a child. Shall I go on? Because there can be about five more charges."
"Where is Darrell? Please find him! Please." Tina sobbed again.

"I tell you what, I'm going to check out your story with this O'Flannery character and, if it's what you say, then you may not be as bad off as we thought."

"Please find my son, Officer."

"The department is making every effort. We have alerted our counterparts in Ontario and they are searching for your son."

"Thank you."

"We'll talk soon."

"Wait! Can I leave now?"

"No, not yet." Donna's face revealed nothing to her prisoner.

*

Scooter cruised along in Mack's tired GMC pickup on Mayer Road, a couple of miles southwest of Smiths Creek, Michigan. Once a thriving railroad stop, the village had been reduced to a bar, a post office, and a dozen rundown homes. The bar, with a pair of massive, pink-concrete elephants out front, thrived but nothing else did.

Scooter was aiming to finish his Saturday lawn jobs for the boss before cutting his G-ma's place, as was his usual routine. He didn't get paid to do his own house, of course, but used the equipment as a bonus for doing all of Mack's other lawns, which Scooter did get cash for.

As Scooter drove he was still thinking about his encounter with Johnny, but more important to him was his long conversation with Angie. He felt like she possessed the ability to undress his emotions like no one else. He loved it, but hated feeling so vulnerable. She was opening up places in his heart which had remained closed for many years. It felt invigorating in some ways, which was unexpected to say the least, and shameful in others.

"Crap!" He slammed on the brakes of the weary white pickup. He had almost rolled past his own house. There was no one on the road, so he backed up past the drive, to be able to pull the truck and trailer in. Thirty feet from the road, he had to stop and force open the rusted metal gate. Swinging it into the drive, he hooked the chain loop onto the keeper post. Not secure to be certain, but this was out in the middle of the sticks and no one had messed with the house in sixty years.

If it ain't broke, Scooter murmured to himself.

The gravel drive was enveloped by foot-high grass and weeds. He was going to have to run the mower down the long winding entry today. It was getting ridiculous.

"There it is again," Scooter said, as the old familiar feeling washed over him. It was happening less often these days but, every once in a while, the wave of childhood excitement and relief of being at G-ma's did push into him. When the emotion overwhelmed him, it happened at this exact spot in the driveway, emerging from the thick woods to the homestead. The apple trees lined the drive with other fruits farther off in each direction. This was his real home.

The two-story, orange-brick house faced west. A wide white porch wrapped two sides, blocking the blazing afternoon sunshine. The portico was covered by more than a roof— it hung thick with memories that still invited him to an afternoon glass of icy lemonade. Scooter's grandparents took long and lavish breaks from working the garden up on the sanctuary, always inviting his younger version inside. The swing that hung from the rafters was gone now, but Scooter was intent on replacing it just as soon as he moved out here full time. Restoration has been his hearts desire since taking possession of the property. Deep inside he knew it was an attempt to force back the hands of time. To return to a carefree life, surrounded by those who loved him best. If he could rebuild this historic place, he could rebuild himself, erasing the decades of mistakes. If.

Scooter stopped the truck in front of the aging barn and just sat for a few minutes, taking in the scene and being enveloped in its peace. This was home.

"You are such an idiot." He was lamenting over the decisions he had made which now kept him from living here. Two D.U.I's was the first obstacle. He was still digging out from the financial ramifications of those stupid choices.

"Broken choices," he corrected himself. Angie would be proud. He glanced at his new *Present* hat in the mirror and remembered his need for a reset.

He had managed to get the roof on the place last year, which saved the old house from impending doom. Installing the white metal roof himself took him the entire summer, but felt like the first positive thing he had accomplished in a very long time.

Now he clicked through ten or twelve other things which had to happen before he could move out here full time, the water well for the house being primary. During the cold winter he survived alone with the hand pump near the weathered barn. It was inconvenient at best, frozen in the coldest months to the point he had to thaw it to get water. The septic field needed to be replaced. The front porch was in disrepair. All of the plumbing and electrical needed updating. The only heat was the wood stove in the living room. The windows leaked air and moisture. On and on, the list kept building— the solutions moved further into his future. Rebuilding his sanctuary seemed impossible.
"Time to mow," he said as a reset, before he was overwhelmed with dread.

The bruised Exmark mower was reliable and sturdy, but Scooter had to walk behind it, so the five acres of cut grass he split up into three areas, tackling one a week. This week he was cutting in front of the house which meant under the fruit trees full of ripening apples and pears. They would be ready in a few weeks. The guys from work would come and gather some to use them as deer bait. Of course Scooter would eat all he wanted. His sister's family would do the same. Keeping the orchard going was one task he had managed to accomplish since his poppy passed.

He figured he had been pruning the fruit trees in the winter for twenty years. The cutting and cleaning up the hellacious mess took three extended days. He burned the branches at the edge of the front yard after the pruning. The trees were all Poppy's doing, planting every one from seed. Poppy loved his orchard, spending hours grafting, trimming, spraying and harvesting. G-ma canned for weeks on end and Scooter ate himself into a bellyache several times a year.

Many of the apple trees had been grafted with different varieties on one tree. Scooter smiled at the memory of Poppy's crooked finger pointing and his voice declaring *"Seed to seed and stone to stone,"* describing the way to graft trees. The finely cut branches trimmed to precise angles were inverted, tied together, and coated with wax so the young sapling would get its nourishment from the older tree. Over a few years, the branches would merge and the cut would heal. The new sapling produced its kind of apples while the rest of the tree produced its own variety. Most of his apple trees in the orchard produced two or three different kinds of apples each.

Scooter would mow the orchard today, circling the twenty-nine trees a couple of times before he could draw the long, straight rows. On the south side of the house, away from the drive, the slanted entry to the Michigan basement had overgrown with vines again so he would need to clean it up. Seeing the doors, he remembered he needed to move the coffee table into the cellar.
"I think I'll just spend the night," he thought, walking behind the loud, red mower.

✳

Scooter rolled into the yard at Mack's Concrete five minutes early on Monday morning. Both Layne and Bull were crawling out of their vehicles in the cramped parking spot just off the driveway. The fence was pulled open, which meant Mack was already on the premises. Scooter had hoped to drop the mower off into the small pole barn and get the trailer stowed before Mack arrived.

He caught a glimpse of Mack's blazing-red face contrasted against the white siding of the new pole barn. The boss was on his phone and appeared to be upset, which did not bode well for the rest of the day— maybe the entire week. They were supposed to have a significant pour today at a church because they had prepped half of a new basketball court last Friday with the hope of pouring the first half this morning, then prepping and finishing the second half this afternoon.

"Something is off," Scooter was thinking, as he backed in front of the door of the work barn.
"Scooter! Get over here," Mack demanded, waving his arms.
"What's up?"
"All of the truck tires have been slashed."
"No kidding?"
"Look at them!"
Mack was right. The trucks were squatting down on their rims, rubber tires mashed under the weight. Mack was yelling, because it was how

Mack dealt with stress. He was right to yell at this mess. Vandals had obviously scaled the eight-foot fence topped with barbed wire and flattened all of the truck tires.

"*Who would do such a thing to Mack, of all people*?" Scooter thought.

"They cut through the sidewalls. The tires are junk," Layne said.

"Looks like they used a drill on some of them."

"How many tires did they get? Bull asked.

"Scooter, go count and write out a list of what we need to get rolling. I have to cancel concrete, call the cops then the tire guy."

"Okay. Don't forget about the insurance company, too," Scooter said.

"Right, he won't be in until nine."

"Like a banker," Layne said.

Mack was deep in anger-laden thought.

"Dang, this is thousands of dollars," Bull whispered to Scooter. "Unbelievable."

"Nice hat, Scooter. Is someone taking attendance today?" Layne asked while Bull snickered, "I'm present, too, teacher."

"Layne, get the jacks out of the barn but don't touch anything, in case the cops need to do something," Mack said.

"On it."

Ten minutes later, two cop cars rolled into the dusty gravel lot. The second car was of the dark, unmarked variety. Donna, the Barbie cop, climbed out of that vehicle a few seconds later.

"Guys! Looks like someone doesn't appreciate Mack's Concrete."

"Hey, Donna," Bull said.

"You keep showing up on our best days," Layne quipped.

"I hope you have better days than this," Donna shot back.

"Hey, Donna," Mack greeted the detective, as he put his phone into his case on his hip.

"So you showed up today and all your tires are slashed?"

"Yep, it looks like somebody broke in and did this."

"Was your gate locked?"

"Yes, we always lock it on the weekend."

"Who was the last one out?"

"That was me, on Friday," Scooter said returning with his list.

"Did you lock it?"

"Yes. I had the white pickup and the trailer with the mower."

"And you locked the gate?" Donna pressed.

"Yes, I did." Scooter looked Donna in the eyes.

"Okay."

"We need to have a look around, Mack. Don't touch anything in case we can lift a fingerprint."

"Got it."

"Do you have any cameras?"

"Yes! Forgot all about them. I had them installed a couple months ago." Mack almost smiled at the thought.

"Great, they'll help. I'll need you to show me the footage."

"It's on a computer in my office."

"Okay."

Fifteen minutes later, Donna strolled out and called for Scooter.

"I need you to look at the camera images."

"Sure."

Layne and Bull elbowed each other as the sexy detective walked past them.

'Sexy Powerful,' is her new name," Layne whispered to Bull and they both laughed.

Walking into the new barn to get in the cramped corner office, the pair stepped around a mess from Mack tearing apart a Georgia buggy. Mack was sitting behind his desk looking grim. The office reeked of stale cigarettes and old man-sweat.

"Play it again, Mack," Donna said, instructing Scooter to get a better view with her outstretched arm.

The dark images flashed across the screen. One guy entered the compound after two a.m. Saturday which set off the motion sensitive cameras. He proceeded to move from truck to truck stabbing with a long military style knife in one hand and a drill in the other.

"You'll notice, Scooter, this guy seems to know there's a camera mounted up on the barn, because the keeps his face turned away at all times. Look, there he looks really awkward— he knows he's being watched."

"Yeah, I see it," Scooter said.

"Do you see what I see?" Donna asked.

"What do you mean?"

"Our bad guy looks like you, Scooter!"

"What?" Scooter bent toward the monitor.

"Seriously, look closer."

"She's right, Scooter," Mack said. "He even has a baseball hat on!"

"I don't care what he looks like— I didn't do this, Mack. I never would. You know me!"

"I thought I did, but pictures don't lie." Mack's cheeks had turned a shade of deep purple.

"I was at home all night. Even backed the truck and trailer up close to my place so there wouldn't be any issues with the mower. I brought the trimmer and blower inside, along with the gas can."

Scooter was explaining with words and his hands. "Why would I do such a thing, Mack?"

"Had you been drinking again?

"No."

"Are you sure?"

"Yes."

"I know you've had episodes where you drank yourself unconscious."

"Yes, a long time ago."

"Not that long ago, Scooter."

"Could it be you got good and liquored up so you don't remember doing it?" Donna asked.

"No."

"Is there anyone who can confirm you being at your trailer home all Friday night?" Donna asked.

"I don't know. All of the neighbors knew I had brought the truck and trailer home. Someone said something about mowing their grass."

"I thought the video said this happened on Saturday?"

"It does."

"Then where I spent Friday is meaningless."

"I'm going to have to follow up on this, Scooter," Donna said noting his objection.

He was silent for a moment. He tried to remember falling asleep on Saturday out at G-Ma's.

"I didn't do this," Scooter insisted.

"The pictures tell a different story. I am going to need your keys until we get this sorted out."

"You're firing me, Mack?"

"No. Not until we get this sorted out! I lost thousands of dollars today. I can't afford to have a guy on my crew who gets so drunk he doesn't remember what he's doing! Now go home and let me think!"

"This is bullshit, Mack! I would never do this to you!" Scooter threw his keys on the desk and turned.

"A sober you would never do this, Scooter." Mack was heartbroken.

*

"Hey, Matt. Can you talk? Give me a call. This is Scooter." The phone beeped in his ear and he closed the phone. He was on his way home, walking east down a congested Lapeer Road. His head was swirling in a chaos of confusion as the morning sun blazed. He was certain he had not climbed over the fence and slashed all of those tires.

The bicycle kid, Ronnie's beating and death, the break-in, now this — to top off an awesome month," he thought. Scooter was feeling like medicating himself and was why he reached out to Matt. He knew he would have to walk out of his way to go to the party store, but it was what his heart wanted to do.

"Angie said that under stress we go back to our preferred default settings," concentrated his thoughts.

His phone rang a few minutes later, and Scooter's direction changed.

"Thanks for meeting me on such short notice, Matt."
The pair were sitting in a corner booth at a local fast-food joint. Matt was nursing a coffee.
"On normal days, I wouldn't be in town. But my son needed some help with a class project at the college, so I had arranged for the day off," Matt smiled.
"That's pretty amazing."
"Indeed. Sometimes we have divine appointments we know nothing about until they happen."
"Huh?"
"I believe God wanted me available for you today, as part of what I was supposed to be doing for Him."
"Oh— that is, I don't know what to say." Scooter shrugged.
"So, what's going on, Scooter?"
"The other day when we first met, I held back from telling you things. Dark things."
"You didn't know if you could trust me. I get it. I didn't tell you all of my horrid stuff either."
"There's been so much going on. I feel like I'm in the middle of a

tornado. I wanted to go drink myself into oblivion, so that's why I called you."

"Thanks for trusting me. What brought it on?"

"I just got fired for something I didn't do."

Scooter spent the better part of an hour telling Matt all of the gory details of his life over the last few weeks. Matt was satisfied to sit and listen, except for a few clarifying questions. Scooter backed up his dump truck of shame and unloaded it on the unsuspecting father of three.

"There. You got the whole enchilada dumped in your lap, Matt. Sorry."

"Don't be sorry, I'm honored you would trust me with your story."

"It's not all of it, but it's enough."

"No one can tell their entire story in an hour, Scooter. What you did tell me makes it easy to understand why you would want to self-medicate."

"I'm sick of being that guy," Scooter said, rubbing his forehead.

"Sick of it is a good place to begin."

"I guess."

"And it sounds like your counselor. . ." He was searching for her name.

"Angie."

"Right. Angie, has been very helpful for you."

"She's been amazing."

Matt noticed a twinkle in his eye when he talked about her.

"There's no way I would have opened up to anyone, other than my G-ma, and told them what I spilled out to you, without Angie. She's changed things. Important things, inside of me."

"Praise God!"

"But I'm still a huge mess," Scooter said and looked toward the worn table.

"You think the enemy is happy about you making progress, Scooter?" Matt asked with his palms up.

"Probably not."

"He isn't. I can say it with certainty. You'll be attacked to bring you back under the power of his delusion. We gotta be present, Scooter," he said, pointing to his own black hat. "So what is your plan?"

*

The knock came loud and long on the damaged trailer door.

Scooter had been sound asleep until the pounding, but remembered to slip on shorts before answering the door. He had to move the board he had wedged between the damaged door and a kitchen cabinet. The handle remained broken since the break-in, so his quick fix was the board he had cut to length.
Another pounding.
"Hang on a second," Scooter said.
Muted noise came from the other side of the portal.
"Yes?" he said pulling the door open.
"Scooter? Do you have an explanation for this?"

Donna McBride did not look pleased at all. Between Scooter and her was a disemboweled cat dangling from a rope in front of his door.
"What the—?"
"Scooter?" Donna held her arms out, eyebrows up.
"I have no idea. It's the first time I'm seeing this, and smelling it."
"Your neighbor called and said the side of your trailer was splashed with blood and guts. I was in the call center when the call came in, so I wanted to see it for myself."
"I had no clue. Like I said, I've been asleep."
"Get some shoes on and come out here for a minute," Donna said and backed off of the metal porch swishing her hand at the stink.
"Okay." Scooter stepped into his work boots behind the door as glass crunched beneath his weight on the carpet. He sidestepped the dangling cat. It was a big cat.
"Will you look at this?" Donna said with one hand on her hip just above her sidearm.
"This is crazy!"
In large bloody letters, distinguished by the three fingers used as a paint brush, the word "MURDERER," was written down the side of Scooter's house.

*

"Nice hat, Scooter!"
"Thanks."
"You've found yourself an accountability partner?"
"Yes, I'm meeting with a guy from church," Scooter said.

"You can call him whenever you need to?"
"He said if he's able to talk, he'll answer my calls. If not, he'll call me back the same day."
"It's a big step forward, Scooter," Angie said.
"Thanks."
"You seem uncertain," Angie said.
"Not about Matt."
"About this?" She turned one hand over, palm up with a slight sweep.
"Yes, a little. I wasn't convinced I was coming back, Angie."
"You're welcome here. Nothing you've said to me has changed that."
He remained quiet.

"Do you understand?"
"I can say I do, but I don't really know if I do," Scooter said without making eye contact.
"Okay. So how about we let that stuff rest for awhile, and work on what you are facing today."
"Yeah." Scooter shifted in the chair and paused to gather his thoughts. "I was greeted this morning by a determined police officer pounding on my door. She wanted to know why I had sacrificed a cat in some ritualistic way and used its blood to write "MURDERER" on the side of my own trailer."
"What?" Angie frowned.
"She wanted to look at my fingernails to see if there was evidence of cat blood."
"You're not kidding," Angie said.
"I wish I was," Scooter said, looking at the floor.
"So what happened?"
"I told her I was sick of the inquisition and wanted her to leave my residence."
"Oh my gosh!"
"What you don't know is I'm the lead suspect in a huge vandalism case at my work. Well my former work."
"Wait— you got fired, too?"
"They think a guy recorded on camera looks like me."
"What happened?"
"Someone broke into the yard and slashed all of Mack's tires."
"No way!"
"Yes, and they're investigating to see if it's me." His stomach turned.
"I am so sorry, Scooter. Why would they think that?"

"Mack seems to think I've gone back to my drinking days. Maybe I blacked out, then went and did the vandalism, subconsciously, or something." Scooter's hand became animated with the answer. He was covering the tremor.

"Does the camera show your face?"

"No. The theory is it was an inside job because the guy kept his face turned away from the camera."

"Wait. So, if I'm understanding you correctly, they are suggesting you became so intoxicated you blacked out and— in this highly intoxicated condition— you kept your wits enough to remember where the cameras were pointing while you vandalized Mack's property?"

"Good point. Want to be my lawyer?"

"No, I can't stoop that low!"

They had a good laugh and Scooter relaxed.

"So, what are you going to do now?"

"I have to fight it. I didn't do this," Scooter said.

"Were you drinking?"

"I had a couple on the night they think I was in some sort of fugue state."

"A couple?"

"I drank two twelve-ounce beers after mowing. I wasn't drunk or looking to be." He looked in her general direction.

A pause from Scooter. "There's something else."

"Really?"

"The night I rode with you to your place. When I got home, my trailer had been robbed."

"You've got to be kidding me! Did you call the police?" Angie sat forward.

"No, I was too exhausted. The thieves never found my important stuff. The whole house was trashed."

"Do you think your friend you were arguing with in the parking lot was involved?"

"It would not surprise me one bit." Scooter looked into her eyes for the first time that day.

"I think you're on the verge of a breakthrough, Scooter and the enemy doesn't want you to find your way to your blessing."

"Matt basically said the same thing. Like I am under some kind of attack."

"I agree. Do you know what it means?" Angie was almost giddy.

"Um, no. Other than it sucks."

"We must keep digging through this stuff, Scooter! We can't stop!"

"Whew, you really like your job."

"I love it! Can we move deeper?"

"Okay." Scooter was afraid.

"I will be gentle-ish."

"Let 'er rip, Doc."

"So you have all of these challenges swirling around you now, screaming for you to go back to the old ways of dealing with things, right?"

"Right. Those default settings."

"It tells me we are close to a genuine breakthrough." Angie glowed. Scooter swallowed hard, gripping the arms of his chair.

*

Looking right, then left, then back to the right, Darrell was ready to spring into action as soon as the next semi-truck passed him. With the resounding roar and accompanying wind, he shot south across Interstate 69. He was leaving behind the sanctuary he had carved out for himself over the previous week. He had managed to raid the log cabin across the lake several times. During his first raid, he stole vegetables out of the garden, a couple of cans of dog food from the shed, along with an ancient, fixed-blade knife. The second day, Darrell swiped more veggies, an old green kiddie pool from behind the shed, and a small hand shovel. Then, on the final mission, he climbed through a window and filled his small bag with all of the food he could carry. On his way out, he grabbed a garbage bag full of empty beer cans. The same day, Darrell left his camp in the woods and went east past the truck stop, to the grocery store on the main road, and got paid ten dollars for the returnable cans.

The pull of the fast-food joint, the one with a yellow arch, next to the USDA site, proved to be too much for him. Darrell got the largest, gooey, grease-dripping, salt-infused, double cheeseburger he could find on the menu, and waited to get back to his camp before he ate himself into a food coma. Later, he was thankful he had grabbed a fistful of napkins. When the greasy gut bomb needed to be released, it forced its way out with violence— which was another reason he wanted to relocate.

The plastic bag from the beer cans proved to be a good find. Gathering returnables was easy and could be done in out-of-the-way places. After crossing the interstate, Darrell found his way onto a rugged billboard road next to the freeway. The two-track snaked along through dense woods at the edge of a swamp. A mile later, a large pond appeared like a rabbit from a magician's hat. The forty-acre lake had a sandy area up from the water's edge on the northeast corner. The entire scene was cut up with deep ruts from quads, ORVs, and motorcycles, which made walking off-trail, through the trees, much easier. Within a couple of minutes, Darrell discovered a tattered deer blind and claimed it as his home for the night. Sleep was pushed off while he searched through his small bag of treasures for something to eat. Choosing one small beef stick. Darrell chewed and tried hard to forget what Ronnie's face had looked like. The brown cylinder of meat reminded him of the metal stake stuck in Ronnie's face. He couldn't shake the vision, or the sudden nausea, and stuffed the salty meat back in its wrapper.

*

"What was your lowest point, Scooter?"
He looked at her for a long moment. She was wearing a shirt with a high neck, unlike the buttoned-up one from the other evening in her car. A tinge of guilt coursed through him for objectifying her body. Scooter knew this was his opportunity for full disclosure.
"Did you know I was married before?" he offered.
"No. You've never said you were married," Angie said.
"I was. It was almost twenty years ago or will be next month."
"Wow," Angie said.
"It's one of the things I'm most ashamed of."
"I'm so sorry. What happened?"
"I loved her more than life itself. Her name was Kim. But I started running with my friends from high school after we were married and became the party guru. It got really bad when she got pregnant."
"Pregnant?"
"Yes. We had ourselves the most beautiful baby girl I've ever seen," Scooter said with a far off look in his eyes.
"Aw," Angie said.

"It was perfect. She was perfect. We named her Bella. My God, I haven't said her name in years. Bella Star Lawrence. She was my beautiful star," Scooter said, and cried at the memory.

Angie fought back tears watching her friend suffer.
"Just the three of us. We lived in the trailer I own."
"You still live in the same place?"
"Yes. It's a real dump now, but I can't let it go, Angie." More tears cascaded. "I can't let them go."
Scooter grabbed for a tissue.
"What happened, Scooter?" Angie asked in a whisper.
"When Bella was three, Kimmy decided she had seen enough of my drunk routine. She got in our car and left. Vanished into thin air while I was at work. Her family all lived out of state and I talked to them but no one would tell me where she was. They all said they hadn't heard a word from her."
"I am so sorry."
Scooter was a broken man all over again. Angie stepped over to him and he stood to meet her. They embraced and cried together. Scooter was washed by wave after wave of despair. Years of stuffed emotions flooded out onto Angie's blouse. She held him close, pulling him in tight.
"I am close to the brokenhearted and save those crushed in spirit—" Angie whispered into his trembling ear.

*

Chapter Nine
*** Star Burst ***

Walking away from the county jail felt like a page was being turned in his life. His one-year sentence had been served, most of those days were spent rotting or fighting in the violent D Pod. It was the section of the jail in which the young, testosterone-driven inmates were held together in four groups of twenty. Three or four fights a day were common in the area, and only the fear of a long stint in solitary kept the masses from killing each other.

The time in the county stockade was hard, with only two hours a day where inmates were allowed outside their pod to walk in circles. Those well-worn paths happened in the common room called *"The Day."* Men walked around the area in as wide an arc as possible, in groups of two and three. All the units in the pod overlooked The Day and many inmates spent their time watching other inmates through wired-glass panels, waiting for a turn around the room, or searching for a weakness in a rival.

If weather permitted and behavior allowed, walking outside was preferred. *"The Outs"* was encased by four twenty-foot-high concrete walls, but it was out of the view of the sixty peering eyes of the pods. James loved to be outside. The view of the sky and the rush of the wind helped him feel alive in a place that reeked of stale air. His outdoor time was spent walking the sixty-by-thirty concrete slab as fast as he could, pushing his speed until he got reprimanded for running, because jogging was not allowed in jail.

With the year behind him, James was feeling overstimulated. The green trees and scent of mowed grass renewed him, as he inhaled long, intoxicating breaths. It was surreal to be walking down the gravel shoulder of the two-lane road in his own shoes, dressed in his former clothes.

James had no need for direction at this point— *"out there"* was enough. A random pickup rumbled by trailing the familiar smell of gasoline, inciting childhood memories. Frogs croaked in the drainage ditch next to him. It was like hearing alien creatures on a distant world. Cicadas in the trees sounded like a far-off tornado siren. All of the forgotten stimuli washed over and through him as he sauntered on.

James was glad for the freedom and something else was unleashed that summer morning— the need for revenge. For a year he had planned what would happen next. The retribution he would exact would be legendary. Lawrence would pay for his sins. Convinced his plan was fool-proof, Moby pointed his feet toward acquiring the necessary supplies.

*

"I think I'll find evidence he was involved in this," Donna said.
"So, the witness you indicated in your preliminary report, who you felt was in '*no way*' a suspect, is now worthy of a warrant?" He looked into her brown eyes, not wanting to get caught by her with wandering eyes again.
"I've got him on camera vandalizing his employer."
"You have an image that looks like him on a very dark recording. Defense attorneys would shred it Donna. Plus he's denying involvement."
"Listen, I think I can find the weapon on the premises. The guy has lived there for years and it doesn't appear he gets rid of anything."
"How do you know that?" he asked, wondering why Donna would want to be a cop when she could model.
"When I was on scene for the brutalized cat, he opened the door and his place looked like it had been tossed."
"There are a lot of weird things swirling around him, I'll give you that." He was thinking the request over. The Prosecuting Attorney for St. Clair County was less than convinced seeking a warrant was the best way forward, primarily because of the implications in Ronnie's unsolved case. It was an election year and he had an eager opponent running against him, which made him hesitant to chase any unsubstantiated theory.

"Listen, Doug, let me check this guy out. Who knows maybe he is a psychopath who has been deceiving everyone around him for a long time." Donna paused to let that sink in.

"Maybe this will be the break we need for both of these cases." Doug
trusted Donna's instinct and knew he was playing it cautious because of
politics. He also knew he had a hard time saying no to his fling.
"Okay, Donna. I'll go after the warrant but it won't be for a couple of
days. Our judge is at a retreat in Charlevoix, and I won't disturb him."
"Really, Doug?" She flashed her incredible smile that melted the man.
"Tomorrow, then." He grinned as she left his office, hoping they would
meet up tomorrow as well, election year or not.
"Thanks."

*

"I've got to fix this thing today," Scooter thought as he looked at his
black mountain bike behind the trailer. Both of the tires were flat and
the front rim was wrecked beyond repair. He drew in a deep breath,
deciding he was going to drop it off at the bike shop downtown before
he saw Angie. The rugged bicycle had been damaged at the beginning
of the summer when he took a fall coming home from work. He
neglected the repairs because his job was so physically demanding— he
was unable to muster up the energy. But now, he needed it fixed and
decided to stop at the gas station to put air in the tires, so pushing the
wobbly rim all the way downtown would be easier. He needed to hurry.

Fifty-five minutes later, he was sitting in the waiting room at Angie's
with his hat on his knee, sweating and sipping on some water Gina had
delivered to him with her charming smile.

He was hoping Mack hadn't cut off his insurance, otherwise he would
have to cough up the hundred bucks from his savings on top of the bike
repair, which he had to pick up tomorrow. Paying up front for the bike
had stripped all his cash, requiring a trip out to G-ma's because he had
relocated his safe after the break-in.
"Funny how things change," he thought. Now, he was willing to make
the long trip to get the cash to pay for the time to see Angie, when seven
weeks ago he almost walked out because of some dirt on the floor.

"Scooter, she's ready for you." Gina leaned out her sliding window.
"Thanks, Gina."He smiled and pulled the door on cue with the buzz.

"Two days in a row— you must be special!" she said, while he walked in.

"No, I'm just really messed up!"

"Hardly. I can spot messed up from a long way off, and you ain't it, mister."

"Thanks."

"Take her a bottle of water, will you?"

"Sure." He grabbed the frosty bottle from Gina's counter. Her fortress smelled of vanilla from a hidden air freshener. His walk down the hall was short and he thumped twice with his knuckles on Angie's sanctuary door.

"Come in!"

Scooter pushed through the door and his breath was removed from his chest. The sunshine was flooding in behind Angie, illuminating her hair with a halo of light, making her appear angelic. Scooter was speechless until she rose and came over to him.

"Is that for me?"

"Ye. . . yes," he said, breaking his gaze.

"Thank you, sir!"

"My pleasure. Sorry for staring. The way the light was bouncing off of your hair, made you look like an angel."

"Aw. You say the sweetest things! Come in and shut the door. I want us to sit on the couch today."

"Okay." He approved.

They sat next to each other for the first time, after Angie had grabbed his growing file and her trusty pad of yellow paper for note-taking.

"Well, I know last night we had an emotional session."

"It was," Scooter said.

"How did you sleep?" Angie asked.

"Like a baby, thank-you."

"Today, I think we need to keep on pushing in deeper, Scooter. We're making so much progress!" She knew it was going to be a painful session for him.

"Whatever you say, boss," he smiled. Sitting next to her was a completely different feel for him. Like she had somehow moved over to his side to be more of an advocate and less of an adviser.

"Are you okay with this setup?" She nodded at the couch.

"Of course."

"Good, because I want to spend some of our time today praying."

"Oh?"

"Yes, and I'll be gentle, I promise!"

"Gentle, yes. Subtle, never," he said, and she looked into his eyes with a nuance he hadn't noticed before. His heart fluttered.

"Can I start us off by praying?"

"Yes." Scooter removed his *Present* hat and placed it on the coffee table.

Angie grabbed his rough and calloused hands into her own.

"Father, thank-you for this good man. Be with us today in our time together. Help him to know your will and experience your presence as we deal with tough things. In Jesus' name Amen."

"Amen." He was tearing up already and took a deep breath. Her soft touch exuded power.

*

Lovely Acres was quiet this early in the morning. James had been sitting in the trees behind the sixth trailer, just off the property line. Birds fluttered in and out of the thick camouflage. Chipmunks chirped, darting across the dark soil. James watched snacking on some peanut candies he had emptied into his hoodie pocket. There had been some movement inside the dilapidated unit in front of his position. A man groaning out a long stretch, doors bumping, toilet flushing. All signs indicating Lawrence was awake, so James reviewed the plan again.

James was sitting in a spot so he could see through the narrow space between the house and shed, all the way to the street. The shed was at the rear of the lot, offset from the house by a foot to the south. The shed's door faced east, toward the front of the property and the street. The green metal building was in line with the back of the trailer so the walls of shed and home created a hidden cove, bordered on the north by several mature arborvitae. Apparent to James, this cove was where Lawrence had stored things that had fallen into disfavor. Out of sight and out of mind. He surmised as long as the neighbors couldn't see the mess, the tenants wouldn't get reprimanded by the park supervisor.

The waiting man took inventory again of the items in the hidden nook. Nothing had moved since his first visit the previous day. The ancient, heavy-duty smoker sat on steel wheels and still held the shiny-white propane tank. There was a bike with flat tires and a bent rim, leaning against the shed. A few pallets tilted against the house along with another propane tank, an old lawn mower, and a wrinkled traffic barrel.

James smiled until Lawrence came out of the door onto his metal steps. He watched him lock the entry with a keyed padlock through a clasp. *"Someone had broken the door handle,"* he thought.
Lawrence stepped away, then made a quick turn out of sight from James' point of view, blocked by the shed. With a rush of movement, Lawrence was standing five feet in front of James, looking at the bike. James could hear his breathing. *"Maybe I should strike now?"* he thought.

"NO! Wait," James reminded himself.
In a quick move Lawrence grabbed up his bike and left, like he was on a mission. James breathed again, unsure as to how he wasn't discovered by his nemesis. A few deep breaths later, he was happy with the way things had turned. Seeing him conjured up the necessary hatred to push him forward with his flawless plan— without acting rash— based solely on emotion.
"Stick to the plan," he thought.

*

"You said your lowest point was when Kim left with Bella?"
"It was the beginning of my trudge through the dark valley," Scooter said.
"Okay. What happened after Kim left?" Angie wrote a note on his valley comment.
"I was a zombie. She left with the money, the car, and my baby girl. I searched so much I ended up losing my job." Scooter crinkled the plastic bottle in his hand and stole a glance at his hat in front of him. "I drank everyday for the first couple of months. I was depressed and angry."
"Angry at Kim?"
"Yes, but more at myself. I was such a terrible husband that she gave up on us." Scooter kept his eyes lowered and Angie could feel the pain in his heart.
"Okay." Angie scribbled.
"My sister didn't give up on me. She knew I was in the process of killing myself. A long, slow, deliberate death."

"What's your sister's name?"

"Jan. She's a couple years older. Stable. Married with kids. Attentive husband who has an excellent career in marketing. Dream house out in Fort Gratiot, in a neighborhood with tons of friends surrounding her. Committed Christian." Silence permeated the office and Angie waited. Scooter looked at Angie. "Everything I have failed at."

"Struggled with," she instructed, not breaking the gaze.

"Right," he said, not believing her correction.

"Go on," Angie said.

"Then I was standing up in church, giving my life to Christ. I was baptized, went to church and Bible studies."

"Okay, so some peace came after the storm?"

"Yes. Then I started working for Mack, which took me out of most Bible studies and I began missing church during the work season. *"I was too tired,"* was my excuse. I went back to drinking here and there. I wasn't really proud of it but I still wanted to *'celebrate'* things."

"This time in your life doesn't sound as desperate as when Kim initially left."

"No, it wasn't," Scooter admitted.

"Had you heard from her?"

"Only because the friend of the court began taking child support out of my checks. That was when I found out she was actually living in New Mexico, not Texas."

"Still no contact?"

"Nope. There never has been from her."

"Never?"

"Not once."

"Have you ever had a visit with your daughter?"

"No."

"Oh my."

*

The cranks that controlled the beveled glass windows were brittle from sun exposure and easily stripped. Using plastic gloves, James forced the bedroom window open without a sound. He reached down, grabbed the two propane tanks and carefully set them inside the home on the floor. The new tank still had the hose connected at the nozzle, while the other end dangled. He had cut the line with the hunting knife he had purchased. After rolling the tanks out of the way, James slithered through the narrow opening and into the back bedroom. He stood still, listening for anything unusual. Nothing changed. He crept toward the front of the trailer, clutching the knife just in case someone was waiting. He doubted the possibility with the way the door had been locked from the outside.

Stepping into the hall, he passed a bathroom, then a bedroom, before the space opened up into the living room. There was crap thrown everywhere. James could see into the kitchen and moved using a path carved through the debris, making sure not to linger by a window.

The kitchen layout was just as he thought, and the stove was gas powered as he hoped. He clicked each of the four burners to life, turning them to high.

Back in the rear of the trailer, he moved the two propane tanks into the bath room and opened the valve of the new tank as far as he could. The hose began flopping violently against the releasing pressure— the rotten egg smell assaulted his nostrils. He pulled the door to the bathroom over a towel leaving a two-inch gap. James closed the back bedroom door, stuffing a blanket beneath and exited through the same window he entered. Stepping down the pallet he used for a ladder, grabbing his green-cloth grocery bag from its hiding place, and pushing through twenty feet of woods into the parking lot of the shopping center, he walked west with haste, between a row of parked cars. Not daring to run because it would draw attention, he scanned his surroundings while waiting for the report behind him.

*

"The absolute bottom was ten years later," Scooter admitted, as he turned his body toward her to relieve the pressure on his neck.
"How many years ago was this?"
"Four."
"What happened?"
"We were working. It was late in the day and we were in the middle of cleaning up after pouring a driveway. I can see it like it happened an hour ago." He gazed out the window behind her desk, in an attempt to stifle his raw emotion.

Angie waited.

"My phone rang— and my phone almost never rang. It was my sister who asked me what I was doing. I thought she was kidding Jan knew I was working. She asked me to sit down because she had some terrible news. She was crying. I could hear her voice tremble and crack. Jan struggled to say the next three words that destroyed me. Bella was dead."

"Oh Scooter!"

"My baby girl was taken away again. This time in a head-on collision in El Paso."

Angie was brought to tears by the pain coming from the broken man sitting next to her. "I am so sorry."

"That's not the hardest part, Angie," he said through sobs.

"You're kidding?"

"No. Jan then told me the accident had happened three weeks before the call. They didn't tell me because they didn't want me at the funeral." Unadulterated shame poured from the broken man. Wave after wave of grief toppled him over on to Angie's lap. "Oh my God! Am I so twisted I couldn't tell my precious Bella goodbye?"

Angie caressed his head while her own tears dropped on the side of Scooter's tormented face, mingling with his.

*

James stepped up on the curb when the violent explosion rocked the trailer park three hundred yards behind him. He never looked back as a gigantic fireball rose from behind the stretch of trees he had left minutes before. Popping the final two pieces of candy into his mouth, he set out for the long walk to Smiths Creek, and the second phase of the plan.

*

"Thanks, Veronica, for letting me ride with you."

"My pleasure, Bee."

"It's so hot in the van."

"And stinky with all of those boys!"

"You have no idea!"

They laughed together in the darkness.

"I've been meaning to ask you all week, why does everyone call you Bee?"

"It was the name my little brother gave to me, when he first started talking."

"Cool."

"We're close." Bee was proud of the fact.

"That's a rare gift," Veronica said.

"It is."

"What's your given name?"

"Bella."

"Beautiful."

"Bella Star," Bee said, and smiled.

"That's pretty. You are a *'Beautiful Star.'*

"I think my dad must have been a romantic." Bee smiled at the thought. Veronica smiled at Bee's statement, but was confused.

"So did you have a good trip?" Veronica asked.

"It was amazing. Life changing."

"Was this your first time?"

"No. I went last summer."

"How do the two years compare?"

"They've been the best two weeks of my life," Bee said.

"Excellent. Why?"

"They have shown me how blessed I am. I look at those kids and realize even though they have nothing, they are happy to be alive."

"I recognized the same thing," Veronica admitted.

"Plus, the fact they're excited to be at church with other Christians. It's way different than back home," Bee said, looking Veronica's way.

"Right. I find myself going through the motions of faith, rather than living it out."

"Me too!"

The pair smiled in unison in the dim dashboard light of the car.

"My hands are sore from all of the hammering."

"My whole body is sore!"

"Well, you are old!" Bee said.

"Funny. Bella Star has jokes!"

They shared a laugh.

"What did you think of the house dedication?"
"It was incredible. You have an awesome voice, Veronica, by the way. The song you sang…, I'll never forget the moment. I never cried so much from being happy. I mean, when do we get a chance to change someone's life?"
"Almost never," Veronica said.

"So, Veronica, was this your first mission trip?" Bee asked like a reporter doing an interview.
"First one since high school."
"Did you go with Brandon?"
"No, Brandon wasn't my youth pastor. I was at another church and went to a reservation in Colorado."
"How was it?"
"It was a good trip. We ran a VBS for Native kids."
"Cool."
"Yes, it was. They were glad we had come. I got close to a little girl."
"How do the two years compare?" Bee smiled.
"I liked both. But we changed a whole family's trajectory by building them a house."
"I agree," Bee said.
"Why is Brandon slowing down?" Veronica was trying to see in front of the fifteen passenger van, but the red trailer was too wide to get a clear view.

It was before sunrise and the group was on a new mission to get back for Sunday's church service so they could report on how their mission trip had gone. Driving north on US 54 from El Paso before sunrise was pushing the tired crew, but Brandon wanted to see if they could make the early service. He wanted to thank all of the people who had supported this year's trip to Juarez. Having led the trip for ten years, he felt this was an important way to thank the people of New Heights Christian Fellowship and show them the difference they were making in the lives of teens and the poor. He would let the students clean up and come back for the late service wrap-up. He had tried this idea a few times in the past but never made the early service deadline, so he smiled at the thought of being on time.

The group in the van he piloted was fast asleep, every seat occupied. Veronica, the other adult leader, was right behind his trailer, a little too close for his comfort. The road was nearly empty, except for the occasional semi truck. Brandon was counting on smooth sailing *for* the ninety-mile drive.

The New Mexico state line intersected northbound US 54 after a sharp jog in the road. Three miles after that jog, was officially the middle of nowhere. Brandon was wide awake drinking his coffee, and listening to a favorite band. He was deciding which part of the trip to highlight to the church as a lone vehicle approached their tiny caravan. He was suspicious of the movement of the southbound pickup truck. The driver was struggling to stay in their lane, so Brandon braked, moving onto the shoulder of the road with a quick jerk. The move sent the back of his trailer veering toward the the oncoming truck for an instant and the intoxicated driver overreacted. The two-ton missile took off the wheel of the trailer and drove head-on into Veronica's sedan.

Veronica saw the trailer twitch an instant before the fender exploded. Her natural reactions pulled the steering wheel down sharply, the car responded, and the incoming truck impacted her vehicle at the passenger corner of the front end with a deafening violence. Bodies are not designed to hit walls at one hundred forty miles an hour.

Bella Star Lawrence was standing in front of the pile of steaming twisted metal and plastic, unsure of what she felt. There was no pain— no actual memory of her soul being thrown out of her body. She walked to the door of the pickup and looked inside at the moaning man who was pinned by the steering wheel. A wave of peace flowed through her heart, a peace unlike any she had ever experienced. Bella knew this was the place her days on earth ended. This chapter of life was closed. She knew the man in the truck would live. Moving to the car that held her lifeless body, she could see movement in the driver's seat. Intuitively, she recognized Veronica's journey on earth would continue.

Turning away, there was a man standing close to her— like he had appeared from thin air— because he had stepped inside of earth's veil the same moment she turned from the wreck.

"Hello, Bella," he said with a deep melodic voice.
"Hello." She was uncertain, but unafraid.

"Do you know what has happened?"

"Yes, I think so."

"Are you surprised?"

"No. My time had come," she said, shrugging.

"Indeed. Who is the other one?" he said, lifting his chin toward the driver's seat.

"Veronica."

Brandon came crashing to the passenger window of the demolished car. "Oh God, NO! Not Bee, God! No!"

Bella thought Brandon sounded like he was on the other side of a thick glass. She could hear Brandon's muffled voice and see his pain, but the intense sadness and visible rage never made its way into her new reality — like the glass was some sort of filter. With the protection, came the recognition and a new confidence. This chaos was not beyond God's ability.

"Why can't I be sad?" she asked her companion.

"What benefit would the emotion bring, in a place where every need is met?"

"I don't know."

"You will learn."

"What is your name, sir?" Bella looked at him.

"Bob."

"Really?"

"Yes. Let me guess— you thought it would be Micheal or Gabriel?"

"Seems more appropriate, doesn't it?"

"I imagine to you it does."

"So, Bob, what do you do?"

"I guide people."

"Where do you guide them?

"Home. I only guide the folks going home."

"Will I miss this place?"

"Not at all."

"What about my mother and brother?"

"The suddenness of the separation will be hard for them."

"Will I miss them?

"Not in the way you imagine. You will wait for them is the best way I can describe it to you."

"Okay. Will I remember them?"

"Of course. They are an important part of your life."
"Will I meet my dad?"
"He is not where you are going."
"I was told he had left already."
"Your mom thought she was protecting you."
"I understand."

Flashing lights were coming from the south and all of the occupants of the van were crying, praying and trying to free the three trapped bodies.

"Are more coming with us?" She held her hand out toward the wreck.
"My orders are to help you, Bella," Bob said, moving closer.
"Okay."
"Can I say goodbye to my best friend, Juanita?"
"Yes, but 'see you later,' is more accurate."
Walking over to her grieving high school friend, Bella smiled, blew her a kiss, and said, "I will see you later, Juanita. Take care of Bobby."

"Ready to go?"
"Yes."
"Take my hand."
Without an inkling of hesitation, Bella reached for Bob's big hand. With his other he pushed and the two stepped through a new opening in the veil, bathed in light. The doorway snapped shut behind them while those gathered around the crash missed the flash in the heavens.

*

Scooter found himself walking next to the river. Wandering really. In and out of consciousness.
"Angie said I needed to face my pain. I had to stop running away, running to medication and numbness." He remembered her words clearly enough as he sat on a bench in the shadow of the Blue Water Bridge.

He stayed and watched the river for hours. The waves and eddies danced across the water as millions of gallons pushed south from the upper Great Lakes through this waterway like a funnel. Boats of all shapes and sizes darted over the water and huge lake freighters lumbered past, blocking his view. He recognized the metaphor. The pain from the loss of Bella was the barricade to the rest of his life.

"All of the wasted years," he heard Angie's voice reminding him— he is here now, not there. For too long, his everyday life was lived in the past, hung up on the unfathomable pain. Stuck.

"Jesus, I don't want this pain to hold me here anymore. Please help me." He didn't even bother to say amen.

Scooter got up and wandered another mile north to Lighthouse Beach then sat at the waters edge. The picture he held was faded and worn from years in his wallet. Baby Bella and Kim smiled back at him from a different time, while he melted into the sand.

*

"Holy crap, Captain!" Donna spoke above the noise into the fire chief's ear.

"It's a bad one, Donna. Three trailers completely gone, five more burning. Not one place unaffected in the entire park. Mostly windows."

"Natural gas explosion?"

"We don't know yet— too early to tell. I had to send a unit around back to the mall to wet down roofs over there. The woods are burning. It's a mess."

"Casualties?"

"We haven't found any bodies yet. I have a lieutenant trying to piece together who lived here, but half of the trailers are rented month-to-month."

"Which makes it a transient community," Donna said.

"Exactly. We could use help in gathering residents over to the east side, so we can get a better picture of who is missing."

"Right. I'll get some uniforms on it."

"What are you investigating here?"

"POI in the kid's death."

"The kid by the pool?"

"Yeah."

"Tragic case."

"Yep."

"What's the address?"

"Number sixty." She knew the number.

"I think the addresses go by tens up the left side," he said.
"Which would make my guy's the sixth one in."
"I believe it's ground zero, Donna."
"Of course it is." Donna shook her head, slapped the captains back, and went to find a couple of uniformed officers to help.

*

"Buddy, you can't sleep here." A large black flashlight was pointing in the man's face.
"Sorry." He tried to block the beam.
"Have you been drinking?"
"No. Thinking." Scooter sat up and put his hat on.
"Looks like you're sleeping to me."
"I guess I dozed off." He handed the cop his faded picture.

"Who is this?" He turned the flashlight to the photo.
"My daughter."
"She's cute."
"She died in a car accident."
"I'm really sorry for your loss. What's your name?"
"Scooter."
"Well, Scooter, the beach closed at ten."
"What time is it?"
"After midnight."
"Sorry."
"Have a good night and I'm sorry about your little girl."
"Thanks. I am leaving."
"I'll make sure you do," he said and walked south.

Scooter breathed in a long invigorating breath. He could no longer see the details of the photo because of the darkness, but it was etched in his memory. Pressing the picture to his lips for an extended moment, he placed it in the bottom of the hole he had dug for his feet, pushing the silky sand over it. Scooter gently patted the grave and kissed his Bella goodbye. "I love you forever, my Bella."

*

James was out of shape. The fifteen-mile walk to the house in Smiths Creek had taken him all day. By the time he remembered the exact location it was getting dark. He paused on the street to ensure his stealth, then stepped around the steel gate, pushing through thick brush. The walk down the winding driveway was quiet, except for the occasional bat fluttering by in its quest for mosquitoes. The orchard looked to be heavy with fruit in the evening darkness, so he paused to find a ripe pear for a snack. Passing the house, James made his way to the shadow of the barn as the stars began to appear. There was a lock on the large sliding door, but the bottom was not held by a guide. It was easy to pull out the door and crawl into the inner darkness.

His feet were throbbing as he tried to see into the pitch-black and waited for his eyes to adjust. The dark was still too dark. After a few minutes, he blindly felt his way forward, bumping into a wall. The ground was clear at his feet, so James sat on the dirt and fell asleep.

*

Young Darrell Patrick was forced from his second hideout because too many people hung around the forty-acre lake. It was an unofficial party spot for off-road seekers from all over the area. It was remote and close, secluded but accessible with the right vehicle. Those whose trucks managed to make it past the obstacles were welcomed into the strange community of like-minded folks. Large fires and late-night skinny-dipping parties happened at least three evenings a week throughout the summer. People camped for a week, fished the lake, and played on their toys, while others just came for the parties.

Darrell knew he had to move away from people. During the middle of the night, he made his way to an asphalt trail marked with letters "*WTA*" and turned east to a main road, then south. Darrell searched for bottles along the route. He had managed to snag a few from the campers at the lake. A couple more miles south, a clerk at a twenty-four-hour gas station gave him seven dollars for his bag of treasure. He bought two hot dogs off of the spinning roller-grille and a chocolate milk. While sitting in the shadow of the station's garbage dumpster, Darrell ate, deciding he never had a better meal in his entire life.

Behind him was a storage area filled with campers, RVs, and trailers of all shapes and sizes. The fence was solid and imposing at the entrance, so he searched the perimeter for a way inside. Five minutes later, he was rewarded when he came across a place where the ground was lower than the bottom of the fence. Darrell rolled inside. He found an unlocked camper door on his third attempt, settled into a full-sized bed, and the best night of sleep in a long, long time.

*

Scooter was walking toward home. It was going to be a couple hour hike, but he was feeling well rested. Emotionally it seemed like a large weight had been lifted from his grieving heart. He figured the crying had helped, along with the sleep on the beach. Walking south past the hospital, he decided Erie Street would be faster, then he could take the Seventh Street draw bridge over the Black River. The trouble with Erie Street was it ran though a poor section of the city. Not only poor, but troubled. So he decided to beat feet and get through as quick as possible, with his head on a swivel.

Five minutes later, he was past the difficult section and walking by the community college as a black truck rolled past him without incident. *"Quite a night,"* Scooter thought. He was thankful for the wave of peace he rode from the beach.

Not long after, coming around an unlit corner beneath a tall oak tree, one block from the bus terminal, Scooter was yanked back into the darkness. A swinging fist hit his unsuspecting stomach forcing all of his air to evacuate his lungs. A knee sank into the side of his head, which sent him to the ground, stars bursting inside his temples. The toes of boots jammed into his ribs. Two, then three kicks were delivered without words or threats— only low grunts of effort were heard during those vicious moments. Dangling between consciousness and sleep, someone asked him, "Do you like what's been happening?"
Then a flash of a boot with silver tips descended on a couple of ribs, snapping the bones under the pressure. His head was lifted from the ground by his hair, as another fist sentenced him to a deep sleep.
*

Chapter Ten
* Shooting Star *

A drum was pounding off in the distance. More percussive thumps were added to the depth of the sound, like a high school garage band was practicing next door. The slow methodical beat grew in intensity and volume. Sharp pain joined the chorus, matching each beat with a jabbing at his skull. The drums closed in on him, encircling his head, while darts pierced his flesh. Boom. Boom. Boom. Jab. Jab. Jab.

Scooter's left eye opened and a yellow finch flew off his forehead, removing the jabbing pain with a few swift flaps of its wings. The drums still rolled unabated, slamming into his skull. He drifted away again.

"If the thumping would quit, I could sleep here forever," he thought.

Deep inside his dreamworld he imagined inhaling a discarded feather from his yellow tormentor, tickling at the back of his throat, causing him to cough. The action sent an electric charge of lightning through his left side, reopening his eye and overloading 125 million sleeping photoreceptor cells in his eye.

The drums were inside his own throbbing head. Scooter tried to force himself awake, but his body protested the call. *"Just a few more minutes,"* was the convincing argument. *"Now!"* came a reply.

He could only command his left eye to open and forced it to focus. The right eye felt like it was trapped under muddy water, unable to detach connected halves of lids to allow light in. He heard his own muffled groan, and it startled him enough to roll over to his back, while he slammed his elbow into a solid surface with an audible crack. The immovable object was a brick wall reaching to the sky. Depth perception was challenged with only one eye functioning.

Then a switch flipped, and the terror of being pulled into a dark corner surged. A replay from his recent past, but like his tainted depth perception, his concept of time was skewed. Touching his side brought intense jolts of pain. Breathing deep was out of the question, as the rhythmic drumming fell into his chest. Rubbing his face released a cascade of dirt down his cheeks and into his ear. His right hand was brushed by thousands of tiny fingers, or needles from a bush, as it came into focus. He momentarily toyed with the idea of death, but figured the green needles confirmed his foggy location was still on earth.

A few minutes later Scooter discovered sitting up was impossible, so he rolled over to all fours and willed himself upright, sitting back on his legs. He was greeted by intense sunshine and a swirling head, but steadied himself with the cool brick wall.

Scooter's right cheek pulsed with a half-inch cut surrounded by dried blood mixed with dirt. His eye was beginning to come online and feed him some information. He recognized he had been hidden behind trimmed bushes. The wall he relied on for support was probably the college field house. The memory of the beating surfaced. Gasping for air, kicking, a question, another kick and lights out.

"But what was the question?" He tried to concentrate, sending the drums off into overdrive.
"Oh Lord."

Scooter lifted his hands and several vertebrae popped in his neck and upper spine, but he could not manage to stretch against the pain in his side.
"Must have broken some ribs," he mouthed.

The front pocket of his shorts was torn. His wallet and keys were gone. The realization sent a flutter of panic. He frisked his shorts, checking for possessions. Everything was missing, including his new hat. His hand tremor returned with his uncertainty.

"They robbed me." With that thought, the urge to flee overtook the pain of movement.
Home called to him like a megaphone. One step, then two. His shirt was torn at the bottom. He thought he looked like a hobo. An hour passed and Scooter had traveled a mile. He turned up Oak Street off of Seventh. When he passed the community food bank, someone asked him if he needed help.
"No, I just fell down," he mumbled and moved on.

The sun was hot on his skin. So intense, he felt as if he were drowning in sunshine. Sweat collected in the small of his back and dirt streaked from his face. Scooter planned to stop at the beer store on the way home — the chaos was too much. Ten blocks became five, then wore down to two. It was at this point the realization struck him— he had no money. Still, his feet pushed toward the door and he would have entered to ask for a loaner, except for the image greeting him on the glass. His own reflection startled him so much he didn't recognize the man. Scooter stared.

A full two minutes passed before he turned for home. At Twenty Fourth Street, Oak Street was blocked off by a row of orange traffic cones and a long string of caution tape. The sidewalk was barricaded on both sides of the street. A couple of kids road up on their bikes, stopping next to Scooter.
"What happened?" Scooter asked, as he feebly pointed toward the wall of cones.
"A house blew up."
"Really?"
"It was a huge fireball. I watched it!" The kids eyes lit up.
"When?"
"Yesterday. I was riding past this corner. It was loudest thing I've ever heard."
"Someone said three houses were wrecked, and a bunch more were set on fire," the other boy said.
"Even the woods burned down."
"The woods behind the shopping center?"
"Yep. They are all gone!"

Scooter turned and left the boys straddling their bikes. He jaywalked across the street, then north one block, knowing the way to circumvent the barricades and get home. He would have to cut through someone's yard, but it didn't matter to him in the moment. Scooter needed to see what happened.

Five minutes later— as if he had taken a hit of smelling salts— Scooter made his way to the fence that separated an empty lot from his trailer park and couldn't believe the scene. He was looking down the street which cut the park in two. He counted trailers on the west side of the road but when he got to six there was nothing. He counted again. There used to be eleven trailers on the west side of the road and his was exactly in the middle. There was no middle. His unit and the trailers on both sides were gone. No sheds, no trees, no grass. Vaporized. The woods behind his place were now random stands of branchless, smoldering charcoal poles, pointing skyward. A couple more trailers on each side of the missing homes were hollow, charred frames, their metal skins folded out.

On the east side of the street, not one window was left intact and the faces of the homes were all charred. Trees were without leaves and lawns had turned to dirt, like God vacuumed the grass away. There was a cop car sitting across the entrance to the park, with a line of wooden barriers blocking the street.

"Crazy thing," came the voice next to him.
"Yeah," Scooter said.
"Sad really."
"How many are dead?"
"The radio is saying only one guy is missing."
"No kidding?"
"He's a person of interest."
"Did he live there?" Scooter asked.
"Guess so. Five are in the hospital, but are expected to recover."
"What happened?"
"They suspect it was a gas leak," the man said.
"It's like a miracle or something?"
"You can say that again— whoo-wee." The man looked at Scooter for the first time. "Are you okay?"
"Yes. I fell and cracked my cheek a good one."
"I'll say you did."
"Hurts," Scooter said.
"You should have it looked at, son."
"You're right."
"Do you need anything?"
"Do you have a bottle of water?"
"Sure, I'll get you one. I'll be right back."
"Thank-you."

*

A bright line of sunshine pierced the interior of the barn. The back wall faced east, having been greeted by the reliable warm orb this morning. The beam of light fell across the face of the only occupant who was sprawled out on the dirt floor, while the sunshine probed the exterior of his eye lids. Dreaming, James believed he was still in jail and sat up wondering if he missed his breakfast tray. Barn swallows chattered in the rafters, as a slight breeze carried the smell of cut hay to his nose. What had been veiled in darkness was now illuminated by the glaring beam of sunrise. The old barn was bigger than he had remembered, but those memories were formed from the exterior.

James stood, stretched, walked over, and peed on the garden tools in the corner with a smirk. Next item of business was some food from his green sack.

As he ate, he walked through the memories which had brought him to this place, feeling the rejection, humiliation, and distrust from his past well up inside him again. Those recurring emotions refueled his desire to finish the plan. His year locked up was a direct result of the distrust and hatred shown him, but this was going to settle the score and tip the scales back toward even. Blowing up the guys house was a start, he figured. Now for some good old-fashioned psychological warfare and James thought he would be satisfied. He wasn't going to kill his old friend— it would break their code— he just wanted to inflict as much pain as he could, for as long as he could. Lawrence dying would be a disappointment; besides, he would have to explain it to the rest of the Denton Boys. Plus, James didn't want to see any of those ingrates ever again. Not one of them had sent him a letter or paid him a visit while he languished in jail.
"Screw them."

*

Scooter had an important decision to make. *"Where am I going to go?"* he thought as he drank from the tepid water bottle.
"Jan." The obvious answer came to him. He turned to walk north on Twenty Fourth Street.

An hour and a half later he was still walking north, but was on Pine Grove, slogging along against the heavy morning traffic. Just as he crossed Sanborn, a car honked and the driver waved. But Matt's face distorted when he recognized how terrible Scooter looked. Matt turned at the next block and doubled back to his new friend, pulling up next to him on the service drive.

"Scooter?"

Matt was out of his car walking over to the man, leaving his door open.

"Hey," was all Scooter could think to say, not wanting to pause his forward motion.

"Where are you going, buddy?"

"I don't know. Jan's."

"You look like you've been run over by a bus!"

"You wouldn't believe it." Scooter stopped walking and turned to Matt.

"You been drinking again?"

"No. I wanted to— after I got mugged, but I didn't have any money."

"You got mugged?"

"Down by the college." He scratched at his dirty neck.

"When?"

"Last night. They took the hat you gave me."

"Why aren't you going home?"

"Strangest thing— my house blew up."

"What? Wait! Your house was in that mess? Oh my God, Scooter!"

"Yeah, my house is gone." His eyes were hollow.

"Hey, come on, buddy. Let me give you a ride."

"Okay. I am exhausted."

"I think you're in shock."

Matt opened the passenger door to help the man into his car. He grabbed his brief case and tossed it into the back seat, and noticed Scooter holding his side.

"Whats going on?" He pointed.

"Got kicked."

"Still hurts?"

"Yeah, I think I have a couple broken ribs." Scooter winced as he sat. Matt ran around to his side and hopped in, uncertain as to what to do next.

"Are you hungry?"

"Man, I'm starving, but they took my wallet."

"I got you. We should call the cops, Scooter."
"Why, Matt? They'll never find them. I was unconscious in the bushes all night."

They drove a mile to a local diner, and Matt suggested Scooter use the bathroom to wash up.
"You will feel better, and can see what I'm seeing."

The water splashing on his face felt revitalizing. He scrubbed his hands and mud rained on the sink and floor. Looking at his face, he saw the growing blue bruise reaching from his cheek to his temple. The cut was filled with dirt and dried blood so he left it alone, not wanting to bleed all over the restaurant. Padding his face with the brown paper towel, he felt more awake. Scooter had enough presence of mind to dry his mud from the sink top and exited toward his waiting friend.

"You look a lot better, Scooter!"
"Feel better, too."

Scooter ate like a starved maniac and asked for more, promising to pay Matt back. He spilled the long tale to his new-found advocate, beginning with his visit with Angie to burying Bella. He included the walk home and the devastation he witnessed.

"You're being severely tested and attacked, Scooter. There's just no other way to make sense of it all."
"It is like a convergence of several nasty things all at the same time," a revived Scooter said, while grabbing for his water glass again.
"That's a good description," Matt said.
Scooter nodded.
"Hey, I was reading this morning in Psalms. Can I share it with you?"
"Sure."
Matt flicked his phone to life and searched for his Bible app.
"This is from Psalm 57:1-3 in the ESV: 'Be merciful to me, O God, be merciful to me, for in you my soul takes refuge; in the shadow of your wings I will take refuge, til the storms of destruction pass by. I cry out to God Most High, to God who fulfills his purpose for me. He will send from heaven and save me; he will put to shame him who tramples on me. God will send out his steadfast love and his faithfulness.'"

"I feel foolish, Matt," Scooter admitted.

"Why?"

"Because it felt like I had this awesome breakthrough with Bella's loss. It was hard and so meaningful at the same time. I knew it was God's doing and I'm grateful, but then something rotten happens and I want to blame God all over again. I walked back toward the bottle— I was willing to give in."

"You've had so many major losses in a short time frame, I am not sure anyone wouldn't be discouraged or even mad at God."

"But I didn't cry out to Him in the middle of it," Scooter said.

"Okay?"

"How could I be so overwhelmed by His grace one minute and completely forget Him in the next?"

"You're human, Scooter."

"I'm so weak." He hung his head.

"Yes, you are. So am I," Matt said.

"It seems like I am the weakest person I know."

"When we're weak, He is strong, Scooter. It's His promise, not mine."

"I feel like I have the market cornered."

"You've been through the fire yet you're still seeking to know God, wrestling with your humanity."

"That doesn't sound screwed up to you?"

"Sure it is screwed up. But we're all screwed up. Wrestling with our humanity is exactly what we need to do."

"Really?"

"You can't put me on a pedestal, Scooter. I'm full of brokenness like everyone."

"I think you're the shadow the verse in Psalms talked about."

"What do you mean?"

"The wings the guy hides under until the destruction passes by."

"Those are God's wings, Scooter."

"Right. But He's used you today to be that for me."

"He used me for your good and His glory. It's all we can hope for."

"Well, thank-you for stopping."

"If you start believing I'm better than you— more godly than you— then you will stop seeing me as an equal. I'm just like you. I may have a few more miles on the journey but it still always comes back to the fact I need Jesus, just as much as you do."

Scooter was fading as the food in his stomach pulled the blood from his brain.
"Do you need a place to sleep?"
"Yes."
"We have an extra bedroom. Can I take you there?"
"I'm exhausted."
"You can rest up at my house until we can figure out your next move."
"Okay. Thanks."

*

"Mom." Bobby walked into the dark room pulling back the curtain and a wave of light crashed in, causing Kim to moan and turn in her bed.
"Mom. Mom, you need to eat. The Andersons brought more food over. It's homemade chicken soup." Bobby was feeling desperate.
"Mom!"
"I'm not hungry, Bobby!"
"You need to eat. It's been two days."
"I'm tired."
"You're depressed"
"What? Who told you that?"
"People at church— they're worried."
"Tell them to mind their own business."

"I'm afraid, Mom."
"Of what?" Kim picked her head up and looked at her son.
"I'm afraid I'm losing you, too."
"What?"
"It's been a week since Bee's funeral and all you do is sleep."
"You've never lost a child, Bobby"
"She was my sister, Mom."

Kim managed to sit up with those words. "I'm sorry. I know how close you guys were." Kim rubbed her face awake.
"Brandon has stopped by every day."
"What does he want?" Kim asked.
"Your forgiveness," Bobby said.
"I don't know if I can."
"I have, Mom."
"Why?"

"Because it wasn't his fault."
"He was in charge of the trip. The safety of the team was his responsibility, Bobby." Her eyes lit up with a hidden fire.
"I know it, but accidents happen," Bobby said.
"He should have been more careful."
"Maybe. The drunk guy is to blame for this." Bobby set the soup bowl down on the nightstand.

"I know you're right. I'm just so angry," Kim said.
"Brandon said I needed to forgive the driver, too."
Kim stared at her son. He looked like he had grown up by five years. There was a maturity behind his eyes which hadn't existed a week before.
"Come here." She held out her arms and he folded into them.
"Mom, I need you. Bee's not here to help me anymore."
After several minutes of weeping, they both wondered aloud how they could possibly produce so many gallons of tears.
"I thought we were out of tissues," Kim said, as Bobby pulled some from the box on the nightstand.
"The Kerns dropped off a bunch of stuff from the grocery store."
"That was kind."
"You won't believe the kitchen," Bobby said and smiled.
"Why?"
"It's packed with food and flowers. So many people have brought stuff over."
"How do you know?"
"I opened the door and talked to all of them."
"You did?"
"Of course."
"It's a lot of work, Bobby."
"I like it. I get to hear so many stories about my sister."
"She was a beauty."
"So many people loved her." He was smiling as more tears bubbled over.

"How is Veronica?" Kim tried the soup.
"Still in the hospital in El Paso, but they moved her out of ICU."
"This soup is really tasty."
"We have a whole pot. I've been writing people's names on the bottoms of the dishes, so we can get them back."

"You've really stepped up, Bobby. Thank-you."
"Bee isn't here to help, so I figured I have to do more."
"I need to get out of this bed."
"It is kind of smelly in here, Mom," Bobby laughed.
"Hey, you!"

*

"Hey, Mack, got a minute?"
"Sure Donna."
Donna pulled her car over behind the concrete truck. The driver of the truck was washing his rig off on the shoulder of the road. Donna met Mack by his favorite orange machine as the truck driver watched her body's every movement with his longing and lust concealed behind mirrored sunglasses.
"How are you doing?"
"We're back working, so that's a good thing," Mack said and smiled. He wasn't blind or dead yet either.
"I'm sure it is. I was wondering if you had seen Scooter around?"
"Nope." The answer was sharp.
"You heard about his place?"
"No."
"The explosion?"
"I heard it was near his trailer."
"It nearly destroyed the entire park," Donna said, sliding her sunglasses up onto her head.
"Really— I thought it was three trailers?"
"Three trailers are completely gone, two more burned to the ground. All of them lost windows and power. The whole place is condemned right now."
"You don't say?" Mack frowned.
"Scooter's trailer was ground zero, Mack, and we can't find him."
"You think he was killed?" A look of horror was on his face when he asked the question.
"I'm trying to piece it all together. I don't know much," Donna said.
"Man, I can't believe it."
"Do you know where he would go if he needed help?" Donna had her notebook at the ready.
"He has a sister."
"Where?"

"Layne! Where does Scooter's sister live?" he shouted over his shoulder.

"What's that, boss?"

"Scooter has a sister, right?"

"Yeah. Jan."

"Do you remember where she lives?"

"Ah, Fort Gratiot, I think. Is he in trouble?" Layne asked.

"Not sure. They can't find him."

"What?" Layne had willingly moved in close to the detective.

"The explosion was his trailer," Donna said.

"No way!"

"Have you seen him, or been in contact with him, Layne?" Donna asked.

"No. Not since the other day when he was sent home," Layne was concerned.

"Do you know his sister's last name?"

"Couldn't tell you— sorry."

"Anyone else he may turn to?"

"He was seeing a counselor."

"A counselor?"

"Yeah. I think she is in the Blue Water counseling place," Layne said.

"Gotta name?"

"No," Layne smiled with the memory from the funeral home.

"What?" Donna asked.

"She is, um—"

"Very pretty," Mack interjected from his seat on the machine.

"We met her at Ronnie's funeral. Well, we all saw her there," Layne said.

"I got it," Donna said and smirked. She held out several business cards to the men.

"Call me if you hear anything?"

The sobering reality sunk in as all the men walked the woman back to her car with their eyes. As she drove off, the concrete truck driver repeated what Bull had whispered to him, "Sexy Powerful!"

*

Twenty-four hours after crashing in Matt's basement, Scooter was in the shower. Matt had left clean clothes stacked on a chair inside the door to the suite. Included in the pile was a new *Present* hat. Scooter guessed he had stayed in a mother-in-law suite. There was a kitchenette, living room with a TV, electric fireplace, and bathroom. In the vanity mirror he studied several large deep purple bruises on his sides. The rib kick was tender to the touch and his face was swollen with a green hue encircling his right eye. The cut had scabbed over.

The steamy shower felt righteous, and Scooter was filled with gratitude for his friend. Yet, in the back of his mind, he was becoming angry. It was as if the anger was a distant cloud in an otherwise blue sky. Behind the cloud was a front, and the front was pushed by a storm, which would soon be crashing in on him— certain to cause havoc. He devoured the muffin Matt had left on the table.

Emerging from the basement suite an hour later, he found the steps. When he opened the door into the kitchen, someone was eating at the table and turned.
"Morning."
"Hey, I'm Matthew, Matt's son." He came over to Scooter.
"Matthew, I'm Scooter." They shook hands. Matthew was working on some homework for college.
"That's right, your dad said you were at SC4." Scooter lifted his head in the direction of the laptop.
"Yep, first year."
"Good for you."
"Thanks."
"Are you hungry?"
"No, I had the muffin. Thanks."
"That was my dad."
"He's a heck of a guy. I am going downtown to pick up my bike."
"I'm sorry to hear about your house," Matthew said.
"Thanks."

Neither knew what to say next and an awkward silence fell over the room.
"Um. Tell your folks that I appreciate them letting me stay."
"No problem. I think they want you to know you can stay as long as you need. The room isn't used much anymore."
"I have another place— my grandparents old place."
"Okay. Cool."

"Well, thanks again."
"Sure."
"Nice to meet you, Matthew."
"You, too."
Scooter left the house.

An hour later, he was getting onto his bike. It was fortunate he had paid the guy up front for the repairs. They refunded him ten bucks because the replacement wheel cost less than they originally thought. As he threw his leg over, his ribs protested in earnest.
"This isn't going to be fun," he thought, turned his hat around, and winced with the first push. Within a few minutes, he realized riding in the street was his only option. Bumps on the bike felt like he was getting punched in the side. Though it was a good feeling to have his bike working again, it was difficult to ride with his injuries.

He stopped and stepped off when he got to the Black River. He needed to think about his options. What was he going to do next? There were ten bucks in his pocket and nothing else. His only option was G-Ma's. He had money in his lock box, along with his birth certificate and important papers.
"Thank you that my house was broken into. Is that a real prayer, God? I wouldn't have moved that box if I wasn't robbed." Scooter was grateful, but he was not looking forward to the next fifteen-miles he would have to spend on his bike.

It was three hours of torture before he arrived at his gate. Slumping against the cool metal, he was sweating and huffing from the ride. The gravel roads had proven to be the most difficult. The fifteen mile journey should have taken an hour.
"Thank you, God, for getting me here," he whispered. The prayers were coming more freely now.
"Just a simple crying out, like Matt had said," he remembered.

Scooter was glad he had decided to stop and spend the ten dollars on some food and water. The plastic bag hung on his handlebars. Lifting the chain, pushing the gate open, pulling the bike through, and resetting the chain, made him feel like he had entered his childhood fortress.
"The moat was crossed— on to the castle," he whispered, and embraced the idea of *G-Ma's castle.*

While pushing the bike through the woods, his own body's stink offended his nostrils. Then out of the blue, the question from the ambush broke through in a flash of memory. *"Do you like what you're going through?"* came the whisper from the dark.
"Do you like what you're going through?" he said.

Through a crack in the barn door, James caught a glimpse of Lawrence pushing his bike up the driveway and smiled while arching his back in anticipation. He made for the green bag, ditching the food out of it into the hay and returned to the inconspicuous lookout.

Scooter stopped at the back door, leaning his bike against its kick-stand. He reached beneath the wood and found the dangling key where he had left it. He stepped up and unlocked the old white door, then replaced the key on the hidden nail. Pulling up on his ten-dollar bag of groceries, he left the bike and headed into the house.

James lost sight of the man after he went inside, so he pushed the door out at the bottom and rolled under, with the green bag in tow. He stepped to the south side of the barn behind the billowing lilac bush and watched. He could see into the kitchen through a small window and the nine panels of glass in the wooden entry door. The screen door must have been a long-lost relic.

Scooter set his grocery bag on the counter. He had no electricity, so the fridge had been propped open and useless for a couple of years. He needed to go dig out his small lockbox from the upstairs bedroom. He kept the spare keys in the drawer next to the sink. He grabbed them and went for the climb.

James saw Lawrence leave the kitchen so he made his move toward the back door. He gently stepped onto the wooden platform, bypassing the two steps in one stride. He placed his ear to the door and listened, hearing footfalls on the squeaky stairway. He twisted the handle and tried the door. A slight creak slowed his progress. The sound of climbing feet never wavered, so he pressed into the room. He stood in the small galley kitchen. A blue plastic bag was dropped on the counter next to him by a dank porcelain sink. The paint was peeling from the walls. The wooden floor was covered in dust and dirt. A grimy refrigerator had a piece of lumber propping the door open.

The green bag was heavy so James set it next to the doorway that led to the rest of the house. Above him the floorboards groaned at the applied weight, while James looked into a dining and living room in the front of the house. A door off to his left revealed a bathroom with the stairs in the far corner from where he stood. The furniture was covered with plastic drop cloths— a couch, a recliner, and an ancient television. The wooden dining room table had four worn chairs surrounding it. There was a wood-burning stove between the two areas directly in front of him.

James moved left, toward the bathroom door, figuring it to be the best place for the ambush.

Scooter found the box in the closet. He had hidden it behind the access door to the plumbing for the upstairs bathroom. He decided to take the box down to the dining room table so he could lay it all out. Descending the stairs was slower than going up. His ribs were throbbing.

He stepped off the last stair and turned for the table, walking past the bathroom. The door swung in after Scooter passed and James drove his unsuspecting adversary into the dining room table with such force it split the base and fell to the floor with a crash. The lockbox and new black hat went sprawling as James began to swing his fists into the man's kidneys with deep thuds. Scooter rolled to his back to face his attacker and was immediately enraged. The man on top of him was an older version of the former friend, but there was no denying who he was, the chipped tooth was a dead giveaway.
"Moby!"
"Lawrence, it's time to pay the piper." James swung wildly and passionately. Years of fury poured out of him as he sought to exploit every weakness he could find.

Scooter was covering up as best he could against the blows, protecting his delicate rib cage and managed to deflect most of the strikes. He felt like a gym punching bag but knew he needed to get to his feet to be able to defend himself. He kicked and connected with his attacker's right knee, sending him spinning and falling face-first toward the floor with a growl.

Scooter rolled away and got himself to his feet. He was the larger man and, because of his concrete work, the stronger man. Without consideration he charged Moby but was met with a prompt boot to his groin, which doubled him over in pain. Moby rose to his feet and delivered a stinging blow to the jaw, which put Scooter down on his back. The next blow, directly to his broken ribs, sent him dizzy and breathless, rolling over in agony.

"Jesus, please help me," was the inaudible prayer deep inside Scooters heart, crying out to God. The prayer was answered by an immediate surge of strength. He grabbed both of Moby's legs and drove forward by pumping his own legs like steel pistons. The move put Moby on his butt with Scooter on top of him. Five solid punches to his face put Moby's lights out. The sixth and seventh were out of pure frustration.

Scooter's sudden adrenaline rush pushed him to his feet. He wanted to bind Moby before he woke up and was headed to the barn when he almost tripped on an unfamiliar green bag. Inside he found everything he needed to do what he wanted— duct tape, a length of chain, and several bolts.

Fifteen minutes later, Scooter had Moby chained up in the cellar. He was face down with his ankles and wrists behind him. The rest of the chain circled over a beam. He tightened the last bolt making sure there was no slack in the chain and kicked him solidly in the side. Scooter spit in his general direction and left without remorse.

Upstairs, he collapsed on the dusty, plastic-covered couch. *"Thank you, Father,"* he said and fell asleep.

A few hours later, he woke up to moaning coming from beneath the floorboards and a wave of fear crashed.
"I should have called the cops," he thought, then remembered he had no phone.
"How am I going to explain this? He's in my house. He just got out of jail, so that would look good for me. He attacked me—he brought the chain and tape. But I tied him up in the cellar."

Scooter didn't know what to do.

"Jan would know what to do," he thought and made plans to leave.
"Maybe I should give him some water?" he questioned himself walking out the back door.
"Hell no!" he said, as he twisted his new hat backward, took his bike from its stand, and left.

*

"Hey, Captain," she said as he walked up to her desk.
"Donna. What is the status of your big cases?" The man looked stressed.
"Ronnie's case had a setback with the explosion. We are back to searching for the lost kid in Canada."
"You're sure he hasn't crossed back over?"
"As sure as I can be sitting here," she said.
"Right."
"Are you getting updates from the RCMP?"
"Every couple of days— saying the same thing. No sign and no trace."
"I can give my counterpart a call to see if we can press them on it."
"I would appreciate it, sir," Donna said, without flashing her infectious smile. She knew doing it had produced an adverse reaction from the captain over the years. It was like he was immune to her beauty.

"So the tire slashing character?"
"Scooter. I received two good leads from coworkers this morning, so, I'll be following up today."
"Do you think he died in the blast?"
"Possibly."
"He wasn't cooking crack in that trailer, was he?"
"No way. He wasn't the type."
"Wasn't?"
"Or isn't."
"What about Tina Patrick?" he asked. The captain was proceeding through his mental checklist.
"She's made claims about a Donny character threatening her and the boy, but we have hit a dead end with him as well."
"Sounds like a theme, Detective." He tapped on her desk.
"Sir."

"We need some movement. I'm getting pressure from above. It appears our fair city is blowing apart, pun intended."
"Yes, sir."

*

So, if Moby gets loose, he can't go to the cops. But he could make another attempt on me," then a bright light switched on.
"Son of a— he blew up my house!" Scooter turned the bike around and pushed for G-Ma's.
"This needs to end."

*

Chapter Eleven
* Day Star *

The train whistle almost blew Darrell out of his comfortable bed. He had completely forgotten the tracks were outside of the window. The sun was high in the sky, so the camper was getting hot. His morning ritual of letting go of built-up stomach gases happened within the first few moments of waking, and today's explosion was particularly rank, obvious revenge from the roller grilled gas station hot dogs. His gas was followed up with the need to empty his bowels so Darrell ran for the toilet. "This beats taking a dump in the woods," he said and smiled.

He cleaned himself with liberal amounts of toilet paper, relishing the convenience, but when he went to flush, nothing happened. There was no water in the toilet tank and none in the sink either. He would have to go back to the gas station to use the restroom to wash.
"I can't stay here. It stinks too much," he thought to himself.

In that moment, Darrell remembered the dream he had about his granny. The vision made him reconsider seeking her out. His dad's mother was as mean as they came, but he figured she wouldn't turn him in to the cops. There would be plenty of food to eat and a working toilet. The scary part would be not knowing if Donny was going to be hanging around. With that thought, he subconsciously touched the seven round scars on the back of his hands and shuddered.

The fear of Donny had kept young Darrell hiding in the woods. He lied to his mom about getting the phone call that night, but he had heard his dear old dad was out of prison. It was a week before he used the unnerving information to get his mom out of bed and into Canada. Darrell knew he could use the fear inside his mother for what he needed. Sitting in the smelly camper, he missed his mom. He wondered where she was, and shed a few lonely tears.
"Maybe it's time to find Granny," he thought.
Darrell knew well enough if he could get out to Smiths Creek, he could find Granny's place. "There are only three streets in the whole town," he reasoned aloud.

He began rummaging through the camper to find anything he could use. He grabbed a fork and spoon, along with a can opener and steak knife. In a closet there was a black day pack on a hook. Next to the sink he found a few cans of food, plus a few dollars in loose change in the bottom of a drawer. Darrell grabbed what was left of the toilet paper.

He decided to go to the station, needing water and a wash for his grubby hands. He had a bad stink rolling off his body, but that would have to wait for Granny's place. Darrell wanted to check out the a huge county map on the wall by the restrooms to help him find Granny's town. With the plan in place, he slipped out into the steamy afternoon.

Walking into the bright building, he passed the newspaper stand and took notice of the bold headline; "Explosion Destroys Trailer Park!" "Wow!" he said, marching on to the back. Pausing at the wall-sized map, he found the red "*You Are Here*" triangle and began searching, but couldn't find Smiths Creek anywhere. Maps were not his strong suit. He gave up a few minutes later and went to use the facilities. Inside the stall he unrolled as much toilet paper as he could stuff into his new pack. After washing he wanted to give the map another look. "Hey, kid, you lost?"
"No, I just wanted to find Smiths Creek on this map," he said to the guy with the gas station shirt.
"Look up. If you follow the railroad tracks, you'll run right into it," he said stepping close and pointing.
"Oh yeah! Thanks!"
"Sure thing."
"My mom is waiting," he lied, and left.

*

"You must wear the all your orange!" barked the deputy from the desk.
"Go back and put your orange county jail top on."
"It's hot in here!" Tina said.
"Oh, I'm sorry! I guess you shouldn't have ended up in jail," the deputy said, sarcasm dripping from his lips.

Tina was not pleased. She was sweating before noon, along with her fifteen roommates. In her mind, the only solution was fewer clothes. She stripped off her white sleeveless T-shirt while facing the wall by her bunk. She pulled her arms from her bra straps, twisted it around her body, and unsnapped the sweaty undergarment. Tina hurried to pull on her baggy orange *county jail* shirt before she caught any flack for going braless. The harassment wasn't what worried her the most, though. The ugly scars carved on her back would make even the most ardent criminal cringe and ask too many questions. This was a place she wanted to blend in, not stand out.

Before she got locked up, Tina had used all of her energy to cover up the pain of those scars, usually through vast quantities of booze and drugs. She knew it made her a terrible mother, but she had no other idea how to live with the pain.
"How do you make it stop?" was the question she never had an answer for.
She was glad to be serving time if it meant she was able to keep her ex away from Darrell. Her boy was still attached to him, and it wasn't safe for him to be near Donny.

Tina sat on her bunk and became consumed with negative thoughts. She routinely beat herself to a pulp for falling for his charm and deception. He was so stinking smooth with his words— he charmed the pants right off of her. Within the first month of them dating she was pregnant. He talked her into an abortion and two more over the first three years. The abuse had started by then, but Tina felt like she was the only one who could help tame Donny's demons. So, she put up with the beatings, because he wasn't angry at her— he was angry with his life, with his disappointments. Tina was convinced Donny was talented, gifted in fact, but he just couldn't catch a break.

He played lead guitar in several bands, doing gigs in local bars. She was so proud when he was on stage. There were many nights he didn't bother to come home, so she knew he was with other women, but chalked it up to his budding popularity. Tina justified the betrayal by reasoning he didn't feel the same about those other girls the way he felt about her. So, she went along to support him, happy to be the most influential woman in his life.

When she found out she was pregnant for the fourth time, she didn't tell him, using the excuse of not wanting to stress him out. Donny finally saw her naked belly and knew. In a fit of rage, he beat her with an extension cord. He laid her back open in long hideous gashes with pain so intense she slept on her side for the rest of her pregnancy. Of course, he had apologized, attributing his violence to the band's nasty breakup.

"It was stress, baby, not you," he whispered in her ear. The phrase still turned her stomach to this day, but not back then. She couldn't see she was in love with a psychopath.

After baby Darrell came along, the glow of his repentant words wore off in a hurry. He was back on the stage again, and women were after him all of the time. Rare was the night he slept at home with her. They had sex all of the time, but when he was finished, he left.

The day everything changed still haunted her. Tina had to help move her grandmother into a nursing home after a stroke. Donny offered a lame excuse for not helping, but she convinced him to keep an eye on Darrell. The four-year-old loved his time with dad. He was his hero— a famous guitar player, the guy who brought him candy and told him crazy stories. However, on this day, Darrell wasn't feeling good and spent much of the time crying, wanting his daddy to comfort him. Instead, the demented prick burnt him with cigarettes on the back of his hands to get him to stop his fussing. Seven times he cried, and seven times he burnt the boy's flesh.

By this point in her parade of shame, both of Tina's knees were pulled tight to her chest and wrapped by her arms. She rocked herself on her bunk, driven by the guilt and shame of what the evil bastard did to them. *"At least he paid in prison,"* the solitary thought her only solace.

*

Scooter had turned himself around three different times. Fighting the pull to go snuff out Moby's life, extinguish him from this world forever, the Scripture about vengeance belonging to God was what ultimately turned him away for the final time.

He was on his way to Jan's house when he remembered she was on vacation somewhere up in the UP. Scooter changed directions and made his way to the library on Allen Road, rolling into the gravel lot a half an hour later. He was glad for the drinking fountain inside the door. The block building was cramped and smelled of bleach and old books. The library catered primarily to children's books and activities, but public computers were available.

He spun his hat around to the front and moved to the desk Scooter was greeted by an energetic redhead with a genuine smile.

"How can I help you?"

"I have a library card, but I don't have it with me."

"Well, I can use your ID to get you what you need."

"Do you have the newspaper?" It was on the counter next to the register. Plastered all over the front was a picture of the charred ground where his trailer once sat.

"Have you read about this?" he asked.

"Yes, its horrible."

"That's my trailer . . . was my trailer."

"No way!"

"Yep. All of my identification went up in the blast along with my phone."

"I am so sorry."

"I need to email my sister to let her know I'm okay."

"No problem. I'll log you on myself." She stepped over to her computer.

"Thank-you very much."

"You bet. You can use number two," she said, pointing at the row of machines.

"Thanks," Scooter managed a smile.

"Can I get you a bottle of water?"

"Sure, thank you."

"No problem." She grabbed one from the mini-fridge behind her and smiled with apologetic eyes.

"Thanks, again."

"You're welcome. Let me know if I can do anything else."

A few minutes later, she brought Scooter two printed pages from the state website about how to get an ID after losing everything.

"Thought this may help you."

"Thank you."

*

"Jan, not sure if you have heard about the explosion at the trailer park or not. I am fine. My house is gone. I have no phone or ID. I'm staying at G-Ma's. I stopped at the library to send this. You don't need to come home I'll be okay. I love you. See you soon. Scooter. P. S. Got my bike fixed, finally!"

*

The bells greeted the desperate man again as he pushed his bicycle inside the counseling office. Gina slid the opaque glass window and her mouth fell open. "Scooter? What's wrong?"

The pain of forcing himself to ride the seven miles from the library without stopping had driven all of the blood from his face, giving him a ghost-like appearance, contrasting with his black hat.
"Gina," was all he managed to say as he went for a chair.
Within three seconds the office door swung wide and Gina came through holding out a bottle of water.
"Scooter, you look awful."
"That's not a positive way to gain customers," he said while smiling through his obvious pain.
"I'm sorry, but you look like you have been in battle or something."
"It's a long story. Is Angie available?"
"You know, you are in luck because her next client just called and canceled. Give me a minute, so I can talk to her," Gina said. She had held the door from closing and turned to walk back through it.
"Thank you," managed Scooter between swallows, raising the bottle in appreciation.
"It's my pleasure."

Fifteen seconds later, Angie pushed through the door and came to sit next to Scooter.
"Hey. Are you okay?"
"I don't know."
"Why do you have your bike inside?"
"So they can't steal it."
"They? Who?"
He wanted to dive deep into the story right where he was sitting, hanging onto his ribs, as his face ran with sweat, but she stopped him from proceeding with a raised hand.

"Let's go back, Scooter. You can put your bike at the end of hallway."
He winced when he stood.
"What's happened?" she said, pointing to his side.
"I was mugged and he broke a few of my ribs."
"Oh my!"
Gina was listening through the glass— not out of nosiness, but from a place of concern.
"Gina," Angie called out and the door buzzed.
Angie stepped aside and let Scooter pass, followed by his bicycle's ticking gears.
Gina held out another water bottle and a handful of fun-sized candy bars to Angie.

Inside the office, Scooter collapsed into his chair as Angie closed the door of her private sanctuary.
Setting the items on the coffee table, Angie sat on the couch next to Scooter's chair. She placed her hand on the man's hairy arm, which was beaded with sweat.

"What's going on, Scooter? It's only been forty eight hours since you left."
"I've been in the fight of my life, Angie," he said, with his hat in his hands. He dove in and told her everything he could remember, holding nothing back, up until the fight with James— as the two held hands in the office.
"So you had your daughter's funeral, got mugged and robbed of all of your personal belongings, your trailer was destroyed, then Matt picked you up and let you stay at his house?"
"Yes, essentially."
"You came from Matt's to see me?"
"Not exactly."
"What do you mean?" Angie looked confused.
"I went out to G-Ma's after I picked up my bike."
"You've been all the way out in Smiths Creek?"
"Yes, but an old friend was waiting for me when I got home."
"An old friend?"
"I used to think we were friends but in all actuality he's been an enemy of mine for years. He is one of the Denton Boys."
"What did he want?"
"Moby wanted to kill me," he said and wiped his forehead.

"What?"

"He jumped me as I walked past the downstairs bathroom. We crashed into the dining room table and it smashed into pieces."

"Oh, no."

"Yeah, we had a brawl right in the middle of my house."

"Are you kidding?"

"I wish I was." He sipped from the new bottle.

"What happened?"

"In the end, just when I thought I was doomed, I cried out to God for help and this surge of energy coursed through me. I can't explain it. I rose up and struck him down, hard."

As Angie ingested the story, she remained quiet.

"I may have screwed up, Angie."

"How?"

"I chained him up in the cellar."

"Oh no, you didn't do that, did you?" Her face was in anguish.

"Yes."

Angie was thinking about the consequences of his actions.

"I left him without water. I turned around several times," Scooter said.

"What do you mean?"

"I was going to go back."

"Why?"

"To kill him. He's the one that blew up my house up." His hand tremor returned.

"How do you know?"

"He just got out of jail. He told me while we were fighting that it was time for me to pay."

"Pay for what?"

"I think it has to do with the fact I had disowned him after I became a Christian."

"I don't understand."

"Being his friend and following Jesus, was impossible . . . is impossible. Moby is sick. Ever since I've known him, he has had a mean streak. That doesn't even describe it well enough. It's like he has zero empathy for anyone. He uses people for his own personal gain."

"Okay."

"It became a real problem after high school. He was always one of those guys you didn't want to spend too much time with, and yet I hadn't completely cut out of my life either."

"Why?"

"I've known him since I was a kid."

"And knowing you, Scooter, you were too nice to be able to tell him to knock it off."

"I guess so."

"It's called passive-aggressive behavior— an unwillingness to confront an obvious wrong face-to-face, so we go about it in round-about ways instead."

"Is that so wrong?"

"Yes, it is."

"Why?"

"Because if you knew he was using people for his own gain you should have called him out on it to his face and cut it off. You may have been able to help many other people."

"I guess you're right," he said, lowering his eyes away from her.

"It's called boundaries, Scooter. You have to define them for people who have no respect and then stick to it."

"I've never been good at that."

"Now, you are paying the price."

"Ouch, Doc."

"Sorry— but not really."

Scooter looked at her.

"What are you going to do?" Angie was concerned.

*

Walking the train tracks for the second day, Darrell's feet were sore. He went back and forth between doing the balance beam trick of walking on the steel rails— which was fun but slowed his progress— and walking on the wooden beams beneath the rails. The timbers were so close together the real battle was not to trip and fall on his face with his heavy backpack, which pulled his sense of balance out of kilter.

The best part of walking the track for Darrell was it was a different world. Through this part of the state the railroad was bordered by trees which gave the illusion you were deep in an unsettled country, free from modern society, until he was forced to scamper through an intersection. Darrell hid in bushes and waited for traffic to clear before racing across, out of sight of peering eyes.

The previous night he stayed in a section of woods a few hundred feet behind a house. During the night, the coyotes howled and yapped so close he cowered motionless beneath a fallen tree. Fear had him clutching his bag of goods and clasping his knife with white knuckles until daybreak, as sleep passed him by.

After eating an out-of-date can of black beans for breakfast, he continued his journey, hoping to find Smiths Creek before nightfall. Back to the tracks he went, climbing up from the ditch to the stone embankment where the rails sat. Darrell was impressed with the railway. Never had he seen so much stone in his entire life. He was guessing the trains were so heavy, they needed something sturdy to travel on.

The sun was over the trees when Darrell felt his feet tingle inside his filthy shoes. Passing it off as exhaustion, he sauntered on, searching for his nirvana. But the vibration was not going away. He stomped his feet on the steel, trying to wake them up. *"Why are my feet falling asleep?"* he asked the wind.

The roar of the horn blast almost sent him out of his shoes, but he froze instead. The second blast came and he felt his eardrums nearly burst from the pressure. He planted both of his hands on the side of his head to protect his ears from the pain, but his feet still didn't want to move. A third and fourth blast were closer as he managed to turn and face the oncoming beast. It was orange and black, spewing a dark cloud from the top of its head as three bright eyes glared into him.

The fifth blast shook his feet free from the bonds of gravity and Darrell jumped to the side, sending him down the stone embankment and tumbling into a wet ditch filled with reeds and cattails. The screaming orange and black beast roared past him, just feet from his head. Darrell had never been so close to anything so massive and powerful. The ground shook beneath him as the steel rails bent beneath the weight. He couldn't move his trembling eyes off of the monster that had nearly devoured his life.

*

"Scooter, something else is going on here."

"What?" He was skeptical.

"I think your past is reaching out to you," Angie said.

"What does that mean?"

"I think you have some unfinished business with the things from your past and it has thrown your present into crisis."

"So, the things I'm going through aren't real?"

"No— they're genuine— maybe more real than our physical world."

"I don't get it, Angie," Scooter said, frustrated.

"People bury traumatic wounds from their past deep into their psyche, reasoning they have dealt with them. Thinking they magically disappear, somehow."

"When you stop thinking about those things, then they're gone, right?"

"Hardly, Scooter. What happens is the way you cope becomes normalized. You believe it's just the *'way life is'* and you think you've moved forward."

"Isn't that the point?"

"Not when you're still carrying the five hundred pounds of guilt and shame on your back."

"I thought you said we were moving on with life?"

"You are moving, but you are hindered at the same time," Angie said. "The addictive behaviors flow from the guilt and shame people carry. Until there is healing at the source, the addiction holds power over you."

"Healing at the source?"

"The very thing you've been running from is the thing entrapping you."

"What?"

"The pain of your shame from ruining your marriage, Scooter."

He stared at her.

"You said to me you were angry with yourself for causing the one woman you loved to *'give up on us,'* Angie used finger quotes.

"Did I say that?"

"Yes, you did."

"Now what?"

"As followers of Jesus, we take the pain and push it into the cross of Christ, knowing it is the place where the Son of God said His work was completed."

"It is finished," Scooter said, as the idea struck a chord.

"Exactly. Then, as we are able, we seek to make amends."

"Amends?"

"You seek to make it right. To apologize and work toward reconciliation."

"From Kim?"

"Yes."

"But she didn't even want me at my own daughter's funeral."

"True. Why do you think that was the case?"

"Because I was a drunken idiot," Scooter said.

"How does shaming yourself now, for broken choices in your past, help you?"

"I don't know."

"It doesn't, Scooter. You just called yourself an idiot."

She sipped from her mug while he tugged on his Present hat.

"Seeking forgiveness is the right move. It destroys the power your past has over you."

"So, you're saying my anger at myself all these years has made me a prisoner?"

"Yes. Unforgiveness is you drinking poison and hoping that someone else will die," Angie said.

"I'm not sure Kim has done anything wrong to be forgiven for."

"You're seeking the forgiveness from her, Scooter, so you can forgive yourself and bury your broken behavior."

Silence filled the air. Scooter's heart pounded in his chest.

"Scooter, sin often causes sinful reactions in others. Only you can own your stuff. You've told me you're ashamed of the way you treated Kim."

"True."

"Then seeking forgiveness is the way to face the pain and work through it, instead of running from it."

"It seems like an impossible task."

"Nothing is impossible with God helping you."

"But I feel so overwhelmed."

"You have many things being thrown at you right now— of course you feel the emotion. And I believe the enemy is attempting to get you to go back to your old ways of coping. The question to people of faith in times of crisis is always, '*Will you trust Jesus*?'"

"I want to," he said.

"There is a little verse in the gospel of Mark where a man facing a crisis says to Jesus, '*I believe, help my unbelief.*' That's in the ESV."
"I believe, help my unbelief?"
"Yes."
"It seems sacrilegious," Scooter said.
"It's the condition of the human heart. God knows His creation."
"I believe, help my unbelief. I believe, help my unbelief." Scooter thought about the statement for a few moments.

"How does it apply to Kim? What do you think?" Angie asked.
"I know what you're asking of me is right and, at the same time, I'm afraid it will be the most difficult thing I have ever done."
"You've faced many difficult things during this season of your life, Scooter."
"True," he said and sipped from his water bottle.
"What am I going to do about Moby?"

✳

The road south was a long, straight, and boring drive. The trio remained silent, while the tires droned on over the hot asphalt. The distant mirage wiggled in the sunshine as heat from the ground rose and distorted their view. The Franklin Mountains grew with each passing mile, as did the dread among the family. Kim and Bobby had invited Bee's best friend Juanita along to travel the sixty-five miles down US 54 on the one-year anniversary of the accident. Bobby was holding fresh flowers for the somber occasion.

"I can't believe a year has passed," he said.
"It's crazy," said Juanita.
"Are you looking forward to your senior year?" Bobby asked, changing the subject.
"In some ways."
"What do you mean?"
"I just want to be done with high school," she said.
"Your mom said you may go into the army?" Kim asked.
"I'm thinking about it. Taking some time to figure out what I want to do before I go to college."
"You may go into the army?" Bobby asked from the back seat, sliding himself forward.

"Yes. Or maybe the air force."

"I didn't know that."

"Are you looking forward to being a freshman, Bobby?"

"Not really," he admitted.

"Bobby has been my Rock of Gibraltar this year," Kim said.

Bobby smiled on the inside, while he gazed out at the passing desert. Tamping down his anger had become normal.

"He's kept us going in the face of all this crap," Kim said.

"It's been the hardest year of my life," Juanita said.

"I'm sorry," Kim said.

"I miss her so much." Juanita began to cry. Kim grabbed her hand, as her own tear factory ramped up production again.

"Why did Brandon leave, Mom?" Bobby asked.

"What did he say about leaving?"

"I know he said God was calling him to Oklahoma, but why do you think he left?"

"I think the accident had hurt him so deeply, he couldn't overcome the pain. I'm sure every time he saw the van and trailer, it took him back to the accident."

"He never really talked to me about it," Juanita admitted, looking out the passenger window.

"It's not you, Juanita. He's hurting like the rest of us."

"I think he blames himself," Bobby said.

"I know Veronica does," Juanita said.

"Poor thing," Kim said. Kim had worked through the anger issues she harbored against the student leadership, forgiving them months ago. She also was aware they had not arrived at the place of forgiving themselves.

"I pray for them all of the time," Juanita said.

"So do I," Bobby said.

The silence returned as the dusty ground raced by.

A half an hour later, Kim slowed the vehicle and guided them to the side of the highway as a semi rolled past. Then, cutting the wheel hard, she pulled a U-turn and got off on the shoulder of northbound US 54. There it stood— the memorial to the broken world. The three-foot-high, white cross contained only three block letters— BEE. Surrounding the cross were the remnants of flowers dropped off over the last twelve months by grieving family and friends. The makeshift memorial reflected the evening sun, glowing against the barren backdrop of sand and sagebrush.

Bobby was the first out of the car. It was his fourth trip to the site. He wanted to clean up the last place his sister had been in this world. He felt like the caretaker now, taking on his sister's role. Trying to step up to be a man had been important to his well-being, and he felt it had ushered him from childhood into adulthood, but he still tripped over his growing anger issue.

He picked up trash which had been trapped in the display, stuffed it into his back pocket, and knelt in front of the cross. "I sure miss you, Bee," he said, and cried again. "This has wrecked our *'you and me together'* promise, sis."
Juanita and Kim flanked the young man and joined his tear making campaign.

A truck rolled by with a gentle double tap on its air horn, a simple recognition of the loss. Up and down the section of highway, this was an all-too-familiar scene.

Memories of the year flooded through Kim's mind and heart. Reading about the man and his subsequent ten-year prison sentence brought little solace. She had to work hard to come to the place where she released her right to get even with the drunk who had taken Bee's life, much like the work she had done to do to forgive the drunk who had given Bee her life.

Kim regretted her decision to exclude Bee's father. She knew she stole from him his ability to have closure. At the time of the accident, Kim felt like she did not have the emotional ability to deal with seeing him again and chose to take the easy way out. She would have to explain to Bobby the fact he did have a biological father living in Michigan. *"I bet he's still in the trailer,"* she thought.

"I'm sorry, Mom," Bobby broke the silent reflection.
"For what?" Kim asked.
"For not being a better son."
"You're a good son, Bobby. I couldn't ask for a better child than you."
"Bobby you are a great kid," Juanita said.

"Sometimes I think if I would have been better, God wouldn't have taken Bee away."

"There are moments I feel the same way, Bobby," Kim said.

"Me, too," Juanita admitted.

"I have learned so much this past year. One of the things is we live in a fallen world that has been wrecked by sin and selfishness. With the sin comes consequences. The drunk guy driving his truck down this road made a choice to get behind the wheel. He made a choice from a place of brokenness to drink himself stupid, and take Bee's life from us. If I focus on the brokenness of the world, I lose all of the beauty it contains. Because I believe God is still involved with us, I can see the beauty. If I'm grateful for the time I had to be Bella's mom, my perspective changes. Yes, I'm sick she is gone. I need to focus on the fact I was able to mother her for fifteen wonderful years. I miss her every day and I will until I die."

"The part that sucks is we have to live with his consequences, too," Bobby said.

"A valid point. We don't live alone. No one can isolate themselves so much they will never feel pain from the fallen world."

"It isn't fair," Juanita agreed, wrapping her arms around herself.

"No, it isn't. The world is not a fair place, but there is still so much beauty if you can get past the pain."

"I don't know if I can," Juanita whispered.

"I'll help you, honey," Kim said.

"Me, too," Bobby said, and hugged his adopted sister. He showed Juanita the special handshake he and Bee shared, completing the adoption process in his mind with the word, "Together."

Kim watched the two kids hug and felt another tug at her heart. She needed to come clean with her son about his father.

"Bobby," Kim said.

Her son was taller than she was now. Kim grabbed his face with both of her hands, wiping away his tears from his three whiskers.

"I love you."

"I love you, too."

"I love you guys, too," Juanita said, the long group-hug on the dusty shoulder of northbound US 54 commenced. With it, Kim's conviction to honesty melted.

*

Darkness had settled over the trees of the orchard like a spring fog. Angie left her car in front of the gate and pushed into the failing light. The surrounding woods were waking to another night shift. Branches creaked, swayed by a gentle Michigan breeze, as crickets and frogs sang their lonely songs. When thick trees opened to the organized orchard, intermittent fireflies pulsed their mating dance as sporadic moonlight illuminated the path. Angie stayed to the side of the driveway, seeking to remain cloaked in darkness beneath the fruit trees. She circled the house, looking for the entrance to the cellar. Knowing ancient farm homes had cellar entries on the exterior, Angie watched for the signature leaning doors.

On the south side of the home, a pair of doors tilted back to face the night sky. The peeling paint was evident even in the low light. Angie found the lock in the clasp between the two doors. It was hanging, not latched, and she smiled knowing Scooter didn't really want to keep anyone prisoner after all. Setting the lock aside, she pulled the handle on the heavy door and it protested against the movement. The sudden noise from the door caused a moan to be released from inside of the cellar, the low bellows echoed in its shadows. Angie began to descend the wooden stairs. Unable to see anything below her feet, she probed with her toe. She held the wall for stability and unconsciously swept her hand for a light switch. The moan intensified.

"Now you be quiet, Mr. Moby," she commanded with a low calm voice. But the commotion only grew from the darkness as she felt for the next invisible step. Feeling the give of the dirt beneath her feet, Angie knew she had reached the bottom, and her hand fell across a switch protruding from the wall. With a flick of her thumb, the scene came to life in front of her. Angie had to hold her hand up to block the rays from the single incandescent bulb aimed at her forehead. The light was apparently powered directly from a car battery on the floor.

There he was— lying on his belly with his arms and feet pulled up behind him, duct tape encircling his swollen head and covering his mouth.
"That doesn't look comfortable, James," she said.

Angie moved closer and grabbed at her pants, pulling a wrench from each of her back pockets.

Moby moaned behind the duct tape again, with squinted eyes fighting against the violating light.
Angie stepped past him to the back of the chain and began to loosen the nut off of the bolt which held the chain over the beam.
"You're going to have to stop your fussing and let me get this chain off," she said.
She kept turning the adjustable wrench counterclockwise, while holding the head of the bolt still with the other wrench.
"Kind of ironic. The very thing you hoped to entrap another is what holds you a prisoner, don't you think, James?"
Moby huffed, spit shooting from the top of the dirty gray tape.

Another minute passed, and the pressure on the chain was released. It unwrapped from the beam and dropped next to the prisoner.
"There, isn't that better?" she asked.

As Angie went to step away, Moby pulled his legs down which released the chain from the loop in his wrists. Angie side-stepped around his movement and, at the same time, he kicked his foot toward her leg. James caught Angie's heel, knocking her over into an antique coffee table, which went sprawling in her attempt to catch herself. She wound up falling headfirst toward the brick wall, nearly knocking herself unconscious, but she caught herself before the impact.

"Will you ever learn?" she asked.
Turning toward Moby, she witnessed him thrashing about, trying to break free of the grip of the chains, eyes wide. In her peripheral vision she caught sight of a dust-caked weight bench. Next to the base were four large steel discs, stacked one upon the other. Angie grabbed a disc off the top of the pile, noticing the painted white letters which read 45 LBS. She walked over to the flailing man dropping the weight on his head. All motion ceased.

Angie paused, then picked up the weight again and slammed it down into his head, bringing a flow of blood from his ears, eyes, nose, and from behind the tape. The third drop was to ensure his demise.
Moby was dead.

With a deep steadying breath, Angie began to unbolt the rest of the chain. Five minutes later she gathered the chain, hardware, and tools from around her, recalling the blinding night to the cellar with a flick of a switch. Retreating up the staircase, she closed the heavy door and walked toward the barn.

In the darkness of the dank cellar, James was gathered in a pile next to his dead body, waiting. It was all he could do. He was stuck between two worlds. A dirty hand from beneath him grabbed at what remained of his gooey essence, scooping him into a container. Angie heard his screams grow distant on her journey to hide the evidence, as James was plunged into utter darkness and despair.

Angie returned for the body five minutes later.

*

Chapter Twelve
* Lone Star *

"Jan. Hello? Jan, can you hear me?"
"W. . . wait," responded the jumbled signal.

"She doesn't have any reception. Just give her a minute, Scooter. She told me she would have to move to be able to talk," Matt said.
"Where are they?"
"Lake of the Clouds."
"Porcupine Mountains?"
"Yes, near Ontonagon."

Matt's phone sounded to Scooter like someone was crunching aluminum foil in the ear piece.
"Should be getting b. . . e . . . tter so. . . on."
"Jan?"
"Yes," huffing and heavy breathing sounds were now making their way through the static. "I am winded. Had to climb to the top of the hill—it's the only place we get reception at the campground."
"It is good to hear your voice, sis."
"It is. I don't know what to say. Matt sent me an email explaining things in more detail. I am so sorry. Please stay at our house, Scooter."
"I have been out at G-Ma's."
"You don't have running water or electricity out there."
"Kinda like camping." Scooter smiled.
"Whatever," Jan knew she wasn't going to convince him.
"I am fine," he said
"You know we will be home by the end of the week, unless you need us now. We can break camp and come back today."
"No need."
"Do you have money?" Jan asked.
"Yes, I have saved for a rainy day."
"This is a little beyond that, don't you think?"
"Yes, just a bit."
"I am so glad you weren't hurt in the blast."
"It's a crazy thing. I had an appointment to see Angie."
"Who is that?"
"My counselor."

"Oh, I didn't know you were seeing one."

"It has been a couple months now. She is helping me.

"Good."

"I think I know who blew up my place."

"Really? So, it wasn't a gas leak?"

"No. It was intentional."

"Who would do such a thing to you?"

"I will tell you later."

"Okay. What have you gotten yourself mixed up in, Scooter?"

"It's not like that, Jan."

"I don't understand, and I need to understand, Scooter."

"I know. I will explain it all."

"So you're not in any kind of trouble?"

"With the law?"

"Yes."

"No."

They both paused.

"Can I borrow the car?"

"Sure, anything."

"I am leaving town for a bit," Scooter said.

"Where are you going?"

"I will tell Matt and he can let you know when you get home. This is something I have do, Jan."

"Is this the right time to be leaving?"

"I need to do this."

"What could be so important?" Jan pushed.

"I am going to find Kimmy."

"What? Why now?"

"It is way past the time to make amends."

"It seems strange, Scooter. With all of this stuff going on in your life right now, it looks like you are running away."

"I am not running away. I am running to the solution."

"I'm not following you."

"These attacks have made it crystal clear, I have waited far too long already."

"How about calling her?"

"Do you have a number?" Scooter asked.

"No. How will you find her?"

"I am going to find Bella's death certificate and go from there."

"It seems like a long shot."

"It is, but this is what I am supposed to do."
There was silence between the adopted siblings.

"Okay. Whatever you need. I am behind you. Bill wants you to know
that the oil was just changed in the car, so you should be good to go."
"Thanks, I appreciate you letting me use it."
"Of course— it's just a car."
"I love you, Jan."
"Love you, too. Keep me in the loop, please!"
"I'll try."
"Be safe out there."

*

The tired city block ran south and had a total of six houses. All of the
homes were neighbors to the tall white church down at the end on the
right. The worn out houses sat just a few feet off of the broken and
heaved sidewalk. Each home had a large front porch facing the narrow
street. Those sacred places used to be filled with the hope and laughter
of happy families who occupied the lone residential street of Smiths
Creek, Michigan. However, the heyday of the tiny village had long
since passed, its sanctity destroyed by an accountant's pen.

All vitality vanished when the railroad cut out passenger stops from
their schedule. It was too close to Port Huron and the end of the line.
The railway abandoned coal for diesel electric locomotives so, Smiths
Creek was left for dead in the wake of the practical decision. The tracks
still bisected the town, and freight trains zoomed through several times
a day headed either for Detroit and its automotive plants or under the St.
Clair River into Canada. All of the trains now rumbled through the tiny
village without a single blink of acknowledgment or nod of gratitude to
its important history.

Darrell came walking into to the center of the tired town in the middle
of the day— even before automobiles began to gather at the watering
hole just north of the tracks. He was lethargic and weary from the
travel. His backpack was biting into his shoulders and sweat streaked
the sides of his face. With both of his thumbs locked behind his hot
backpack straps he turned onto Granny's street, uncertain of what he

may find. He determined to walk past her house on the other side of the street so he could see from the church if Donny was there. A hundred steps later Darrell, was slowly walking in front of the church, peering into Granny's house. It was closed up as usual and no cars were sitting in the narrow gravel driveway. He thought the house looked like it had fallen apart even more since his last visit.

Walking around the back of the church he stood in its shadow, watching the house for any signs of life. Next to him a water spigot was inviting him over to take a drink. He gulped down the mineral-laced liquid that smelled of sulfur. Then he let the water wash over his head and splash down his back, the sudden coldness causing Darrell to gasp. He scrubbed the dirt from his face with his cupped hands, rinsing himself over and over, willing vitality back into of his travel-weary bones.

The church had significant evergreen bushes along the back entrance and Darrell hid his backpack beneath the thick branches and walked to the street. Scanning up and down the road for movement he paused while his heart thumped inside his chest. As he approached Granny's porch he remembered the second step creaked and bypassed it. On the porch he looked into the windows, hands cupped around his face, hoping to catch some movement through the thin curtains. Nothing. The screen door spring announced his arrival. Darrell turned the handle and stepped inside the dank house.
"Granny?" He paused. "Granny, are you home?"
"Who . . . who is it?" Asked a shaky voice.
"It's me, Darrell."
"Darrell? What on God's green earth are you doin' here?"
"I need your help," he said, taking a few more cautious steps into the living room.
"Come in here, boy, let me have a look at 'cha."

*

"Thanks for letting me use the phone, Matt."
"You bet. How is Jan?"
"Concerned, but I think I convinced her not to come home early."
"Okay."
"I am heading out of town, you probably heard," Scooter said.

"Where to?"
"I am going to find Kim and make things right."
"Really?"
"Yes. I want to ask her to forgive me."
"Wow. Big step," Matt said.
"Yes. Angie seems to think some of the upheaval in my life can be traced back to the open wound. She said it has been festering for a long time. So, I need to seek some closure and make amends."
"Do you need anything?"
"No. I am going to ride out to Jan's and borrow her car for the trip."
"I want to help you, Scooter."
"I don't know how, other than praying for me. I don't have many clues to finding her."
"I am praying and will continue to ask God to guide and protect you. We are all praying for you, Scooter."
"Thank you," he said, while looking at the ground.
"Can you give me what you have about Kim, and I can do some internet searching while you are on the road?"
"Sure. I appreciate it."
Matt reached for his pocket and pulled out some folded bills. "We want to bless you with this, too. It isn't much."
"I can't take that."
"Why not?"
"I don't know. It doesn't seem right."
"Like the hat, it is a gift. Let me bless you."

Scooter hesitated while looking at the man.
"We want to bless you, and this will help you to get to Texas and back."
"Well thank you, I will pay you back."
"It is a gift. Bless someone else when you are able," Matt said.
"Thank you, Matt. You have been a lifesaver."
"God is good. I am glad we could do something."
Scooter looked at his own feet, overwhelmed by his friend's kindness.
"I think making peace, with your past, will help you."
"I know it's what I need to do, Matt."

*

"Hey, Gina, is Angie available for a few minutes?"
"Sorry, Scooter. She's not in today," Gina said.

"Really?"

"She took the next few days off for personal reasons."

"Oh, okay." Scooter turned for the door, confused by the news. Angie had always been available.

"Take care now." Gina smiled and slid the window closed.

Scooter waived and walked out to the familiar chime from above his head.

About the time he reached the black car, Gina had caught up to him.

"Hey," she whispered to his back.

"Gina?"

"I can't say anything other than, Angie wanted you to have this." Gina turned over a small, nondescript box wrapped in brown paper to Scooter.

"What is it?"

"I don't have a clue. The only thing she said to me was there would be a message on your birthday."

"What?" Scooter was confused and irritated by the secrecy.

"It's all I know. I have to go now, Scooter. Good luck to you, young man." Gina smiled, and squeezed his arm.

Inside the two-seater car, a disappointed Scooter turned the box over a few times and placed it in the center console. He was annoyed but would deal with that mystery later. He dropped his hat on the passenger seat and fired the throaty car to life.

The vehicle was compact and lightening quick. He had driven it one other time, when Bill had thrown him the keys after he had a larger turbo installed as a "gift" for Jan. Scooter knew this was Jan's car from before their marriage, but Bill had adopted it as his own after the wedding vows. He covered it all of the time with a custom cover and made sure to drive it only on days without a chance of rain. During the winter, the four tires were removed and placed in the basement. A few years after the new turbo, he put a furnace in the garage under the guise of improving his man cave, but everyone knew it was to keep his *"Night Sky"* from freezing. The Sky had thirty-five thousand miles on the odometer and not a single speck of dirt inside or out. The interior still held a new car smell from regular doses of "new-car" fragrance.

Jan must have insisted her brother be allowed to take the car, because Scooter knew Bill would have rather driven him all the way to Texas himself. Sky rumbled out of the lot, the front end bouncing a bit as Scooter got used to the tight clutch and narrow shift pattern.

"This is no pickup truck," he said with a smile, while launching off from a green light with tires squealing, heading to the westbound ramp of Interstate 69.

*

Donna found the address on the tattered mailbox across the street from the house and pulled her unmarked cruiser into the gravel drive, stopping as her lights caught the rusted steel gate protecting the property. Undeterred, she climbed out and examined the chain lock on the post. The lock looked new and the gate was secure. She was going to have to ignore the impediment and proceed to gather her intel in a less "official" way. She convinced herself she was merely concerned for Scooter's safety and needed to inspect his premises to gain information on his whereabouts, or for evidence of foul play. Her boss would look the other way if she could catch a break on the case, as he had several times before on issues with less gravity. Plus, she knew Doug would have her back, no matter what. The thought of him brought a smile and stirred passionate memories from the previous evening's interlude. She was falling for the man and willingly gave herself to him as often as they could arrange the discreet meetings.

Turning her car off, Donna shook herself from the powerful memories. Stepping out, she made her way around the metal gate, through the woods and back to the driveway. She was walking at a deliberate pace, hoping her eyes would adjust to the complete darkness the low cloud cover provided. Gravel crunched beneath her feet as she crept along. Five minutes in, walking among the rows of trees, she smelled fruit hanging above her head. A dog barked off to the south and bats fluttered through the still air above her head. With her eyes adjusted Donna could make out the large covered porch on the house. The windows were enveloped with blank darkness. There wasn't a light to be found in any direction, not even a small indicator LED every home contained for a smoke detector, television, or microwave clock. She decided to walk around the house to make sure nothing was out of place, even though the whole situation was making her skin crawl. Stoking childhood fears, she tromped through tall grass.

Around the south side she ran into a scent, beginning at the front corner of the house and the intensity grew as she made her way back. The nauseating stench announced something living had died. There was no denying the smell of death and it was emanating from a set of ancient doors to the cellar.

Donna flicked her flashlight on and kept one eye closed to maintain partial night vision. The lock in the clasp was secure and the doors would not budge. She pointed the beam into the bushes and flower beds in the area and could not see any bloated animals, which could explain the source of the stench. She went back to the barn and walked around without the benefit of her light. Within five minutes she ended up back at the cellar. She considered the trouble she would create cutting the lock off of Scooter's doors. Donna decided against the move, but would push for a warrant with Doug. It would have to wait until first thing in the morning, because he was home with his family while she was alone in the dark. Donna made for her cruiser.

*

"All of these bags have to be loaded on this truck."
"Okay," Bobby replied to the intimidating man with the dark Zia tattoo on his forearm.
Bobby thought there must have been at least thirty burlap bags in the pile and they all had "100 Pounds" printed on their side.

The man left and Bobby began hefting the pistachio nuts onto the edge of the flat bed then climbing up to slide the bag to the front of the truck. After five bags, Bobby was drenched in sweat and needed to figure out a more efficient way of loading. He settled on lifting four bags then climbing up on the truck and pulling them forward. He was trying to keep the stack neat and orderly for his intimidating boss, Poncho.

The sun was just coming over the front of the ancient truck and beginning to boil the young man's forehead, as he struggled against the weight of the bags. He was thankful for the new job Juanita had helped him secure, but he didn't realize how hard it was going to be.

Thirty minutes later, Poncho returned, as a soaked Bobby was heaving the final bag onto the truck.

"Bobby, this looks real nice."

"Thanks, Mr. Rodriguez."

"You can call me Poncho, son."

"Okay."

"And you are hired."

"I wasn't before?"

"This was your final interview. Too many young people these days don't want to do the hard work. They want to push buttons or be on their phones all of the time."

"Yes, sir."

"Work means sweat, and having a job around here means you will be working, not standing around looking at social media."

"Okay."

"Do you have one of those fancy phones, Bobby?"

"No, I don't have a phone, sir."

"Good. Why?"

"Never had the money to get one."

"Well amigo, now you can earn one, if that's what you want."

"I'd rather have a pickup truck."

"That is a good goal to have." Poncho smiled for the first time, revealing his silver tooth. "I was sorry to hear about your sister."

Poncho had placed his hand on the young man's sweaty shoulder, taking him by surprise.

Bobby's eyes lowered and he nodded his head in appreciation without words.

"So do you have your driver's license yet?"

"I turn sixteen in a few weeks."

"Let's get you some practice, son. I want you to learn how to drive this truck."

"What?"

"Yes. You can stay on ranch property and travel between our three pistachio stands. You are going to have to load and unload these bags. This is our supply barn and from here we keep the stands filled with everything they need. We call this place '*The Nut Shed*' or just, '*The Shed*.' You will be the one driving and delivering everything to them. I have other things to do."

"Okay." Bobby was excited and nervous to drive.

"The truck is old, but she is our trusty '*Mule.*' Most of the time you treat her like your abuela, but there are occasions you have to get a bit mean and force her through the rough places."
Bobby was not sure what he meant, and secretly hoped Poncho would demonstrate before he wanted him to drive her.

"You get behind the wheel."
Bobby gulped, and moved to the *Mule's* driver's door. The door sank and groaned at her hinges as Bobby tugged it open. Cloth was torn from the massive bench seat and pieces of foam were missing. Bobby's backside fell into the seat and he naturally tilted away from the door because of the missing foam. He felt like he was too short for the truck and wanted to sit higher. Poncho led him through the function of the controls of the stick shift and manual breaks.
"There is no radio, no air conditioning, no heater of any kind. You have to check the oil level twice a day out here at *The Shed*. The oil is next to the door in the drum. You also have to make sure she has water in the radiator, which is next to the oil."
"Got it."
"Have you ever checked oil in a vehicle before?"
"Yes, in my mom's car, all of the time."
"Good. You have already surpassed most of the kids in your generation. When we get back I will show you how to check the radiator."
"Okay."
"Let's go." Poncho pointed forward.
Bobby gulped and tried to start the truck without pushing in the clutch, and she lurched forward.
"Ah, lesson number one, amigo— push in the clutch before you turn the key."

*

"Afternoon, how can I help you?"
"Hey, where am I, exactly?" Scooter tightened his hat on his head, scratching at his greasy head.
"You are in Clovis, New Mexico, sir."
"Sorry I'm kinda tired."
"Been driving for a while?"
"Yes, left Michigan yesterday."
"Michigan! Wow, you should be tired."

"I am."
"So, what can I get you?"
"How about a number two with a chocolate shake to drink?"
"Okay, anything else?"
"Directions?"
"Where are you headed?"
"El Paso."
"El Paso del Norte."

Scooter didn't know what she meant. "How far until the alien city?"
"Roswell is about a hundred miles south on US 70."
"Okay, thanks."
"You had better make sure you fill your gas tank. There is nothing between Portales and Roswell."
"Thanks for the tip."
"Sure. If you want to get to El Paso just stay on 70 all the way to Las Cruces, then head south."
"Sounds like a plan. Thank-you."
"Sir, your food is ready." Another girl brought the red tray.
"Thank-you."

Scooter's head was still buzzing with road noise as he ate his burger. It was the first meal he had stopped for the entire ride. The last twenty-six hours had been spent making a mad dash across the country. He had never driven so far in one sitting and was enjoying the sights of the open road. His sister's car was fast and great on gas, but the short wheel base gave it a rough ride, especially on the crummy roads around St. Louis. Scooter's ribs were throbbing again.

He planned on washing up in the restroom before he pressed further west. Scooter knew he was going to have to stop for some sleep before he made it to El Paso, but he wanted to get closer than Clovis. Now, he would have to fill up the car too.

Two and a half hours later, after seeing all of the alien decorations in Roswell on light posts and buildings, Scooter was having a ball, blasting through the curves in the mountains of south central New Mexico. Then, in Ruidoso Downs, Sierra Blanca commanded the skyline and he pulled over to get a better view of her.

"That might be the most beautiful thing I have ever laid my eyes on," he whispered to himself, leaning into the open doorway and pushing the bill of his hat up. He decided to pay for a room at a mom and pop motel a few miles down the road, just outside of town.

From the wooden chair out front of his unit, Scooter watched the sun go down behind the white peaks. He felt this was the first time in weeks he could breathe, although his ribs still reminded him of his recent battles. The bruise was gone from his eye, and the bone was still tender to the touch, but the mountain views washed his concerns to the back of his brain, while peace gripped at his heart.

"This is right where I am supposed to be." He was convinced.

*

"Juanita, where do you want me to put the delivery?"
"Hey, Bobby. Are you here on your own today?"
"Yes, first solo mission."
"When you come to the north stand all of the deliveries get left inside the back door, to the right." She pointed to the spot.
"Good to know."
"If you have a special order, then you have to tell the manager."
"What about the main store?" he whispered.
"Up there you always let them know when you arrive. They will give you a printed invoice. Occasionally they will have you deliver directly to either the north or south stand."
"Okay, I hope I can remember everything!"
"You will have it all down in no time, Bobby."
"I hope so."
"Did you bring the chile with you?"
"Yes, both red and green."
"Good. Can you take one of the big bags of pistachio's up front so we can fill the "Grab-N-Go" bin."
"Sure," Bobby said.

*

Descending the mountain switchbacks into the wide-open spaces, Scooter was amazed by the morning sun reflecting off of a distant band of glistening white sand. With the car windows down, he raced along assisted by the constant, unseen pull of gravity. The breeze buffeting his ear drums and dancing through his blonde hair. The peace from the previous evening was still ruling his heart, even though so many things could have been bothering him. Scooter felt free and let his left arm dance out the window, carried on by the breeze.

Twenty minutes later, traveling south on US 54 he noticed several signs for pistachio stands, with a gigantic green cracked nut for a logo. He was looking for the store as he came around a bend and pulled into the large sandy lot. The intense lime-green building sat a hundred feet from the road. It reminded him of a farmer's fruit stand with all of the produce in an open-air setting resting in the shade of a flat pavilion which extended from the building. The only vehicle he could see was an ancient flatbed, jutting out from behind the building.

Shutting off the motor, Scooter stepped out into the warm sunshine and stretched loud and long. He covered up his wind tossed hair with his favorite brush, his Present hat.

Juanita, from behind the Grab-N-Go bin, almost fell over looking at the stretching man next to the black car.
"Oh, my gosh! Bobby? Is Bobby still here?" she asked the woman sitting at the register.
"I think so," she said.
"Look at the guy by the car and tell me if that isn't an older version of Bobby!" Juanita was trying to be discreet and failing miserably.
"Oh, my goodness. What is that word when two people from different parts of the world look alike?" she asked Juanita.
"Doppelganger."
"That's it!"
"I am going to find Bobby so he can see his long-lost cousin!"
"He doesn't have a license plate on his fancy car," the cashier said.
"Hmm. I wonder why?" Juanita raced through the back door. "Bobby!" Juanita turned the corner as Bobby was getting into the *Mule*.
"Are you calling me, Juanita?"
"Yes. You have got to come up front for a second and see this."
"What is it?"

"It is crazy," Juanita grabbed Bobby by the hand and yanked him into the building. By this time the man from the car was beginning to look through the selection of the stand.

Scooter glanced at the two young workers in the lime green shirts as he turned to look at some of the different flavors of pistachio's.
"Hello," he said.
Bobby stopped in his tracks when he saw the man.
"Can I help you find something, sir?" Juanita asked.
"Just looking around, miss. I needed a break from driving."
"If you need any help, please ask."
"Sure thing. Thanks," Scooter said.

Bobby looked as if he had seen a ghost and the spirit looked just like him. It was an eery feeling for young Bobby to be looking at an older version of himself on his birthday, and he retreated.
"Sir, can I ask you a question?" Juanita returned to the doppelganger.
"Sure."
"You're not from round here?"
"How do you know?"
"You don't have a license plate on your car."
"Ah. I do, but where I am from, they only have them on the back."
"Where are you from?"
"Michigan."
When that word came out of Scooter's mouth, Bobby's head spun and he looked directly at him.
"We only have plates on the rear because of the car companies in Detroit."
"Oh. Well, I was noticing you look just like one of the guys that works here."
"Really?"
"So much like him you could be his brother."
"Bobby. Bobby, come here," Juanita called to him to come out from behind the wall. "Could I ask you for a favor?" she asked Scooter. "It is his sixteenth birthday. Would you take a picture with him?"
"Sure, I can."
"It will be fun!"
"Bobby, come here."
"What do you want, Juanita?"
"Excuse me, what's your name?" Juanita asked Mr. Doppelganger.

"Scooter— my friends call me Scooter."

"I am Juanita and this is the birthday boy himself— Bobby."

"Happy birthday, Bobby." Scooter stuck out his hand toward the uncomfortable kid.

"Thank-you, sir." They shook hands.

"I want to take a picture for your mom. She will get a kick out of this, Bobby."

"She is not going to take no for an answer, son. We may as well get this over with."

"Yes, sir. She is relentless."

The unsuspecting pair posed uncomfortably next to each other with exactly the same silly grin on their faces.

"Thank-you so much, Scooter. You have made my day!" Juanita said with a wink and a smile.

"Happy birthday, Bobby." Scooter nodded.

"Thank-you. I have got to get on the road, Juanita. Poncho is going to kill me."

"Go, birthday boy. Get out of here!"

Turning back to Scooter, Juanita said, "I can get you a discount on anything you want in here, Mr. Scooter." She winked again and bounded away as her shiny, black hair swayed, glistening in the sun.

*

"Kim!"

"Juanita, what are you doing here?" Kim hugged her like she was her own long-lost daughter and Juanita, returning the embrace, relished the affection.

"I have got to show you this."

"You made a trip out to the hospital just to show me something?"

"Yes. You are not going to believe it!" Juanita grabbed for her phone.

"What is it? My break is almost over."

"I will be quick. A man came into the north stand today."

"Was he cute?"

"Yes, but that's not the point."

"It is always the point, Juanita." Kim laughed at her own joke.

"I made him take a birthday picture with Bobby." Juanita handed over her phone.

Kim almost fell over and had to sit down.

"Where did you take this?" Kim asked in slow motion.

"At the north stand, a few hours ago."

"Oh, my God!"

"I know, right? He looks just like Bobby."

"It looks like Bobby is standing next to his father." Kim said.

Juanita couldn't understand the expressions passing over Kim's face as she expanded the photo with her fingers.

"Can you send this to me?" Kim asked.

"Sure."

Silence ruled while Juanita made the necessary clicks to send the photo to Kim's phone.

"What are you doing tonight for dinner?" Kim asked.

"Nothing."

"Can you come over, please?"

"Can we sing happy birthday to Bobby?"

"Yes! I am picking up an ice cream cake after work."

"Sure! It will be fun."

"Great. I have got to get back, but thanks for showing me the crazy picture."

They hugged and left in opposite directions, each filled with confusing emotions over the encounter.

*

For Scooter, the ninety-mile drive south from Alamogordo passed by in a flash, as he was consumed with negative thoughts about his ragtag life in Michigan, and doubts assaulted the validity of his mission.

"Finding Kim is going to be impossible!"

"What are you even doing out here?"

"Jan was right— it feels like I have run away."

These questions and others ping-ponged around Scooters mind. The serenity of the previous day was gone, replaced by indecision and naval-gazing. The realization struck like parting storm clouds; he didn't own the peace he had experienced, but the peace itself had possessed him. On yesterday's porch of the motel, watching the sun set behind the mountains of New Mexico, he had experienced a certainty of being in perfect harmony. God had gifted peace to his weary heart.

"Where has it gone, Lord? I need to find Kim and make this right," Scooter prayed and proclaimed.

Forty-five minutes later he had checked in at his El Paso motel. It was the one he looked up at Matt's house. Then, he remembered the box Gina had given him from Angie, in the console. His heart jumped thinking about what Gina had said to him. *"Something about a message on my birthday,"* he remembered, wiping the chile and lime flavoring from his pistachios onto his pants.

Retrieving the box, he went back to his room in the motor lodge. It smelled of sweat and cologne but was clean, as far as he could tell. The package was the size of a box of checks, which was exactly what was beneath the brown paper skin. Inside the box was a black flip phone wrapped in bubble wrap.

Turing the unit on, it sprang to life and worked to connect with the area network. After a minute a signal sounded the completion of the start-up process. Scooter opened the phone to a striking picture of Port Huron's Blue Water Bridge. He investigated through the programs and the contacts page. There were only two listings— "Friend Work," and "Friend Best." A yellow telephone icon flashed in the lower left corner and he pressed the button, which called voice mail. The inbox needed a four-digit code to open it.
"Why would she give me a phone with a message and not let me access it?" he thought and closed the unit in frustration. He flipped on the television to escape.

A couple of hours later, his mind was numb from the dancing images on the screen, it hit him! *"My birthday!"* He was in.
Angie's voice greeted him, "Scooter, this is Friend Best, and I hope you are well. If you need to talk, you can call me anytime from wherever this adventure takes you. Be careful. Bye for now."

*

"Happy Birthday to yooooou!"
"You guys are weird!" Bobby said, unable to conceal his appreciative smile.
"Hey, we are singing our hearts out here!" Juanita said.

"Happy Birthday to yooooou!"

"The coyotes appreciate the mating call!" Then Bobby howled, mouth pointed to the ceiling.

"Happy Birthday, dear Bobbyyyyy!" Kim was all in on the exaggerated song.

"You are so mean!" Juanita said. "Blow out the candles!"

Tears welled in Kim's eyes watching her son. "I cannot believe you are sixteen!"

"You are not going to get all sentimental on me now, are you?"

"I will if I want to— it is my right."

"The cake is melting," Juanita said.

"Right." Bobby extinguished the candles with one swipe of his breath and the girls clapped.

"I would like a monster piece, Mom."

"Anything for the birthday boy."

"A truck would have been nice." Bobby smiled.

"Open your real present now, the fantasy present later," Kim said pointing with the knife to the package on the table.

"Thanks Mom. I am certain you didn't get a shrink ray and make my truck small enough to fit in this box."

"You are so smart for your age, Bobby!"

They all had a good laugh.

"Fog lights! Cool! Thanks Mom!"

"Sorry, I can't afford the rest of the truck, kiddo."

"I know you can't. I have a job now and am going to save my money."

"See, the way it is supposed to happen," Kim said.

"Blah, blah, blah. Not in Juanita's house!" Bobby said and poked at his best friend.

"She is a spoiled kid. What can I say?"

"Hey now, I am right here." Juanita smiled then stuck out her knuckles toward Bobby.

"Together," they said in unison.

The cake was cut and leftovers were slid into the freezer.

"Bobby, I want to talk to you about something and I want Juanita to listen," Kim said while nibbling at the frozen cake.

"Okay."

"No, he hasn't asked me out on a date, Kim," Juanita laughed.

"You are both my kids and my kids don't date each other. This isn't Kentucky," Kim said.

"Gross. You are a twisted woman," Bobby said.

"Seriously. I have been keeping something from you, Bobby. And now you are of age, it is time I told you the truth."

"What?"

"All of these years I have worked really hard to protect you and Bee. The whole reason we came west was to get you away from a dangerous situation. I was pregnant with you when I left your drunken dad back in the trailer in Michigan."

"I know all of this," Bobby said and shoveled another bite of cake into his face.

"No, you don't."

"He got killed a few years later in a drunken car crash," Bobby said.

"That was the story I told," Kim said and drew in a deep breath. "I knew he would try to come and look for us, so I ran as far as I could. I even changed my name."

"You did?" Juanita said.

"So you changed my name, too?" Bobby frowned.

"Yes."

Bobby stood up. "What is my real name, Mom?"

"You were born Bobby Lawrence."

Bobby sat back down with a blank expression, as his mind churned. "There is more."

Juanita was sitting still, watching the drama unfold.

"Your father is not dead," Kim said and tears ran from her eyes.

"What the hell, Mom?"

"I am so sorry. I thought I needed to protect you and Bee."

"Does this father of mine know about Bee's death?"

"Yes. I talked to his sister."

"I have an aunt, too?"

"And cousins."

"This is messed up. I don't know what to say." Bobby's head was spiraling.

"I know. I am sorry, Bobby. When I saw the picture of you and your doppelganger, it reminded me I had to come clean. I made those decisions as a single mother running from an abusive drunk husband."

"He used to beat you up? You never told me that!"

"He never hit me, but he would push me around. I was scared to death for my kids."

238

Bobby was stunned.

"There is one more thing I need to tell you," Kim was sobbing now. "I didn't want him to come to Bee's funeral."

"Why?"

"Because he didn't know about you, Bobby. I left when I found out I was pregnant. He doesn't know you exist. I didn't call Aunt Jan until three weeks after Bee's funeral." Kim's head dropped to the table and her insides coiled up fetal, in shame.

"Why would you keep this from me? The only thing I ever wanted was a father! I can't stay here with you! You are not my mother!" Bobby raged, threw his remaining cake against the wall, and stormed out into the night, nearly ripping the screen door off its hinges. He paused only to scream as loud as he could on the front porch, his hands balled into tight fists. Juanita put her head down on the table and joined the heartbroken elegy.

*

The three days in El Paso were frustrating, as Scooter ran into dead end after dead end. He was unable to find information about his daughter's death in any Texas record or newspaper. The days melted into one disappointment after another. So in defeat, Scooter headed north out of town early on a calm Sunday morning. As soon as he got away from the glow of city lights, the sky revealed the millions of lights of the Milky Way. The sun was going to be coming up in an hour, so Scooter pulled over and took the removable top off of the car. "*They named the car Sky for this reason,*" he thought while fighting to store the roof panel in the tight trunk.

US 54 made a sharp jog right after he got back to driving and he decided to open the motor up to relieve some pent up frustrations. The turbo spun up and forced him back in the seat. As he reached to shift into third gear, something popped with a loud hiss. Smoke rolled from beneath the hood and Scooter was forced to the shoulder, where he turned the car off and imagined Bill's certain cringe.

"Perfect! Where are you now, God?" Scooter shouted up through the open sun roof while smacking the leather encased steering wheel. The stars' blank expressions didn't respond to his anger and he felt lost. A couple of minutes later, he set the car's flashers and opened the hood to have a look. He remembered he had a flash light in his overnight bag and retrieved it. But it was dead and Scooter threw it as far as he could into the desert night with a primal scream. He was stuck. Scooter sat down and waited for the daylight as weariness and disappointment surged.

Just as the circle of the sun broke the distant mountain tops a tow truck appeared and pulled over in front of Scooter's broken car.
"Hey, am I glad to see you," Scooter said.
"You might not be so happy when I tell you that I am only going north. My garage is in Alamo and I have to be there in a little over an hour."
"The Alamo? Isn't it somewhere in Texas?" Scooter was unaware of the local idiom.
"Alamogordo is where I am going."
"I am still happy!" Scooter said, smiling.
"Tom is my name. It's going to be $150 for the tow."
"Works for me, Tom. I am Scooter."
"You don't sound like "yer from Texas, Scooter." Tom was playing.
"No, I am from up north a ways."
"Your plate says 'Pure Michigan.' Tom was moving out of his truck.
"That's right."
"I do love these vintage Saturn's."
"I do, too, or at least I did."
"What's wrong with her?"
"Think I blew a radiator hose or maybe the radiator itself."
"Okay. Nothin' to get your shorts in a knot about."
"I suppose you are right, Tom."
"I will hook her up and we will be gettin' on our way," Tom said.
"How can I help?"
"Keep the heck out of my way, yankee!" They both laughed.
"If you can get inside your car, I can tell you when to release the brake and take it out of gear," Tom said.
"On it."
The car was loaded, Scooter joined Tom in his cab seven minutes later and the pair was off.
"You been at this for long?"
"Yes, my whole life. My daddy owns the rigs and the garage where we're goin'."
As the tow truck got up to speed, it passed by a white cross surrounded by fresh flowers.

"That has to be the tough part of the job." Scooter nodded to the cross on the shoulder.

"Yes, it is."

"Can't imagine."

"That wreck there was a few years back and if I'm rememberin' right a young girl was killed by a drunk driver."

"You're kidding?"

"Nope."

"Did you go on that call?"

"No, my daddy did. I recall him talking about it though. More people are killed on this road than anywhere else in New Mexico."

"Wait— we are in New Mexico?"

"Yes. The jog in the road a little way back is the state line. The signs got taken out by an accident a few years back."

"You've got to be kidding me?" Scooter said.

"No, why?"

"It's a long story."

"I am all ears Scooter, for the next sixty-five miles. You can start by explainin' your hat."

Scooter filled him in on his tale of woe in El Paso, of Bella and the Present hat.

"A real sad story, Scooter. Do you know why I am hurrying to get back to the Alamo?"

"No clue," Scooter said.

"I play drums at church. The guy who is supposed to be playing decided to have a baby a week early."

"He decided?"

"Well, God did."

"Gotcha. I am a Christian."

"You can come to church. If'n you're not busy, I mean." Tom smiled, enjoying the banter.

"My jammed schedule has recently had an opening for Sunday morning."

Both men laughed.

"It may be Tuesday before we can get your parts to fix her, just being honest."

"Figured it would be something like that."

"We could tow you back down to El Paso this afternoon. They may be able to get you fixed up quicker."

"No, I have had enough of El Paso, Texas."
"If you want to come to church I will give you a ride."
"I am going to need a motel, too."
"I can fix you up." Tom smiled.
"Tom you are a life saver. Let me guess— your daddy owns the motel too?"
"No, that would be my auntie."

*

"I think I saw you sitting by yourself in church today, young man." Scooter looked up from his plate of eggs, bacon, and hash browns to the elderly man standing over him. "You did?"
"I am Willie— most folks call me Old Man Willie but for the life of me I can't figure out why." His smile was broad and bright, revealing a missing front tooth.
"Willie, I am Scooter. Would you care to sit?" He pointed to the empty seat across from him.
"Sure, Scooter, what brings you to our fair city? You should have gotten your breakfast Christmas style," he whispered like the information was a guarded regional secret.
"What does 'Christmas style' mean?" Scooter had leaned forward to ask.
"Both red and green chili sauce smothered over everything, for double the burn." Willie winked and smiled.

"Willie, do you want your breakfast over there?" The waitress was poking fun at the unofficial traveling community relations officer.
"Yes, ma'am, I believe I will."
"Don't be callin' me ma'am, I am not that old, Willie!" She smiled and kept on walking, doing rounds with her coffee pot.

Willie looked back to the man in front of him as he finished up his plate of food.
"My car decided to have its radiator blow, down on 54. Tom towed me here."
"Well Tom does bring in lots of folks to our church that way." Willie beamed with his infectious smile.
"Strays, you mean?" Scooter said.

Willie laughed loud and long. "That's funny. We are all kinda strays until Jesus gets a hold of your heart."

"True," Scooter said. "I have been a stray even after Jesus got me," he added.

"We all learn the hard way, Scooter."

"I know I have spent too much time running away, rather than running to."

"A preacher I heard recently said somethin' 'bout that," the old man said with a snicker.

"You mean today?"

"You are a good listener, young man."

"I am trying to learn, Mr. Willie."

"Sometimes tryin' is all we got. Yes, sir."

"Amen." Scooter nodded.

Silence reigned for a few awkward moments.

"Was you on vacation, down in El Paso?" Willie asked.

"No."

"Not too many folks do that, I suppose." Willie smiled again at his own joke.

"I was looking for my ex-wife."

"Why on earth would you be doing that, Scooter? Most men want to run from those memories." Willie laughed loud and long.

"It's been too long. I need to make things right between us."

"She lives in El Paso?"

"No. I don't know where she lives."

"Oh." Willie paused to think.

"Where are you from?"

"Michigan."

"Michigan! You drove all the way to west Texas without knowing where your ex-wife was located just to tell her you are sorry for the way you treated her a long time ago?"

"That's the crux of it, Willie," Scooter said and pushed his empty plate to the side. "This trip has proven to be another long and dusty dead end road. The story of my life."

"Man alive!"

"Crazy, I know," Scooter said.

"My friend, that is the opposite of crazy— it is an act of present faith!"

"Not too sure about all of that. I know I was an ugly husband back in the day and she never deserved to end up with a man like me," Scooter said.

"Looks to me like the 'old you' got left behind in the dust, a long while back." Willie pointed over his shoulder with his thumb.

"Well I hope and pray it is true, no matter where I call home."

"So, how was you goin' to find this mystery woman?"

"Not too sure. The only clue I had was a few years old and it turned out not to be an accurate assumption on my part."

"Sorry to hear that, Scooter. Real sorry to hear that. Yes, sir."

"Thanks, Willie."

Willie sipped at his coffee, and Scooter swept up his crumbs with his napkin.

"If you don't mind me asking, what clue were you following?"

Scooter looked long and hard into Willies big brown eyes before he said a word.

"My fifteen-year-old daughter was killed in a car accident on US 54 about four years back. I cannot find her records in Texas. Tom said it may have happened across the border in New Mexico, so I have not given up totally on the idea."

"My God, Scooter, I am sorry. The Lord works in mysterious ways, son."

"It must be true, because I don't understand any of this, and I was certain He had me come out here for this reason."

"What if God had a better plan all along?" Willie asked.

"I am praying He does, Willie. I feel like I have been in the fight of my life and now I am swinging at shadows."

"Scooter, I am certain He does! Yes, sir."

*

Chapter Thirteen
***** Star Gazing *****

"Excuse me for a minute, Scooter. I need to talks with someone. I will be back," Willie said.
"Sure thing."
The man struggled to get up from the narrow booth, showing his age. He shuffled across the floor and out of sight.

"Refill on the water?"
"Please."
The waitress returned with a carafe to pour water into his glass. Ice plopped into the cup, splashing speckles of water on the table.
"Where did wandering Willie get off too now?" she asked, and set Willie's hot food plate down.
"I am not sure— he went in that direction," Scooter said, and pointed.
"I will go track him down and let him know his food is not gonna stay hot forever."

Five minutes later the steam had stopped rising off of Willie's Christmas style egg dish. Then he reappeared with a tall slender fellow.
"Scooter, I want you to meet Pastor Jerry."
"Don't get up, Scooter. Can I sit for a minute?"
"Sure. Willie needs to eat. His breakfast is getting cold," Scooter said.
"Don't you worry about that none," Willie said and sat.
"Willie has told me some of your story, Scooter."
"Okay."
"I want you to know there is no judgment from me on any of it," he said with both of his hands raised in front of him.
Scooter nodded his appreciation.
"Can you fill in a few more blanks for me?"
"I have got nothing left to hide, Pastor."
"You can call me Jerry."
"Jerry it is."
"Okay. What did you say that your ex wife's name was?"
"I don't think I said her name. . . maybe I did. Her name is Kim Lawrence, or at least it was Lawrence.
"She came to Alamogordo from where?" Jerry asked, as he leaned in.

"All that I know is she left me in Michigan over sixteen years ago," Scooter said.

"Do you know what she would be doing for a living?"

"I haven't had any communication with her since she left."

"Oh, I see."

"I know she had taken classes back home to become a nurse, but she wasn't finished by the time they left."

"Nursing?"

"Yes. What is this about, Jerry?"

"I have someone in my congregation who might fit the description you gave, but I have to be careful, you understand?"

"Kim won't want to talk to me," Scooter said.

"Sixteen years is a long time, Scooter. What would you want with her if not to talk?"

"I only want to tell her I am sorry and ask her to forgive me for my brokenness."

"Sounds honorable."

"I could just write it down and let you give it to her. If this really is her." Scooter's heart raced.

"So, you are not trying to meet with Kim?

"I would love to see Kim, but I never imagined she would want to talk to me. Heck, I wasn't sure I could find her. I just know I needed to try, so I could tell her. Closure, is what my counselor calls it."

"Okay. Okay." Jerry was thinking. "You told Willie you had children with her?"

"A child, Bella, our daughter. Did Mr. Willie tell you Bella was killed in an accident somewhere on US 54 about four years ago?" Scooter asked.

"Yes he did. I am sorry for your loss. So, no other children with this Kim?"

"No," he said.

"Did you pay child support for your daughter?"

"Yes, still do."

"Really, why?"

"Penance," Scooter said and shrugged.

"How much do you pay, if you don't mind me asking? It could help us make sure."

"I understand. Like I said, I have nothing to hide. I pay $352.00 a month."

Jerry was taking notes into his phone. "Okay. I need to make some phone calls."

"Okay," Scooter said.

"Willie here, said your car broke down?"

"Yes, sir. Tom towed me in and it is at their shop. I imagine it will take a couple of days to get the parts before I am on my way."

"Where will you be stayin'?"

"Tom said his auntie's place. I have no idea where it is."

"Oh, I know. Their motel is north of here. Tom will be over in a bit, I think they are almost finished setting up at church."

"Okay. Thank you. Everyone has been real nice, Pastor Jerry."

"I am glad you have fallen into our laps, Scooter, and I like your hat."

"Thanks," he replied, not knowing what the first phrase meant.

"I will be in touch."

*

"Darrell, you gotta get goin'." Granny was shaking the boy back into this world with both of her scrawny arms, the excess skin under her biceps flapping with the motion.

"What do you want?" protested the boy.

"I want you out of my house and don't you come back anytime soon, you hearin' me, boy?"

"Granny, what did I do?" Darrell rolled over, rubbing the sleep from his eyes.

"Nothin', but you have got to go. Donny is on his way over and he is looking for you."

The fuse ignited in Darrell's heart, and he sprung out of bed.

"He's coming here?"

"Yes. There is a sack of food 'n' stuff for you at the front door-- now you get." Granny had her hands on her hips.

Darrell remained silent as he tugged at socks, pants, and shoes, imagining Donny's face if he caught him.

"Don't you travel on the roads— keep to the woods. Don't look back, son. There is nothin' here for you."

The screen door crashed behind Darrell, as he jumped from the porch and ran to retrieve his backpack from the bushes behind the church. Within moments a car rumbled into Granny's place. Darrell crept to the edge of the bushes, in the shadow of the church, to take a look at dear old dad. Fear surged and pressed against his chest.

Across the street Donny slammed the door of the rusted out beast and bounded up the porch, yelling as he entered. Darrell finished putting his supplies from Granny in the pack and backed away from the building. He made sure to keep the church between him and the snarling monster. He cut through a neighbor's yard, causing a dog to bark. This noise inspired Darrell to run for the woods a hundred yards away. Sliding in behind thick bushes, he tried to catch his breath and watch if anyone had followed him.

"What a way to start the day," Darrell said. He laid on the ground, chest heaving, looking up through the trees, wondering why God hated him so much.

*

"Kim, this is Jerry," he said into the cell phone while walking in circles outside behind his house.

"Hey, Pastor."

"I noticed you sitting in an unusual spot this morning."

"Yes. I needed some alone time," Kim said.

"Is everything okay? I have been trying to call you for hours."

"No, not really," Kim said as her voice cracked.

"What's going on?"

"It's Bobby."

"I am sorry to hear that. What's the problem?" Pastor Jerry asked.

After a pause, Kim said, "I told him about his father."

"What did you say?"

"His dad isn't dead. I had lied to him his whole life. The story I made up was he had been killed in an accident. I have been lying to everyone." Tears fell onto her phone.

"Why did you do it?" Jerry asked.

"Because I needed to protect them." Kim sniffed at the thought.

"I know you, Kim, and I know your desire to protect your kids is who you are. You are a good mother."

"Right now, Bobby thinks I am a monster."

"I am sorry. I don't believe it for a minute and neither does he. He is hurting and he lashed out."

"Thanks. I am sure you are right. What did you want, Pastor?"

"You are not going to believe this. I am not sure if I do, and I met the man."

*

"Millie and Don's Roadside Inn, Tularosa, New Mexico," Scooter said into his "Angie" phone.
"Scooter, I am glad you have landed somewhere," Matt said.
"I am happy I wrote your number down in the front of my Bible."
"Me too. At least New Mexico is a beautiful state to wait for your car to be fixed."
"It is." Scooter shook his head, as he glanced up to the mountains behind the motel.
"I will let Jan know and text you her cell number."
"Thanks, Matt. I appreciate it."
"Talk to you later. Get some rest!"
"Thanks, I will. Bye now."

"Excuse me, sir, I couldn't help but over hear you say the name Scooter. Were you talking to Scooter Lawrence by any chance?"
"Yes."
"I grew up with him. We went to school together," the smiling man said.
"He is a friend of mine, too."
"Small world, standing in line at the grocery store."
"It is."
"I forgot to get bread. You have a good day!"
"You, too," Matt's eyes narrowed.

*

Scooter spent his Sunday afternoon taking naps and staring at the small television screen. Tom had set him up at his aunt and uncle's place for next to nothing. They attended a different church, a Lutheran church in Tularosa but shared his Christ-following faith. They welcomed Scooter with open arms, even brought him a one-person fruit basket to his room, complete with a bag of local pistachios.

At ten after six, a white SUV with blackened windows pulled in front of Scooter's room. Pastor Jerry climbed out from the passenger side and walked over to his door. Scooter pulled on his hat and opened his bright red portal before the man had a chance to knock.

"Hello, Scooter."

"Pastor Jerry, fancy meeting you here." Scooter smiled as uncertainty flooded his eyes and thoughts.

"Yes. I was wondering if we could talk somewhere, outside?" Jerry asked.

"Sure. I noticed a picnic area out back."

"Great. I won't take up too much of your time."

"Okay. What is this about?" Scooter pulled his door closed and walked side by side with the man.

"Well, I wanted to continue our conversation."

"My search for Kimmy?"

"Yes."

They each took a side of a picnic table. There were four wooden tables in the area, all painted a bright red, each facing their own direction with a small play ground for kids in the middle of the arrangement. The large stand of elm trees kept the sun at bay as the men faced each other, alone in the park. Birds fluttered about the trees, inspecting the intruders. The sun was retreating, sending long shadows across the dusty ground. The air was warm, dry, and still, but filled with uncertainty.

"I don't know how to say this to you without sounding crazy," Jerry said choosing his words carefully.

"I can handle crazy— heck— I think I wrote the book," Scooter said with a shortened smile.

"This whole thing has been something." Tears pushed into the corner of Jerry's eyes.

"You can say that again and again. I have not told you half of the things that have been going on in my life lately, Jerry."

"Well this is miraculous— like I have a ring side seat and I am watching from the front row."

"What is?" Scooter asked.

"This whole day."

"It was a good service," Scooter said.

"It was fine, but this thing God is clearly doing here is amazing."

"Okay, time to share." Scooter looked into the man's eyes.

"I talked to a woman I thought may be your ex-wife," Jerry said.

"She doesn't want anything to do with me. . ." Scooter tried to finish Jerry's sentence.

"No. The opposite in fact. I brought her here with me."

Scooter stood up.

"Wait, Scooter! She wants me to make sure this is safe for her," Jerry said, motioning for him to sit.

"Okay, how can I do that?"

"We brought dinner. A couple of big friends and I are going to eat right over there at that table." Jerry pointed.

"You and Kim are going to meet here at this table, then depending on how it goes, you will eat with all of us," Jerry smiled. "Scooter, if any harsh words or raised voices happen, this will all be over, and you will never find her again. We are going to do everything possible to protect Kim, you need to understand."

"I agree. It is fair."

"Okay."

"I can't believe it." Emotion bubbled over, and Scooter started crying.

"I have said those words a hundred times today, Scooter."

"What do you want me to do?"

"Stay here. We are going to bring out the food and when Kim is good and ready, she will come out."

"Sounds good." Jerry dropped a couple of tissues onto the table in front of Scooter.

"She may talk to you or she may not be able to. Do you understand?"

"Yes. Completely."

"I have to make sure she is safe. Can one of my friends pat you down?" Jerry looked into his eyes.

"I have nothing to hide."

"He is a retired cop."

"Okay."

The next four minutes in Scooters mind took two hours. A stern looking bald man came to the table and asked Scooter to stand while he searched him over. He had him empty his pockets, turning them inside out. He felt down his each of his arms and legs, then under his arms and around his waist. The man was professional and without emotion.

"Thank-you," he nodded and moved away giving Jerry a concealed thumbs up.

"Thank-you, sir." Scooter was too nervous to sit.

Then a parade of people carrying food dishes came around the corner, along with cups and drinks. Two women organized the items, as Jerry and a couple men brought more containers from the truck.

"Hi, Scooter. We sure hope you're hungry," said one of the women with a broad smile.

"I am, but I have butterflies and I can't eat just yet."

"Don't you be nervous. Can I pray with you?"

"Yes, please."

She drew up close to him, her fresh vanilla scent preceded her arrival. She placed one hand on his shoulder, raised the other palm up out to her side and bowed her head. "Lord, I thank you for bringing this man to us. We pray you will bless his time with Kim, our precious sister you dropped into our care thirteen years ago. Thank you, God, for allowing us to be witnesses to your mercy and grace today. Bless their time. In Jesus' name, we pray. Oh, and please, bless this food as well. Amen."

"Amen."

As Scooter opened his eyes Kim was standing ten feet in front of him. "Oh, my God." He bent over at the waist, lost his hat and began sobbing. "Oh, my good God."

Scooter wanted to turn from her presence, but knew he needed to face her with all of his emotions.

"Kimmy, you haven't changed a bit," Scooter managed to get out.

"I didn't know if it was you," she said. "They were calling you Scooter, not Ronny."

"The old me— he died a few years back, so everyone calls me Scooter now— well my friends do, at least." Scooter wiped at his face.

"Can I call you Scooter?"

"Please."

"It will be like I am meeting a new person," Kim said.

"You are, Kim."

"Nice to meet you, Scooter. My name is Kim." She smiled, without showing teeth.

"Pleasure to meet you, Kim. Would you like to sit down?"

"Yes, I would."

The ladies in the kitchen crew were already crying, holding their hands over their mouths to avoid interrupting the beauty of the scene.

"Can we wait to eat? I have something I need to tell you," Scooter asked.
"Okay."
"We are going to wait a bit before we eat, but you guys please go ahead and get started," he said to the observation team.
"Okay, Scooter," Pastor Jerry replied and led the troops back to the food table. Two security men didn't budge, but simply stood with their hands in front of them watching Scooter's every move, like they were in the secret service and Kim was their charge.

"Thank you for coming to meet with me, Kim, I know this is a lot to ask."
"I can't believe the timing of this myself," Kim said.
"Up until this morning, I had given up all hope of finding you," Scooter said. "I was headed back home— my plan had failed. Once again God brought me to the end of myself and is showing me good things happen in His time."
Kim listened without reacting.

"Kim, I am sorry for the way I treated you. I was never angry at you. I was a broken man and had no idea what that even meant. I drove you away. I want you to know it was my fault our marriage was destroyed. I did it. It was my selfish attempt to bury my pain. I have no excuse. I am sorry, Kim. I am so, so sorry."

"I cannot imagine the pain you went through in raising Bella alone. Then, to have her taken from you by someone as broken as I was, had to have been devastating. I have no feelings of ill will toward you for not inviting me to the memorial. I have been angry with myself, for being the type of person who drove the love of his life to such a desperate state she had no option but to run away from her drunken husband's issues." Tears and snot ran down Scooter's face.

The praying woman placed a box of tissues on their table, along with his hat, and walked away. Scooter blew his nose free of the mess.
"Sorry. So, with all of that, I pray one day you will be able to forgive me Kim. I know I cannot expect you to, but I hope you will."

Scooter looked up into her eyes, and Kim was crying too.

"Ronny, um, Scooter. Thank you for saying those things to me. It means so much to hear them come from you rather than reading them on a page. The first reason I have agreed to meet with you today is I want you to know I have forgiven you. It took a long time for me to work through it and I still struggle with parts of that life, but overall, I have forgiven you. I chose to forgive you. I know now, when feelings surface from my past, I have to run to the cross to remember whose I am."

"Oh, thank you, Kimmy." His head went down to the table as the five-thousand-pound weight was lifted off his shoulders. Scooter cried without shame.

"You have helped me so much today, Kim. I want to thank you."
"I will need your help, Scooter."
"Name it— how?"
"Don't be so quick to volunteer for this one."
Scooter looked into her tired, red eyes.

"When I left you, I was determined I needed to get away from the partying."
"I know you did."
"I need you to sit and listen, Scooter," Kim looked into his eyes with a determination he had never witnessed before.
"Okay."
"Because I have done horrible, broken things in my life, too."

He opened his mouth and then shut it without a word, trying to give her space. Her blonde hair was cut shorter now and she had put on a few pounds, but this was the miracle he had been dreaming about, and praying for, for the last fifteen years.

"The one thing that made me finally decide to get out was. . . was, the fact that I was pregnant again. I left you to protect a new child. To keep him away from all of the chaos."

Scooter was certain everyone heard the bomb go off inside of his head. He leaned back to take in the thought and looked up to the green canopy

254

above him. He noticed the audience of birds above him but couldn't
hear their songs.

"Yes, Scooter, you have a son I have never told you about."
"I don't deserve this," he said.

Kim had no idea what he meant. "What do you mean?"
Tears streamed down Scooters face as he looked to her.
"This is a gift you have given me. I don't deserve this mercy from God,
or from you."
Now Kim joined the crying.

A minute passed.
"What's his name?"
"Bobby."
"What?"
"Yes, you need to see this." Kim pulled out her phone from her back
pocket and found the picture from Juanita.
"Oh my God. That's my son?"
"You can't deny he looks exactly like you." Kim laughed through her
tears.
"You are right. I was so fixated on finding Bella's death certificate, I
didn't think too much about it."
"You just thought it was a weird coincidence?"
"Yes, and I was tired from driving. But the odd thing, or maybe the God
thing, is I felt none of the peace I had experienced coming into the day
after I left the stand. If I would only listen to Him more, Kim."
"I know just what you mean. I was supposed to tell Bobby about you a
long time ago, but I waited, being stubborn— always finding an excuse
to not do the hard things."
"So, he doesn't know I am his father?"
"No. Not really. Let me explain."

Kim guided him through the story up until Bobby ran out of the house.

"You haven't seen him in a few days?"
"No, but I have a good spy. She knows where he is holding up."
"And?"
"And he needs a little time to process through my deception."
"Okay, I understand."

"He trusted me and I betrayed him. He has always longed for a father. Bobby is a good kid and he needs his dad," Kim said.

"You trusted me, Kim, and I betrayed you a thousand times."

Kim looked through Scooter, trying not to focus on past pain.

"What ever you want to do," he said.

"He needs a healthy dad, Scooter. Ronny has to be dead. I have to make sure it is true before I let you in."

"I get it. It's my fault, Kim, not yours. I would have kept Bobby away from Ronny, too."

"Thank you for saying that," Kim said and grabbed a tissue.

"Thank you for telling me about Bobby."

"Can you forgive me for running away and lying for so long?" Kim asked.

"I will never forgive you for running away, Kim, because you did the right thing."

"I have struggled. I have struggled with the decision."

"Will you forgive me for hiding for so long and not coming after you sooner?"

She thought about that for a few moments. "I wasn't ready," she said. "It wasn't the right time."

"I wasn't ready, either," he said.

They both laughed at the irony.

"I can't believe how God made all of this happen— the timing was perfect."

"Us either!" people eating in the group said.

"Can I bring you some food?" asked the praying lady.

"Yes."

"Sure."

*

The black pickup sat idling in front of Millie and Don's Roadside Inn at 3:30 a.m. Inside, four Denton friends hatched their plan.

"I know that is the car Lawrence left Port Huron in," Tums said, pointing to the two door coupe.

"It confirms the call I got is accurate," Johnny said.

"If you are sure, I want Johnny and J-Law to go welcome our former friend to New Mexico the proper way," Jet sneered.

"On it boss!" J-Law said.

"Are you certain this is our best play?" Johnny Dog questioned Jimmy.

"This is only our first play, Dog. Now go make it happen— I am counting on you. We need Mr. Lawrence to be on his way, headed out of town, before he gets any more crazy ideas rolling around in that tiny little brain of his."

Both of the passenger doors opened and yet the interior lights remained off.

"You ready for this, Dog?" J-Law asked.

"I have been waiting for this moment for a long time."

"Yeah. My legs are numb from that long ride."

"Who runs away to Texas, anyway?"

"Right?"

"So, are we going in the front? Or do we sneak around back?" Dog asked.

"Front. He will be sleeping. We will be on him before he knows it."

"Look what I have for our old friend." The brass contours around his knuckles sparkled in the streetlight.

"He will never know what hit him," they laughed together with a nervous edge. The two Denton boys approached the third door on the left, across the parking lot from the office.

"Ready?"

J-Law reached for the handle, twisted, and pushed the door into the darkness. A beam of low light followed them from the motel sign on the front lawn, splashing inside the room. The pair stepped inside and eased the door shut behind them, cutting off the light. They stepped closer to the first bed and listened for breathing rising from the pile of blankets, over the hum of the air conditioner beneath the window. The curtains ruffled in the breeze of the blowing fan, and the pair didn't hear any of the rhythmic breathing they expected.

As confusion spread over them, an intense beam of light lit up their faces in the darkness, temporarily blinding the stalkers. Some people say there is a slight whistle that forms when a baseball bat is swung hard enough, not usually heard until the split second before the wood connects with the ball. There was no baseball in the room. Scooter was prepared for the onslaught and met it head on. J-Laws melon was the first target for the slugger and the bat cracked his forehead so hard parts of his brain were launched out of his ears. He fell with an abrupt thud to the carpet.

Johnny dove for Scooter's injured ribs with his shoulder, slamming the man back into the television, knocking it onto the floor. Just before the contact Scooter was able to protect himself by lowering his arm to cover his wound. Scooter grabbed a hold of his attacker, riding him to the ground with his momentum. What Johnny had forgotten in the rush was the bat Scooter clung to. Scooter allowed his hand to slide up the shaft closer to the barrel, shortening his grip. They fell on their sides facing each other, and Scooter began slamming the bat into the back of Dog's head. Three, four, five hits and Johnny was losing his grip on the target and his own vision.

"How did you know?" is all Dog could manage to get out of his mouth. "You guys are so predictable. I was ready for you this time!" Scooter's exclamation point was on the side of Johnny's temple, silencing him. He stood over his Denton buddy, raised the bat over his own head and drove it down into Dog's face three times.

Scooter slouched to his bed, breathing heavy, and nodding at his bat in appreciation.

*

"Poncho, I know he is out here." Kim pushed past the muscular man, who was conceding ground to the determined mother. "Bobby, I know you are here. I need to talk to you. I am not asking you to come home. I need to tell you what has happened."
Poncho walked away from the pole barn, knowing better than getting in the middle of a family fight.

"What do you want, Mom?"
"Please come here. I need to talk to you for a couple of minutes, then I will leave you alone."
Bobby came out from the shadows of some stacked pallets of bagged pistachios as ordered.
"What is it?" he said, trying to remain ambivalent.
"I have some news."

"About?"
"I don't know how to start."
"You came to me, Mom."
"It is a miracle in my mind, and in the minds of a lot of people we know."
"What is a miracle?"
"You know what we talked about on your birthday?"
"How you lied to me?" Bobby said, as his anger flared.
"Yes, I did lie because I was trying to protect you."
"I should have been able to make my own decision, Mom!"
"You are right. I was supposed to tell you when Bee died, but I was too afraid and I chickened out."
"Not cool." Bobby folded his arms in front of his chest.
"I know. I am sorry."
"I am really struggling with this." Bobby's face fell.
"I know you are."

He looked at the dirt around his boots while leaning against the stack of burlap bags.
"You know how Pastor Jerry says God works things out in His way and at His time?"
"I guess."
"Ask me who I meet yesterday? Go on ask me."
"Mom, I don't want to play your little guessing games right now."
"Okay. Well, I sat and talked, for the first time in over sixteen years, with your father."
"What? You called him?"
"I ate dinner with him."
"I thought he lived in Michigan?" Bobby's eyes grew wide.
"He does."
"I don't understand."
"Let's just say, God brought him to us."
Bobby didn't know what to think or say, while his eyes darted at the information.
"I wanted to tell you and not hide it from you. Let you make your own mind up. Would you like to talk to him?"
"More than anything."

*

Fifty yards beyond the playground, surrounded by the four red picnic tables where Scooter had reunited with Kim eight hours before, a deep ravine ran east to west. During the rainy season it roared with frothy mountain water, cascading over scattered boulders. Scooter grunted as he hauled his two lifeless friends, one at a time, to the edge of the precipice. With two swift kicks, he knocked each of the bodies over the edge of the canyon, into the blackness below. They bounced and rolled down out of sight, swallowed by the abyss. Scooter erased his footprints with a tree branch and paused in the shadows to make sure no one had been watching. After he caught his breath, he made his way back to his room, where he gently clicked the deadbolt and fell into a deep, dreamless sleep.

*

Chapter Fourteen
* Rising Star *

Pale dust billowed out behind the car as it raced up the winding road. Scooter was searching for the trailhead Kim had texted him about an hour ago. The road was rough, not the kind of surface the low sitting coupe was built for, but Scooter didn't care one bit. Kim had invited him for a morning walk and he was determined to make it on time. The directions he had scribbled down lacked a few details, like distances between turns. So Scooter was frustrated with himself and pushed Jan's repaired car up the washboard road.

"Bridal Veil Falls— thank you, God!" he muttered as he read the brown sign.

He turned north and pulled into the parking area two minutes later. He was the only vehicle and thought he had arrived first, except for the attractive blonde standing by the trailhead sign with a smirk. Scooter smiled and locked the car.

"I thought I beat you up here," he said smiling.

"I bet you did," she said.

"How did you get here?"

"My best friend, Patty, dropped me off."

"Are you okay with just the two of us walking out here?" he asked.

"You haven't turned into an ax murderer have you, Scooter?"

"Not this morning." He smiled at her again.

"I am packing, just in case you did."

Scooter did a double take at the thought of his ex-wife with a handgun.

"So, is that your car?" she asked.

"No, it is Jan's."

"Really?"

"Yeah, she splurged after college and bought it, then she met Bill, who became her husband. He has taken over the care of it. He treats it like it's his baby."

"He would love how clean it is right now." She smiled, and looked at her feet.

"No, but he would be more appalled at how hard I drove on the road to get up here," Scooter said.

"So, how is Jan doing?"

They began their walk, which was a seven-mile loop and would take them four hours to complete. Kim was hoping to get a better feel for how her ex-husband was doing, away from the crowd of the community dinner a few nights before. She knew this man a long time ago and loved him with his flaws, up until he became the monster who almost destroyed her life. Now armed with her faith, a few good friends, and a pistol, she wondered what God was doing.

"Do you remember the trailer we had?" she asked.
"I still own it."
"You are kidding me?" Kim was only slightly stunned.
"Nope. But there isn't anything left of it right now."
"Huh?"

The explanation surrounding those events took almost two miles of trail to work through. Kim had many questions along the way, and Scooter did his best to answer them for her.

"I want to tell you the whole story surrounding the chaos and what brought me to trying to find you and I will do that when you are ready."
"Okay," she said. "Jerry said you were going to counseling?"
"Yes, and she is the reason I am standing here."
"Why?"
"Angie is tough. She never lets me wallow in self-pity. She asks insightful questions, things I have run away from my whole life. We have talked about everything, even things I didn't know were bothering me, back from when I was a kid."
"What does it have to do with today?"

"She taught me our coping mechanisms are formed early in our lives and influenced by many factors we don't always have control of. So, because of that, I have spent much of my life allowing my eight year-old self to dictate how my adult life was lived. It's only when I began getting some healing from my past hurts that I could fight against the constant pull back into addiction every time something went wrong."
"How does it work, Scooter?"
"When I experience a stressful event, I have to allow myself to feel the emotions. I do that by saying what I am feeling, out loud. Like, "I feel abandoned again" and admit it to God. Knowing my emotions don't

make God mad or disappointed, I am free to be honest with Him and myself."

"That's a good thing. Is that what the hat is for?" Kim said, while lifting her chin toward his head covering.

"Yes, I need to be present, but it's not the most important thing."

"What is?"

"The most important thing is hearing the truth from God about who I am, in the middle of feeling those negative emotions."

"Okay," Kim said.

"I need to remind myself all of the time of who I really am, in God's view."

"Hmm." Kim was considering the thought.

"Angie has taught me to ask myself, 'How does God view me right now?'"

"Does it help?"

"It has made all of the difference, not in asking the question, but in the answer of how God sees me."

"Why the distinction?"

"Asking questions is important, but hearing what the King of the Universe thinks of me, is life changing. The challenge is believing what God says about me, not what my circumstances say."

"So how do you know what He is saying about you?"

"Time in the Word, being quiet and present before Him. A good accountability relationship is key."

"It sounds like Angie has helped to you."

"She has and so has Matt."

They arrived at the falls and paused at the sight of the cascading water.

"I need to tell you about the little boy at our work site," he admitted.

"Okay."

Scooter went into detail describing the events surrounding the boy's death, finding him stuck on the stake, the police questioning, and falling off of the wagon.

"So what was all the Angie stuff about? I thought she helped you?" Kim pushed, as the old familiar feelings invaded.

"She did, Kim. I failed."

"How many times have I heard it before, Ronny?"

"Too many to count." Scooter winced at the slight.

"I thought you put that way of life behind you?"

"I have and I am. I could have lied to you like I always did in the past. I told you, Kim, because I am committed to not keeping secrets."

Kim was quiet for a time, watching the water splash on the rocks and foam in the pond beneath the falls.

"I am not asking you for anything other than forgiveness, Kimmy— which you have said you have already done. I am eternally grateful. I want to be honest with you and I promise I will be. I am not perfect. I still struggle with things in my life but I am so blessed you would ask me here today."

"You are right. Ronny would have never told me anything bad about his life. Thank you, Scooter. I am not your judge and I am not your wife."
"Thanks."
"Thanks for being honest with me. I was worried you would paint too rosy of a picture of your life. I am trying to look out for Bobby."
"It has been anything but rosy lately, and I know you love our son."
Scooter liked saying the term, "our son."

"Ready to finish the loop?" Kim asked.
"Sure."

"Why do you still wear the wedding ring?" Scooter asked.
"Keeps the weirdo's away!"
They laughed together.

*

"I went on a hike with Kim today."
"No kidding? How did it go?" Matt asked.
"It was good, really good."
"How long of a hike was it?"
"We were out about four hours. There is something she told me— it shocked me."
"What?"
"When she left me, it was because she was pregnant. As it turns out, I have a sixteen-year-old son."
"No way! How do you feel about that?"

"Well, I am going to meet him in about fifteen minutes, but I was overwhelmed. It's a blessing for me, I hope it will be for him, too."
"We will be praying about your meeting, Scooter. What's his name?"
"Bobby."
"So, are you angry about the time you missed with him?"
"Only at myself. I wasn't ready to be a father when we had Bella."
"Are you beating yourself up?"
"Not really. I had some attacks last night I had to fend off. It was intense, but I was more prepared for it, like you told me to be."
"Knowing how your enemy attacks your weaknesses is important, and responding with the truth is your best weapon against them."
"I am beginning to grasp the concept."
"Good, and you cannot let your guard down, Scooter."
"Thanks for praying, Matt, and for the money and the hat. It helps remind me. I am using some of the money to take Bobby pizza."
"You're welcome, Scooter. Have a good time tonight."
"I will. Talk to you soon."
"Later, buddy."

*

The nights were beginning to get cool, too cold to sleep under the stars without any protection, so Darrell was looking for a place to hole up for a while. He was moping through a section of woods a few miles from Granny's place, wondering what had come of his mom.
"She would look for me," he muttered, then he thought of the danger she faced from Donny and he wanted her to steer clear of him.
"Granny knows how crazy he is, but even she wouldn't stand up to him for me. I am a worthless piece of crap," he thought, as tears ran down his face.

He came to the edge of a farmer's field. It was filled with a dark-green plants and bounded by thin rows of woods on two long sides. Off in the distance was a sun bleached barn and a house. Darrell decided to keep to the woods and get as close to the barn as he could. It was raining out and his clothes were soaked.

Twenty minutes later he was perched below a pine tree watching the house and barn for activity. There was a small orchard in the front and on the south side of the house, with more trees beyond that. He couldn't see any roads, only a driveway interrupted the woods in front. Darrell was cold and wet below the tree. He only waited ten minutes before making his way to the barn. He stood in a large bush at the corner of the weather-beaten building for a few minutes. He saw the lock on the sliding barn door and his heart sank. A stiff wind was blowing and Darrell was ready to give up. He sat with his back against the old wood and put his face into his hands.

"Why do you hate me? Why do you all hate me so much? I didn't mean for him to die. I even tried to help him. He was dead already. He was dead, with the one in the head." His angry line from shadows of the garage echoed through his heart again. He could feel the knife in his hands. *"Two in the chest and one in the head."*

Darrell fell over on his side as fat rain drops pelted his face, mixing with his salty tears. A gust of wind shook the barn behind him and the sliding door slammed against its frame. Another blast, another knocking of the door. Darrell looked down the wall and along the underbelly of the slider. The next gale pushed the bottom away from the side of the barn and his head tilted with a thought. The blowing continued and it brought him to his feet. He was certain no one was home and the trees blocked the neighbors view, so he walked over to the sliding door and pulled out as low as he could. The door was heavy but it moved with his tugging. He removed his pack and set it next to the him. Darrell pulled the bottom and kicked his pack behind the opening he made. A smell of hay puffed out from the portal as he forced his way in over his backpack.

A half an hour later he had fought his backpack up into the loft and collapsed on a stack of rectangular hay bales. As rain pinged out nature's sonnet on the metal roof above him, Darrell's broken heart was hypnotized into a deep sleep.

When he woke, hunger churned inside of him and he dug through the pack for a cold can of ravioli from Granny. The pull lids made making dinner easy. After licking the can and his spoon clean, Darrell went exploring in the expansive barn. In a corner of an old stall he found a small pile of canned goods, jerky, candy bars and multiple varieties of sports drinks. It was a gold mine of good fortune and Darrell couldn't believe his luck.

"Thanks," is all he could manage to say to the metal ceiling high above his matted head.

*

As Scooter pulled in front of the building with *"Nut Shed"* painted on the front, he took a deep breath, uncertain of what awaited him. A broad Hispanic man was in front of the same truck Scooter had seen before. The man was at the entrance of the open sliding door standing below his sweat-encrusted, dingy-white cowboy hat. He was visibly wary of Scooter, like he was protecting his prized employee from an unknown predator.

"Hey, are you, Poncho? I am Scooter."
"Hello."
Scooter was holding two pizza boxes and a plastic bag with three soft drinks.
"Bobby is inside. He is pretty nervous to meet you," Poncho said.
"Truth be told, so am I."
"He is a good kid, and he works hard."
"I am glad to hear that. Thank you for looking out for him," Scooter said.
"It is my pleasure. It is hard to find young people who want to work hard these days."
"True. We can't find any in my trade."
"What do you do?"
"Concrete work."
"Hard work."
"It is, and not many want to do it."
"Let's go inside so you can set that stuff down on the bench," Poncho said smelling the food.
"I brought enough for all of us Poncho I hope you will join us."
"Gracias, señior."

They stepped through the cavernous opening and twenty feet back was a ten foot long, well organized workbench, complete with an ancient vise on one end and a drill press on the other.
"You can set it there," Poncho said, and pointed.

"Bobby!" Poncho called out through cupped hands, into the depths of the darkened building. Off in the opposite corner was a pickup truck with the front end hoisted up on ramps.
"He is changing the oil in the pickup truck."
"Great."
"Bobby!"
"Yeah?"
"Someone is here to see you and he brought food."
"Okay. I will be right there." Bobby came sliding out from beneath the truck on a creeper, while holding a blue rag and grease gun. Wiping his hands on another rag he approached Poncho and the man he posed in a picture with.
"There is no denying the relation," Poncho said with a smile and laughed a deep belly laugh.
"Hi, I am Bobby. It's nice to meet you— again."
"Hello, Bobby. I am Scooter— the pleasure is mine." He offered his hand to the younger version of himself, with a smile.
"My hands are greasy." He hesitated.
"I don't mind one bit."
The two shook hands and looked at each other for a long moment before letting go.

"I want to tell you I am sorry, Bobby."
"For what? I just met you."
"Sorry for being a messed-up guy."
"I don't know much about you," Bobby said and stuffed the rag into his back pocket.
"I know you don't. I made many poor decisions for too many years. It got so bad a pregnant young woman had to run away from her husband. So I did change your life."
"It was always normal to me," Bobby said, and shrugged.
"All I am saying is, I wish I had my stuff together a long time ago-- because I missed so much of your life." Tears slid down his cheeks.
"Thanks."
"Are you hungry?"
"Always."
"Do you like pizza?"
"It is my favorite food group."
The two laughed and Poncho faded into the background.

"Poncho, I brought enough for you, too," Scooter said.
"Thank you, I will grab a piece, then I have to make a phone call."

"Take a pop, too."
"Pop. You two even sound alike," Poncho said.
"They call it soda out here."
"They are wrong," Scooter said with a smirk.
"I keep telling them," Bobby said.
"You have a Tigers hat," Scooter said.
"Yeah, my favorite team."
"Cool. Mine, too."

There were two stools in front of the work bench and the men sat and ate their first meal together. They spent the afternoon talking and laughing about many things, including Bella. The stories caused another level of peace to fall over both of their wounded hearts. God, in His timing, brought renewal through this connection of two lonely men.

"I hear you are angry with your mom."
"I was. She has lied to me for my whole life."
"If you want to be angry, that is up to you but you need to know I was poison, and she was right to run away to protect you kids. I was acting like an idiot— a broken man— by being a drunk all of the time."
"She didn't have to lie to me."
"You are right."
"I am having a hard time letting it go," Bobby admitted.
"I am sure. When people close to us act out in broken ways, it hurts."
"Yep."
"Do you normally run away for days on end?"
"No, I never have."
"You are making my point," Scooter said.
"How so?"
"Your mom got married to me and we were in love, then I betrayed her trust and she was crushed everyday for years. So, she ran away, something she had never done before and never had intended to do before I had hurt her."
"So, I am her now?"
"No, you aren't, but brokenness hurts people, Bobby."

He thought about what Scooter had said.

"I love her, and I really wanted to know my dad."

"You seem like a good kid, Bobby, and I want to be a part of your life but I can't force my way in. I want to know you. But it is not all rainbows and butterflies. I have been a horrible person for most of my life, and God in His mercy never gave up on me. For me, meeting you, is a new lease on life. There have been a lot of miles of pain to get me here today, and I never want to go through it again, but I am here right now."

"I am thankful you are. It is an answer to a prayer I have been saying my whole life."

"I am sorry I was so bull-headed that God had to break pieces of me off before I was ready to be your dad, to be Bella's dad."

"I am glad you are here now," Bobby said.

"So am I. I think your mom deserves your forgiveness, too."

"She does."

"When we are done, I will drive you home, if it's what you want."

"I am sick of sleeping in this barn."

"I bet you are. So tell me about the truck you are working on."

*

"Cut the lock," Donna called to the uniformed officer standing by the metal entry gate.

The three cars rolled onto G-Ma's property with no fanfare or flashing lights.

"We are gathering evidence for the investigation into the missing child, the death of another child and the explosion at the trailer park. We are not— I repeat, we are not— tossing the place in some sort of vendetta. Do I make myself clear?" The officers nodded in agreement.

Darrell heard Donna's announcement from inside the barn and ran back to his belongings in the loft. Frantically he moved a couple of bails of hay and ditched his stuff beneath. As he moved the second bale, an idea came to him. If he switched the direction of two bales over the top of a missing bale in the stack it would created a place for him and his pack to fit beneath. Darrell deposited his pack in the space, got in, and pulled the bale over his head, hoping he had remembered to pick up his mess.

"We need to start over at the cellar entrance. There was something stinking up that area."

Two minutes later, the cop with the bolt cutters snipped off the lock to the cellar. Another officer pulled open the tilted door as a third cop trained his weapon into the dark space. The stink was overwhelming.
"Detective, we have located the source of the odor."
"What is it?"
"A dead raccoon, ma'am."
"What? How would a raccoon get trapped in the cellar?"
"Do you want me to cuff him?" All the cops busted out laughing.

"You have jobs to do— get to it," Donna barked.
"Bolt cutter guy, go get the barn opened up."
"Yes, ma'am."

Darrell was restless in his hideout. Then it hit him— the empty ravioli can with his spoon was sitting out next to the beam. He pushed hard at the bale and it slid off of the other. Darrell looked like a scarecrow with all of the hay sticking to his head as he tiptoed over to the pole. As he reached to grab the can, he heard a loud metallic snap coming from the front of the barn. Peering down into the open area the door magically slid open, bathing the interior in afternoon sunlight. An officer was looking up in the boys general direction and Darrell froze. The cop continued scanning the interior of the barn, not noticing the scarecrow of a kid and his wide eyes in the loft. Darrell slid behind a bale and made his way back to his hideaway, his heart beating out of his chest.

Two hours later, Donna had more questions than answers. The barn looked clean but it was filed with hay. The weights in the cellar were recently cleaned off. There was a damp spot that smelled like bleach in the dirt next to a round circle made from one of the weights, which were neatly stacked next to the bench. The dining room table lay smashed to pieces on the main floor, pointing to a recent altercation. The place was a wreck, but there was only circumstantial evidence pointing at nothing conclusive.

"Where are you, Scooter?" Detective Donna McBride was stumped. Leaning up against her squad car, she reread her note book for anything she may have missed. Ten minutes later Donna realized she did have an open lead she had failed to write down. *"I need to find the counselor."* She scribbled the word "counselor" and circled it five times with three bold exclamation points.

In the barn, after the last car rolled out of the yard, the young runaway had spent his waiting time planning. He was going to build a hidden area he would use as a safe house. Darrell envisioned tunnels and rooms deep down inside the pile. He figured it would give him something to do instead of thinking about his mom and Ronnie all of the time. The recurring dreams were appearing every night and he wasn't getting enough sleep. *"At least I am warm and dry,"* he thought, while crunching through his third fresh apple. Now he needed to build his hideout so no one would ever find him again, then he would go explore the house.

*

The triple black Saturn Sky Coupe sparkled in the early morning light. Scooter had spent a couple hours on Saturday cleaning the car inside and out, even waxing the exterior. He thought it looked better than when he had removed the cover in Jan's garage a week ago. He was a man on a mission this morning, knowing he only had fifteen minutes before he needed to meet Kim in front of their church.

Twelve minutes later, he rolled into the parking lot and chose a spot in the far corner to back into. There, a small tree would keep the morning sun from overheating the interior of Bill's sparkling baby.

Scooter was carrying a coffee and a hot chocolate as he walked toward the front doors. The church was nontraditional in its appearance, looking like it had been transformed from an old strip mall into the church campus. Large-lime green and yellow signs welcomed everyone, directing the foot traffic inside.

Scooter was wearing the best clothes he could come up with on short notice. Kim had invited him last night to attend the morning service with her and Bobby. He ended up running to a gift shop, and settled on the emerald green polo shirt embroidered with "White Sands National Park" over the heart, along with some new deodorant. He decided the people of Alamogordo wouldn't mind his Present hat, so he wiped it free of dust and put it on.

Just inside the open doors Kim was waiting with Bobby at her side. She had a breezy summer dress on along with make up and curled hair. Scooter noticed those things first off. He was still deeply attracted to her but needed to remain focused on reconnecting.

"Morning guys,"
"Morning," they both replied.
"Coffee, Kim?"
"Yes, please," Kim responded.
"I'm not a coffee person," Bobby said. To which Scooter produced a cold pop from his back pocket.
"How about this? I am not a coffee guy either."
"Sure, thanks."
"Thank you," Kim said.
"My pleasure."
"You weren't kidding in your text describing this place as not looking like a church building. I was here last week and didn't notice those things. I came with Tom and we were talking and I wasn't paying attention.
"Right. Tom knows how to talk! Just a few years ago, this was a strip mall that wasn't doing so well. The church started with one storefront fifteen years ago. Then the owners of the property died and his kids wanted out, so they sold it to the church for a deal."
"Nice."
They all sipped at their drinks.
"How was sleeping in your own bed, Bobby?"
"Amazing."
"Are you two doing any better?"
"Yes, we had a few long talks. Thank you for bringing him home," Kim said.
"I was nervous you wouldn't be ready for me to know where you live," Scooter said.
"It is not hard finding where people live these days, plus did I mention I have a gun?"
"That is true, I suppose, even though I am not good at computer stuff and, yes, the gun has come up a few times."
They chuckled.

"Hey, Scooter, good to see you here with these guys," Pastor Jerry said. He was already wearing a lapel mic.
"So, you are on today?" Scooter looked to the mic.
"Yes, I speak most of the time."
"Good to know," Scooter said.
"How are you doing, Bobby?"
"Good, Pastor. Thanks."
"I will catch up with you guys after the service?"
"Sure," Kim said.

During the next few minutes of small talk Scooter couldn't help but notice many people were watching and glancing over at the three of them. He caught several making comments to significant others while pointing with their eyes.
"Looks like the new guy is the talk of the town," Scooter whispered to Kim and Bobby.
"They are calling you the miracle dad."
"What? Why?"
"Just how God worked everything out, with the timing and all."
"They should be calling God the miracle worker," Scooter said.
"They recognize who is responsible," Kim said.

Scooter never had been involved in a miracle before and he smiled at the thought. Standing in front of him was Kimmy and a son he never knew he had. One week ago he was retreating from El Paso an angry defeated man, wondering where God was.

"Who is this young man you have with you, Kimmy?" Kim was going to introduce him to Scooter but Willie grabbed onto the man with a happy hug.
"It is good to see you today, Scooter!"
"Thanks Willie. It's good to be seen."
"You two know each other, I take it?" Kim asked, with a raised eye brow.
"Yes, we had breakfast together last Sunday."

"Hey, Scooter, how you doin'?" Tom held out his hand.
"Morning, Tom. Not working today?"
"Nope. Someone else is picking up the strays on 54."

"Funny, real funny." Scooter said.
"I gotta go play. Talk to you later?"
"Sure."

"My, aren't you Mr. Popular?" Kim said with a grin.
Bobby and Scooter laughed with exactly the same cadence, volume, and sound.
Kimmy rolled her eyes, and went toward the bathroom.

*

"Hello?"
"Hello, Scooter!"
"Hi, Angie. How are you doing?"
"I am good. I was just wondering about you. How are things?"

Scooter could not contain himself and gushed over with stories for the next hour, giving Angie all the details he could remember from his ten day adventure.

"That is miraculous, Scooter."
"Indeed," he said.
"So, what are your plans now?"
He hadn't spent too much time on thinking about the future when the present was so ripe with newness and optimism.
"I am not sure what to do next," he admitted.
"One step at a time, my friend," Angie said.
"I want you to know how appreciative I am for all that you have done for me, Angie."
"You have done the work."
"You have been my guide through my broken wilderness."
"You are a good man, Scooter, and I want you to be reminded God didn't waste His time investing in your life."
"Thank-you, Angie."
"It's been my pleasure."

*

"Patrick!"
"Yeah?"

"Pack your rack."

"What?" Tina asked.

"Pack your rack— you are getting out of here. Your bond was posted."

"Yes, ma'am!"

Tina's head was swirling. This proclamation came out of left field. She had resigned herself to spending the entire time in jail while she awaited trial. But someone had made her bail.

Who?" was the nagging question, as she stripped off her orange county jail suit and slid back into her own clothes. The deputy watching and waiting for her to finish held a clip board. Tina assumed it had her information on it.

"Does it say who made my bail?" she asked, while buttoning her stained and faded blue jeans.

"Not on this paperwork. You can ask at the front desk."

"Okay."

"You should be happy you are getting out of here."

"I am, but my ex is looking for me. It's not good."

"I am sorry."

"Thanks."

"Ask Cindy up front, she should be able to tell you who made your bail. If there is a problem we can help you sort it out— just let us know."

Out in front of the county correctional facility, sat a four-door, rusted out, beast of a car, with two occupants, both smoking cigarettes, and waiting.

*

Chapter Fifteen
✳ North Star ✳

The campfire crackled with life as the dried kindling did its job. Sparks flew skyward, racing into the cool, clear night. Two one-person tents were set up fifteen feet from the fire ring, as flickering shadows danced their way across the green and beige nylon. The bed of the pickup truck held a face cord of wood, and a white cooler was perched on the tailgate. It had taken Scooter considerable time to get the fire going Bobby reminded him they were camping out at almost 9,000 feet, so fires were harder to start with the the altitude and higher humidity of these mountains.

"Were you in Scouting?" Scooter asked.
"Yes, for five years, through the church."
"Then what was I doing lighting the fire?" Scooter smiled.
"It seemed like you wanted to do it."
"Man-pride thing, I guess. I am sorry— I should have let you build it."
"No big deal," Bobby said.

The pair settled in after getting their camping oasis organized over the last hour. Now relaxing by the fire, they were silent for a few minutes, enjoying everything about the moment they shared.
"The sky is clear tonight— should be lots of stars."
"Alamo gets three hundred sunny days a year. It rains more up here in the mountains, but there are always great nighttime views."
"I like Alamo. It's a small city, like Port Huron," Scooter said, as they both glanced toward city lights which were visible to them, glowing a soft white, near the western horizon.
"We don't have any big water like you do," Bobby said.
"Lake Huron does makes it a special place to live."
"I would like to see it," Bobby said.
"I was sitting on the beach a couple of weeks ago."
"What were you doing?"
Scooter paused as he considered the memory. He knew he needed to let Bobby in.
"I was finally saying goodbye to your sister."
"Really?"

"I know— you are probably thinking it took me a long time."
"I just never considered it would be difficult for someone so far away, I guess," Bobby said.
"You didn't know us, but the accident hit us hard."
Bobby retreated into his own thoughts.

"It had been weighing on me since it happened, and I had never taken the time to officially say goodbye."
"So, you said farewell at the beach?" Bobby asked.
"Yes. It is one of my favorite places."
"What did you do?"
"I carried a picture in my wallet of her and your mom ever since they left. I laid it to rest in a sandy grave as the waves rolled in."
A moment of silence followed, as Bobby considered what his father was saying.
"Is the water freezing cold?"
"Not this time of year."

The two stared into the fire for a few minutes without talking.
"You know, if Mom was here, there would never be any quiet moments."
"She doesn't like silence, does she?"
"No, usually there is music or the TV playing in the background. When Bee was alive, those two would never stop talking— it drove me crazy."

Scooter smiled and poked at the logs with a stick to rearrange them.
"Did you and your sister get along?"
"She was my best friend. Bee was fierce and stood up to anyone she thought was giving me crap for no good reason." Bobby told the story from the bus stop and how he knew from then on she was his hero.

"That is really cool, Bobby. She always was determined, even as a little girl."
"So how did you hear about the accident?" Bobby asked.
"My sister, Jan, called me at work one day and told me to sit down because she had some bad news."
"That sucks."
"I went numb," Scooter said.
"I just got angry at everyone," Bobby said.
"Really? Your mom said you were her rock."

"She needed help because she didn't deal with it very well. So, I did the things around the house to get us through, but inside I was furious."

"Furious?"

"With the drunk guy, with Brandon the youth pastor, with God. It took me a year before I worked through it all. I had said I forgave them early on, but it turned out I had to keep forgiving them whenever it came up."

"A hard lesson to learn. So, you're not angry anymore?"

"I wouldn't say that. I just don't get stuck on angry for very long now."

"What changed?"

"Pastor Jerry reached out to me. We started taking walks up here in the mountains a couple times a month."

"Cool!"

"Yes, he has been kind to us. He is a good man."

"Why don't you get stuck on angry anymore? I guess I'm asking about your reaction to your mom the other day."

"I was more hurt than angry. I didn't see it coming. Then you showed up." Bobby smiled.

"I showed up all right. My plan didn't work, Bobby."

"But you are here now."

"True, but I was headed home without any clues. Our time together is a pure act of sovereign grace. The fact I am sitting here with you is all God's doing."

"I think you had something to do with it."

"God brought me out here to look for your mom. Then I tried to tell Him how I was going to do it. My plans burned to the ground, like most of my ideas, I guess. He had a better way and invited me to walk in His will, but I ignored Him. So, He let my car break down at just the right spot, and He arranged the perfect guy to pick me up."

"Are you saying we don't have any choice?" Bobby asked.

"Sure we do, and the only reason we do is because when God's timing is right, then we can see and receive, His blessings."

The smoke from the fire swirled a bit, bending to a gentle breeze.

"I am not the savior here, Bobby. My plan didn't work. God is your only hope."

"I learned that lesson when Bee died," Bobby said.

"Now you get to see it again. God has allowed me to see different angles on the same lesson many times."

"Yeah, I guess you are right."

"Not having a father is tough, but you do have a heavenly Father who loves you more than I ever could. I didn't know you existed ten days ago, but He knows all of the hairs on your head and all of your thoughts. He has to be your north star, Bobby, not me."

"He has brought you into my life."

"Which is a huge blessing for me."

"And me," Bobby said, glancing over at the man next to him as the shifting light danced across his face.

"A blessing from His hand. Did you know I spent time in an orphanage as a kid?"

"Mom told me."

"So, I developed this idea women were going to save me from the rejection I felt from not having my biological parents in my life. Women can't save you or me. Neither can any man. The only true Savior is Jesus, Bobby."

"I know about His death and resurrection and stuff."

"That is where He starts."

"Starts?"

"Starts changing us from the inside out. Starts bringing our thoughts and desires in line with His."

"What about the year that I was so mad with Him? I felt like I had walked away."

"Did He use your rebellion to change you?"

"Yes, I guess he did."

Scooter flipped the logs over and added two more from the pile between them.

"It was more than just walking away. I ran away from God for the entire time," Bobby said.

"I have ran away for over forty years."

"Why do we do it?" Bobby asked.

"Because we are weak and rebellious. On top of the fact we are stubborn, thinking we have the right plan for everything, when in reality we are just trying to make God in our own image. He won't be made. As near as I can figure, He lets us run away for a time and then woos us back."

"I could never be so patient with rebellious children," Bobby said.

"Me neither." They laughed.

Later that night, after the fire was only smoldering embers, Scooter laid on his sleeping bag beneath the Milky Way. He watched the cosmos slow dance above him. Tears of gratitude streamed down his face as he lifted his hands toward the heavens in worship and thanked a merciful God.

*

Jimmy the Jet and Tums clicked their doors shut on the truck a half mile from the campers.
"We are gonna scare the crap out of them," Tums whispered.
"No, we are here to do more."
"Right, boss man."
Jet loved it when his buddies called him by that name.
"I can't believe we found him out here in the mountains."
"Of course, we did, Tums. He can't get rid of us. We made him who he is— don't you forget it."
"I know he attacked both Dog and J-Law the other night."
"No way. Ronny Lawrence doesn't have the guts."
"Then explain how Dog and J Law are sprawled out in the bed of the truck with dented heads."
"I think they ran into something powerful, got roughed up, and needed to sleep it off," Jet said.
"Did you get a look at their heads? I don't think they are making it back, or waking up."
"You don't know that. We just found them in the dark. The idiots must have fallen down the ravine."
"No way. Those wounds are intentional," Tums said.

Jet was quiet as he thought about the ramifications.
"We need to be ready, in case Ronny. . ." Tums didn't finish his sentence for Jet—, he didn't have to.
"Yeah," said Jet, while choking back a rising fear. "Just in case."

The pair slowed and crept along the road.
"There are a lot of steep cliffs out here, Jet."
"Places to get tossed, like the Rat did."
"The Rat? You mean the ugly kid in Denton? I haven't thought about him in years."

"Me neither. Not since I threw him down those stairs," Jet said and sneered.

"I thought it may have gone down like that."

"He bounced all the way down."

"Look, there is the old pickup."

"Grab some rocks. We will lure him out. Once we start, we can't let up."

They both picked up a couple rocks each and stepped closer to the truck. Jet touched his partners arm to get him to stop moving. Laying in the shadows, next to the subtle glow of a burnt out fire was the guy they were looking for. Jet made hand gestures for Tums to work around the outside of the campsite, then they would attack from two sides, pelting him with rocks and race in for the up close and personal.

Tums was clumsy. As he walked away he was making too much noise for Jimmy's liking. Jet figured Tums had given his position up with his stupidity. He was counting on the element of surprise against Lawrence. The moon had already descended beyond the horizon, so seeing his partner's signal was going to take concentration. Tums readied himself, waving both arms over his head and Jimmy responded in-kind. As Tums stepped back to blast Lawrence with a baseball-sized rock, he inadvertently stepped off the edge of a cliff and fell three hundred feet in the darkness. His tumbling corpse hit the first rock the same time Jimmy the Jet hit Lawrence in the thigh. Another throw from Jet just missed Scooter's head. Scooter spun around, removed his hat, and fell on his knees to pray.

A powerful hand pushed in through the veil and grabbed Jimmy the Jet's seething head. The massive being was birthed through the portal to bludgeon the night stalker into submission, knocking him unconscious. He had been summoned, and arrived at just the right moment. The other-worldly being threw Jimmy's limp body away from the camp and left him immobilized in the stone on the side of the dusty, two-track road.

The next morning, on the way to another campsite, Bobby was concentrating on the trail map. Scooter steered the truck over the top of Jimmy the Jet's head with a crunch. A deep sense of satisfaction poured into Scooter's soul, as he thought his final Denton nemesis was extinguished. A quarter of a mile later, Bobby pointed out a black pickup, pulled off on a trail, with its tailgate down revealing the empty bed.

*

Before the campers returned to town the following day, they stopped to top off the tank in the borrowed truck. Both of them went inside to grab a cold drink. The woman at the register appeared to be ambivalent and uninterested in her job, but she took notice of the two men in front of her because they looked so much alike.
"Are you guys brothers?" she asked.
"Something like that," Scooter said.
Bobby read her name tag, but wasn't sure, because the woman standing in front of him looked like she had aged at five times the normal rate.
"Are you Veronica?"
"Congrats, you can read," she said, without looking up at him.
"I am Bobby, Bee's brother."

The realization hit Veronica hard, she covered her mouth and took a step back from the register.
"Hey, listen— I want you to know I have forgiven you, Veronica. I don't blame you."
She could not speak as powerful emotions erupted from a long-buried volcano inside of her heart.
"I want you to meet my dad."
"Hi, I am Scooter."
Veronica silently nodded as tears fell from her face.
Bobby whispered to Scooter, and identified Veronica as driving the car when Bee was killed.

"Veronica, I want you to know, what happened was an accident and I have forgiven you as well. Something tells me you are having a hard time forgiving yourself."
"I am so sorry." Veronica's face fell toward the floor in shame.

Both of the men came around the corner of the counter, and reached out to her wounded heart. Unbeknownst to them, the timing of the chance meeting was another perfect divine interruption, as Veronica was planning to end her own life after work. The guilt and shame had been winning, but God had a different plan.

*

"Where are you now, Scooter?"
"I am eating dinner with Kim and Bobby."
"Hi Jan!" Kim said, overhearing the question as she set the plates out on her table.
"Hey, Kim," Jan replied. Inside, Jan was put off by the new information which had been held back from her about having a sixteen-year-old nephew. She refused to confront the issue at this time because of her brother and all he had been through.
"Have you been keeping up with the news from here?" Jan asked.
"No." Scooter replied.
"You are still considered a missing person and a person of interest in the ongoing investigations."
"Do you mean more than one?"
"Yes, three are listed in the Times article today."
"What? Makes no sense to me."
"Your trailer blew up, and no one has seen you since."
"Okay."
"You need to come home and talk to the cops, Scooter."
"I will come home."
"The article says they served a warrant on G-Ma's house, looking for evidence."
"Not good," Scooter said.
"No kidding. They are going to ask me questions and I don't want to lie for you."
"There is nothing to lie about."
"You need to get back and fix this."

This was not the news Scooter wanted to hear, or even think about, at this point.
"Thanks for letting me know, Jan. I will keep you informed."
"Okay. Thanks. I am afraid for you, brother."
"I know you are. This is going to work out. I am learning to trust God's timing."
"Your faith really has grown. Give my love to everyone out there."
"I love you."

"Love you, too."

The phone clicked in his ear.

Immediately Kim had a dozen questions, most about timing and details of his intense story. After spending the entire dinner discussing the matter, Scooter acquiesced.

"You guys are right. I need to head back home and face the music."

"I know we can't begin again with things like this hanging over our heads."

"You are right, Kimmy."

Bobby relished the thought of his parents talking about beginning again.

*

Inside, the weather-beaten barn had undergone a radical transformation. Darrell invested three difficult days into moving and stacking bales of hay. It turned out he possessed a knack for making hideaways. Both of his entry tunnels had a door inside and out. A simple idea which used a bale to move into position after he entered or left. Inside, he army crawled down a fifteen-foot passage into his living area, which was high enough for him to sit up. Darrell had arranged the bales on the roof in such a way as to let in daylight. He built two emergency escape areas hidden behind specific bales, which anyone else would crawl past without detecting.

The only difference from the outside of his hideout was the pile of hay that appeared like it had grown in volume. He made traps to warn him of intruders and two weapon systems to protect himself. He rigged the chain fall, used for hoisting things into the loft, by pulling it up tight to a beam and tying it off with twine. A small hatchet was left below the string to be able to release the heavy pulley and send it swinging across the barn. Darrell tested the weapon and it slammed into the sliding barn door leaving a significant gouge. He reset it with a smile, and sank the blade of the rusty hatchet into the beam.

Darrell designed a pit four bales deep in the loft, concealing it with branches and loose hay. Later he updated his trap design to include sharpened sticks pointing up from the bottom of the hole. He remembered the trick from an ancient Vietnam war movie.

By the end of his project, Darrell felt prepared. His next challenge was food. He was out and the prospects of his mom rescuing him dimmed by the day, so he turned toward the unexplored house.

*

The panhandle of Texas was a long and lonely part of the drive back with mile upon mile of scrubland and canyons. From Amarillo to Oklahoma City, Scooter relived his time in New Mexico, like rewinding an old VHS movie. The final hug from Bobby, and then Kim, stood out among the highlights.
"I have missed you, and I will miss you more," Kim had whispered into his ear with the final embrace. Replaying the special moment brought tears to his eyes, even in the middle of nowhere.

Scooter was spent, unable to push through. He relented and stopped in Joplin, Missouri. He sent Kim a quick text from the parking lot of the motel:
Scooter: *"Spending the night in Joplin, MO. Thank you for caring."*
Kim: *"Glad you are safe. Get good rest."*
Scooter: *"Night."*
Kim: *"Night."*

It was in those closing moments of the day, Scooter sat at the warped desk and used the motel note pad to write Kimmy a letter. He filled the pad as he poured out his heart to her. At the end, he signed his new name on the cardboard backing. Scooter tucked his masterpiece in his duffel bag and went to bed. Before he drifted away, Scooter thanked God again. He hoped God would go further and allow him to fully reconcile with Kim.
"I could live in New Mexico," was his final conscious thought of the day.

He slept like a baby in the worn-out motel room, even though there was a pile of uncertainty awaiting him in Michigan, and a black pickup idling in the parking lot. Peace held on.

*

The bells above the door signaled her arrival. Before she got to the opaque glass reception window it was slid open by the woman sitting at the desk behind it.

"Good morning, how can I help you?"

"Good morning, I am Detective Donna McBride."

"Detective, what can I do for you?"

"I have a few questions for one of your counselors on staff."

"Who are you looking for?"

"There was a man who claims he comes to your facility for counseling and I am trying to corroborate his story."

"Sure, I can help you." She swiveled in her chair to face her computer screen.

"His name is Scooter Lawrence."

"Scooter?"

"Yeah, it's his nickname. I can get his given name off of the report in my car."

"I don't recognize the name Scooter."

"What about Lawrence?" Donna asked.

She tapped away on her keyboard for a few moments.

"We had a Lawrence, but it was a Shelly."

"No, he is definitely a man," Donna said.

"Okay. Um, what about his counselor?"

Donna flipped through her small notepad searching for the information.

"A coworker told me he was seeing someone named, Angie."

"We don't have anyone here by that name." The receptionist was smiling.

"What is your name?"

"Judy."

"Judy, you are telling me definitively you do not have Scooter Lawrence as a patient?"

"Yes. I have no record."

"And you are saying you don't have any counselor named Angie who works out of this office, maybe from home or another location?"

"We do not employ any staff members named Angie."

"Do you have a last name for her? Maybe Angie was a nickname?"

"That's all the information I have. Are there any more counseling offices in this plaza, or close to here?"

"Not that I am aware of."

"Okay." Donna scribbled.

"There is another place on the north end of town, on Krafft Road."

"No, this was the location mentioned, with the correct name on the sign."

"Sorry."

"Thank-you for your time."

*

The rear door of the house was being held shut by yellow caution tape. When the police raided the home they had destroyed the latch with an entry tool. Then, before they left, they had tied the rear door closed with the tape by stretching it from the door's handle out to the hand rail.

Darrell slid the improvised rope from the top of the rail and entered the home through the squealing door. He searched every cupboard and closet, trying to find anything that would help him live in the barn. He managed to wrangle up seven cans of soup, three microwaveable rice packages, cracker sticks with cheese, and five protein bars. In his search, he also found a New Testament which he decided to confiscate for reading purposes.

Pleased with his haul, he placed it in a green cloth bag which he found on the floor. The bag contained a couple of bolts. Sneaking out, he replaced the police rope and took his provisions to his hidden lair in the bowels of the barn.

Lunch was his first meal in two days. His pants were growing around his waist, and Darrell was concerned. *"How long can I wait for mom to find me?"* he thought. After a nap, he drank the last of his water, knowing he would have to fill his empty bottles under the cover of darkness.

He had found living the "hiding out" lifestyle was filled with long periods of boredom, which got briefly interrupted by moments of sheer terror. Officially this was a boring day. Eyeing the little book from the house, Darrell moved himself up to a place with more light on the top of the pile and began to read. Three hours later, he was wondering why the story of Jesus had repeated for the fourth time, although the John section had some different tales about the Son of Man. It was at this point a worn pamphlet entitled "Romans Road" fell out of the pages from the back of the book."

There in the outskirts of Smiths Creek, Michigan, on top of a pile of hay, Darrell Patrick prayed his first real prayer and asked Jesus to forgive his sins, like the pamphlet said. He cried hard, thinking back to what he did to Ronnie, beating him to a pulp. Then the night he watched him die. Ronnie was dancing around like no one could see him on the sidewalk with the stars. Darrell could hear the sickening sound of his head hitting the stake when Ronnie tripped.
"I wanted him to die," he admitted, reminded of his mantra.

Darrell figured those two acts of pure hatred would be the reason he would experience the wrath of God. They were the sins which living a good life could never make up for. He sobbed over his running away from his mom when she needed him the most, and all of the hiding from the police bothered him too. But the one thing he was not sorry for-- that he refused to confess as a sin, was running away from Donny. His dad was bad news, just like his mom had told him a thousand times before.

"Okay, God, thank-you for not hating me because of what Jesus did on the cross. Help me know what to do. This is Darrell, by the way, in case you're busy with other people wanting something from you. Amen"

*

"Ma!" Donny yelled, and the screen door slammed behind him.
He charged into an unexpected scene. Tina and his mom were talking at the dining room table, but before Tina could jump up to run from him, he had discovered their secret meeting.

"Well, well, well. The criminal returns," he said, with a sardonic grin. Granny's eyes narrowed, watching her son reappear like an April thunderstorm, wondering where she had gone wrong.

"Ma, I never thought you would betray me like this," Donny said.
"I haven't betrayed you. I have protected you."
"This doesn't feel like you are protecting me right now, Ma."

"This isn't her fault, Donny. I just got out of jail and I don't have anywhere to go," Tina said.

"Sounds like you have some real issues, like I have been saying all along."

"No kidding." Tina glared at Donny, and he promptly backhanded her across the face, knocking her off of the chair for the insolence.

"Haven't had anyone to beat up lately, Donny? You stop it right now!" Granny said.

Donny shot over to her, lifting her frail body up by her neck.

"You listen to me, you old wench. I will kill you just as quick as look at you. You betrayed me for the last time by protecting this whore."

"She is the mother of your son, Donny. Please. Please don't hurt her anymore." Granny choked out the words though gritted teeth, while pulling at his strong hands.

"Why, Ma? Why are you taking her side?"

Granny only gurgled out a string of nonsense.

"She is hiding him from me!" Donny raged, and dropped his mother to the wooden floor.

Grabbing Tina up by the nape of her hair, Donny yanked her off the ground and threw her onto the couch. He knelt on her chest, forcing air from her lungs and grabbed her face, avoiding her attempts to bite him.

"You are going to tell me everything," he commanded, with vicious eyes.

"I am not telling you anything about Darrell," Tina managed.

"Oh, you will talk."

The beating began in earnest as Donny's fist rapidly struck the unprotected woman's face. An awakened Granny tried to stop him, thinking he was on the verge of killing Tina on her couch. She hit Donny over the back with a broom handle. In response, he threw her to the floor, knocking her out cold in the process.

He returned to the couch, intent on demonstrating another lesson in control before he beat Tina unconscious. She was half out of her mind with pain as Donny ripped off her pants and underwear. Tina tried to fight and kick him off, but he was too heavy, and her sanity evaporated in the assault.

Donny had knocked the mother of his son unconscious in his rage, pummeling her face with countless blows after the sexual assault. Now, except for her blood-stained shirt, Tina lay bleeding, disfigured, and half naked, in the back seat of his rusted-out boat of a car. He was driving the back roads of the Smiths Creek area in concentric circles. Before Tina had acquiesced to the force of his blows, she admitted their kid had stopped out at Granny's and been given some food. Supposedly, he ran off just before Donny pulled in when he first came looking for him.

Donny was driving and thinking like his twelve-year-old son, while his tires crunched down the gravel roads. He knew the kid was street-smart and would choose to hole up somewhere close to Granny's house, especially if he thought his mom would come looking for him.

So onward he drove, doing ten miles an hour down every road, studying each driveway for clues. He crisscrossed the areas on both sides of the railroad tracks, to no avail. He thumped the tobacco down in another pack of smokes and lit one up. Few people took notice of the brown car crawling down their road, and only two paid any attention to its slow passing with a wave of their hand.

Several hours later, Granny woke up feeling nauseous. There was dried blood on the side of her head from a split in her cheek, and her shoulder had bruised over to a deep shade of purple. Tina and Donny were both gone. Only the blood stains on her couch, and Tina's torn clothes on the floor, testified to what had taken place.

*

Chapter Sixteen
* Star Struck *

The final hundred miles proved to be the most difficult for Scooter. He had pushed hard from Joplin all day, but after driving for over fifteen hours, he hit a wall and had to pull out all of his tricks. He ate sunflower seeds until the insides of his mouth were raw from the salt. The action of cracking each shell and using nothing but his tongue to fish the tiny seed out, usually kept him going for hours of mindless driving. When the salt became an issue, he switched to sweet chocolate-covered peanuts, eating one at a time without chewing, until the peanut remained.

During long-distance junkets of the past, he kept his drinking down to a minimum to lessen the number of pee stops. Today, he had to resort to drastic measures, like splashing his face with cold water, removing his hat, rolling the window down, and pushing his head as far out as he could while in motion. The final step would be stopping and doing push-ups on the side of the road, or next to the car as he filled up with gas. If he was forced to give in to his body's demand for sleep, a twenty-five-minute power nap was used. Those naps usually bought him some relief and a few more hours of driving.

All of the techniques had been deployed in his battle to get back to G-Ma's in one piece. His forehead was numbed by a long blast of cool Michigan air over the final twenty miles on Interstate 69. It was after midnight when he pulled into his drive and an open gate. Scooter had nothing left inside to motivate him to get out of the car and close the entry barrier behind him. He turned the black Sky off in front of the barn while his ears buzzed with road noise, and his body felt like it was still in motion.

Scooter affectionately patted the dash board in thanks. Because everything was pitch black he grabbed his duffel to get out his new headlamp. In his fumbling, he knocked his letter to Kim on the ground as the door opened. With the open door, the smell of ripe fruit on the trees greeted him and reassured him he had made it home in one piece.

"Thank-you, Lord," he said, as he stood up to stretch his weary body. His spine and neck popped and cracked with the movement. He clicked his head lamp on so he could see his hands in front of his face, and noticed the pad of hotel paper containing Kim's letter on the ground. The gravel was a long way down, but he reached and stuffed the letter in his back pocket. Moving to the back porch the light hit the reflective caution tape and the yellow jumped out at him. With the sight, a sense of foreboding overtook the previous moment's reassurance from the smell of the orchard. Scooter drew in a deep, long breath. He knew his call to Detective Donna McBride was hanging over his head, but it would wait until morning.

Breaking through the plastic rope, his door greeted him with the familiar squeal. He decided to set his bag down behind the wooden portal to hold it closed, and he headed for the plastic-covered couch in the living room. Scooter yanked off the drop cloth and fell into the cushions. Sleep came without any effort as the relentless black pickup rumbled past his gate.

*

An hour before Scooter arrived at G-Ma's, Donny crept up the driveway in his junker. He was looking toward the barn, thinking his son, Darrell, would be attracted to it for a hideout. It appeared no one lived in the house— it was impossible to see the house from the road or any neighbors from the house, because of the all of the trees. The metal gate kept everyone but the most determined out, so Donny had settled on this place being one of the strongest possibilities for Darrell's hideout.

Cutting the motor, Donny left the lights shining on the large sliding barn door. Knowing the history of his car, he knew he only had five minutes to have a look around before the battery would become compromised. He reached over the seat and slapped Tina on her backside. He tugged upward on her T-shirt and smiled at the sight of his handiwork on her back. His warm hands glided over her smooth, raised scars, and his sense of invincibility grew.
"I think I've got that kid of ours cornered. Maybe you won't need any more of these," he sneered.

Tina only moaned. Donny had been feeding her drugs in between the brutalization sessions throughout the day, and she needed him to think she was still out of her mind. In reality, Tina had been trying to plan for the moment Donny grabbed Darrell. Her hand rested on a cool tire iron on the dirty floor of the car. Tina figured she only had the strength for one attack, and it would have to come after Donny brought Darrell to her.

Donny opened the door of the car, but did not close it. He figured if he could catch the kid sleeping then he would have a better chance of not chasing him through the woods. Forcing the barn door open, light flooded across the dirt floor. Donny's mind was racing to find the boy, eyes searching for the places he could hide. If the roles were reversed, he would hide up in the loft under some of the hay.

He climbed the ladder without making noise, pausing at the top to let his eyes adjust to the darkness of the loft. Some light was making its way up to him, but it was through a dim reflection. Three cautious steps forward on the tight bales and he paused again, straining to see.

Inside the pile of hay, Darrell was holding his breath as he peered between two bales at the feet of his father. He knew it was his dad, because of the shiny steel toes of his cowboy boots. Fear gripped Darrell and he willed himself to remain perfectly still, hoping to have a chance of surviving this encounter with the crazed man.

Donny's next step forward was unexpected for him. The floor fell out from beneath his feet and he surged downward through cracking branches, yelling and grabbing at the air. As his body slammed into bales, a sharpened stick pierced through the meat of his left thigh, halfway between the knee and hip. The force of his weight coming to a sudden stop, broke the dried wood off and Donny screamed in pain.

Darrell, on one hand, did everything he could not to hoot over the success of his trap, but on the other, an unexpected memory sent flashbacks of Ronnie falling on the stake. The thought sent a shudder down his spine. He couldn't see his dad in the bottom of his trap, but he could hear his thrashing and screaming like a wild animal, so he knew the Ronnie incident hadn't repeated itself.

Donny tried to clear the panic from his mind. He needed to get out of the hole he had fallen into. So he began pulling bales of hay into his pit and was able to drag his way out. In the dim light at the top of the ladder, he could see the sharpened end of the one-inch-diameter stick protruding out of the back of his leg. Donny knew he needed to take care of the wound before he could catch the kid.

Several minutes later, Donny announced to the darkness, "Tina, let's go. I don't think he is here," and slid the barn door closed, hoping to antagonize the hiding derelict who set up the trap. Moving the door nearly caused him to pass out from pain.

In the gaze of the dimming headlights, Donny reached down and pulled the wood from his leg, doing everything he could not to scream out. He dropped the crude weapon, and limped into his seat as sweat poured from his body and blood from his two new holes. In the back seat, Tina celebrated with a silent, hidden smile.

*

Donna sat rubbing her forehead at her kitchen table. New yellow sheets of paper were scattered over her work surface. There were lists on each sheet with corresponding numbers. The numbers indicated other facts and evidence in all three of her open cases. Her head was pounding with the complexities of possibilities and cross references.

After talking to Matt and Jan on the phone, she sat down for a few hours, trying to piece together what she knew as actual, provable facts. She was forced to admit their story was a credible alternative to what she thought had happened. Over the last couple weeks, she became more convinced Scooter was at the center of the entire affair, instead of trusting her gut about the man.

"Have I allowed my emotions and personality to get involved to the point where I skewed the evidence in this case?" The question was the cause of her headache.

Donna, not knowing the answer, decided to head off to bed to get some sleep before her meeting with the captain in the morning. Her phone vibrated to life in her hand, and a smile stretched across her face when the new text appeared. A warm prosecuting attorney was going to be joining her for the night.

*

"Hey, Mom?"
"Bobby, Scooter made it home. Just got the text."
"Cool, he drove a lot today, I tracked his route on my map." He pointed to the highlighted route.
"I guess he did. You've been working, and haven't told me about your camping trip," Kim said.
"It was amazing. I really liked it, and him."
"What did you guys do? Details!"
"Guy stuff. You know— camp fires, fishing, eating, throwing rocks, telling stories, hiking trails."
"Sounds like guy stuff to me."

Bobby got up from his bed and walked to his mom. She was standing just inside his bedroom door when he threw his arms around her. He was six inches taller than she was now, and he enjoyed the height advantage. Since starting his job, he had gained muscle and girth. Kim recognized her boy was becoming a man and sighed at the passage of time while inside of his embrace.
"I love you, Mom. I am sorry I ran off. I didn't mean what I had said to you," he whispered.
"I am sorry I lied to you. I love you, too," she returned the whisper.
"Can you believe what has happened?" he asked.
"No. I am still shaking my head."
"Dad said it was an act of pure grace."
Kim pushed away to look at his face. "Dad? You are calling him Dad now?"
"Yeah." he shrugged. "Why not? He's the only one I've got, here on earth, anyway."

Kim began to cry, and hugged her son even tighter. "I'm sorry I kept him from you."
"I want to go visit him."
"It's a long way."
"Yeah, but I need to go, Mom."
"I know you do."

"Do you want to come along?"
"Yes, at some point," Kim said.
"Is there a chance with you two?"
"A chance for what?"
"I don't know." Bobby didn't want to come right out and say.
Kim pushed away again, wanting to look into his eyes.
"For your dad and me to get back together after so many years apart?"
"Yes. Why not?"

The long pause ended with a smirk on Kim's face.
"Maybe." She shrugged. "I am trying to wait to see what God has in store."
"You didn't say no."
"I have never stopped loving him, Bobby."
"Really?"
"Yes, really," she wiggled her head.
"All these years?"
"I have prayed for him for a long time."
"I never knew," Bobby said.
"True enough."

*

As Donny sat on top of Tina, he forced more pills down her throat. The pain from his wound didn't allow him to remain in the back seat for more than a minute. After he got off and slammed the door shut, she turned and gagged the pills onto the floor in the darkness. Tina recognized the sound of the screen door slamming and knew they had returned to Granny's. Her head was still spinning and groggy but she knew Donny would go back to the barn to find Darrell. Tina needed to be ready, and reached for the blanket at her feet. Rest would be her best friend in fighting back the fog from the drugs. She forced herself to sleep so she could be ready to help her son.

Inside the house, Donny went to find the medicine to help him fix his wound. The pain he had already addressed with an Oxycontin from his stash. It was just beginning to make a difference, taking the edge off of the nasty wound. He sought out the medicine cabinet in the bathroom.

Yanking the peroxide and gauze from the shelf, he dropped his pants and used the hand towel to remove the blood from his leg, then Donny dumped the foaming clear liquid over the hole and screamed in pain. He repeated the self-torture on the back of his thigh and wrapped the gauze around his leg, using the entire roll. His head was filled with crazy pain.

On the way to the living room, Donny did not bother to look in on his mom, figuring she was out for the night. He decided to lay down for a few minutes to give the drugs some time to overcome the throb in his thigh. He fell fast asleep.

Granny came into the living room ten minutes after he stopped moving, with her shotgun in tow. She was wallowing in self-pity over the fact her son was a loser. She had tried hard her whole life to give him everything he needed, but had failed at every turn. She didn't want to kill him while he slept, so she sat in the lone chair across from him and watched him sleep. Waiting. Soon her eyes could no longer remain open, and Granny drifted off.

*

Donny put the shot gun in the front seat, after taking it from his sleeping mother's lap. When he cracked the woman's skull with the butt of the gun, he knew it was for her own good.
"If you call the cops, I will kill you," he whispered to her lifeless body on the living room floor and left for the car.

Seeing Tina sleeping in the back seat aroused the twisted man again and he took full advantage. Tina endured his attack, focusing on playing like she was still drugged from the pills he had given her. She feigned the stupor, knowing her son needed her. The anger that built up inside her, had to be put away, stuffed down until later. So, Tina play-acted and encouraged the monster to finish.
"I knew you wanted it," he slobbered into her ear, with heavy breathing.

Donny wasn't sure of the time, as he left Granny's street, driving for the barn which was only a few miles away. The sky was brightening from the impending dawn as he crept down the wooded drive, through the orchard and toward the barn. In an instant, the tires stopped rolling from his pressure on the brake pedal.

"What is this?" Donny was looking at the back of a black car parked in front of the barn. He rolled up next to it and turned his clunker off. Looking back, Donny noticed Tina had been forced to the floor with the sudden stop. She appeared to be sleeping, probably from the drugs, he figured.

Donny checked to make sure his gun was loaded by racking a round as slow as he could into the chamber, as he exited the vehicle. The sky was brightening to the east and his cover of darkness was evaporating. He noticed the bright tape on the back stairway and decided to enter the house to look for the visitor.

Gun to his cheek, Donny limped across the yard as Darrell scampered back up to his fortress inside the barn. In the house, Scooter never heard a noise as his duffel bag was pushed across the kitchen floor. The door chose not to squeal because of the back pressure applied by the skidding bag behind it, and Donny walked inside unhindered. He remained still for a few minutes, then noticed a slight snore emanating from the next room. His leg throbbed as he stepped toward the couch and the sleeping figure.

Peering over the back of the bulky antique furniture, Donny found an unsuspecting Ronny Lawrence sleeping right before his eyes.

"We meet again!" Donny thought and rose the shotgun over Scooter's head. He blasted the butt of the gun behind his ear, and Scooter fell off of the couch with a grunt. Donny pressed in as quick as his leg allowed. Scooter tried to focus his eyes as he raised his head. Donny promptly stuffed the butt of his gun into his forehead, snapping the man's head against the floor. Scooter was out, and Donny knew it. He would have to finish the job after he flushed Darrell out of the barn. He didn't want a gunshot scaring the kid off.

Donny retreated through the kitchen, and watched the space between the buildings for movement. There was nothing happening, other than birds dancing and singing at the sight of the daylight. He moved down the steps, one at a time due to the renewed pain in his leg, and limped to the barn door. He was forced to lean the gun against the weathered siding in order to push the big door open with only one good leg.

Inside the car, Tina was looking at the back of the psychotic maniac as he struggled against the heavy door. She held on to the tire iron with a death grip, and clicked the latch with her free hand as Donny groaned out loud in his push.

Darrell came out of hiding in the hay and made his way to the beam where his final weapon was still loaded with kinetic energy. He kept to the shadows as the door rolled open in front of him. Donny was in the opening, but not near the place the heavy pulley would strike. Darrell remained quiet behind the beam with his hatchet in hand.

Donny yelled Darrell's name into the dark space.
"I have got your whore of a mom right here, and if you ever want to see her alive, you need to come out of hiding, boy," he raged at the culmination of all of his effort to find his kid.

He failed to see Tina get out of the car. She crept around the back of the vehicle, clutching the cold tire iron with both hands. She noticed the gun was still against the barn and decided to let her boiling anger spill out in the form of rage.

As Tina stepped from behind the car in bare feet, Scooter pushed through the back door of the house. He didn't bother with any of the steps as he ran in full sprint toward the screaming man at the door of the barn. He saw a woman without pants rise up from behind the car at the same time he hit the gravel. Donny turned and faced the noise coming from Scooter's footfalls. At that exact moment, Tina drove the tire iron into Donny's bandaged leg with as much force as she could muster, which produced a scream bordering on insanity.

Donny managed to punch the top of the screaming woman's head as he fell back toward the barn in front of his car. His leg exploded with pain. His gun was less than three feet from his outstretched hand. His thigh was on fire, but his drive for self-preservation kicked in, and Donny lunged for the gun.
Scooter was now within ten feet of the insanity, and wanted to protect the woman from the crazy man in front of the car.

From his perch in the loft, Darrell thought his mother was in shorts, and she hit his yelling father in the leg with something hard. Darrell was paralyzed with fear. Then the man from the house came into view, just as Donny grabbed the gun while lying on the ground.

The twelve-gauge shotgun roared to life, blowing out its double-aught buckshot into the chest of Scooter Lawrence. The steel shot ripped through Scooter's heart and lungs, forcing their way though his body, killing him on the spot. His blood poured from his wounds, staining the ground of his earthly home for the final time.

Donny stood up, with the gun in his hand as Scooter's limp body skidded to a stop at his feet. He racked another shell and turned toward the stunned woman on the ground. He lifted the gun to his cheek. As his finger moved to the trigger, a one hundred-pound block of steel and cable crashed into the back of his skull. The gun roared again, this time sending the nine pellets into the gravel at his feet.

Donny was dead before his body hit the ground. Darrell slid down the ladder from the loft, running toward his mother.

Two county sheriff cars rushed onto the scene as Darrell crashed into his mother, who was sitting on the ground, trying to kick Donny in the bleeding head.

"Mom! Mom! Mom! I am here," Darrell screamed.
"Oh, my God, you are here," she said, as they grabbed for each other.
"Put your hands up!" barked the deputy.
Darrell reached for the shotgun that was next to him in the gravel.
"Gun! Gun! Gun!" yelled the one Deputy to the other.

Ten minutes later, two more cars rolled into the yard. The first was Detective Donna McBride, followed closely by Scooter's friend, Matt. It was Matt who had received a call from Scooter from the living room floor after Donny's attack. Matt called 911, and then Donna.
The pair were followed up closely by an ambulance.

*

The midnight-blue beings slithered their way upward. They had been summoned to the surface to collect another offering. The pair sensed they were drawing close, because the volume of the screams increased.

As their spindly fingers pushed up through the limestone gravel, they were warmed by the sun of another world, a foreign place. The black iridescent pile of goo felt their arrival and shouted against them with as much force as he could muster.

"Donny, is that you?" One of the creatures asked the shimmering man-pile with its gravely voice.

"Get away from me! Leave me alone!" Donny shrieked.

"What are you going to do? Your soul has no form here anymore."

"Get away!" Donny screamed in absolute terror.

"This is what you have wanted," said one beast.

"This is what you have earned," said the other and both nodded in unison.

"No! No!"

"Yes, Donny. Thank-you for your offering."

The two scraped up the goo into their containment jar, and the noise ceased when the lid was clasp shut.

"It is much too bright here, don't you think?" said the one to the other.

"I do, indeed." They left the way they had arrived, through the gravel driveway.

*

Tina was dressed and drinking a bottle of water. Donna had given her a pair of sweat pants from her gym bag in her squad car. She sat on the bumper of the ambulance, as Darrell munched away at a protein bar which Matt found in his lunchbox. Tina was pawing at her son's filthy hair, pulling at pieces of embedded hay, and Darrell was savoring the maternal affection.

Matt sat on the back steps of Scooter's house, crying over the scene. He had been trying to call Jan for the last ten minutes, but hadn't dialed the number. He didn't know what to say to her. His confused prayers were flooding the gates of heaven, and his broken heart overflowed through his eyes and shaking hands.

After talking with the captain, Donna was busy taking pictures of the bloody chain fall, while one of the sheriff deputy's was crawling over the bales of hay looking for evidence to corroborate the kids wild tale. The other Deputy had covered the heads of the fallen men. Donna studied the scene and noticed the wallet in the front of Donny's pants pocket. She had already removed the one from his back pocket a few minutes earlier. This wallet carried Scooter's picture on the license and verified the mugging both Jan and Matt had informed her of.

Donna was frustrated with herself for not seeing the obvious signs, and moved to the ambulance.

"Darrell, I need to ask you a few questions."
"Okay," he said.
"I need you to tell me what happened the night Ronnie died."
Darrell looked up at her through squinted eyes. The sun was behind the police woman's head. Realizing her position, Donna knelt down beside the grubby kid.
"Whew, boy, you need a bath," Donna said.
"I know," Darrell said, and jumped into his story from the beginning.

*

Seventeen hundred miles away, the sun had not yet crested the Sacramento Mountains of south-central New Mexico when Kim's cell phone rang. Wrapped in a towel, just out of the shower, she decided to answer the strange number, because her phone indicated the call was from a Michigan area code.
"Hello?"
"Kim, this is Jan,"
"Jan?"
"Are you sitting down? I am afraid I have some terrible news."

*

Chapter Seventeen
* Star Shine *

The directive was plain and simple. He was required to get both of the people on the list to the front door before he went through. Outside the portal, without people to tag along, he felt competent— loved his job, in fact. But finding people on the inside intimidated him, because of the myriad of places they could be, and he was on a strict timetable this morning. Everything needed to be in place and ready to go, before he could step through the veil. He knew he would have to ask for help to be able to pull it off. He sent out a notice for assistance to a few of his coworkers, and had several offers to help before he was able to put his device back into his pocket.
"Thank-you, Lord!" he said out loud.

Moments later, his device buzzed to life with a new message— his two subjects were being brought to the gate and he celebrated with a deep invigorating breath.

*

Double aught buckshot has the nasty ability to separate a person from their body with one close-range blast. Scooter found himself on the ground in front of the back porch at G-Ma's house. He knew it was his house, but he had always preferred to call it by her name. It brought him comfort when he thought of it in those terms. He had been launched free of his physical being by the blast of the gun, forced from the bonds that tied him to the material world.

There was no discomfort in the new reality. Seconds before, he was running toward an enraged man with a shotgun. Now, he was standing up behind his home. Technically, the building he had an affinity for was his earthly home only for a short time, but it was where he felt the most accepted his entire life. Even though he was adopted, his grandparents' attitude made him feel as if he was a part of the family all along. This was the place where the seeds of faith were planted in his heart and now had been brought to its conclusion. Scooter's earthly journey was complete.

Walking over to his former body, Scooter felt weird— not uncomfortable, mind you— but different, odd, out of place. Looking upon the body one had occupied from outside of its physical constraints was a new and unique experience. A large hole was evident in the back of the corpse. He assumed the gunshot exited from the space.
"Never had a chance," Scooter said.
"No, you didn't," said the figure standing next to him.
Scooter felt like he should have been afraid of the sudden appearance of the stranger, but he felt no fear or apprehension. Perhaps it was the deep baritone voice had soothed him.

"Did you see what happened?" Scooter asked.
"No, I just arrived through the portal," the being said.
"Oh." Scooter was uncertain of the meaning.
"Are you in pain?" He chuckled at his own comment.
"No. Why are you laughing?" Scooter asked.
"It's an inside joke. You can no longer feel pain like you did before."
"Explains a lot."
"Do you know what happened?"
"Yes."
"How do you feel about it?"
"I'm not sure. But I feel it's the right time for me to be leaving."
"Indeed."
"Who are you?"
"Scooter, my name is Bob."
"Bob? Really? Just Bob?"
"Why not?" Bob asked.
"I guess I would have thought it would have been different."
"I hear that a lot," Bob said.
"So why are you wearing the tie, Bob?"
"It's your special day," Bob said, and pulled at the knot of his black tie.
"What's your job in all of this?"
"I lead folks home."
"Oh. So, we are going to leave this place?"
"When the time is right. Does leaving make you sad?"
"No. But I am curious about what is next," Scooter said.
"I have found some people need to have a final look around, for closure. When you are ready, we will take our leave."
"What if. . ."

"It cannot take too long, Scooter." Bob smiled, having read his thoughts, and because he had heard it a million times before.
"I want to say goodbye to my friend."
"If you want to be accurate, you should say, '*until we meet again.*'"
"Right, yeah, that's right," Scooter said.
"I believe he is moving this way." Bob pointed with a lift of his chin.

Matt was walking toward the back porch. Scooter recognized his distress, like Matt's heart was made more available in the new reality. "Thanks, buddy. I appreciate you and your friendship." Scooter went to touch his friend's shoulder, but his hand passed through the man instead.

"So, Bob, was this closing scene just for me?"
"Yes."
"Okay. I trust everything is taken care of."
"Indeed."
"How is it I can see into Matt's heart?"
"Humans could always perceive one another, but now the veil of pretense is gone, removed from you."
"Now I can see more clearly?"
"Yes, precisely."
"*The former life was a shadow of the things to come,*" Scooter realized.
"Are you prepared to take our leave?"
"Yes," Scooter said.
"You will have to hang onto my hand as we step through."
"Is is a door?"
"More like a curtain, so to speak."

With one glance back, Scooter looked for the final time on his G-Ma's place and gratitude overflowed his heart. Bob used one of his hands to push into something like a heavy curtain. He held it back as Scooter stepped off of the earth and onto another shore. With his entry into the new world, familiar bells chimed above his head and he glanced up, as feelings of acceptance surrounded him.

Even though it had been daytime on earth, the old world's light seemed like darkness in comparison to the new reality behind the curtain. He was momentarily dizzy and out of sorts, as all of the new information assaulted his senses simultaneously. As Scooter's new world came into focus, there were two people standing in front of him. He stopped and blinked his eyes in an effort for clarity. It appeared they were standing on a patch of emerald grass, next to a field of the most radiant flowers he had every laid his eyes on. *"Vivid,"* was his initial thought, but the word didn't do the experience justice. It was as if all of his senses, which were set to a certain level on earth, were now being turned up a hundred-fold. The scene continued to grow in front of him as he became more aware of abilities to see, hear, and smell, in ways he never considered possible. Then, like a powerful electromagnet, his heart was drawn to the angelic young woman in front of him. She was glowing with a soft radiance and gazing directly into his essence, warming his soul.

"Bella? Bella!"

"Daddy!"

"Oh, my precious girl." They fell into each others arms. "I have missed you so," he said, spinning her around, absorbed in the embrace and she screeched with delight.

"And I have been waiting for this moment," Bella whispered. "When I first arrived, I thought you were already here."

"Mom was trying to protect you and Bobby."

"You got to meet Bobby?"

"Yes. God performed an amazing miracle."

"Abba is like that." Bella smiled so bright Scooter could see inside of her.

"I forgot about this part of the covenant, where we would be with others."

She grasped the meaning of his statement intuitively.

"There are many who wait with a growing anticipation for their reunion with you, Daddy."

"I can only imagine," Scooter said and tears of joy ran down his face. While he rejoiced, he was enveloped by the scent of the flowers, like their scent increased in reaction to his joy. The fragrance of an eternal springtime brought a flood of hopeful emotions.

"It takes getting used to all of the new and delightful things." She had read his sensations, like they had been written on a momentary glint of his eyes— because they had been. It always had been available to see and read, but for him, now, there was nothing constraining the full expression of his heart.

"There is someone else who wants to greet you." Bella pointed to the boy behind them.
"Ronnie!"
"Hi Scooter! Welcome home!"
"My little buddy!" Scooter bent down to look him in the eyes.
"Can I tell you something? I have wanted to tell you since I have arrived."
"Anything Ronnie!"
"There really were stars in the sidewalk, Scooter— it was magical!"
Rapturous tears flowed as Scooter embraced his friend again.

*

Eight days after the tragic shooting at the barn, family and friends gathered inside a church in Lakeport, Michigan. The funeral for Scooter Lawrence was to take place at noon, and people began to gather at ten o'clock to pay their respects.

Mack walked inside the building, even though he was afraid he would burst into flames, or the ceiling would fall on them all. "It's a Catholic thing," he said to Layne.
"You look good all cleaned up," Bull said to his coworker while holding the door.
"I don't swing that way, Bully-Boy," he quipped back, so only the three of them could hear the joke as they walked in.

"Thanks for coming. I am Matt, a friend of Scooter. How did you guys know him?" he asked the trio.
"He worked for me," Mack said.
"We worked with him," Layne said, including Bull with a hand gesture.
"Oh, I am sorry for your loss."
The three shook hands with Matt.

"I still can't believe it," Mack admitted.
"It seems so surreal," Layne added.
The four of them stared at the tile floor for a few moments.

"Were you guys close?"
"Yeah, but with all of the weird stuff happening, I hadn't talked to him since he. . ." Layne trailed off, not sure how to end the thought. He

wanted to go on a rant against Mack for firing him, but knew this wasn't the right place to do it.

"I feel guilty as hell about all of this," Mack said, with tears flowing freely.

"Why is that?" Matt asked.

"I never should have fired him. In my heart, I knew it wasn't him who slashed those tires."

More awkward funeral home silence ensued.

"For whatever reason, there was a purpose. He needed to go on this journey. It's confusing for us on this side of eternity why it ended the way it did."

"You can say that again," Bull said.

"Makes no sense to me," Layne said.

"Have you been busy pouring concrete?"

"Yes, real busy."

"Good for you. Thanks for coming out. I appreciate you guys being here. I am certain Scooter would as well."

A few minutes later, a ragtag coalition from Alamogordo walked through the doors and were greeted by Jan and Bill.

"Kim, my gosh, you have not changed a bit!" Jan said, and hugged her sister-in-law.

"I was thinking the same thing about you, Jan."

"Aren't you so sweet when you tell stories?"

They all laughed.

"This is Bobby. Bobby, your Aunt Jan and Uncle Bill."

"It's so nice to meet you, Bobby." Jan began crying, seeing so much of her brother in him.

"You, too," Bobby managed.

"I cannot believe how much you look like your father."

"It was one of the obvious signs— made it impossible to ignore," Bobby admitted.

"This is Juanita," Bobby said, as he pulled her forward by her hand.

"Thank-you for making the long trek, Juanita. How do you know these guys?"

"I was Bee's best friend and as soon as he gets around to it, I will be Bobby's girlfriend."

Bobby's face turned red.
Kimmy laughed with Juanita and the rest.
"You have to admire a girl who knows what she wants," Bill said.
"This is Tom. He did most of the driving. He also owns the tow truck," Kim said.
"Tom, were you the man that picked Scooter up in the desert?" Jan asked.
"Yes, ma'am. Your brother was a real honest guy, and I am sorry for your loss."
Jan could only nod her head and hug the man, not believing he would make such a long journey on a whim.

"How was the drive?" Bill asked.
"It was a marathon," Kim said.
"You all came in the church van?"
"We sure did. Everyone took turns driving."
"How long did that take?"
"Thirty-two hours from door to door," Bobby said.
"I was glad for the hotel last night," Tom said.
"Did you get to see the water yet?"
"It's what Bobby wanted to see the most," Kim said.
"Did you go down to the river, Bobby?"
"Yes, sir. The river and the beach by the lighthouse," Bobby said.
"Great."
"My dad and I talked about that beach when we went camping."
"I am so glad you got to go camping together," Jan said, with new tears, holding onto her nephew's arm.
"So am I," Bobby said.

Pastor Jerry appeared from the restrooms, and began introducing himself around as Scooter's New Mexico pastor friend. The first couple he talked to was Dell and Sharron, and they told him the story of how broken up Scooter was when the accident happened.

*

Sunrise was glorious over the lake. The orange orb broke through a sparse set of eastern clouds, as the still waters greeted the group gathered on the beach. New Mexico phones were grabbing images of the iconic waterway as shafts of light pierced through a few clouds on the distant horizon. Orange, purple and yellows danced across the morning sky. The air was crisp as Bobby walked into the lake with Pastor Jerry beside him. Gulls cawed at the intrusion. The calm water was warm in comparison to the cool air. The current in that slice of the lake pulled constant and strong toward the mouth of the river to the south. This was the point where the three upper Great Lakes empty into the St. Clair River, pushing toward Detroit and the lower lakes.

Lighthouse Beach was the place Bobby had asked Jerry to baptize him before they left for home. He explained this was the location his dad spoke so fondly of. Now, he would make the vow to follow Jesus in front of family, friends, fishermen, and a dozen unhappy seagulls.

Kim smiled from the beach, noticing a large number of fishing boats dotting the lake near the mouth of the river. She aligned her current view with a similar scene in her distant memory. Kim removed her shoes, wanting to feel the sand between her toes, like a part of her needed to connect in a physical way to this spot on the globe again. She chose to sit and record the moment on her phone.

"Bobby Lawrence, do you believe Jesus Christ is your Savior?" Jerry asked. Kim noticed Bobby's name selection.
"Yes, I believe."
"Do you confess your sins, knowing the blood of Jesus removes them forever, as far as the east is from the west?"
"Yes, I believe that, too."
"Good, one more."
"Okay."
"Do you wish to be baptized into the Christian faith?"
"I do."
"Bobby, based on your proclamation of faith, I baptize you in the name of the Father, and the Son, and the Holy Spirit." Jerry painted the sign of the cross on Bobby's forehead with water. Bobby plugged his nose as Jerry laid him back, submerging him beneath the surface of the crystal clear water. Jerry helped the young man up from the depths, and Bobby was met by enthusiastic cheers, whoops, and clapping. Some fishermen took notice and honked air horns.

Bobby's own joyous tears mixed with the water cascading from his hair. He grabbed a hold of Jerry, soaking up against him with his wet shirt, and whispered a genuine thanks into his ear.

"You bet. Thanks for wanting to do it here. It means so much," the teary-eyed pastor said.

Kim got all of it on her phone, despite catching her own snivels in the process. Her feet were already covered with sand, as she turned her device off and leaned back. As she did, her right foot fell upon a corner of a sharp object buried in the sand. Sitting up and reaching toward the source of the pain, the back of a photograph was revealed and her heart skipped a beat. Shaking the grains off and turning the old photo over, she saw young Bella and her own image staring back at her from the past. It took her breath away.

Bobby ran to her dripping wet and tearful. Kim stood to embrace her son, with the tattered picture of Bella in her grateful hand.

"Look what just showed up! It was in the sand, buried beneath my feet."

"You have got to be kidding me! Dad told me he had a funeral for Bella on this beach. He said he buried an old photo." They hugged again, and Bobby ran off to show everyone the baptism gift from his dad.

Overwhelmed, Kim felt led to remove the envelope from her back pocket. She had received it from the detective after the funeral service. Donna McBride had found it in Scooter's pocket and wanted Kim to have it before she left for New Mexico. Kim had waited to read it, knowing it had come from him. She felt like she wasn't ready for the words in the moments after the memorial service. Now, standing here on Scooter's beach, after finding his buried treasure, and watching her son become a man of faith, Kim knew it was time to listen to his final words to her.

"Dear Kimmy,
Thank-you for not shutting me completely out of your life. I am truly sorry for what I put you though and am grateful to God for watching over you during my absence. Thank-you for forgiving me. I do not deserve such love.

I am thankful for the things God has taught me over the years. Lately He has been speaking like never before. He arranged our meeting, He revealed our son to me, and has given me hope for the future.

I have always loved you and never wanted anyone else. I realize now, I never deserved you.

When I lost you, I knew it was my fault and did a good job beating myself up over it. Many years later, I learned forgiveness has to include me forgiving myself at some point in the process. If God wasn't counting my sin against me, why should I? Now I know you don't hold it against me any longer, I have finally forgiven myself.
Thank-you for this incredible gift.
Always yours,
Scooter."

*

As Bobby came out of the brick building which held the bathrooms and changing areas, he was pulling on his new, black, 'Present' hat from Matt, when a woman met him just outside the door. Bobby was drawn to her radiant eyes.
"Hello," she said.
"Hi."
"What were you doing out in the water so early in the morning?"
"I got baptized."
"Why did you do it?"
"Because I wanted to publicly declare I am a follower of Jesus."
"That is brave."
"Thanks."
Then she leaned in close to Bobby, so close he could smell the fragrance flowing from her hair.
"Your daddy wrestled his demons. Everyone has demons to fight and they don't die easy, Bobby, but I will never leave you," she whispered.
Bobby's eyes grew wide with recognition, and Angie vanished into a mist.

*

❋ Sequitur ❋

"Put to death, therefore, whatever belongs to your earthly nature: sexual immorality, impurity, lust, evil desires and greed, which is idolatry. Because of these, the wrath of God is coming. You used to walk in these ways, in the life you once lived. But now you must also rid yourselves of all such things as these: anger, rage, malice, slander, and filthy language from your lips. Do not lie to each other, since you have taken off your old self with its practices and have put on the new self, which is being renewed in knowledge in the image of its Creator." (Colossians 3:5-10).

Warning! Spoiler Alert! Warning! Spoiler Alert! Warning! Spoiler Alert! Warning! Spoiler Alert!
(If you read this section before reading the book, it will change your experience— but hey, it's up to you!)

As I considered the implications of the above verses in Colossians, I asked myself what it would look like if I took the admonition seriously? This story evolved from my attempts to understand.

The fictional story of Scooter's reach for God, while running away from Him in the next moment, is my story. His desire to make things happen in his own timing, is a direct reflection of my futile attempts to control God. Scooter's insistence on living with the things which were killing him, is a mirror, reflecting my image as I have toyed with dangerous addictions. His running away from difficult realities is a condemnation of my evasion techniques. I am a mess, but it's not the end of the story. I am a mess loved by God. Gaining an understanding of the boundless love of our Father has helped me work through the living, breathing dichotomy of me.

For dramatic reasons, I wondered aloud what it would look like to personify the things we are trying to put to death in this life of following Jesus? I have learned one of the jobs of the Holy Spirit is to equip us in the faith, and the task is done across the scope of our entire life. The Holy Spirit molds us, breaks pieces off, and challenges our preconceived notions of the definition of a godly life. At times in the Christian life, we must move and initiate, and other times, we must be still, waiting for Him to move.

Scooter's "old Denton friends" in the story are his personal demons—the things he must learn to put to death. We all face ours each and every day. Often, they become our comfortable way to cope, our hidden, pet sins. Many Christ-following people feel stuck when it comes to finding victory over these powerful forces. There is hope, and there is freedom as we learn to press into Jesus for all of our needs.

Then there are the "Donnys" who threaten us— the dangerous people who oppose us in this life. I portrayed this character as a psychopath because many people face an incomprehensible evil in our fallen world, an evil that cannot be reasoned with. It only responds to holy confrontation.

Miss Angie, the attractive counselor in the narrative, is a personification of the Holy Spirit. She knew what to say and when to say it, but Scooter struggled to follow in his own strength. He learned his issues were rectified as he leaned on God. Now, to take my own advice.

Some have asked me why Scooter met his end. I have been asked, "Won't it cause people to not want to grow?" Fear of death motivates us to react in many negative ways. I wanted to describe death as a mere step in our existence as Christ-followers. When life on earth concludes for those who are gripped by faith in Jesus, they are ushered home, through the veil. In the in-between time, "Let us fix our eyes on Jesus, the author and perfecter of our faith. . ." (Hebrews 12:2a).

Much peace to you and yours,
Craig Matthews
April 2021

*

The Stars in the Sidewalk